UNNATURAL AFFECTIONS

U*N*NATURAL AFFECTIONS

WOMEN AND FICTION IN THE LATER 18TH CENTURY

George E. Haggerty

INDIANA UNIVERSITY PRESS / BLOOMINGTON & INDIANAPOLIS

This book is a publication of

Indiana University Press
601 North Morton Street
Bloomington, Indiana 47404-3797 USA

www.indiana.edu/~iupress

Telephone orders 800-842-6796
Fax orders 812-855-7931
Orders by email iuporder@indiana.edu

The paper used in this publication meets the minimum requirements of American
National Standard for Information Sciences—Permanence of Paper for Printed Library
Materials, ANSI Z39.48-1984.

Manufactured in the United States of America

Library of Congress Cataloging-in-Publication Data

Haggerty, George E.
Unnatural affections : women and fiction in the later 18th century /
George E. Haggerty.
p.   cm.
Includes bibliographical references (p.   ) and index.
ISBN 0-253-33389-X (cloth : alk. paper). — ISBN 0-253-21183-2
(pbk. : alk. paper)
1. English fiction—Women authors—History and criticism. 2. Women and literature—Great
Britain—History—18th century. 3. English fiction—18th century—History and criticism.
4. Domestic fiction, English—History and criticism. 5. Gothic revival (Literature)—Great
Britain. 6. Friendship in literature. 7. Family in literature. 8. Desire in literature. 9. Love in
literature. 10. Sex in literature. I. Title
PR858.W6H34 1998   97-39448

1 2 3 4 5 03 02 01 00 99 98

For Philip

"Brother and Sister!—it was unnatural"

—David Simple

CONTENTS

Contents

ACKNOWLEDGMENTS

I have been unbelievably lucky in the colleagues and friends who have made contributions to my critical and theoretical thinking since I began this project some time ago. Colleagues at the University of California, Riverside, who have made life in the Inland Empire an intellectual experience of unexpected richness, include Jennifer Brody, Sue-Ellen Case, Joseph Childers, Carole Fabricant, Susan Leigh Foster, Stephanie Hammer, Katherine Kinney, Carole-Anne Tyler, and Traise Yamamoto. All of these colleagues have read and commented on my work and made helpful contributions. Other colleagues in eighteenth-century studies and lesbian and gay studies who have encouraged my work include Carolyn Allen, Terry Castle, Lucinda Cole, Pat Gill, Shawn Lisa Maurer, Eve Kosofsky Sedgwick, Ruth Smith, Kristina Straub, James Thompson, Hans Turley, and Liz Wood. I have also received rich and at times challenging readings from a number of scholars in the field. Nancy Armstrong, Felicity Nussbaum, Joseph Roach, and Patricia Meyer Spacks have all commented helpfully on this project. As a reader for Indiana, Claudia Johnson offered a complex and encouraging response that I found nothing less than inspiring. It is an exciting moment to be working in this field.

I am grateful to the Regents of the University of California for providing a context in which I am able to work on projects like this one. I find that research support, sabbaticals, and other released time, such as that at the Center for Ideas and Society, have made this project viable. I would also say that my experience in teaching undergraduate and graduate students at the University of California, Riverside, has given this work special meaning. I would especially like to thank my research assistants John Beynon and Ashley Stockstill, whose energy and enthusiasm for this project have kept me going. Other students who have actively participated in my work include Geoff Cohen, John Jordan, Erik Kruger, Peter Morgan, Katharine Morsberger, Terri Nickel, and the late Aaron Walden. Equally important are friends such as Bob Glavin, Bill Kinnucan, and my sister, Pat DeCamp, who have helped to put this project in perspective.

Acknowledgments

The staff at Indiana University Press have been enormously helpful. I would like especially to thank Joan Catapano, senior acquisitions editor, and Grace Profatilov, her assistant. The copy editor, Stephanie G'Schwind, also deserves a special word of thanks.

Thanks also go to the editors of the following journals for allowing me to reprint material that appeared in earlier and at times much different form in their pages: *Genders* (chapter 5), *Studies in English Literature* (chapter 2), and *Tulsa Studies in Women's Literature* (chapter 4). I am also pleased that Columbia University Press has allowed the reprinting of material that, in its earliest incarnation, appeared in *The Columbia History of the British Novel,* edited by John Richetti (chapter 3).

I could never say enough to thank my partner, Philip Brett. Like many academic couples, we spent several years commuting between campuses of the University of California; but this book has been written since he relocated to the Music Department at U. C. Riverside. Many of its virtues are the result of his constant presence. He has always offered inspiration and support, but lately he has been more like a collaborator, a partner in crime. This book is dedicated to him.

U*N*NATURAL AFFECTIONS

INTRODUCTION

Women, Novel-Writing, and Culture in the Later Eighteenth Century

SENSIBILITY AND SEXUALITY

During the half-century or so that is known as the Age of Sensibility, women established themselves as novel-writers with amazing alacrity. Cheryl Turner, who documents this phenomenon, speaks of a "dramatic, unparalleled surge" in women's novel-writing in the middle to late years of the eighteenth century;[1] and it is reasonable to assume that access to novel-writing placed women in a relation to the culture of the period that was different from what would otherwise have been possible. Any selection of novels from these years would tell a unique tale about women's concerns and their willingness or unwillingness to challenge convention or articulate female-directed concerns.

The novels that I discuss are interesting primarily because of the ways in which they have been able to tell a different story from that which culture at large has seemed to tell. These novels were written by some dozen different women in the second half of the eighteenth century. Each tells a carefully constructed story and each offers a distinctive account of female experience and the terms of female success. In doing so, each of them articulates a distinctive set of obstacles to a uniquely realized understanding of female desire. Together, these novels defy attempts to generalize about women's writing in the later eighteenth century. From another perspective, however, they tell one very complex story about female subjectivity and the options available to women in the age of sensibility. To articulate the common concerns of these very different works and at the same time to reveal the significance of their differences are the aims of this study.

By looking at some of the most popular works of the period, I have uncovered a surprising consistency of interest in transgressive desire of various kinds. The affections that are articulated here are "unnatural" in the sense that they defy cultural taboos and challenge what are seen as "natural" boundaries. These situations abound in the works I am going to discuss, and as a result these novels offer a complex understanding of the role of gender and the articulation of female desire in the age in which women came into their own as novel-writers. I am not saying that (all) these works are "feminist," or even "lesbian," although recent work has made the case that at least the second of these terms was available for identification in the later eighteenth century.[2] I am nonetheless interested in the ways that these novels resist heteronormative values in general and articulate various forms of female-female desire in particular. I am also interested in how male characters function in these novels: either as objects of what is rarely articulated as uncomplicated (and more often appears as transgressive) female-male desire, or as either insignificant in various ways or significant only as they enable the articulation of different kinds of relations among women.

The kinds of cross-gender relations that I read as transgressive are several, and their transgressive quality of course depends on the specific circumstances in which they are articulated. Incest offers perhaps the most common transgressive trope—not only, as in the case of the situation represented by the epigram for this book, when it is threatened or suspected, but also, as frequently in Gothic fiction, when it is achieved. Other modes of cross-gender transgression include relations which bring characters of different social status together, a frequent enough trope in comedy but one that can give rise to distressing consequences when dealt with in a serious context. Relations across racial lines are also marked as transgressive, as a novel like Dacre's *Zofloya* makes abundantly clear. Heteronormativity, then, almost

Introduction

by definition excludes various forms of hetero-directed desire, and I hope to show both how such desire is coded in these novels and how the dominant fiction of the age, the fiction of increasing femininity and ever more rigorous domestic ideology, has excluded the stories that these women took such pains to tell.

Slavoj Žižek's notion of the symptom can be useful in this context. He argues that when bourgeois society comes into its own in the eighteenth century, "the relations between domination and servitude are *repressed:* formally, we are apparently concerned with free subjects whose interpersonal relations are discharged of all fetishism; the repressed truth—that of the persistence of domination and servitude—emerges in a symptom which subverts the ideological appearance of equality, freedom, and so on."[3] I would like to argue that female sensibility is one such symptom, but I would extend the range of what it represses to include not just relations between domination and servitude, increasingly repressed within the rhetoric of female liberation and domestic ideology, but also the impossibility of female desire itself. In Žižek's terms, any ideology necessarily contains a fissure that exposes its hidden agenda and at the same time gives the ideology its substance; this is the "symptom." Female sensibility—the extremes of feeling (tending toward madness) and of bodily dysfunction (culminating in death)—is one of the fissures in the bourgeois ideology that emerges in the later eighteenth century. In time, as sensibility's influence became more pervasive, sensibility itself became a symptom of nervous disorders of various kinds. The later eighteenth-century medicalization of emotional pleasure, however, disguises the ideological symptom with which it is identical. Far from allowing us to diagnose only individual psychological complaints, that is, sensibility offers a means of diagnosing a culture's refusal to acknowledge the repression inherent to its hegemonic realization.

I have previously theorized varieties of the male response to sensibility, and I have shown how sensibility fails because of the rock of the "real" of desire that breaks through all attempts at generosity and subverts goodness with pleasure.[4] This tells only part of the story, however. As historians of sensibility have repeatedly made clear, sensibility was both coded as feminine and increasingly seen as degenerate in the later eighteenth century.[5] What happens when women explore subjectivity from the perspective of sensibility? It might not be as susceptible to the criticism, often leveled at male sensibility, that its benevolence is no more than a performance that reasserts the superiority of the "giver" to the poor receiver of generosity.[6] By the same token, female explorations of the thrill of feeling uncover more symptomatic expressions of female desire itself. For Žižek "it is precisely the symptom which is conceived as . . . a real kernel of enjoyment, which persists as surplus and returns through all attempts to domesticate it, to gentrify it (if we may be permitted to use this term adapted to designate strategies to domesticate the slums as 'symptoms' of our cities), to dissolve it by means of explication, of putting-into-words its meaning."[7] Will female desire be written into these accounts, will the rock of the "real" return through all attempts to domesticate it in these works? I think that it is safe to answer yes and to claim that various attempts to articulate the "real" of female subjectivity are everywhere apparent in the works I am discussing.

Women novelists are very good at diagnosing the ills of sensibility, as I will show; but they are also adept at recovering the female body from its status as object in works of male sensibility. In fact, these writers depict the female body and its often transgressive desires in complex and at times almost mesmerizing ways. Interestingly, they do this at the precise moment of cultural history at which gender roles were being codified. That is why men are so interesting in these works. I would go so far as to claim that the symptom of female desire will be discovered, among other figures and other situations, in the figure of the man as he is depicted in these novels. To be sure, men who professed sensibility were always suspected of passivity, effeminacy, or worse.[8] In novels by women, such gender confusion can be exhilarating or disgusting, as the extremes of Radcliffe and Wollstonecraft might suggest; but, I will argue, it is also the key to the cultural significance of the specific works in question. I am interested in each woman's portrayal of the male and modes of male response because of what it says about her ability to imagine a different world for herself. The opportunities for subverting male privilege and particularly odious forms of gendered male behavior are rarely neglected in the works I am going to discuss. At the same time, however, these figures say as much about various kinds of female-female and male-male desire as they do about any relation between men and women.

The culture of sensibility suggests the outlines of what Foucault calls "a completely new technology of sex" that emerged in the later eighteenth century.[9] What this means culturally is a new mapping of the female body and the medicalization of various forms of female desire that can be traced to their origins in the medical and scientific literature of the age. Throughout the later eighteenth century, the body becomes an agent of sexual response in its very emotional organization. For the woman of feeling, affections carry with them an unmistakably erotic charge, and different forms of friendship and even familial bonds can become, in various circumstances, the carefully articulated substitute for sexual activity itself. "Romantic friendship," mother-daughter bonds, and sisterly relations are all charged with erotic significance in the novels I discuss. Relations between men and women, moreover, which are only intermittently erotically suggestive, challenge cultural expectation in various ways: incestuous desire, emasculated heroes, and even Gothic villains begin to reorder the parameters of female desire in these works. By considering the language in which such transgressive desire is expressed and by relating that "expression" to the larger concern of ideological appropriation, by which language is marked, gestures are coded, and feelings are mediated, I will show how this kind of sensibility offered new options for female sexuality at the same time that it exposed a threateningly repressed and repressive system of control.

Sensibility suggests more about subjectivity than it does about sexuality, and the discourse of female subjectivity that emerges in this period hints at the potentially radical implications of a new kind of self-awareness.[10] The tension between the ideological imperatives of the age and the local pockets, as it were, of resistance, expressed in terms of bodily reality and sexual urgency, seems at times to promise an avenue of subversion or liberatory politics. The drama constituted by the emergence at one and the same moment of a sexuality and the appropriation of private feeling, the tension surrounding the sacrifice of privacy and the codification of sexual response, the tragedy of domesticity and the sexualization of the family—all of these issues make the literature by eighteenth-century women fascinating for those of us studying the histories of culturality, if I may coin an expression, as well as sexuality. The implications for the history of fiction are likewise profound.

WOMEN AND FICTION

Nancy Armstrong makes the point that novels *about* women and those *by* them participated alike in the process of feminization that began in the later eighteenth century. She argues the "degree to which the gender of representation is in fact bound not to the author's sex, but to the institution of the novel as well as to changing social attitudes."[11] Because the novel began to have institutional force by the end of the eighteenth century and because women as well as men could be seen in general to be inculcating the values of the bourgeois ideology of the woman's role in the family and in the home, we should look again at some of the novels that fulfill this cultural role with enough formal uneasiness to have been marginalized in literary history since the early nineteenth century.

The role of women in the production of fiction in the second half of the eighteenth century has by now been richly documented and persuasively theorized. According to Cheryl Turner, there were over four hundred novels written by women between 1696 and 1796, and studies such as those by Ros

Ballaster, Mary Ann Schofield, Jane Spencer, Janet Todd, and Turner herself have offered us a revised, female-oriented history of the novel in the eighteenth century.[12] More specific works of critical and theoretical analysis— such as those by Nancy Armstrong, Terry Castle, Margaret Doody, Julia Epstein, Catherine Gallagher, Claudia Johnson, Felicity Nussbaum, Mary Poovey, Patricia Meyer Spacks, and Kristina Straub—have deepened our understanding of what can be at stake in novel-writing and why the position of women in the novel enterprise of the later eighteenth century is of deep cultural importance.[13]

The critical and theoretical studies that have redefined the field in this way have raised a range of questions about the position of women in later eighteenth-century society. They have described the increasing restrictions on female behavior, the "constructed nature of female consciousness," the commodification of innocence, the codification of "femininity," and the exclusively domestic range of "proper" female endeavor. They have also suggested that female-female desire has largely been overlooked in these works and that the most distinctive women writers are also often the most distinctly at odds with the dominant values of contemporary culture.[14] I will return to these ideas again and again throughout this study, for together they provide as rich an account of the cultural role of women novelists as that available for any period. At the same time, I cannot help but feel that this very rich context leaves me free to develop my argument at the margins of these feminist projects and with a slightly different emphasis. Each of the novels I discuss in this study seems to me distinctive in the way it tells its story, just as it is distinctive in what it says. In this study, I will argue that these novelists both are excruciatingly aware of the limits of novelistic convention, culturally as well as formally, and exist in an oblique relation to the cultural norms that determine the limits of subjectivity itself. If these works strike us as "queer," as in various ways they must, that is because they are challenging the assumptions of female sexuality and attempting to chart new areas by means of which female desire can be articulated.

In her study of women writers in the marketplace in the eighteenth century, Catherine Gallagher explains a great deal about how the market works to make use of women's talents at the same time that it denies women any position in the world beyond that of female author, a position both disembodied and displaced in ways that makes the woman herself virtually vanish.[15] Even more remarkably, however, Gallagher makes the point that "[f]ar from being the descendent of older overly fictional forms, the novel was the first to articulate the idea of fiction for the culture as a whole." She says further that "[t]he most radical and least explored distinction between prenovelistic and novelistic narratives is that the former often claim particular extra-textual reference . . . and the latter normally do not."[16] If a culture can be known by the stories it tells, not only the narratives that it creates about itself but also the stories that it suppresses, then how much more useful are fictions that need no "extra-textual reference" to be given cultural meaning? But Žižek's comments help us to see that even the most ungoverned expression of fictional "truth" can only replicate the system of ideological control that represses its most basic Truth in the guise of creative freedom. Women could create any fiction they chose, to be sure. But every story would, after all, be part of the larger fiction that the culture told itself. Even the stories they told about the "nobodies" of their own creation fit the culture's idea of itself.

Women novelists did much more, however, than this cultural function suggests; they went so far as to prescribe new terms for female behavior and to codify femininity itself. In *The Sign of Angellica*, Janet Todd emphasizes the "constructed nature of female consciousness," which, she claims, was "formed . . . to an extraordinary extent through fiction."[17] Nancy Armstrong, too, sees fiction as central to the process of "feminization" of domestic culture that separated the woman from politics and history in exchange for the myth of authority in the home.[18] If Cheryl Turner can cite over 170 women novelists writing in the eighteenth century, and if Gallagher can claim that from mid-century most of these novelists would have been writing self-proclaimed "fiction," then one might wonder why they did not do more to change the position of women in later eighteenth-century culture. As my comments above suggest, however, the proliferation of fiction by women cannot in itself shake ideological control. Indeed, just as women gained the access to power that novel-writing might suggest, their own position in the cultural context, indeed their own identification as women, became less clearly defined. As Claudia Johnson says, sentimentality involved the masculinization of feminine gender traits.[19] It is almost as if, in giving woman a place in fiction, the age of sensibility took away her place in the world. This is the "vanishing act" that Gallagher describes, and it is the strange equivocation that Johnson explores.

This loss of femininity, however, is double-edged. By assigning feminine gender traits to the "man of feeling," women novelists of the later eighteenth century place gender identification on hold. For men, this could mean, as Johnson's comments imply, a feminization of masculinity; but this is not always an affront to female prerogative. In some cases, it allows women more, rather than less, freedom to experiment with gender roles. The absence of the aggressive male encourages "romantic friendship"; absent fathers facilitate mother-daughter bonding, and maternal fathers at least provide intriguing role models.[20] Sisterly relations develop when men are unsatisfactory, and many of the male-female relations are brotherly and tender in surprisingly erotic ways.

The writers I discuss in this study were to a certain extent aware of the ideological implications of fiction in general and their own novel-writing in particular. While in various ways these writers contribute to the creation of an ideology of the feminine in the later eighteenth century, they also reappropriate the cultural conclusions that even their own works might suggest. In other words, the formation of a politics of gender is an active concern in the works I have gathered for analysis here. The cultural construction of gender, moreover, is the subject of these works as well as, inevitably, their process. In their different ways, these writers, all of them female, reveal their uneasiness about the cultural situations in which they find themselves; they react to these situations in ways that defy gender expectations—for masculinity as well as femininity; and they challenge the status quo. I am not alone in thinking that it is possible to understand the radical modes of resistance in these works as a kind of queer politics. The "unnatural affections" that I describe in the chapters below cannot adequately be described in heteronormative terms.[21]

If these writers all intimate a distrust of language, of literature, and of culture, then it seems to me that they also express that distrust in their fictions and that they do so in a variety of ways and by means of a variety of techniques. If Gallagher is right to say that this is the first generation of writers to have "fiction" available to them, then it seems to me that the details of this "fiction" are of the highest cultural significance. I hope to show that in these dozen cases, the fictions that emerge are neither fully articulated attempts at political resistance nor slavish reinscriptions of dominant values, and that instead they represent, in their various ways, significant attempts to challenge the cultural status quo, to supplement the dominant fiction, that is, with fictions of their own.

Women are often seen to be in collusion with the force of ideological control in the later eighteenth century. In *The History of Sexuality*, Michel Foucault depicts women as the perpetrators of cultural harm, in the police state known as family life, or as victims of medical diagnosis, in what he calls the "hysterization of women's bodies."[22] Foucault's notion of cultural resistance, like that of Althusser, is bleak and unforgiving; to him all attempts at resistance are immediately accommodated by the system of power that determines discourse. One way to understand this idea in terms of the women novelists of the later eighteenth century would be to say that culture not only allowed but even welcomed these veiled challenges to its absolute control, for by allowing the "fiction" of resistance to be articulated in these novels, it could turn the screws of dominance all the tighter. It would be naïve to claim that any novelist can "resist" cultural ascendancy just because he or she wants to, and I would argue that even the most political of the writers I am considering, such as Wollstonecraft, were doomed to failure, as Wollstonecraft herself failed, and that an inability to write themselves out of their position within the "abodes of horror" is what haunts their imaginations.[23] Fiction, after all, is just what the dominant culture excels at appropriating for its own ends.

What these novelists learn to do in their different ways, then, is not openly to challenge hegemonic value in the stories they tell. Instead they find the mode of resistance to lie in the way their stories are told. Female desire, that is, cannot be articulated directly in a culture that has always given precedence to male subjectivity, but it can be articulated nonetheless. Women novelists seem to acknowledge that there is only one story to tell, but they nevertheless insist that there is more than one way to tell it.

NARRATIVE MYTHS

In the essay "Desire in Narrative," Teresa de Lauretis argues "that many of the current formulations of narrative process fail to see that subjectivity is engaged in the cogs of narrative and indeed constituted in the relation of narrative, meaning, and desire; so that the very work of narrativity is the engagement of the subject in certain positionalities of meaning and desire."[24] In discussing the role of myth in the construction of culture, de Lauretis cites a ritual that Lévi-Strauss describes in which a Cunan shaman uses incantations to help a woman overcome the pains of childbirth. According to de Lauretis, expectations of a female hero for the childbirth ritual are doomed to disappointment: "[n]ot only is the hero a male, personified by the shaman, as are his helpers, also symbolized through decidedly phallic attributes; but the very working of the incantation promotes the childbearing woman's identification with the male hero in his struggle with the villain (a *female* deity who has taken possession of the woman's body and soul)."[25]

For de Lauretis, the "subject" in this process is necessarily male, and the woman is always, at best, the object: "The story of femininity, Freud's question, and the riddle of the Sphinx all have a single answer, one and the same meaning, one term of reference and address: man, Oedipus, the human male person. And so her story, like any other story, is a question of his desire; as is the teleology that Freud imputes to Nature, that primordial 'obstacle' of civilized man."[26] De Lauretis is saying here that any story in Western culture turns on the pivot of male subjectivity, male desire. This is neither a casual observation nor a careless one. It strikes me, on the contrary, as almost irresistibly persuasive:

> The end of the girl's journey, if successful, will bring her to the place where the boy will find her, like Sleeping Beauty, awaiting him, Prince Charming. For the boy has been promised, by the social contract he has entered into at his Oedipal phase, that he will find woman waiting at the end of *his* journey. Thus the itinerary of the female's journey, mapped from the very start on the territory of her own body . . . is guided by a compass pointing not to reproduction as the fulfillment of *her* biological destiny, but more exactly to the fulfillment of the promise made to "the little man," of his social contract, *his* biological and affective destiny—and to the fulfillment of his desire.[27]

De Lauretis's argument is both subtle and profound. If myth subtends narrative, or if, even more to the point, myth depends on narrative, then the stakes in any culture would be as high as they are in the cultural situation that she describes here. If the ritual that is described seems an exact match to fictional situations which are familiar—I would point to van Helsing and company's shamanistic impalement of Lucy in *Dracula* as an almost literal recreation of the scene that Lévi-Strauss recounts—it must be true too that women were not free, could not be allowed to be free, to appropriate the terms of narrativity for themselves.[28] De Lauretis claims that "the female position in narrative is fixed by the mythical mechanism in a certain portion of the plot-space, which the hero crosses or crosses to."[29] Her chapter makes a convincing case that narrative itself works to exclude the female from the position of subject in Western culture.

The privilege assigned to masculine subjectivity in de Lauretis's account has a kind of mythic function throughout this period. In his study of early-eighteenth-century "fictions," *God's Plot and Man's Stories,* Leopold Damrosch argues that a Christian "myth" offers early-eighteenth-century fiction "a structure of meaning." He defines "myth" as "the total structure of meaning that a culture accepts, which in the case of Christianity is a body of narratives and prophecies . . . that are interpreted through theological exegesis and also through other narratives." His study articulates persuasively how myth and novel are in various ways disjunct, how myth "impose[s] meaning on naive imitation" and "atemporal structures on temporal ones."[30] For female novelists writing in the later eighteenth century, the myth against which they articulate their fictions is also a structure of meaning; structured, that is, in narrative and interpreted at an atemporal cultural level. The myth they confront, however, is not God's but Man's—the myth of male superiority and the complacency of Christian belief in the secondary status of women in an ordered universe. The plots they develop often artic-ulate a fantasy of female self-expression; but often this fantasy is little different from what culture has already determined as woman's place. That place, as determined by the implicitly patriarchal cultural agenda, is both strictly delineated and rigorously controlled.[31] According to Patricia Meyer Spacks, "Eighteenth-century novels contain their society's myths: the virgin and the whore, the wise father, the fortunate orphan. But by the patterns of action they represent, they also modify the meanings of those myths."[32] I think it is more difficult to modify the meaning of myths than this quotation suggests, but I agree that novels often attempt to do so.

Much of the work that has been done on "romance," the putatively "female" form, has had also to admit that even the most wild expressions of female license could not have a liberatory effect on female readers precisely because they understood the terms of fictional negotiation. Later in the century, even Gothic fiction, as critics such as Tania Modleski and Kate Ferguson Ellis have argued, served to delineate rather than defy the limits placed on female desire.[33] The promising but ultimately ineffectual Countess in Charlotte Lennox's *The Female Quixote* puts this case succinctly for an entire age:

> And when I tell you . . . that I was born and christen'd, had a useful and proper Education, receiv'd the Addresses of my Lord—through the Recom-mendation of my Parents, and marry'd him with their Consents and my own Inclination, and that since we have liv'd in great Harmony together, I have told you all the material Passages of my Life, which upon Enquiry you will find differ very little from those of other Women of the same Rank, who have a moderate Share of Sense, Prudence, and Virtue.[34]

What would be clear to anyone reading such a passage, as it is shockingly clear to Arabella, the heroine of the novel, is that any story, for a woman, will be the story of transgression.

In her famous essay on female spectatorship in film, Laura Mulvey has claimed that "sadism demands a story." Teresa de Lauretis has reworked this idea for narrative in general: "'Story demands sadism, depends on making something happen, forcing a change in another person, a battle of will, strength, victory/defeat, all occurring in linear time with a beginning and an end.' All of which is, to some extent, independent of women's consent."[35] What does it mean, though, to consider these perceptions when reading novels written by women for women in a period during which gender distinctions were still under cultural negotiation? It would be naïve to think that because women were writing these works, the essential nature of narra-tive would shift. Again and again women novelists force their characters into the kind of suspended animation that de Lauretis describes. Indeed, the great success of women novelists in the eighteenth century suggests that perhaps they bought too quickly into the system of fictional narrative that would betray them.

In her study of women's novel-writing in the eighteenth century, Cheryl Turner argues that

> The conversion of both sexes to an acceptance, even approval, of female authors . . . was indeed carried forward during the eighteenth century. This was achieved through the promotional activities of the book trades, by the advocacy of the writers themselves, and by a number of important changes in the literature market which extended women's access to literature, increasing their familiarity with the work of the past and current female writers.[36]

This transition could hardly have taken place if the work of female writers was considered in any way a threat to established values. The fictions that these women created, in other words, could not directly challenge the fiction that circulated about the culture itself. I am not saying that the culture was inherently misogynist, but rather that women's role in later eighteenth-century culture was circumscribed enough to make direct attempts to "vindicate the rights of women" seem both radical and, finally, misdirected. Fiction could not simply posit a female protagonist and hope that a new narrative of female subjectivity would emerge.

"Her story is a question of his desire": again and again in the chapters that follow, "her story" cannot be told because of the degree to which it is formulated as an expression of "his desire." This comes true in Charlotte Lennox's tale of romantic fantasy as well as in Burney's bourgeois novels of education; it comes true in Radcliffe's version of bloody sensibility as well as in Dacre's lurid nightmare of miscegenation; it comes true in the form of the male narrator in *Millenium Hall* as well as in the pathetic deaths of *David Simple*. But most of all it comes true in the narrative resolutions of almost every work I will consider. It is almost as if narrative takes control at a certain point in these works. The novelists seem powerless to resist the dictates of narrative resolution. Still, these writers manage to register their frustration and despair at the limits of narrative in terms that eventually work to subvert that implicit cultural expectation. No final subversion of cultural imperatives as deeply felt and pervasively exercised as those controlling the place of women in society is ever possible; but these women create situations in which it can at least be imagined.

In the novels I am considering, they do so in a variety of ways. Primarily, they shift the emphasis from endings and the resolutions of plots to the

Introduction

processes by means of which plots are developed. Often women are independent agents for long stretches before they are forced into narrative closure in marriage. In many cases, the "story" is in essence the story of avoiding the narrative closure of marriage. This is as true of *The Female Quixote* as it is of *Sense and Sensibility*. Other novelists transform the haven of domesticity in various ways: at times incest problematizes family relations to the point of public scandal or private misery; at others, maternal or paternal affection is rendered ineffectual or even villainous; at still others, family intimacy becomes the stiffest barrier to self-realization. All the novels I am discussing see the family more as a problem than as a solution. Another ploy that helps women novelists to tell a different story revolves around the uses of "romance": female fantasies are given freer play in romance, and romance effects are often used to undermine "realism" and insist on fictional possibilities. Gothic writing, "female Gothic" as it has traditionally been called, carries romance techniques into magical and threatening other-worlds that allow female characters a surprising degree of initiative and a range of victimization that could be in certain ways described as an attractive alternative to passive femininity. Radcliffe, often considered a conservative writer, gives her heroines more freedom than most of her contemporary novelists ever attempt. If she does this in the context of a Gothic plot, all the more reason to admire the lesson of female independence she so vividly teaches and the mechanics of plot that she so effectively manipulates. Finally, the works I am discussing often emphasize female-female relations in ways that defy narrative expectations. The signal work in this regard is of course Sarah Scott's *Millenium Hall,* but novels by Wollstonecraft, Austen, and Radcliffe all use the trope of female friendship to counterbalance the male trajectory of narrative desire. Most of the works I am considering here use a combination of techniques to tell their remarkably complex stories. Even when they are telling the least exceptional tale of female education, they find ways of renegotiating the terms of female experience. This is true in spite of the tendency, in some of these works, to marry off their heroines to the highest bidder.

One technique that has not been as fully explored as the others I list is that involving male characters in these works. In her analysis of gender, politics, and sentiment in the 1790s, Claudia Johnson makes the point that the codes of sensibility and sentimentality challenged gender definition in the later century:

> Under the sentimental dispensation contemptuously referred to by Wollstonecraft as the "*manie* of the day," gender codes have not simply been reversed. They have been fundamentally disrupted, and this is why

> Wollstonecraft's intensely homophobic phrase "equivocal beings" is so
> germane. . . . [T]he conservative insistence upon the urgency of chivalric
> sentimentality fundamentally unsettled gender itself, leaving women with-
> out a distinct gender site. Under sentimentality, all women risk becoming
> equivocal beings.[37]

If women are "equivocal beings," so are men, often and in ways that
Johnson's use of the term "homophobic" suggests. The disruption of gender
codes that rendered male same-sex desire as a structural impossibility begins
to suggest the possibilities of transgressive desire for men as well as women.
If these novels abound in fops, men of feeling, ineffectual heroes, and men
whose gender identity has been compromised in various ways, then these
men have a lot to tell us about the way that women attempted to redefine
their cultural role in the later eighteenth century. I feel that the emasculated
males that proliferate in these novels perform more roles than even Johnson's
study suggests. To be sure, the lachrymose male in more than one case and
in more than one political situation did usurp the position traditionally
allotted to the female. But in the novels that these women write, as I will
show, the lachrymose male can perform a more complex function in the
narrative of female desire than has been acknowledged.

Wollstonecraft's contempt notwithstanding, there is more than one role
for the effeminate and emasculated male to play in women's fiction of the
later eighteenth century; the degree that the gender system ceases to be a
binary system in these works is not always a sign of equivocation. The degree
to which the gender system is disrupted, that is, can also be the degree to
which men and women are offered a different kind of relation than what is
otherwise presented in the fiction of the period. Tearful fathers and ineffectual lovers, I would argue, do not so much usurp female prerogative as
redirect male desire itself, displacing the usual trajectories of narrative into
transgressive but nonetheless sympathetic directions. These works articulate
cultural myths with every possible slant in gender coding, personal relations,
family life, female and male desire, and female subjectivity. These are the
issues that I will explore in the pages that follow.

THE LAW OF DESIRE

The story of the inculcation of female virtue in such nonfictional writing
as conduct books and treatises on female education has become fairly
familiar.[38] At the same time, it must not be forgotten that an entire arena of
public attention was paid to the possible negative example of the divorce
court and other forms of criminal prosecution. The fiction of female trans-

Introduction

gression was here spelled out in more thrilling detail, as the trial records published and disseminated from about mid-century attest.[39]

The widely popular *Trials for Adultery,* for instance, "taken in SHORT-HAND, by a CIVILIAN," according to the title page, were meant to titillate the interest of a growing reading public. They do in effect use narrative to shape history as a way of controlling judgment and heightening scandal in a way that twentieth-century readers might associate with tabloid journalism. Increasingly in the eighteenth century, historical record becomes a version of "fiction" with narrative rules that govern the outcome. In these trial records, it also becomes increasingly clear how simple the contours of a woman's story can be when it is subjected to the rigors of patriarchal law.

The preface to the first of these seven volumes suggests the terms of the cultural agenda operating in the later part of the century, and "the Editor" makes it clear what priorities are at work:

> It requires little or no apology for the publication of these trials. It may . . . deter the wavering wanton from the completion of her wishes; it may be of service to the practicers in the law; . . . it will shew to the world in general by what gradual steps affection sinks into indifference, indifference into disgust, and disgust into aversion: the consequences of which are but too apparent from the perusal of these volumes. When a Woman (especially of the superior class) has lost that inestimable jewel, virtue; alas! how is she fallen! her nobility no longer claims our reverence; her coronet ceases to be enviable; her birth (which she has disgraced) but adds to her offence; as, from her situation, it was incumbent on her to have been an example of purity to the rest of her sex: she is indeed become the object of the scorn, pity, and derision of her relations, her former associates, and the public.[40]

After such a preface, it would be impossible to imagine that any account contained within these seven volumes could be written from a perspective sympathetic to the female point of view. How easy it is to see prejudice working through a narrative scheme such as those produced repeatedly here. The cases, in fact, seem but an excuse for the presentation of primarily female transgression, with rhetoric that excoriates not only the crimes but also female identity itself. As Miss Milner discovers in *A Simple Story,* female transgression has identificatory power: when a woman falls, as this preface suggests, she becomes "the object of . . . scorn, pity, and derision," less herself than an abject parody of the woman she was.[41]

The most striking feature of these "trials," however, is the absence of men: husbands are invisible here, and even adulterous male liaisons are presented as little more than the occasion for female transgression. At the (literal or figurative) trials, by which women are judged, men are usually present only in the obscure position of judge and (often) jury. What these narratives show is precisely what de Lauretis has argued. The story of female transgression is the story of male desire, but here the female becomes the object of cultural contempt, the body over which the story is told: a story that demands sadism. If similarly transgressive moments occur repeatedly in the fiction I am going to discuss, if women transgress in the ways that these adultery trials suggest and in other ways too culturally obscure for public trial, then they do so in the presence of men and with the complicity of men, before, during, and after the act of transgression. The man who writes this preface vividly suggests the impossibility of imagining any narrative but one where adultery bespeaks female villainy. By placing this narrative in a court of law, moreover, he can silence the female, as she is silenced in the culture at large.

Law itself, of course, has something of the status of myth in Western culture. Rachel Blau DuPlessis is one of several feminist theorists who have argued that the "dominant" cultural conventions have mythic status. She notes that "no matter what notion of the sex-gender system one uses to explore the relation of women and men, and of women to society, the reproduction of these relations in consciousness, in social practice, and in ideology turns especially on the organization of family, kinship, and marriage, of sexuality, and of the division of all sorts of labor by gender." In short, this reproduction happens in the "plots" of fiction: "Romance plots of various kinds, the iconography of love, the postures of yearning, pleasing, choosing, slipping, falling, and failing are, evidently, some of the deep, shared structures of our culture."[42]

In other words, these plots have the status of myth in our culture, the culture that was being formulated in the later eighteenth century and that is reflected in the novels I am going to discuss.[43] What DuPlessis calls "romance plots" form the basis of several of the novels I consider below. In them, the mythic status of narrative expectation is acknowledged and resisted. In many cases, these are novels about novel-writing and novel-reading, novels about trying to make sense out of the improbabilities of fiction, novels about attempting to articulate a female sensibility in a man's world, novels about how to tell a female story within a male plot. To the extent that romance is coded as female, moreover, either in its "realistic" form of the "marriage-plot" or in its more extravagant chronicle of female excess, the more effectively it circumscribes female experience and sets the limitations on female self-expression. If it grants a kind of authority to women who write and read novels, it also determines in what very specific ways that authority can be used.[44]

For DuPlessis, "One of the great moments of ideological negotiation in any work occurs in the choice of a resolution for the various services provided. Narrative outcome is one place where transindividual assumptions and values are most clearly visible, and where the word 'convention' is found resonating between its literary and social meanings."[45] I agree wholeheartedly with this argument, but I think it can be usefully extended "beyond the ending" in the direction of literary form itself. That is, narratives can only resolve themselves (or not) in terms of what they set out to accomplish.[46]

There is more than the ending at work in activating ideological negotiation in novels written by women in the later eighteenth century. I am tempted to see queer politics at work here because these novelists attempt to subvert a binary sex-gender system in various ways. Since literary and social "meanings" are under negotiation throughout these works, moreover, and since more than the ending determines the cultural significance of any literary endeavor, I argue, in this chapter and in more specific ways in the chapters that follow, that these novelists found ways to tell their stories within, around, and beyond the plots that were culturally available to them. The politics of novel-writing is never transparent, and even the most committed political novels can quickly be accommodated into an overarching cultural agenda. Nevertheless, many of the novelists I am discussing seem aware of the inherent contradictions of their position and still seem interested in challenging the status quo.

Of course I am not arguing that the later eighteenth century is essentially more or less misogynist than other periods of English or American history. But the stakes in the later eighteenth century, as Claudia Johnson and others have shown, are especially high.[47] Women were for the first time finding themselves at the center of a cultural vogue and at the same time being given a political function in a revolutionary culture.[48] But still, if Foucault and others are right to say that the "hystericized" female has her origins, as it were, in the eighteenth century, as countless medical and social tracts will attest, it is precisely in these novels by women that a complex understanding of female bodily self-awareness may be found. This self-awareness is often expressed in terms of female-female desire. Emma Donoghue has recently documented a rich and previously under-theorized trove of eighteenth-century writings by and about women that address their physical and emotional love for one another. If there is one common thread throughout the works I discuss, even in the most male-directed of these works, it is the thread of female-female desire. I am not claiming that such desire is by definition subversive or that one woman's love for another would be enough to rewrite the cultural narrative of the period. But Donoghue's work makes it clear that there is a vast body of cultural material concerning the possibility—the danger from the dominant perspective—that women might step out of the sex-gender system and into one another's arms. Donoghue says that "[t]hough gender is central to *Passions between Women,* I see same-sex desire as disrupting the conventions of femininity rather than denying womanhood itself." Such disruptions are what interest me here. According to Donoghue, the woman who felt desire for another woman "may have thought herself odd, sinful, unwomanly, even monstrous; she may have been ready to pass as a man, crossdress, or send out some signals of masculinity; but surely she would not simply have equated her desire for women as maleness."[49] In the chapters that follow almost all of these expressions of sexual self-awareness are put to use. But gender *is* under negotiation in various ways and with various results in each of the novels I discuss. What is common to them all is a willingness to rewrite the cultural meaning of female desire with whatever means available.

Throughout this study, I try to concentrate on one or two novels by each writer I discuss. (The one exception to this rule occurs in the "Female Gothic" chapters, in which, as I explain below, I attempt to look at a range of techniques in the work of several novelists.) Throughout, I very much want to construct an argument that is in touch with the complexity of development that a novel represents. The story that I want to tell makes sense only in these terms: narrative development is part of what I am getting at here. Too often these works are discussed in a cursory way, in a survey format, as if a summary of their plots explains what they are trying to say. I believe that novels such as these are sophisticated enough to benefit from the close attention that I offer them here.

Part One ("Family Values") discusses various works that address the signal complications of family life—incest and various corruptions of family feeling, in particular. The first chapter examines Sarah Fielding's *David Simple,* explaining how Fielding manages both to explore incest and its consequences and to rewrite Augustan value in the novel's shockingly deflating sequel. This novel begins with a betrayal of sibling trust and repeatedly displays representations of paternal villainy, the most telling involving a suspicion of sibling incest that is both cruel and debilitating. Even happy families are subject to the whims of fate, and an almost incredible series of deaths bring the novel to what can only be considered a gloomy close. Fielding's novel is a profound comment on the received wisdom of resignation and a complex challenge to the increasingly circumscribed possibilities for women. "Unnatural affections" are the ground of the narrative and they help offer shape to later narrative claims of resignation and contentment. The second chapter in this section addresses questions of female abjection and father-daughter love in Elizabeth Inchbald's *A Simple Story.* The family again plays a central role in determining the dimensions of female desire, both determining the objects of affection and assuring that they are both literally and figuratively taboo. What begins as a story of female transgression and ends as a fantasy of family romance exposes the abjection to which a woman is victim and explains why and how that can be the only desirable choice after all. Finally, in "Female Gothic (1)," I discuss Clara Reeve's *The Old English Baron,* Charlotte Smith's *Emmeline* and Sophia Lee's *The Recess,* three novels that together defy generic assumptions concerning female subjectivity and the contours of female desire. These works begin to give a sense of how "female Gothic" is grounded in feminine sensibility and to what degree it can be read as a symptom of the denial of female desire in hegemonic culture. They bring the various strands of romantic and transgressive expression—"unnatural affections"—together and begin to suggest a female resolution to many of the questions that other novels in this study continually raise.

Part Two ("Love and Friendship") considers three writers in whose novels various modes of utopian fantasy and female-female desire play against a series of debilitated heroes to produce a radical revision of gender relations and, in one case at least, an attempt at wholesale revision of the sex-gender system itself. First, I consider Jane Austen's *Sense and Sensibility,* a work which has recently given rise to complex reading of sisterly affection and which challenges attempts to assert confidence in its heteronormative conclusion. The love between the sisters, Elinor and Marianne, is played out against a demanding assortment of family and social obligations, and it is threatened by a set of singularly unimpressive male suitors. Austen reworks the relation of male and female in this novel, however, to suggest both the strength of female bonds and the insufficiency of happy endings. The next work to be discussed in this section is Sarah Scott's utopian vision of *Millenium Hall,* in which female-female desire is articulated in terms that defy the dictates of patriarchal narrative. *Millenium Hall* attempts to rewrite narrative and refuses to allow marriage to be a solution for its heroines. Instead, women find solace in their relations with one another and, with the help of a suggestively enabling Italian, redefine eroticism in terms that are neither predictable nor uncomplicated. In the last chapter of this section, the focus shifts to Mary Wollstonecraft's *Mary* and *The Wrongs of Woman.* These works, with their vivid dramatization of female victimization, attempt to challenge the dictates of law as well as narrative. *Mary* tells of the impossibility of friendship and the disappointments of narrative expectation. *The Wrongs of Woman* begins in a mental institution and ends in a court of law: the woman placed there is a symptom of the culture itself. The ends of narrative effectivity are apparent here, as are the very details of cultural arrangement that make feminism, female desire, and female-female bonds so difficult to achieve.

Part Three ("Erotic Isolation") will look at several novels that explore romantic and Gothic extremes of female experience, which both challenge convention and redefine the limits of female desire. In the first chapter I consider the romance of transgressive female desire in Charlotte Lennox's *The Female Quixote*. Arabella, the heroine of this novel, writes her own escape from the tawdry details of her daily life. In doing so, she defies the limits that are placed on female emotionality and reimagines female fantasy as self-directed. The ecstatic experience of self-love is a source of conflict in the novel, to be sure, but the novel celebrates female subjectivity in startlingly unmediated ways throughout. The chapter that follows articulates the brutal isolation that Frances Burney's heroines face. In this chapter I look at the second of Burney's three vast novels of her maturity, her astonishing *Camilla*, to see what options for female self-realization it entertains. In this novel of female education, I address the issues of masculinity and deformity, both as they are brought to life in the characters of the excruciatingly passive hero, Edgar Mandelbert, and his "rival," the effeminate fop Sir Sedley Clarendel. I also try to show how Burney uses these defective heroes to redefine female subjectivity and how here, as in *Millenium Hall*, female "deformity" becomes a help rather than a hindrance to self-fulfillment. Finally, the excruciating isolation of the heroine creates a fictional situation that defies narrative expectation and eroticizes sickness, hysteria, and the limitations of domestic life. The next chapter considers Ann Radcliffe's *The Romance of the Forest*, a work that defies critical attempts to explain the interactions between gender and culture in her work. In this novel, the bloodied and victimized male becomes a kind of erotic totem, both eliciting female desire and releasing it from the sadistic objectivity of narrative expectation. The three works in this section describe the pain of female experience, even as they tell of romantic success and personal happiness. I want to look at this pain to attempt to understand it as a symptom. Finally, I look at two later novels, Mary-Ann Radcliffe's *Manfroné* and Charlotte Dacre's *Zofloya*. Both these works redefine "female Gothic" and attempt to use transgressive desire as a means to effect social change. In their violence, brutality, and undisguised sexual irregularity, these novels set a standard of explicitness that is rarely matched, before or after. In a sense, they send a challenge that resonates well beyond the nineteenth century. But then all these works do. This is not the story of the end of narrative possibilities for women; rather, it is a new account of narrative beginnings.

Part One

FAMILY VALUES

ONE

Brotherly Love in
David Simple

FAMILY ROMANCE

David Simple is a novel about family.[1] At one point in the novel, Cynthia, a central character, exclaims: "I have made it my Observation, in all the Families I have ever seen, that if any one Person in it is more remarkably silly than the rest, those who approach in the next degree to them, always despise them the most; they are as glad to find any one below them, whom they may triumph over and laugh at, as they are envious and angry to see any one above them."[2] The novel dramatizes this observation in several ways. Dissension and nastiness are assumed to be inherent to family relations, and the family never functions as an unalloyed source of pleasure. When family relations are intimate, moreover, and mutually supportive, they become suspect in a culture that is just learning how to police private affections. Here is no idealization of the domestic: family life is inevitably vexed and painful in often surprising ways.

The novel begins on a note of fraternal distrust and betrayal. Daniel Simple rewrites his father's will in an attempt to ostracize his more honest brother, David, in a plot that fails so quickly that it is often overlooked. These opening scenes of fraternal discord serve immediately to suggest the kinds of betrayals possible within a familial structure. The betrayal matters because it is the family that is affected. David *feels* this loss because he has been betrayed where he most has trusted. This examination of family tension insists on the duplicity inherent in the representation of sensibility, a duplicity which threatens to undermine the value of the private world from within and without: for whatever one feels, sensibility can be measured only in its representation. It is a performance: Robert Markley calls benevolence "the affective spectacle of benign generosity."[3]

Even within the intimacy of family life, the facade of sensibility cannot be penetrated; yet it is the only value possible in a world of false feeling and emotional corruption. When Daniel is exposed, the family suffers, for David sets out on his own to find a "true friend." There is nothing merely sentimental about this portrait of family life, and Daniel's betrayal of family trust is the first of several such betrayals in the novel. Sarah Fielding's unidealized portrait of family life has broad implications for all the works in this study. These women novelists seem committed to a deconstruction of the ideology that celebrates the family for its own sake. They understand too well how the family can become little more than a trap for the underprivileged.

Cynthia's own story tells of familial contempt and betrayal with a Richardsonian intensity. Her parents were "continually teazing" her, and her sisters "took an inveterate hatred to" her, all because of her "wit" (101–102). The contempt her family feels for her is more irritating because her sensitivity is informed by her intelligence. The family situation is described as irrational as well as unfair. Kate Ferguson Ellis has discussed "the language of domestic violence" in the writing of the Gothic novelists of the 1790s.[4] Domestic violence is no less present in this "sentimental" novel of mid-century. I would argue, moreover, that the violence itself has an even greater valence in a novel like this one, purporting to treat everyday experience.

The irrationality of Cynthia's situation is heightened to the point of madness when she is subjected to the attentions of a presumptuous suitor. In Cynthia's case, the arranged marriage is so clearly a business transaction that she mocks her suitor as he soon as he begins making his proposals: he "made me the polite Compliment, of telling me, *that he supposed my father had informed me that they two were agreed on a Bargain. I replied, I did not* know my Father was of any Trade, or had any Goods to dispose of; but if he had, and they could agree on their Terms, he should have my Consent, for I never interfered with any Business of my Father's" (108). When he corrects her, she goes on to articulate her estimate of his proposal: "I made him a low Court'sey, and thanked him for the Honour he intended me; but told him, I had no kind of Ambition to be his *upper Servant*" (109). She admits to David that *"I shall always call it Prostitution, for a Woman who has Sense, and has been tolerably educated, to marry a Clown and a Fool"* (109). The feminist implications of such a stance are clear, and Cynthia may well be functioning as Fielding's own mouthpiece here.[5]

By equating marriage and prostitution, Fielding attempts to challenge the status quo. Cynthia is intelligent and clear-headed enough to resist this brutalizing transaction, and she cuts through the sentimental code of family intimacy by seeing things clearly and by giving her feelings a meaning that she herself controls. She escapes the misery of familial abuse, in other words, by gaining control of the "marriage-plot" that would make final her victimization. Cynthia places the family itself at the center of social conflict, and in doing so she undermines the ethos of domestic harmony and challenges the tenets of domestic ideology. Fielding is not the first novelist to bridle at restraints placed on women, but she goes to great lengths in this novel to dramatize the effects of familial abuse. Cynthia is strong enough to resist in this situation, but her status in the family is clearly marked.

Marked, too, is the maternal position, as the story of Camilla's mother's death makes clear. This poor women has an accident that has an emblematic power. She steps on a thorn one day when she is out walking with Camilla, and the wound becomes so infected that the surgeon recommends amputation. Camilla's mother complies and is subjected to the horrifying operation; but the amputation is without effect, and soon after she dies. It may not be entirely insignificant that Camilla's mother is subject to this violent dismemberment as the result of a puncture wound or that the wound becomes infected while she "went about the House, only a little limping, without any great Complaint, for four days" (136). The wound is fatal because the woman attempts to fulfill her duties as wife and mother. She suffers, that is, because of her position in the family. The wound itself—"the Point of the Thorn was just visible; all around it was very much swelled, and in the middle was a great black Spot" (136)—could be thought to represent the "wound" which in a patriarchal culture every woman bears and which marks her secondary place. If for Camilla's mother this "wound" is fatal, so it is for countless other young girls who are analogously wounded and condemned to die. Alike infected with the culture itself, that is, they are left its most insignificant victims.

In discussing the symbolic significance of the wound, Žižek says, "the wound is 'a little piece of the real', a disgusting protuberance which cannot be integrated into the totality of 'our own body.'" Žižek would say that it is a materialization of that which is destroying her, "but at the same time it is the only thing which gives [her] consistency."[6] For Camilla's mother, the wound that destroys her also gives her consistency. What is more "maternal" than this sacrifice to family and home? Her death is symptomatic: Camilla's story begins with physical pain and psychological agony, and proceeds to dramatize an allegory of womanhood that shows this suffering to be constant.

INCEST AND INTIMACY

Camilla's family history, more harrowing than Cynthia's, centers on incest, the taboo that by definition problematizes family. "Sibling incest" is unusually common in the eighteenth-century novel—in this study, it appears in Fielding, Lee, and Dacre as a central trope, and it is suggested in Smith and Burney. Of course it is also centrally present in the novels of Behn, Defoe and Fielding, and Walpole and Lewis, and it is mentioned in a range of novels too numerous to mention. In each of these novels, incest is used for "shock value" and to suggest the threat or thrill of transgression in a world of sexual ambiguity. When Moll Flanders learns that she has been married to her brother, her narrative shifts from the picaresque to the paranoid, and when Ambrosio, the monk, discovers that the victim of his brutalizing lust has been his own sister, his cataclysmic punishment seems assured.[7]

In certain cases, however, especially in *David Simple* and other novels by women, sibling relations seem not only *not* transgressive but even, to a certain extent, ideal. Who is a better partner, after all, than the brother who shares a sensibility toward the world in general and toward women in particular? He offers a kind of maturity that seems impossible in the public world of rakes, aristocrats, and other villainous types. The brother is eroticized and other male relations are fraternalized, as it were, not to diminish their sexual charge but rather to increase it. That this would be possible in an "age of sensibility" makes perfect sense, and the so-called "weak" heroes of a range of fiction from Fielding to Burney to Radcliffe suggest that a sibling relation is the only conceivable male-female relation that is neither abusive nor victimizing. These novels could be said to be incestuous in spirit, even if they are not in fact. As Terri Nickel says in a recent discussion of *David Simple*, "incest registers the demand for sympathetic identification—that one desires in the other some model of oneself." Nickel sees this trope "at the same time marking the inevitable self-destruction of such empathy"; but it seems to me that punishment from without forges even tighter sibling bonds.[8]

Culturally speaking, "sibling incest" occupies an odd position in relation to the incest taboo itself. The twentieth-century approach to incest, in books such as *Incest: A Family Pattern, Betrayal of Innocence: Incest and Devastation,* and others, stresses father-daughter incest almost to the exclusion of other forms. When these books do include a chapter on "sibling incest," moreover, they argue for instance that "siblings are generally so inclined to experiment sexually that some experts estimate that at least casual sibling contact occurs in nine out of ten families with more than one child. Sibling incest is by far the most widespread form of incest, though it often goes unreported, even when discovered." And: "Under certain very specific circumstances sibling incest may not be a traumatic, or even unpleasant, experience."[9] This author, Susan Forward, goes on to explain circumstances in which such incest is traumatic—a brother uses a sister as a "guinea pig" or a much older sibling abuses a young child—but the force of her and others' arguments is to suggest that sexual experimentation between siblings of the same age is neither uncommon nor automatically abusive. Why then the taboo?

It is helpful to remember that the incest taboo has more to do with male control/exchange of women than with "natural" male-female relations. In *The Elementary Structures of Kinship,* Lévi-Strauss says that "the prohibition of incest asserts that natural distribution should not be the basis of social practice regarding women. . . . Considered as a prohibition," he says, "the prohibition of incest merely affirms, in a field vital to the group's survival, the pre-eminence of the social over the natural, the collective over the arbitrary."[10]

Incest, in other words, is a cultural taboo, rather than a "natural" one. But Emile Durkheim, working a generation earlier than Lévi-Strauss, tells a different story. For him, the taboo depends on a connection of the female with blood, which, for various deeply cultural reasons, the different groups that he studies fear and totemize:

> [E]very time that the blood of a member of the clan is spilled, it results in a veritable public danger, for a terrible force is thus liberated which threatens the entire neighboring area. That is why various means are used to contain and to disarm this force. . . . One begins to see here the origins of exogamy. The blood is taboo in a general way, and it taboos all that enters into contact with it. . . . The woman is therefore . . . taboo for the other members of the clan. A more or less conscious anxiety, a certain

religious fear, cannot fail to be present in all the relations which her companions can have with her, and that is why these relationships are reduced to a minimum. But those which have a sexual character are still more strongly excluded than the others. . . . Furthermore, the organ involved in such relationships immediately becomes the center of these terrible manifestations. It is therefore natural that the feelings of distance that the woman inspires at a particular point reach their greatest intensity. That is why, of all parts of the feminine organism, the sexual is the part most severely restrained from any relationship. It is from this that exogamy and the serious penalties which sanction it are derived.[11]

Durkheim's description of the incest taboo is as "cultural" as Lévi-Strauss's. But it helps to explain the "abomination" in specific, and perhaps recognizable, terms. The recent theorist who attends most specifically to the connection between blood and female exclusion is of course Julia Kristeva, whose *Powers of Horror* makes the following gloss on remarks such as those by Durkheim: "Excrement," she says, "and its equivalents (decay, infection, disease, corpse, etc.) stand for the danger to identity that comes from without: the ego threatened by the non-ego, society threatened by its outside, life by death. Menstrual blood, on the contrary, stands for the danger issuing from within the identity (social or sexual); it threatens the relationship between the sexes within a social aggregate and, through internalization, the identity of each sex in the face of sexual difference."[12] In this description of social and sexual identity as a threat to the relation between the sexes, Kristeva could be describing the incest taboo itself. Incest as an abomination is tantamount to heterosexual panic, or, simply, fear of the female.

As I have suggested, the eighteenth-century novel offers a chronicle of incest situations and incest solutions. Usually the force of the taboo is elaborately articulated, if not deeply felt. At times, however, the question of incest is raised to challenge its function as a taboo in Western culture.

In *David Simple*, "The History of Camilla" addresses the question of familial intimacy and its cultural implications in an imaginative and illuminating way. (This is not surprising in a novel that repeatedly problematizes family.) Early in her narrative, as I mentioned above, Camilla loses her mother after a bizarre accident and finds that except for her brother Valentine, she is without a friend in the family. We might call him her "valentine," remembering that in the eighteenth century one's valentine was the first member of the opposite sex that one saw on the appropriate day.

Camilla's father eventually courts another bride, who although friendly at first quickly becomes Camilla's bitter enemy: "Thus my Father's House, which used to be my *Asylum* from all Cares, and the Comfort of my Life, was converted by this Woman's Management into my greatest Torment; and my

Condition was as miserable, as a Person's would be, who had lost the best Friend he had in the World, and was to be haunted hourly by his Ghost" (145). The stepmother is of course the stuff of fairy tales, but what Fielding manages to do is to turn that fairy-tale fantasy into the real hideousness of actual events. In other words, she looks into the classic configuration and discovers what is really threatening about the perversion of the family. When the situation has gotten to a point of outright physical violence— Camilla's father strikes her in an expression of frustration and rage at her disagreements with his wife—Fielding carries the tale of familial torment in a surprising but at the same time particularly appropriate direction.[13]

As I have said, Camilla's chief support at this time is her brother Valentine: he has suffered with her at the hands of the father and stepmother, and vows, she says, that "he would never forsake me" and "that he would accompany me wherever I pleased, and be my Support and Guard to the utmost of his power; for that he valued his Life no longer than it conduced to that end" (159). When they escape to the house of a friendly aunt, they are almost immediately denounced as illicit sexual partners. The accusation resounds with a significance that is hard to contain within the confines of its structural function as yet another in a series of familial outrages. It insists upon itself as *the* central outrage, around which all other familial concerns revolve. In other words, incest becomes a kind of explanation for what is wrong and what is right about all the familial groupings we are presented in the novel:

> The next day she [the aunt] went out, and at her return came into the Room where we were, with the greatest Fury imaginable in her Looks; and asked us, "What it was we meant, by telling her a Story of *Livia*'s ill Usage, and God knows what; and endeavouring to impose on her, and make her accessory to our wicked Conversation with each other: Brother and Sister!—it was unnatural, she did not think the World had been arrived at such a pitch of Wickedness." She ran on in this manner for a great while, without giving us leave to answer her. . . .
>
> Then she launch'd out into a long Harangue on the crying and abominable Sin of Incest, wrung her Hands, and seemed in the greatest Affliction, that ever she should live to hear a Nephew and Niece of hers could be such odious Creatures. At last I guessed what she would insinuate; but, as I knew myself perfectly innocent, could not imagine how such a Thought could come into her head. (160–61)

The accusation of incest is fitting because it is the sin which only family ties make possible. In a novel which is as concerned with the violence of family as any Gothic novel, it is appropriate that this trope for familial corruption is ushered forth. The fraternal incest that is articulated here is central to the literature of sensibility. For relationships that have meaning in this culture are first and foremost fraternal relations. When those relations are proven strong and enduring, they are sexualized; and in every case, there is something almost incestuous about the resulting bond. What happens in *David Simple* is that Fielding articulates exactly this configuration. Camilla and Valentine are model siblings in this world. They are mutually sympathetic; they have similar tastes; they will support one another in times of stress. Their relation is therefore *unnatural*, and whatever they come to mean to one another, publicly they are understood as an abomination. Romantic friendship between members of the opposite sex, friendship even between siblings, is an impossibility. Incest labels such friends as outlaws, just as the world of sensibility gives little priority to a kind of relation that does not assure the ascendancy of the father. Men of feeling, women of feeling, each shifting slightly into the sexual role of the other—all such characters are outlaws, and incest is a convenient label to suggest their relation to society. As Terri Nickel argues, "[s]ibling affection here is the ground for any exogamous love. . . . Valentine and Camilla must first of all find partners who will listen to their story and imagine their suffering. Those listeners also must marry them as a 'sibling unit.' Thus, Fielding creates a community grounded in both identification and pain. . . . Moreover, metaphoric incest is a form of the sympathetic identification necessary to the family in Fielding's work."[14] I would add only that what the family requires it also rejects: Camilla and Valentine must constitute a new family if they are to survive.

The central characters in *David Simple* live, as it were, outside of law. They are certainly outside of convention. And it is their unwillingness to conform that makes them threatening to society. Those of us who are queer might want to claim them for our own. (The happy ending that Fielding provides for them in *David Simple* is in *Volume the Last* reversed, and both these characters, among others, die unceremoniously and abruptly.) Personal relations are sexualized as a way of maintaining control over them. What Fielding has done is to have given the position of heroes and heroines of sensibility a label that approximates the loathing with which they are held in patriarchal society. If they are taken seriously at all, they are taken as a threat.

Foucault argues, in his *History of Sexuality*, that in the nineteenth century, "sex gradually became an object of great suspicion; the general and disquieting meaning that pervades our conduct and our existence, in spite of ourselves; the point of weakness where evil portents reach through to us; the fragment of darkness that we each carry within us: a general signification, a universal secret, an omnipresent cause, a fear that never ends."[15] What we can see happening already here in the mid-eighteenth century is

an articulation of "Sin" that traps individuals in a discourse about themselves. When Camilla and Valentine become the odious creatures that her
aunt describes, they have been written into a discourse of the "unnatural"
that reaches out to include all those who do not participate unthinkingly
in the mechanisms of patriarchy. That no man or woman of feeling can do
so unthinkingly is the measure of the pathology of feeling and an approx-
imation of its most lethal dangers. Camilla is pushed to the very margins of
society, and even when she is little more than a beggar, she is robbed and
beaten and threatened with death: "Alas, Sir," she says to David, "there is no
Situation so deplorable, no Condition so much to be pitied, as that of a
Gentlewoman in real Poverty" (169).

Camilla and Valentine must both suffer for the crime they have not
committed. Or have they? Fielding has articulated an ideal of brotherly
love and labeled it "incest"; she has constructed a world of almost inter-
changeable brother-sister characters in an arrangement of mutuality that
resembles nothing more than a thoroughly eroticized family; she has evoked
the cultural "taboo" in order to expose its meaninglessness in a world
structured around female desire; and she has rewritten masculinity to account for this shift in subjectivity and to accommodate her characters to a
position at the margins of a culture that is looking only for objects.

Given the popularity of incest as a fictional trope, it is not surprising that
there are a number of "incest" cases in the notorious annals of the Old
Bailey; but these cases are exclusively of the father-daughter variety. There
are others, many of them harrowing, in which a young girl is sexually
abused by an older boy; but I found none in which the sibling relationship
functioned. "The Marriage Controversy," as it has been called by Trumbach
and others, flourished in tracts at about the same time that Fielding was
writing *David Simple*. John Fry's *The Case of Marriages between Near
Kindred Particularly Considered* (1756), for instance, focuses on sibling
incest as a constant preoccupation. Fry, in his preface, suggests that "some
Marriages which have been commonly censured as unlawful, are not only
lawful, but under some Circumstances fit and expedient: and, in particular,
that such as are contracted between an Uncle and a Niece, and with the Sister
of a deceased Wife, may be sufficiently justified by the Authority of the Law
of Nature, and the Laws of our National Constitution." Fry then proceeds
to a careful examination of those chapters in Leviticus that seem to address
the question of incest. He argues from biblical evidence, starting with the
injunction "A man shall leave his Father and his Mother and cleave unto
his Wife"—suggesting the "Unlawfulness of Marriage between Parents and
Children; and I think with good Reason"—but, going on to collateral
marriages, he argues that Eve "was truly a Part of [Adam's] Flesh before she

became his Wife"; and that "by making at first but one Pair, and command-ing them to multiply, so that all Mankind might descend from them; it became absolutely necessary, that the next Marriage should be between *Brother* and *Sister,* and that by the sovereign, and righteous Will and Ap-pointment of God himself." He then turns to various marriages between brothers and sisters in the early books of the Bible, culminating in the injunctions against such marriages in the eighteenth and twentieth chapters of Leviticus. By means of ingenious close readings of biblical passages, he argues that there is no injunction against "marriage" between such close relations, but only against unclean acts, such as adultery or fornication.[16]

The interest of Fry's argument is not whether he has made a convincing case about "marriage to near kindred," but that he has made the case at all. His argument is based on a reading of Scripture that makes it clear that marriages between brother and sister were divinely ordained from the first days in paradise and that only a misreading of Scripture has resulted in the law that prohibits such marriages. Fry does not go so far as to argue for marriage between brother and sister, but he does argue cases that were considered tantamount to the same in the eighteenth century, particularly the marriages between a man and his deceased wife's sister. Fry's tract, and others, suggest that the terms of the taboo were being renegotiated for reasons of cultural urgency.[17] It is surely no accident that Fry is writing just as "sensibility" is reordering domestic space and resexualizing familial relations, as *David Simple* makes clear.

If brother-sister incest becomes a constant motif in eighteenth-century fiction, then Sarah Fielding participates in this debate as energetically as any novelist of the age. It cannot be argued that she is encouraging incest. At the same time, she allows her central characters to be victimized by such an accusation in order to emphasize the inequities of a cultural system that both sentimentalizes the female and demonizes her. Incest is the most convenient trope for articulating that double female bind. That a woman of sensibility would eroticize the man of feeling who is her brother is understandable in a culture as ruthless as the one depicted here. "The abominable Sin of Incest," however, labels that desire for a gentle male companion as one further indication of female sexual voracity. The weak, fraternal hero may provide a different idea of domestic happiness for the woman of sensibility, but that ideal is mocked by culture and proscribed by law.

VOLUME THE LAST

Dissatisfaction with the original ending would be reason enough for the sequel, but in *Volume the Last,* Fielding does everything she can to make her re-vision of the earlier novel complete: she reconceives the world of fiction and exposes its very fictionality. In her preface to *Volume the Last,* a "Female Friend of the Author" says that "our Author was willing to exemplify the Behaviour of a Man endowed with such a Turn of Mind as *David Simple,* in the natural and common Distresses of this World, to illustrate that well-known Observation, that 'The Attainment of our Wishes is but too often the Beginning of our Sorrows'" (309). If this attitude was implied at the end of *David Simple,* it was implied by the indirection of a dissatisfying and in some ways false resolution. Fielding seems prepared to redress the balance here by developing her characters beyond the false resolution into some further adventures more in keeping with the darker mood of the earlier volume. Rather than see what follows as a punitive retribution, however, we should understand that Sarah Fielding is rethinking her relation to fictional narrative itself. In any case, although a "well-known Observation" is cited, it is not an observation that usually falls within the purview of fiction. One is tempted to ask what happened to Sarah Fielding between 1744 and 1753 to evoke this odd reversal of the terms of her most popular novel.

The loss of her three sisters and the illness of her brother Henry may to a certain extent account for the change in tone between the two works. Of no less importance, however, might be her friendship with other female writers, Jane Collier (the "Female Friend" of the preface) especially, and her consequent rethinking of the terms of narrative convention to which she earlier subscribed. As Jane Spencer has argued, *The Cry* (1754), which these two women jointly authored, clearly articulates a criticism of one version of female experience. Fielding and Collier make an impassioned plea against romantic notions of marriage and paint in vivid colors the fate of the unhappy wife.[18]

Spencer suggests that "they criticize the romantic illusion that obscures masculine power, not the power itself."[19] But as *Volume the Last* suggests, the undermining of romantic expectation, the deconstruction of the "marriage plot," is a form of resistance that explodes the fictions according to which women are asked to organize their lives. Romance and marriage have simply but unmistakable ideological force, as I argued above. Rachel Blau DuPlessis could be speaking for the eighteenth century as well as the twentieth when she says that "the romance plot . . . is a trope for the sex-gender system as a whole."[20]

Fielding has played according to the rules of the "romance plot" and has found that her fictional instincts were more than the form could bear. Hence the discomfort with the resolution of the novel and the sense that she has raised more ghosts than she has been able to quell. Spencer talks about Fielding's "need to conform," but *Volume the Last,* while not wildly radical, does challenge the assumptions beyond the patriarchal myth of "happily ever after."[21] In *Volume the Last,* Fielding attempts to write an ending appropriate to her subject, neither comic nor tragic, but not simply pathetic either. In other words, she is looking for an ending appropriate to female experience in the world. If in *David Simple* Sarah Fielding depicted a sort of heterosexual panic at the implications of family intimacy, in *Volume the Last* she exposes the lie of domestic harmony itself. Even happy families face suffering and death with almost tedious regularity. It is as if she takes us "beyond the ending" of a romance narrative to show the grueling details of family life.

Volume the Last begins with loss and continues in misery. Not long after the group of David and Camilla, with Cynthia and Valentine, have set themselves up in a country setting, David finds that he has lost his inheritance. The ill effects of the suit are compounded by David's agreeing with his lawyer to pursue the case in court. As his family grows—several children are born in a few years—his luck goes from bad to worse, and at the end of the first book, financial reversal, at least, is complete. After confronting the facts of their financial situation, Cynthia and Valentine decide to go off to Jamaica, where Valentine is promised he will be able to succeed as a lawyer. When Valentine and Cynthia leave, they leave behind their small daughter, Cynthia, who is showing signs of ill health. Cynthia falls ill in their lodgings at Bath, and she dies shortly later: "*David*'s little Family much lamented their Cousin, for she was a pratling spritely Child, and innocent of one Thought of Offence towards any Mortal" (347).

Soon Camilla's father, who had been restored to her in the resolution of *David Simple,* begins "bowing downward to his native Earth with Infirmities" (359), and he dies shortly later, "as if he was only falling into a refreshing Slumber" (360). Almost immediately after this loss, David and Camilla's youngest daughter, Fanny, "just opening to her Parents a Disposition to their hearts Desire, was taken from them by a violent Fever" (374). And before there is time to think, David and Camilla receive a letter from Cynthia announcing the sudden death of Valentine from a "raging Fever" (378). Peter, their son, dies shortly later from smallpox, and David and Joan, two more of their children, are carried off in a bout of measles. These deaths are dealt with summarily, but the narrator stops to explain: "But by passing quickly over all the Sorrows that affected *David* and his *Camilla* I would not be understood as if they felt not the paternal Concern for such Children being torn from them. The true Reason why I dwell not on that Concern, is, that Words cannot reach it—the sympathizing Heart must imagine it—and the Heart that has no Sympathy, is not capable of receiving it" (412).

Brotherly Love in *David Simple*

The literary imagination, an imagination expressed in language, is helpless before the human pathos that the novelist depicts. She implies that an imagination of "Heart," a sympathetic feeling, must supply what words cannot express. Fielding is in touch with a wide range of mid-century philosophy in her position here.[22] As Leo Braudy says, "the sentimental novel asserts the superiority of the inarticulate language of the heart to the literary and social forms" and such novels "attempt to create literature of emotional intensity that rejects traditional forms."[23] Fielding challenges her readers to understand the personal misery of loss and the power of inarticulate grief. At the same time, she makes them rethink their assumptions about the fictional enterprise. These deaths are neither sentimentalized nor are they dismissed as unimportant (as they are, say, in novels like *Moll Flanders*). Fielding gives the lie to fictional convention by asserting a "sympathy" that reaches beyond the confines of her plot. At the same time, the point that Fielding makes is not solely a point about the limits of fictional convention. She is saying something about family life as well. The deaths of children become symptomatic of what even the happiest family is powerless to prevent. The real that obtrudes in this situation is not the real of sexual desire; it is the real of death. Žižek claims that "the 'death drive', this dimension of radical negativity, cannot be reduced to an expression of alienated social conditions, it defines *la condition humaine* as such." He adds that "[a]ll 'culture' is in a way a reaction-formation, an attempt to limit, canalize—to *cultivate* this imbalance, this traumatic kernel, this radical antagonism through which man cuts his umbilical cord with nature, with animal homeostasis."[24] Fielding approaches the trauma of death with the surgeon's knife. She knows that death has a most profound effect on life, and she is ready to "cultivate" the imbalance that this knowledge implies. She uses her position as a woman and a novelist to rewrite cultural values. What difference does it make to face death as directly as she does? It makes all the difference.

When Camilla dies, it feels as if we must be reading a parody of sentimental fiction: "But whatever were the Pains of Mind or Labour of Body that *Camilla* underwent, they were too much for her Strength, and she survived her Child but two Months" (413). The idea that Camilla is overcome by her suffering is not unusual, but her death, dramatized here as yet another scene of giving birth, makes it seem as if Fielding has something more than a sentimental tale in mind. Camilla dies because she has been suspended in a romance structure that has proven its falseness to her and finally to her husband. In other words, the happiness which she enjoyed at the end of *David Simple* has proven a lie in *Volume the Last*. Fielding may not assert a feminist position as positively as some other eighteenth-century writers, but she does suggest the ways in which women have been victimized in conventional romantic fiction.[25] Camilla has entered her union with David with all the promise of a fictional resolution. In *Volume the Last,* she bears five children, loses four of them, and then succumbs herself through mere exhaustion as much as anything else. It is not only narrative convention that has been false, however; it is the promise of happiness that forms the basis of bourgeois culture.[26]

When she dies, her husband, the eponymous hero who very shortly dies himself, simply gives thanks that her sufferings are at an end: "as soon as he heard that his *Camilla* was out of the Reach of Pain or Sorrow, he thanked God, and felt a Peace and Calm that his Mind had been long a Stranger to" (413). "Happily ever after" now seems to mean the happiness of loss, the happiness of seeing an end to suffering. This is a bitter reversal of the earlier hopeful close, and it forces its readers to question not just that hope but the social assumptions that make such hope possible.

"But now I will draw the Veil," the narrator says after David's own death, "and if any of my Readers chuse to drag *David Simple* from the Grave, to struggle again in this World, and to reflect, every Day, on the Vanity of its utmost Enjoyments, they may use their own Imaginations, and fancy *David Simple* still bustling about on this Earth" (432). These direct words challenge the very fictionality of fiction and in doing so mock the brutality of the convention, which demands "resolution," at the same time that they challenge the symbolic myth of personal happiness. Earlier in the novel, it was clear that personal happiness must be sacrificed to a public good. Now it seems painful to hear her character say: "The same natural Desire for Happiness actuated me with the rest of Mankind" (430). Fielding shows how this "natural Desire" is perverted in a culture that functions at the level of the symbolic: natural desires will always be coded as unnatural when they challenge culture at its very roots.

TWO

Female Abjection in
A Simple Story

If Sarah Fielding's *David Simple* tells a story that victimizes the female because of sibling affection, then Elizabeth Inchbald's *A Simple Story* (1791) rewrites the family romance from the inside out and produces a profound tale of female abjection. Incest is again the central trope, but in this case the transgressive desire is seen as the foundation of female subjectivity. The generation that separates these two novels does not belie the similarity of their arguments or the "simplicity" of their vision. In both novels, female experience can be described only with tropes as taboo as they are symptomatic.

Recent theories of abjection articulate a post-Freudian description of the abject individual, and studies such as those by Julia Kristeva and Judith Butler have redefined how subjectivity and abjection intersect in contemporary culture. The concept of abjection can also open up a range of later eighteenth-century fiction and poetry that is otherwise inaccessible. As recently theorized, abjection describes a state of self-awareness that could in a patriarchal culture be ascribed without revision to the female. Kristeva describes literary "abjection" as follows:

> In a world in which the Other has collapsed, the aesthetic task— a descent into the foundations of the symbolic construct—amounts to retracing the fragile limits of the speaking being, closest to its dawn, to the bottomless 'primacy' constituted by primal repression. Through that experience, which is nevertheless managed by the Other, 'subject' and 'object' push each other away, confront each other, collapse, and start again—insepa-rable, contaminated, condemned, at the boundary of what is assimilable, thinkable: abject.[1]

I quote this passage in part because of the eloquence with which Kristeva explains the sources of abjection and in part because this analysis offers a valuable insight into Elizabeth Inchbald's extraordinarily complex story of daughter-father love, *A Simple Story* (1791). What could more vividly represent the "descent into the foundations of the symbolic construct" than this irresistible attraction to the father? What is more primal to the construction of the individual in patriarchal culture? Daughter and father: "'subject' and 'object' push each other away, confront each other, collapse, and start again—inseparable, contaminated, condemned, at the boundary of what is assimilable, thinkable."

A Simple Story exists precisely on this boundary. The novel tells—obliquely at first and then directly—of a young girl's love for the Jesuit priest who is her guardian; of her defiant behavior when she finally wins his love (after he has been allowed to give up holy orders); of her guilty flight after an "unforgivable" transgression; of her husband's cast-iron rejection, first of her, then of her daughter; and of that daughter's suffering at his rejection and her final acceptance into the paternal bosom. The novel is broken neatly in two: the first half leads up to the marriage of Dorriforth and Miss Milner; the second begins seventeen years later, after the first heroine's "fall," when her daughter is at the age she was when the action first began.[2] For Terry Castle, the second half of the novel is a "displaced recapitulation" of the first half, and it has been difficult from the first for critics to pay the second half of the novel the attention it deserves. Yet, like *Wuthering Heights,* this is a story that has to be worked out over two generations, following the frustration, disappointment, and even the malevolence of a passionate and self-important man and his effect on two or three relatively helpless victims.[3] Inchbald's double narrative insists, moreover, on abjection as implicit in the position of the female in a patriarchal culture.[4]

This first half of the novel tells a simple story of female fallibility. Throughout the early sections of the novel, Miss Milner's love for her guardian, Dorriforth, puts her in a state of suppressed agony that only gradually becomes legible to a reader.[5] In the second half, Miss Milner's daughter, Lady Matilda, experiences similar agony because of the systematic rejection at the hands of the same man, Miss Milner's estranged husband and Lady Matilda's father, now Lord Elmwood. This doubly articulated attraction for the inaccessible father borders on the Gothic. The darkly threatening paternal figure is a familiar trope in eighteenth-century fiction, by 1791 especially; and, as I argue in my discussion of Radcliffe's *Romance of the Forest,* it is often assumed that such figures are attractive to the heroine.[6] Gothic novelists often equivocate over the bond between the heroine and the "demon-lover," but Inchbald leaves us no room to speculate over the intensity of the erotic attraction that Miss Milner and her daughter feel in turn for the imperious Dorriforth. Instead, she anticipates a whole range of nineteenth-century fiction by domesticating this dark figure as a stern mentor and at the same time making him utterly inaccessible. Inchbald, in other words, takes pains to literalize the demon-lover-mentor in the figure of Dorriforth, who, as Miss Milner's guardian after her father's death, is a vaguely transgressive choice as love-object; but as a Catholic priest, he is utterly, even thrillingly, taboo.[7] For his daughter, Lady Matilda, he is more literally taboo; but in her case as well, he becomes the sole object of desire. Indeed, it seems as if the young woman can really love only the one man who is inaccessible to her. The abjection implicit in the paternal object-choice is my topic here.

Miss Milner's love for her priestly guardian borders on a sacrilegious as well as an incestuous passion. Castle aptly calls the novel a "rhapsody of transgression."[8] Of course there are enough qualifying circumstances to render her love superficially acceptable or even ennobling. After all, Miss Milner's hopeless passion for an inaccessible lover, as problematic as it sometimes seems, is almost a romantic cliché. But Inchbald's insistence on the transgressive quality of her desire reminds us that she is questioning both fictional conventions and family structure in her "simple" progress from daughter to wife. With Lady Matilda, too, Inchbald eroticizes the relation between father and daughter in ways that make her concerns unmistakable.

That both Miss Milner and her daughter feel desire for this father-figure defies novelistic propriety at the same time that it mocks the fictive quality of fiction. In other words, the conventions of romance are subjected to a scrutiny of their underlying gender-power relations that few other novelists approach. At the same time, by eroticizing the "father," Inchbald unapologetically cuts through the tenets of sensibility, which paint the father as a superior being endowed with saintly grace, and proposes a domestic scene that is neither simple nor in any conventional sense "happy."[9] What makes this unusual plot device particularly remarkable, however, is the easy equation it assumes between female desire and pain.

The most obvious terms for understanding the situation that develops between Dorriforth and his "ward" and between Lord Elmwood and his daughter are those offered by Michele A. Massé. In discussing the familiar configuration in Gothic fiction, which she labels masochism, Massé explains that the "heroines of the Gothic, inculcated by education, religion, and bourgeois family values, have the same expectations as those around them for what is normal. Their social contract tenders their passivity and disavowal of public power in exchange for the love that will let them reign in the interpersonal and domestic sphere." As I have just suggested, Miss Milner and her daughter literalize "bourgeois family values" in a particularly telling way. They do so, moreover, in the terms that the culture has provided for them. As Massé explains, in culture as it was being codified in the later eighteenth century, "the father is the daughter's familiar, promising power through love if she maintains the self-abnegation that is her part of the bargain. Yet he or his surrogate is only a representative for the deep structure of patriarchal exchange systems."[10] This "self-abnegation," masochistic in its outlines and "romantic" in its intent, seems to me closer to the quality of abjection than to masochism itself. Indeed, abjection, as described by Kristeva and others, could be seen as formative of a culturally determined female identity. Miss Milner's love for Dorriforth, as transgressive as it is, is so deeply rooted with her own personal history, her devotion to her father, and her attempt at discovering an identity of her own, that Kristeva's description seems uncannily appropriate. Kristeva sees incest as the unthinkable sexual encounter, a life-stopping defilement that, for figures like Oedipus, equates pleasure and death.[11] If the genders are reversed, however, and the female subject dares to harbor incestuous desire, an even more rigorous defilement of the terms of cultural coherence threatens. In the case of Lady Matilda, a kind of "primal repression" is at work. The novel, to a certain extent, reenacts the unthinkable desire for the father in its curious doubling of mother and daughter, and it insists on the paternal as the inaccessible, the unsatisfying, but the only choice for the desiring female.

What is shocking, then, about Miss Milner's story is neither its intensity nor its debilitating power, but rather her ability, when she sees a chance of achieving her "romantic" aim, to cease to be the abject daughter and to exercise some of the power with which her guardian's love finally invests her. As she says to Miss Woodley when the latter is berating her for her high-mindedness and refusal to obey Dorriforth: "As my guardian, I certainly did obey him; and I could obey him as a husband; but as a lover, I will not."[12] As Massé's comments suggest, this attitude is already accommodated within a patriarchal system: her defiance only reinforces Dorriforth's arbitrary power. Inchbald allows Miss Milner to exercise her female prerogative in order to demonstrate just how profound the limits to that power really are. His love gives her the power to transgress normative boundaries, but it also ensures that certain other limits are securely in place.

Dorriforth seems at first to admire his young ward, and he tries to be helpful to her in little ways throughout the early chapters. But he hardly ever succeeds. He has more than his vow of chastity to keep him distant from her. His own spiritual guide, the priest Mr. Sandford, is outwardly hostile to the girl as a ploy to curb her willfulness and teach her the error of her ways. But Lord Elmwood is in fact more aloof and more implacable than any demon-lover in Gothic fiction. He is arbitrary in his displays of power and his peremptory demands of obedience, a "tyrant," in Jane Spencer's phrase, who finds himself immune to the petty personal concerns of those closest to him. "It is male behaviour," Spencer says, "not female, which appears fascinating, wayward, and contradictory in this novel."[13]

"There was in his nature shades of evil" (33), the narrator tells us. In something like a trial run of his rejection of his wife and his daughter, Lord Elmwood has rejected a sister "who married a young officer against her brother's consent" (34). As Sandford tells Miss Woodley, "He loved his sister too, tenderly loved her, and yet when he had taken the resolution; passed his word he would never see her again; even upon her death-bed he would not retract it—no entreaties could prevail upon him" (144). For a young woman of Miss Milner's make-up, it is easy to discover what Lord Elmwood's evil means: from her deathbed as well he remains aloof. His love, that is, is totally selfish; it has no meaning beyond its ability to bring him self-gratification, self-congratulation. It isolates him as the figure of authority and objectifies him as the one who cannot afford to feel.

At various points in the novel, we are reminded of Dorriforth's inflexibility, as if it were a fact of life. Miss Milner is warned, advised, mocked, urged to change in various ways in order to avoid offending him. He is above correction, however, and only his own will determines him to be kind or brutal in turn. But this defines "paternalism": female fortune depends on paternal will in more ways than one in this novel. Miss Milner suffers because of her love for Dorriforth. Early on, she earns his displeasure because she seems to equivocate—seems to dare to be less than absolutely straightforward—on the question of the objects of her affection. Anyone reading the scenes, for instance, in which she professes to love the nit-wit Lord Frederick Lawnly (later Duke of Avon) must squirm at Dorriforth's triumph over her equivocation, since it has been made clear that only her love for Dorriforth has caused her to behave as she does. Dorriforth, after all, has hot-headedly assaulted the young aristocrat when he dared to address his ward against his will, and she pretends to love Lord Frederick only in order to prevent Dorriforth from risking his own life in a duel.

Miss Milner's situation becomes abject as a result of Lord Elmwood's arbitrary tyranny. Because she cannot love him, she loves him more, and she turns his uneasiness on herself. And when he professes to love her, she challenges his love with taunts disguised to establish her own independence. This behavior on her part, however, might be seen as an understandable reaction of someone who has been at his pleasure either outcast or intimate. For it is in the nature of patriarchy to arrange relationships just so. Paternalistic control, in other words, yields an incoherent response that is gauged primarily as resistance. But abjection only plays at resistance; it is after all committed to the subjection that it has isolated as desire. For Lady Elmwood, happiness is never enough. She always destroys it because, in her abjection, "happiness" always implies its loss, and freedom from constraint means only that the next set of bonds will be tighter.

The form of Miss Milner's resistance, then, is also the form of her abjection: in this case, the behavior of a coquette. If her defiant flirtations are alone the measure of her ability to defy paternal protection and prove its arbitrary nature, then they at the same time produce the violent response that Miss Milner's cultural position causes her inevitably to desire. Her later, tragic marital infidelity is not so much a fall as a fulfillment of the dangerous quality that Lord Elmwood's treatment has already presupposed. If, in any case, her coquettish behavior earns her nothing less than Lord Elmwood's contempt, then her infidelity earns her his implacable hatred: "Lord Elmwood's love to his lady had been extravagant—the effect of his hate was extravagant likewise" (197). By falling in love with the man who is literally her father-surrogate, who is at the same time because of his "orders" as inaccessible as a father would be, Miss Milner exposes the particular virulence of a patriarchal system.

When Miss Milner provokes Lord Elmwood by persisting in her plan to attend the masquerade and when she is seen there (however innocently) with Lord Frederick, who "hands her to her carriage," Lord Elmwood cuts off their engagement. What might be interpreted as wild jealousy and the ruthlessness of male prerogative, Lord Elmwood calls "prudence":

> That you still have my friendship [he writes to Miss Milner], my admiration, and even my love, I will not attempt to deceive either myself or you, by disavowing; but still, with a firm assurance, I declare, Prudence outweighs them all, and I have not, from henceforward, a wish to be regarded by you in any other respect, than as one "who wishes you well." . . . [F]or a single week, do not insult me with the open preference of another. —In the space of that time, I shall have taken my leave of you *for ever*. (174–75)

This letter, which mortifies Miss Milner and breaks her spirit, is a breathtaking articulation of the freedom with which the patriarchal figure assumes the control of language itself. By using prudence as a substitute for vanity, jealousy, and contempt, Lord Elmwood makes his action seem honorable. This passage is central to the reworkings of the power relations between Milner and her guardian, and through it abjection is refigured. Miss Milner's desire for Dorriforth becomes equivalent to her rejection by him. If we remember that Miss Milner has been under the absolute control of Lord Elmwood for some time and that her defiance of her guardian, although questionable behavior for a dutiful daughter and wife, was merely an attempt to test her independence—she is seventeen or eighteen at the time— and when we remember that Sandford has all along been campaigning against Miss Milner as an object beneath contempt, exposing the collapse of familial relations in an implicitly homosocial patriarchy, then we may recognize that her situation has in many ways been structured as an impossibility. Lord Elmwood's "prudence" represents his best chance to preempt any articulation of female subjectivity that is not directly under his own control. While Miss Milner sobs abjectly in hopes of being forgiven, Lord Elmwood ignores her or bows stiffly from the waist. He understands the dynamics of abjection and although not entirely immune to its effects, he wields the kind of power that redirects his own abjection onto his fiancée. Wollstonecraft wrote in *The Analytical Review* that "the vain, giddy Miss Milner" is presented in too favorable a light;[14] but Inchbald creates a character whose giddiness is the result of a cultural refusal to grant or acknowledge her ability to judge for herself. Dorriforth creates the circumstances in which she can fail, and indeed he could be said to desire her failure. For his authority is guaranteed only to the degree that she does.

It is hardly surprising, then, that their wedding itself is a time of mourning: in finally gaining Lord Elmwood, Miss Milner loses herself. After their marriage—the pathetic and tearful scene that ends volume II—and after "four years passed in the most perfect enjoyment of happiness" (196), Lord Elmwood travels to the West Indies, where he remains for several years. While he is there, he falls ill, and decides not to communicate with Lady Elmwood because of a "too cautious fear of her uneasiness" (196). This recalls the "delicately nervous friend" who concealed her father's illness early in the novel, "lest it might alarm a mind she thought too susceptible" (6). In both cases, this contempt for female understanding and control has dire consequences. In the early case, "this refined tenderness gave poor Miss Milner the almost insupportable agony, of hearing her father was no more, even before she was told he was not in health" (6). Miss Milner, it seems, is the victim of her sensibility, or rather the "sensibility" of the age, that refuses to permit local female suffering while at the same time taking the fact of "female suffering" as its most basic cultural tenet. That suffering is given special form when the wife is outcast and rejected.

Miss Milner's unhappiness in love returns to haunt her after marriage, just as her status in the Dorriforth household has always suggested that it might. In this case, however, her guilt and her desire are given their usual eighteenth-century configuration, and the "rhapsody of transgression" takes the simple form of adultery.[15] When Lady Elmwood transgresses—during her husband's prolonged absence she renews her acquaintance with Lord Frederick, now Duke of Avon, and succumbs to his assiduous advances—her husband asks for no explanation, makes no consideration of extenuating circumstances, and allows no communication of any kind. As various critics have argued, adultery was in the eighteenth century a uniquely female fault. In the infamous *Trials for Adultery: Or, the History of Divorces* (1779), six and a half of the seven volumes contain tales of female infidelity luridly told and brutally concluded.[16]

Inchbald focuses not on the fact of adultery, but rather on the treatment that her heroine receives at the hands of her never- forgiving husband. At the same time, Lord Elmwood is at least partially responsible for his wife's error, and he is entirely responsible for the misery of her last dozen years. It is he who sits within culture in judgment on her who has violated its terms. Culture allows her no way to ask forgiveness, however, and she can ask nothing for herself. The pain involved, the implicit masochism of her position, is a feature of her place in culture. Massé says that "the heroine of marital Gothic will always reawaken to the still-present actuality of her trauma, because the gender expectations that deny her identity are woven into the very fabric of her culture, which perpetuates her trauma while denying its existence."[17] Gender expectations define the terms of Lady Elmwood's abjection as well. The trauma of her loss is measured as guilt, and the misery of her circumstances marks out the features of her self-contempt.

Lady Elmwood's isolation is the most profound feature of her altered circumstances, and her situation is described in terms that suggest a nightmare of Gothic dimensions:[18]

> In a lonely country on the borders of Scotland, a single house by the side of a dreary heath, was the residence of the once gay, volatile Miss Milner— In a large gloomy apartment of this solitary habitation (the windows of which scarce rendered the light accessible) was laid upon her death-bed, the once lovely Lady Elmwood—pale, half suffocated with the loss of breath; yet her senses perfectly clear and collected, which served but to sharpen the anguish of dying. (199)

Inchbald calls to her aid the conventions of Gothic fiction in order to underline Lady Elmwood's position as a tragic victim of unfeeling tyranny. Inchbald seems to feel that only in the sublime violence of the Gothic can Lady Elmwood's suffering be evoked in anything like its full emotional dimensions.

Lady Elmwood dies without seeing her persecutor or knowing that there will be any forgiveness for herself or her daughter. Her lord, in his inimitable unreasonableness, has cast out his daughter with his erring wife: "Beholding himself separated from her by a barrier never to be removed, he vowed in the deep torments of his revenge, not to be reminded of her by one individual object" (197). She dies as outcast: as a female, she sees this as her natural fate. Culture determines that it is she who will fail, she who will transgress, and she who will suffer. Men, it seems, know and conspire to protect and nurture their own power; women err and are pushed to the margins, where they are "free" to succumb to the Gothic nightmare of their own sexual creation. Even as she lies near death, Lady Elmwood scribbles a note to her arrogant husband to plead for her child, in hopes that he might recognize her, love her. Still, that is, she plays the abject victim who tries to create an identity out of her lack.

The second half of the novel works at reintegrating this Gothic split in two ways. First, Rushbrook, the lad whom Miss Milner rescued from avuncular neglect, finds himself in love with the outcast Lady Matilda, Lord and Lady Elmwood's daughter. Second, and more compellingly, Lady Matilda hopes to overcome her father's injunction against her and somehow to be not only forgiven but also loved. According to Castle, "Matilda's story combines folk motif and family romance in ways prefiguring the starkly supercharged structures of Romantic poetry and fiction. . . . In the figure of the now-terrible Lord Elmwood, a man paralyzed by compressed love and rage, in Matilda's Oedipal absorption with this invisible tyrant-father, we see the outlines of classic Romantic psychodrama, from *Prometheus Unbound* to *Wuthering Heights*."[19] Lady Matilda offers Inchbald the opportunity to extend her tale of quasi-Gothic horror and to redirect its force. That she does so without qualifying her indictment of patriarchy is a measure of the novel's power.

Lady Matilda finds herself in a situation strikingly similar to that of her own mother: she is rejected by a stern father-protector for no reason that she can discern, and she must puzzle out how to please him—for his pleasure motivates all action in the novel— without overstepping her severely circumscribed bounds. She is never to be seen by him, although at his whim he may choose to inhabit the very house where he has placed her, nor can anyone even mention her without risking dismissal from the august presence of the lord forever. He commands the space in which she lives and the language in which she is or, more precisely, is not mentioned.

The collapse of father/lover is so thoroughly affective here that even Rushbrook understands his position to be second to that of Lord Elmwood. Lady Matilda's simpering displeasure with her situation is hardly a surprise. Lord Elmwood, in his paternal position, is carefully eroticized for the girl: she glimpses him, or almost does, in the distance and feels her heart pound; she confronts him accidentally on the stairs and collapses in a swoon into his arms; she is forbidden his presence and she moves dutifully to a neighboring farmhouse with the perverse hope that he will love her more. It is peculiar to the abjection portrayed in this novel that abuse yields greater devotion, as it does in this case. "Given oppression as a premise," Massé says in her study of female victimization, "masochism can work to create and preserve a coherent self, to control the repetition of trauma, and to regulate others as well as the self. . . . The repetition of masochism is not simply a gendered death-drive but the individual's fight for life and a future."[20] Matilda's abjection before the idea of her father seems merely self-destructive until we consider how thoroughly this abjection is, like the masochism Massé describes, an attempt at survival. More than a psychological state, that is, abjection prescribes the very mode of action that culture has coded as female. Massé's masochist avoids conflict between assertion and recognition "by demanding that others recognize and love her precisely for her *non*assertion. Her silent suffering becomes her claim to fame."[21] This closely describes the behavior of Matilda: shut away in a few rooms of Lord Elmwood's house, she hopes secretly that her refusal to be seen will be recognized and appreciated. Sandford suggests to her at one point that "his thinking of ye at present, is the cause of his good spirits." "'Oh, heavens!' cried Matilda, lifting up her hands with rapture" (225). This is typical of Matilda's relation to her father. It is a portrait of abjection itself: "the abject," Kristeva says, "is the violence of mourning for an 'object' that has always already been lost."[22] Matilda mourns for the father she has never had; she feels rapture at the thought that he might think of her; and she lives in panic that he might see her by mistake.

This version of the family romance is as powerful as anything in the first half of the novel. Miss Milner, after all, at least imagined that a kind of resistance was her prerogative; but lady Matilda offers no resistance at all. Her story is also more clearly abject than her mother's, for the premise of the second half of the novel is simplicity itself. Should Matilda present herself to her father, the object of her desire, she will be banished from his home. As the now kindly Sandford says, "'What recompense would his kind thoughts be to you . . . were he to turn you out to beggary?' 'A great deal—a great deal,' she replie[s]" (225). In speaking of the masochist, Massé says that "[h]er acceptance of the suffering others impose is necessary to her psychic and physical well-being: she, like all of us, must have whatever form of 'love' is available to create and preserve a coherent identity."[23] For Matilda, this love is paternal, incestuous, and totally destructive, as well as being the only thing that can give her a coherent identity of any kind. Rather than resist her culturally determined role with an already fruitless gesture of defiance or self-determination, she makes her oppressor the object of her love. The only possible object of her desire, that is, the one other that can ever give meaning to her self is her father. "To each ego its object, to each superego its abject," Kristeva says.[24] This is the structuring principle of *A Simple Story*; this is its form.

The father's rejection of Lady Matilda, his almost apoplectic fury when her name is mentioned, suggests an obsession that could hardly be considered "natural." The one time she meets him and collapses in his arms, he "presse[s] her to his bosom," and she mutters the hopeless, "Save me":

> Her voice unmanned him.—His long-restrained tears now burst forth—and seeing her relapsing into the swoon again, he cried out eagerly to recall her.—Her name did not however come to his recollection—nor any name but this—"Miss Milner—Dear Miss Milner." (274)

The very thought of a reconciliation with his daughter "unmans" Lord Elmwood: his masculinity itself depends on the distance that her abjection has implied. In this scene he articulates an incestuous longing that is stifled as soon as it is uttered. His inability to distinguish his wife from his daughter is not so surprising—his wife was after all his "daughter" before she became his wife. His attitude toward her, moreover, is more that of a spurned and furious lover than that of an alienated father. In his terms, in the culture's terms rather, the two cannot necessarily be distinguished. Castle says that this sequel is a "spectral reenactment of its utopian original."[25] As such it spells out in more romantic extravagance the underlying implications of the first story. Here we have the totally self-abnegating heroine falling into the destructive yet welcoming arms of the father in an embrace that defies patriarchal control at the same time that it articulates it in all its ruthlessness.

I have mentioned Lady Matilda's obsession with this man and her ever-vigilant attention to the implication of his whims, insofar as they are communicated to her. She hovers just outside his awareness whenever he has been in Elmwood Castle, and she allows herself to follow him in and out of rooms he has inhabited. She can allow herself only the ghostly outlines of contact with her father, the absent presence that haunts her private moments:

> In the breakfast and dining rooms she leaned over those seats with a kind of filial piety, on which she was told he had been accustomed to sit. And in the library she took up with filial delight, the pen with which he had been writing; and looked with the most curious attention into those books that were laid upon his reading desk. (245–46)

"Filial delight" hardly needs a gloss in a novel which has eroticized authority and rendered it problematic. Lady Matilda fetishizes these leavings and plays with his pen because patriarchy itself has made any other relation to power utterly pointless. She does not so much reject suits for her hand as not even notice them: she has eyes for one man only, the father who refuses to see her.

The only character in this second part of the novel who dares to question paternal whim and even challenge its authority is Rushbrook. As adopted son of the lord it almost seems a right, if not a duty, for him to make his challenge. We repeatedly hear that he is Lord Elmwood's heir only by the lord's pleasure and that a rash gesture on his side could cause him to lose his favored position. He is emasculated by Lord Elmwood's preemptive behavior, and his attempts to articulate an independent position are mocked and held under suspicion by his lord and master. That he chooses to defy the divine right of fathers through his love for Lady Matilda brings into high relief the complexities of the Oedipal structure at work in this novel. His attempts to speak up for the dispossessed girl earn him threatening looks and promised "vengeance" (289) that Lord Elmwood had threatened to exercise on anyone who mentioned her name in his presence. The look of vengeance begins to suggest the power of the repression that Lord Elmwood experiences, and it also places him in a position that Matilda has already imagined.

Rushbrook expresses his own desire for his sister-cousin in terms that the novel has already provided: "Lady Matilda . . . is an object that wrests from me the enjoyment of every blessing your kindness bestows. —I cannot but feel myself as her adversary—as one who has supplanted her in your affections—who supplies her place, while she is exiled, a wanderer, and an orphan" (289–90). Rushbrook is vying with Matilda for a place in Lord Elmwood's affections, just as he vies with Lord Elmwood, later, for a place in hers. Triangulation of desire, an oddly inverted family triangle in this case, becomes the norm.[26] No sooner does Rushbrook articulate these home truths about his awkward position in this inverted triangle, than he turns his outrage on himself:

> [H]e beheld himself as a barbarian, who had treated his benevolent and only friend, with an insufferable liberty; void of respect for the gnawing sorrows which had imbittered so many years of his life, and in open violation of his most strict commands. —He felt he deserved all he was going to suffer, and he fell upon his knees, not so much to deprecate the doom he now saw impending, as thus humbly to acknowledge it was his due. (291)

So effectively has Lord Elmwood exerted his paternal power that his self-abasing would-be hero finds himself on his knees and doomed. No less ready than his cousin to suffer at the hands of this magnificent benefactor, Henry Rushbrook attempts to break the pattern of paternal abuse with his own attractive but insufficient form. Abjection becomes for him too the only response that a ruthless patriarchy, almost deliriously sadistic, can allow.

The intensity of this encounter, which ends with Rushbrook's being ordered from the house and protection of Lord Elmwood, suggests how high the stakes between these two men have become. Rushbrook loves Matilda, but obviously he also sees his love as a way of challenging and breaking through the reserve of his foster father. Matilda becomes a pawn in a game they are playing. At the same time, Rushbrook's daring to challenge Lord Elmwood with his love for his daughter challenges patriarchal control precisely where it seems most secure. Both Matilda and Rushbrook are dispossessed and entirely dependent on the will of the father.

FAMILY VALUES

The timid and despairing Rushbrook and the battered and broken Lady Matilda are a couple familiar from Gothic fiction. And like their Gothic cousins, they offer to wallow in their doom perhaps to underline the horror to which they are subjected. Inchbald protests paternal authority, in other words, in terms that put the lie to notions of paternal "goodness" and domestic virtue. The brutality of Lord Elmwood and the abjection that both Matilda and Rushbrook experience before him suggest the ways in which the Oedipal family is writ large in culture. The symbolic Law of the Father is represented here by a father who makes his own laws and enforces them peremptorily.

As if concerned that we not miss her point about paternal villainy, however, Inchbald subjects Lady Matilda to one further outrage before the inevitable reconciliation can transpire. Lord Margrave, one of Matilda's "rejected" suitors, pursues her fruitlessly for some time until finally his friends convince him to abduct her by force. She is carried off almost effortlessly, and Lord Margrave has the suffering heroine under his own power for several hours before anyone comes to her aid. Lady Matilda is such an easy target, as the novelist reminds us, because she has been cast aside by her father and has no one else to "defend her honour." The abduction finally raises Lord Elmwood out of his lassitude, and he rescues her. Notice, though, that he chooses not to protect her from the abduction but rather to rescue her after it. He chooses, that is, the role of lover—he leaves Rushbrook at home while he sets out fully armed—a heroic rescuer rather than the more prosaic but infinitely more comforting role of father. When he rushes into Lord Margrave's bedroom to save his daughter, his role is clear:

> That moment her father entered—and with the unrestrained fondness of a parent, folded her in his arms.
> Her extreme, her excess of joy on such a meeting; and from such anguish rescued, was still, in part, repressed by his awful presence. —The apprehensions to which she had been accustomed, kept her timid and doubtful—she feared to speak, or clasp him in return for his embrace, but falling on her knees clung round his legs, and bathed his feet with her tears. —These were the happiest moments she had ever known—perhaps the happiest *he* had ever known. (328–29)

The lord here asserts his heroic posture and her abjection without even thinking. The act of "folding" his brutally rejected daughter seems to assume that no explanation of his past behavior is necessary —she becomes in any case a mute object. She "represse[s]" the "excess" of joy she is meant to feel on this occasion precisely because it threatens her predetermined position in this particular family romance. Rather than speak, she falls to her knees in a gesture of submission that cannot be misunderstood in present company. She has reason to be happy: she has found that she can experience the pleasure of rejection even as he accepts her; he has reason to be happy as well: finally he has a woman where he has always wanted one.

The happiness is so intense—her abjection so complete—that it is difficult to see this as anything but the resolution to the novel. Once again a tearful father-daughter embrace, with him of course on top, brings the promise of a tentative resolution. This admittedly leaves little room for Rushbrook, and his attempt finally to assert himself as a lover for the reclaimed daughter is almost an afterthought. It seems so much less important than the paternal resolution, moreover, that Inchbald feels that it is better to hint at it as a possibility than to claim it as a fact. We are told only that when Rushbrook makes his final plea that "whether the heart of Matilda . . . *could* sentence him to misery, the reader is left to surmise" (337). In her abjection, it seems, she is unable to articulate active desire even in the novel's final moments. Inchbald is not being coy here; rather, she is reminding us of Matilda's own misery at the same time that she admits formally that Matilda already has the man of her dreams. Because of the energy of the primary relationship, there is little more that she dare say.

The feminism of the novel, as Castle and Spencer in their different ways argue, is unmistakable. It is Inchbald's stifled cry of protest at female victimization as well as her bold attempt to articulate what she must see as the basic truth of female desire. By telling her story twice, moreover, Inchbald avoids a "happy ending" two different times. I have quoted Castle as suggesting that the novel "alters the ideological force of the marriage plot itself."[27] The tenor of this alteration is implicit in the resolution I have just described. On one hand, it offers the perfect resolution to what has been a novel about the abjection of the female in a patriarchal culture. On the other hand, it invests the marriage plot with terms that undermine its force and question its significance. The act of patriarchal exchange is enacted in both plots, and in both there is a single male figure. This gives the lie to the "bargain," in which the female is given a degree of power in the domestic sphere. Inchbald insists that all female power is illusory, even that power she so infamously wields over male desire.

THREE

Female Gothic (1):
Friends and Mothers

At a climactic moment in *The Castle of Otranto* (1764), Horace Walpole dramatizes the flight of Isabella, his vulnerable heroine, within the gloomy confines of the castle's subterranean regions. In so doing, he opens an area of investigation that later writers explore with enthusiasm:

> The lower part of the castle was hollowed in to several intricate cloisters; and it was not easy for one under so much anxiety to find the door that opened into the cavern. An awful silence reigned throughout those subterraneous regions, except now and then some blasts of wind that shook the doors she had passed, and which grating on the rusty hinges were re-echoed through that long labyrinth of darkness.[1]

Walpole may not have known that he was offering terms for what would come to be known as "female Gothic"; but he did understand that female vulnerability was an area of great fictional potential. I shall not spend time here on Walpole's version of female experience, but I would rather like to turn my attention to the phenomenon of women writing novels in which they are at times brutally victimized and always threatened.

Tania Modleski argues that "the female Gothic . . . expresses women's most intimate fears, or, more precisely, their fears about intimacy—about the exceedingly private, even claustrophobic nature of their existence." "Furthermore," she says, "female Gothics provide an outlet for women's fears about fathers and husbands."[2] In so stating the case for female Gothic fiction, Modleski suggests that by offering their female readers this "outlet" for anxieties about their position in late-eighteenth-century patriarchal society, female Gothic writers were, perhaps unwittingly, working out a system by means of which they could be accommodated to their fate. Female Gothic, in Modleski's terms, works in the way that Fredric Jameson describes in his discussion of "mass culture": mass culture, he says, performs "a transformational work on [real] social and political anxieties and fantasies which must then have some effective presence in the mass cultural text in order subsequently to be 'managed' or repressed."[3] Female Gothicists, according to this analysis, would be "transforming" the very real anxieties that they and other late-eighteenth-century women experienced within a patriarchal system into a "cultural text" by means of which the anxieties around the issue of victimization could be "managed." The writers themselves, the argument might go, are unwittingly performing a cultural function that results in their own oppression.

While such an argument works well for twentieth-century popular Gothic, its effectiveness is limited when applied to eighteenth-century female Gothic. In the first place, women were so silenced and their desire so discounted that these expressions of female anxiety and female desire have an almost immediate political significance. Anne Williams has noted the almost too obvious fact that female Gothic fiction, "organized around the female perspective, . . . necessarily views the male as 'other.'"[4] Ideological conditioning, however, can make this reversal much more difficult than it sounds. The novelists I discuss in this chapter were themselves often aware of their ideological conditioning and, in more than one case, dedicated to resisting hegemonic control. Finally, the supposed victimization is not always as simple or as one-directional as critics such as Modleski make it sound. As I will demonstrate in this chapter, victimization itself can become a form of resistance in these works.[5]

Jameson's repression model is directly opposed to a Foucauldian reading of history, in which discourse, akin to Jameson's "cultural text," neither manages nor represses matters of sexual urgency but rather encourages, even demands, their wider and more vociferous expression. As Foucault explains in *The History of Sexuality,* late-eighteenth-century culture becomes increasingly sexualized in even its most intimate forms.[6] This sexualization of the family, hysterization of the female body, and eroticization of various social forms is central to the work of female Gothic writers. Their own awareness of this process suggests, however, that an element of protest underlies their brilliant expressive extravagances. Foucault would argue, of course, that no matter how deeply felt their protest, these authors and their Gothic imaginings were already accommodated within a system of power deployment. I would insist that these works are never fully accommodated within any cultural system and that they push culture to its limit, and beyond. That is what makes these works Gothic and what convinces me that these women are by no means satisfied with the status quo. They are attempting always to do something more than culture allows them.

In another essay I have argued how various elements of the cult of sensibility can be seen as symptoms that expose the underpinnings of the emerging bourgeois culture that embraced them.[7] Female Gothic fiction can be seen as symptom as well, not just of the "real" of female desire, but also of the reason that female desire must take this Gothic form. Slavoj Žižek notes that a symptom is "a particular, 'pathological,' signifying formation, a binding of enjoyment, an inert stain resisting communication and interpretation, a stain which cannot be included in the circuit of discourse, of social bond network, but is at the same time a positive condition of it."[8] Female Gothic fiction is a positive condition of the "social bond network" that controls female desire for the purposes of domestic regulation. The "angel of the house," in other words, can have meaning only to the extent that her bleeding Gothic sisters lie huddled in the corners of dungeons that the nineteenth-century bourgeois imagination refused to conceive.

Female Gothic novelists began consciously imitating the early practitioners of Gothic writing, especially Horace Walpole, and in doing so, they helped to codify a set of narrative conventions which could be recognized and indeed marketed as "Gothic." Walpole had articulated in *The Castle of Otranto* the possibility of a fiction that at once defied the limitations of realistic expectation while subscribing to the basic terms of narrative convention. Hence he produced a novel in which the "everyday" quality of fiction was violated in countless ways but which also conformed to a plot whereby the female was both brutally victimized and ritualistically married—in some cases, of course, these fates are the same. Walpole's claim, in the preface to the second edition of his novel, that "the great resources of

fancy have been dammed up, by a strict adherence to common life," sometimes masks the fact that his females are one-dimensional and useful really
only in the degree to which they can suffer.[9]

Several writers took inspiration from the historical setting of Walpole's
work and the narrative possibilities of an inherently threatening past—
abandoned rooms may be haunted, locked chests may harbor dreadful
secrets, tattered manuscripts may divulge horrifying transgressions. Although different from one another in countless ways, these writers share
the tendency to use the conventions of Gothic fiction to add excitement to
tales that are primarily historical (and sentimental) romances, committed
more to the heroine's tears than to her terrors. Often, they use a heroine's
own suspicions as a way of instructing her as to the foolishness of Gothic
imaginings: the ghosts that wander unchecked in *The Castle of Otranto*
here turn out to be explainable in physical terms, in obedience to rules of
realism—"the limits of credibility," Clara Reeve calls them. Gothic writers
like Clara Reeve, Charlotte Smith, and, to a degree, Sophia Lee were un-
willing to violate these limits, and they use Gothic effects simply to heighten
the moral lessons of otherwise sentimental tales. This version of female
Gothic is corrective: it finds Gothic effects attractive but resents the ways in
which it has caused a disruption in narrative decorum. That these women
wrote Gothic fiction at all, however, is a measure of their attraction to this
"dangerous" form. Whatever else is true, it offered them a chance to escape
into a narrative mode of violation: that they pull back from that mode so
successfully is a measure of control. In most cases, however, it is a control
that is thinly disguised attraction to the transgressive possibilities—in narrative and social terms—of Gothic experience.[10]

MEN IN LOVE: *THE OLD ENGLISH BARON*

Reeve called *The Old English Baron* (published as *The Champion of
Virtue* in 1777) "the literary offspring of the *Castle of Otranto*," but it is a
far cry from Walpole's lurid masterpiece. In it she tells a tale of wrongful
usurpation and uses some of the less shocking devices of *Otranto*, such as
"incoherent dreams," a "haunted" chamber, even "ghosts" and a skeleton.
But her imagination is less engaged by scenes of haunting than by the legal
squabbles of a group of petty aristocrats, and her attempts to articulate
"sentimental" codes of social interaction seem far more deeply felt and
dramatically persuasive.

James Trainer argues that "without her decisive intervention to make
possible supernatural fiction which does not do violence to human reason

the new direction taken by Ann Radcliffe would have been unthinkable." Trainer argues that Reeve finds a way to suggest the presence of a supernatural world in her work: "By bringing this other world into the lives of simple men and thereby allowing them a momentary *frisson* which could quickly be banished by appeal to their Christian faith. . . . This ambivalence, the simultaneous attraction and repulsion which may be caused by some external phenomenon, is what Clara Reeve was struggling with in her theories to reconcile the marvellous and the probable."[11] Reeve's "ambivalence" about her Gothic project suggests an uneasiness at the heart of female Gothic itself. It is not just the uneasiness, however, over how to "reconcile the marvellous and the probable."[12] For Reeve, as for her imitators, the marvellous and the probable, the worlds of fantasy and reality, could never be adequately reconciled from a female point of view. The unknown is attractive because it is different from what is known: it might be a place in which female power has some viability. For Reeve, as we shall see, the world that is known is almost entirely male. Maybe the other world harbors some secret female power after all.

The Old English Baron concerns Edmund Twyford, an admirable peasant youth who proves to be the rightful heir to the Lovel title and estate and who earns his right through the help of Sir Philip Harclay, a friend of his murdered father. Early in the novel, Sir Philip begins to suspect foul play when he has a dream in which his deceased friend Lord Lovel leads him "into a dark and frightful cave, where he disappeared, and in his stead he beheld a complete suit of armour stained with blood, which belonged to his friend, and he thought he heard dismal groans from beneath."[13] Reeve's Gothic technique places such effects in a dream, and when this dream material finds its equivalent in reality, as it does in the "haunted" chamber in which Edmund is forced to spend a night to prove his bravery, it takes on the character of a heinous crime rather than a supernatural occurrence: Lovel was murdered in his armor and buried beneath the floor of the room in question. This is the technique known as "explained Gothic": whatever supernatural elements heighten suspense throughout the tale are always accommodated to naturalistic explanations before matters are brought to a close.

Many critics have suggested that "explained Gothic" is deflating and that writers such as Reeve, and after her Radcliffe, raise expectations so high that the explanations inevitably disappoint. Yet even a writer like Reeve is forced into incestuous longing, fraternal murder, and familial secrecy as a way of "explaining" the few groans that she allows herself. In other words, it seems to me that the explanations are more harrowing than critics have given writers like Reeve credit for. Moreover, the story she tells, although predictable in its general outline, shocks in some of its specific detail.

More importantly, Reeve's insistence on "natural" explanations opens the way for the uncanny to enter her text. As Terry Castle argues in *The Female Thermometer*, "At numerous points in [Freud's] 'The Uncanny,' . . . it is difficult to avoid the conclusion that it was during the eighteenth century, with its confident rejection of transcendental explanations, compulsive quest for systematic knowledge, and self-conscious valorization of 'reason' over 'superstition,' that human beings first experienced that encompassing sense of strangeness and unease Freud finds so characteristic of modern life."[14] Clara Reeve is a mistress of the kind of strangeness that Castle explores here, and she works to show that strangeness is indeed an integral part of everyday life.

Interestingly, this tale, one of the first "female Gothic" efforts, concerns itself almost exclusively with the behavior and the relations of men. Female characters in *The Old English Baron* are either murdered, like Edmund's mother, or ignored, like Lady Emma, his eventual wife. Reeve attempts to create some love interest around the figure of Lady Emma, but her effort is perfunctory. The few scenes between Emma and Edmund, are stilted and ineffective—trembling, confusion, and silence is their frequent mode—and even the moment of their betrothal is severely compromised:

> Come hither, my Emma! said the Baron. She approached, with tears on her cheek, sweetly blushing, like the damask rose, wet with the dew of the morning. I must ask you a serious question, my child; answer me with the same sincerity you would to Heaven. You see this young man, the Heir of Lovel! you have known him long; consult your own heart, and tell me whether you have any objection to receive him for your husband? I have promised to all this company to give you to him; but upon condition that you approve him: I think him worthy of you; and, whether you accept him or not, he shall ever be to me a son. . . . Speak freely, and decide this point for me and for yourself. The fair Emma blushed, and was under some confusion; her virgin modesty prevented her speaking for some moments. (143)

Here, as elsewhere, Emma's demands and disappointments seem secondary to the display of male affection. Even when she does manage to articulate her desire in this scene, it is through that of her father: "As I am called upon in this public manner, it is but justice to this Gentleman's merit to declare, that, were I at liberty to choose a husband from all the world, he only should be my choice, who I can say, with joy, is my father's also." (143)

Reeve rises much more effectively to the task of discussing male rivalry and the struggles for power amid this group of petty landowners. More energy, for instance, goes into the description of the arrangements for a duel between Lord Lovel and Sir Philip than into any detail of the relation between Edmund and Emma. More to the point, the attachment between Sir Philip Harclay and Edmund shapes the narrative: Sir Philip notices the youth when he first visits the seat of his deceased friend and he tries to carry Edmund off as his own servant; later he greets him as a long-lost relative, virtually adopts him as his own son, and gives him his mother's family name; then, of course, he fights for him (in the duel mentioned above), defeats his enemy, and procures him a name and estate; then, conveniently, he gives away his own home and moves in with Edmund and his wife, where he lives "to extreme old age in honour and happiness" until he dies "in the arms of his beloved Edmund" (153). Edmund, for his part, never seems happier than when "on his knees" before Sir Philip—a suggestive posture—in token of his love and submission to his dear friend of his father: "As he drew near he was seized with an universal trembling; he kneeled down, took his hand, kissed it, and pressed it to his heart in silence" (85).

Reeve eroticizes male friendship because it helps her to dramatize the emotional intensity behind male relations and the male claim to power. Later, when Lady Emma is proposed as a compromise solution for Baron Fitz-Owen, she seems to function as little more than a pawn in the male power-game. Sir Philip initiates the following negotiation with the Baron:

> Cease to look upon Edmund as the enemy of your house; look upon him as a son, and make him so indeed!—How say you, Sir Philip? my son!—Yes, my Lord; give him your daughter: He is already your son in filial affection! your son William and he are sworn brothers; what remains but to make him yours? He deserves such a parent, you such a son. (125)

These are not the negotiations of men who see women as anything more than a means to get closer to one another. What is striking, however, is the degree to which this *male* quality of the Gothic world is heightened and emphasized in Reeve's account. The author, that is, may be mocking male relations at the same time that she seems to celebrate them. ("My Lord, I am yours!" Edmund says to the Baron, "all that I have is at your devotion! dispose of me as it pleases you best." [142]) She may be marking the dimensions of a network of patriarchal relations at the same time that she silences and marginalizes the females in her text. *The Old English Baron* is a story of corruption and intrigue—the corruption and intrigue of an "old" order. Reeve's "new" order, barely articulated, is one in which male relations are eroticized and/or domesticated, while fraternal relations between men and women are acknowledged as potentially something more than that expression implies. If her vision is predominantly *male,* her narrative voice undermines the usual male pretensions to power. Reeve equates the patriarchal and the Gothic in a particularly illuminating way. Eve Kosofsky Sedgwick has suggested that "in any male-dominated society, there is a special relationship between male homosocial (*including* homosexual) desire and the structures for maintaining and transmitting patriarchal power: a relationship founded on an inherent and potentially active structural congruence."[15] Reeve may not have intended to expose the underpinnings of culture so ruthlessly, but she does expose some of the most harrowing features of the male-dominated society in which female Gothic fiction emerged.

VISUAL PLEASURE: *EMMELINE, THE ORPHAN OF THE CASTLE*

Charlotte Smith, in such novels as *Emmeline, the Orphan of the Castle* (1788), *Ethelinde, or, the Recluse of the Lake* (1789), and *The Old Manor House* (1793), brings the use of setting to a new level of Gothic sophistication. As Lévy says, "No one before Radcliffe could better transcribe the secret impulse of terror felt by a young girl given up to an architecture, where the softest sound and the lightest shade are amplified by the resonance and obscurity of the vaults to fit the dimensions of a nightmare."[16] In the first of these novels, Smith tells the story of a persecuted heroine, Emmeline, and her rakish lover, Delamere. Less interested than Walpole in the Gothic dimensions of her plot, she still uses techniques such as seemingly supernatural events and unreasonable persecution of the heroine to heighten the emotional intensity of her tale. In doing so, she also insists on female education and the importance of female clear-headedness. In anticipating some of the central concerns of later writers in this way, Smith suggests the intersection of Gothic and sentimental fiction more vividly than her contemporaries. Her novels also help to demonstrate the degree to which the Gothic became a crucial element in female education, and at the same time they help to explain what may have inspired some of Radcliffe's less satisfying turns, especially in the direction of "explanation."

Smith shifts the focus of Gothic from character to setting, and in doing so she establishes the area in which the first generation of female Gothicists were to excel. Classic male heroism has little place in Gothic fiction. In order for a hero like Edmund, in *The Old English Baron,* to be a hero, he must dismiss the superstitions that haunt a wing of Castle Lovel, and the energy of the tale is spent in dismissing ghosts as the rightful heir reclaims his throne. Later female Gothic substitutes for such bravery a kind of fear that in the late eighteenth century was almost programmatically connected to the female. Gothic novelists rewrite male heroism as well, of course, but it was in the realm of female response that they were to establish Gothic most effectively. There are many reasons for the female nature of the Gothic; preeminent among them is the very process of gender categorization that was extending its influence in areas as diverse as medicine, aesthetics, psychology, and economics. In addition, of course, the novel had proven that the suffering female could, as in the case of *Clarissa*, be a source of almost unending expressive power. Finally, theories of the sublime had established a certain vocabulary of terror that place the female experience of quasi-sexual assault among the more exotic areas of terrific effect.[17]

When Emmeline, the title character of Smith's first novel, looks out from the turret in Mowbray Castle, where she hopes to escape the assiduities of an unpleasant guardian, she looks with an eye especially sensitive to picturesque effect.[18] What the "view" does novelistically, however, is to capture an emotion in the landscape. Smith is not the first to have done this, but she does it in such a way that thrilled her readers; and she manages to suggest the sensibility of her heroine and her "visionary" power:

> the beautiful prospect it commanded between the hills, where suddenly sinking to the South West, they made way through a long narrow valley, fringed with copses, for a small but rapid river; which hurrying among immense stones, and pieces of rock that seemed to have been torn from the mountains by its violence, rushed into the sea at the distance of a mile from the castle.[19]

The scene is gentle, but it contains the surging river at its very heart. Like Emmeline herself, in other words, the scene vibrates with emotion—with hopes and fears—that the novel proceeds to analyze. The "violence" depicted here, moreover, is a harbinger of the psychological and emotional violence that the heroine will undergo. Her attraction to these things in the landscape is a measure of her power to overcome them in her life.

Smith uses the castle to provide Walpole-like effects, and even when Emmeline is not in imminent danger, the castle sets a mood that creates the ominous feeling that characterizes so much of Gothic fiction:

> A total silence had long reigned in the castle, and her almost extinguished candle told her it was time to take some repose, when, as she was preparing to do so, she thought she heard a rustling, and indistinct footsteps in the passage near her room.
>
> She started—listened—but all was again profoundly silent; and she supposed it had been only one of those unaccountable noises which she had

been used to hear along the dreary avenues of the castle. She began anew to unpin her hair, when a second time the same noise in the passage alarmed her. She listened again; and while she continued attentive, the great clock struck two. (31–32)

At first glance, this passage could come right out of *The Castle of Otranto*, but it seems to me that there is none of Walpole's lurid amusement at the plight of the female and more real sympathy for the actual situation in which Emmeline finds herself. Smith's Gothic effect depends on female vulnerability, to be sure, and Smith suggests that vulnerability even as she has Emmeline reason herself out of her fears. Smith, that is, creates the Gothic effect of the scene by playing on our sense of the position of the female in a male society, even as she argues for female independence and self-determination. When, shortly after this, the door to her room is opened violently and Emmeline confronts the frantic Delamere, who is pouring out his love for her, Smith's uncanny Gothic technique is further revealed. It is no ancient ghost that stalks the halls of the castle but a young and impassioned suitor who threatens Emmeline more than any ghost ever could.[20]

Another way of putting that would be to say that Smith creates a character who undergoes some of the real terror behind Gothic effects. Walpole's Gothic character exists only to convey those effects to the reader. Smith's "female Gothic" reclaims emotion for her female character. The dread Emmeline feels is the dread of her vulnerability. In *The Female Thermometer*, Castle says that Freud's central insight is "that it is precisely the historic internalization of rationalist protocols that produces the uncanny." This insight, Castle claims, "offers a powerful dialectical model for understanding many of the haunting paradoxes of eighteenth-century literature and culture." She says, as Freud does in "The Uncanny," that "the more we seek enlightenment, the more alienating our world becomes; the more we seek to free ourselves, Houdini-like from the coils of superstition, mystery, and magic, the more tightly, paradoxically, the uncanny holds us in its grip."[21] Emmeline realizes this dynamic as she gazes into the darkness that surrounds her. As the ghosts are dispelled, the real fears only begin to emerge.

Landscape can also help to register this protest whenever Emmeline is in emotional or psychological distress. Smith is always careful to remind us of not only her own descriptive powers but also both how sensitive Emmeline is to her surroundings and how essentially threatening even a natural landscape can become. Passages such as the following suggest a sensitivity to landscape, a "female" sensitivity that is to be celebrated, at the same time that it suggests a sense of loss and impending doom. That Emmeline can recognize these things is to her credit; that she must suffer them is inherent in her ability to recognize their power. When Emmeline sets out from Mowbray Castle to escape Delamere, Smith paints the following picture:

> The road lay along the side of what would in England be called a mountain; at it's [*sic*] feet rolled the rapid stream that washed the castle walls, foaming over fragments of rock; and bounded by a wood of oak and pine; among which the ruins of the monastery, once an appendage to the castle, reared it's broken arches; and marked by grey and mouldering walls, and mounds covered with slight vegetation, it was traced to it's connection with the castle itself, still frowning in gothic magnificence; and stretching over several acres of ground: the citadel, which was totally in ruins and covered with ivy, crowning the whole. Farther to the West, beyond a bold and rocky shore, appeared the sea; and to the East, a chain of mountains which seemed to meet the clouds; while on the other side, a rich and beautiful vale, now variegated with the mellowed tints of the declining year, spread its enclosures, 'till it was lost again among the blue and barren hills. (37)

This is description for the sake of description—where else, one might ask, had women been given the opportunity to paint such vivid pictures as these—but it is also a Gothic description insofar as it reminds us that Emmeline is a character under threat from a tradition, mouldering and ruined as it is, that still exerts its control over such as she. Smith makes the connection between the picturesque landscape and the threatened heroine almost automatic. The reader is asked to understand the landscape, that is, through the heroine; and thus one of the central Gothic conventions is established.

Emmeline's connection to the landscape is also an interpretive connection. Her visionary power invests her with a subjectivity that her cultural objectification would deny. That is why so much energy goes into landscape in female Gothic: it offers the female herself a center from which to view the world and it grants her a visionary power that officially belongs only to the male poets of the age. In this case, of course, the description centers around the Gothic castle itself, here represented as "totally in ruins and covered with ivy": Smith manages, as Lévy suggests, to invoke the implicit threat of the Gothic setting at the same time that she distances it and places it in "perspective." It is threatening to the heroine, it seems, except in the degree to which she can *see* it in its diminished power. This is one of the features of Smith's Gothic, of course, the manifestations of power are everywhere, but they diminish in importance if the heroine can exercise her own powers of observation and judgment.

After the opening scenes set in her childhood home, however, Emmeline, the "orphan of the Castle," has to make her way among less obviously

Gothic effects familiar in the sentimental world. Throughout the central sections of the novel, the tragicomedy in which she participates is never far from its Gothic underpinnings. Here, for instance, is a description of her abject state after Delamere has carried her off, for marriage or worse:

> Her cheek, robbed of it's [*sic*] bloom, rested on her arm, which appeared more bloodless than her cheek; her hair, which had been dressed without powder, had escaped from the form in which it had been adjusted, and half concealed her face in disordered luxuriance; her lips were pale, and her respiration short and laborious. (154)

Such a description is reminiscent of *Clarissa*. This careful study of disorder reminds us of both the violence she has suffered and the gaze to which she is subjected. This pale and exhausted form is the victim of male aggression, to be sure, but this is also the image of female power in a patriarchal world. "Disordered luxuriance" suggests the erotic threat to which she has succumbed; but it also suggests the degree to which she retains control. Emmeline is constantly victimized, in other words, but she is never a victim. Delamere never forces her to acknowledge his desire. She remains her own woman in spite of all his attempts to make her the object of his desire. Her visionary power has made this self-possession almost inevitable.

The other side of female sensitivity—the horrid Gothic side—is expressed in the person of Lady Montreville, the mother of Delamere. She holds Emmeline in contempt and uses everything in her power to control the passion of her son. Her motherly "affection" is so intense that when she hears (mistakenly) that he has been wounded in a duel, she gives way to a kind of hysteria that was increasingly codified as female. As her daughter writes to Emmeline:

> Her distorted features; her hands contracted, her eyes glazed and fixed, her livid complexion, and the agonizing expression of her countenance, were at their height when Delamere was desired to go into the room. (194)

The pain at the loss of a child is not to be underestimated, of course. But Lady Montreville has overreacted and indeed manipulated her emotions so often in the novel, that it seems as if Smith is making a point about female sensibility itself. When Lord Montreville speaks to his son, he uses his wife's illness to press his point about filial obedience, for he too disapproves of his son's interest in Emmeline: "If you would not be indeed a parricide, shew Lady Montreville that you have a sense of your errors, and will give her no farther uneasiness" (195). The family politics here are intense, and Smith has found a way to naturalize, as it were, the frequent Gothic device of the parricide. Delamere will "kill" his mother by resisting her will. By domesticating parricide in the form of female hysteria, moreover, Smith shows how "real" such Gothic devices can be. Lady Montreville's hysteria is used in an elaborate ploy to control her son. When, sometime later, she does die, after a series of nervous collapses, Smith insists on the consequences of her emotional self-indulgence. Cruel and vindictive she might be, but her death is a measure of how totally the female has been given over to emotion. Unlike Emmeline, who retains composure in extreme situations, Lady Montreville behaves as a female was supposed to behave; and as a result, she dies.

Adeline, the other nearly purely emotional character in the novel should die as well. Not only is she married off to a man twice her age who is brutal and villainous, but also she becomes involved in an adulterous affair and bears a child that is not her husband's. In the fiction of sensibility, she could surely be pitied, but she would also be doomed. This remarkable character is the sister of Emmeline's friend (and eventual suitor), Lord Westhaven and Godolphin. Her love for the rake Fitz-Edward, which is an embarrassment to all who know her, almost kills her. More than once she languishes in fitful delirium, and more than once she seems certain to pass out of this world. But she survives, and by the end of the novel she is even allowed to hope that she and the repentant Fitz-Edward may someday be united. Early critics of the book, including Mary Wollstonecraft, who reviewed it for the *Analytical Review,* were appalled at this generosity to an adulterous woman. But clearly Smith was interested in rewriting morality: the outwardly virtuous Lady Montreville dies a sinner; the sinful Adeline is virtuous enough to be rewarded with survival. This is a feminist stance, and even Wollstonecraft revised her attitude before too many years had passed. Smith is using the license of the Gothic to make claims for female sexuality that would not otherwise be possible.

In the drama of personal fulfillment and sexual threat, the landscape seems to offer a context in which a woman's physical presence can be naturalized. Not fainting or fleeing but in touch with the world around her, the female becomes something more than a male possession. Sensitivity to nature also allows her to see, where other women might be blind. Smith's heroine does not succumb to fear, nor does she allow herself to become the victim of darkness and gloom. She internalizes the uncanny, that is, as a way of triumphing over the threat of the unknown. Her imagination gives her control of the world around her, and it also places her in spectral relation to all that she sees.[22]

At the end of the novel, Emmeline returns to Mowbray Castle, her home. What the novel has taught her, more than how to choose the right husband, is how to live in the world. Gothic trappings frighten her into a confrontation with her deepest fears about her illegitimacy. But what Emmeline finds is not just a mother as well as a father—her illegitimacy is disproved when she finds proof that her father actually married her mother before his death, making her the rightful heir of Mowbray—as the book rushes to its conclusion. She also finds, as the passage quoted above demonstrates, a self that will make her tenancy in the castle a real possibility.

Emmeline is among the first Gothic heroines, and her position may help us to determine central features of female Gothic itself. Emmeline is vulnerable in the ways that a helpless and orphaned female can only be in a patriarchy. She is victimized by the attentions of others—almost always unwanted—and she is in actual physical danger more than once. The forces moving against her—moving villainously and without her knowledge to deprive her of her natural rights—are constantly threatening, so much so that even her most comfortable moments are threatened by an abuse of power. In spite of all this, Emmeline succeeds to determine her own fate and to make choices for herself.

Several critics have suggested that female Gothic articulates a fantasy of female power.[23] Emmeline's success against all these odds, suggests that there is an element of truth to that claim. Smith, after all, who had been bitterly unhappy in marriage, was now writing to support herself and her many children. She had scores to settle with men in general, and with the particular kind of man who was her husband.[24]

At the same time, and perhaps for similar reasons, there appears to be, in female Gothic fiction, an attraction toward suffering. Even in *Emmeline,* we might note the exhilarating detail with which the heroine's various failures are articulated. Her fears are given ample coverage, and even descriptions of nature could be said to put her in a vulnerable position. The attraction of weakness and vulnerability is something I will attend to more carefully in chapter 9. It seems to me too easy to say that these works express a fantasy of female power, without stopping to consider what other kinds of fantasizing they might express. Michelle Massé argues that the passivity of Gothic heroines is overdetermined, "engendered not only by some single representative of authority but also by larger social institutions that reproduce themselves by what Nancy Chodorow calls 'legitimating ideologies.'" For Massé, these heroines are trapped: "their social contract tenders their passivity and disavowal of public power in exchange for the love that will let them reign in the interpersonal and domestic spheres. . . . Yet, like Dora," she says, "they are surrounded by couples who testify to the transaction's failure. What *is* gives the lie to what they are told *should be,* and they are haunted by the discrepancy. . . . The Gothic plot is thus not an 'escape' from the real world but a repetition and exploration of the traumatic denial of identity found there."[25] Female Gothic, as *Emmeline* suggests, sometimes manages to challenge this denial, and in doing so it transforms suffering from a repetition of the traumatic denial into a celebration of the possibility of escape.

MATERNAL LONGING: *THE RECESS*

One of the most intriguing of recent feminist rereadings of the Gothic, Claire Kahane's "The Gothic Mirror" articulates a position which challenges previous modes of understanding the Gothic. In her essay, Kahane suggests that the Gothic castle offers the typically motherless heroine a setting in which her own victimization can be confronted and somehow overcome. She does this by "maternalizing" the space which threatens her: the subterranean regions of the castle, these secret spaces, dark and womb-like as they are, come to represent the maternal space that the heroine both desires and fears. Kahane says, "What I see repeatedly locked into the forbidden center of the Gothic which draws me inward is the spectral presence of a dead-undead mother, archaic and all-encompassing, a ghost signifying the problematics of femininity which the heroine must confront."[26]

This kind of interpretation offers a great deal to critics who are attempting to understand what kind of attraction Gothic fiction might have held for the thousands of females who read and wrote them. It is too easy to say that female readers are attracted to the thrill of illicit sexuality or the masochistic enjoyment of their victimization that the Gothic everywhere represents. Kahane's position offers another way to understand what is attractive to women in these works and why the plight of the Gothic heroine might have such seemingly universal power.

A key work in this regard is Sophia Lee's Elizabethan romance, *The Recess* (1783–1785). The peculiar space signified by the novel's title comprises a set of subterranean chambers constructed under an abbey, which in the near-past of the novel is a retreat in which the sister-heroines of the work, Matilda and Ellinor, spend their childhood. Formerly a convent, the space is cavelike but consists of various rooms, centered on "a vaulted passage" whose light "proceeded from casements of painted glass, so infinitely above our reach we could never seek a world beyond."[27] This remembered space assumes a suggestive womblike quality, and the distinctly charged memories of this childhood world are suffused with the idea of the girls' mother, the majestic but threateningly distant (and doomed) Mary, Queen of Scots. Just as Mary is a mother both inaccessible and dangerous—should the girls be acknowledged publicly, their lives would surely be in danger—the maternal space is the scene of horror (the incestuous relation of their foster parents, their own brutal incarceration and near-rape) as well as love (both between the sisters and among them and their historically important male companions, Leicester and Essex). The tale of unhappiness and loss that besets them—each is doomed to misery in love and wretchedness in life—returns repeatedly to this exotic space and the ominous happiness that it represents. In the end, however, it can only torment these girls with all they lack. The literally "absent" mother, glimpsed distantly only once before her execution, hovers over the work with a similarly threatening presence that always seems to promise happiness but in fact brings misery and despair. If later Gothicists create maternal specters to challenge heroines with the limits of their own subjectivity, Lee tries to maternalize history itself as harrowing and fraught with danger in a particularly female way.

Perhaps one of the most interesting Gothic features of *The Recess* is its handling of incest. The novel, so carefully set in a romanticized past, wastes no time in establishing relations that are sexually charged in obviously transgressive ways. The opening pages of the novel, in fact, suggest that the appropriated history will allow the author license in creating a world that is erotically charged as well as politically dangerous. The sisters, Matilda and Ellinor, emerge from an eroticized space and eroticized circumstances, in other words, in their bid to eroticize history itself. This may seem an odd "politics" for the mid-1780s, but what Lee seems to be claiming here is a space for the female not just central to political intrigue but its very cause.

The woman that the sisters know as mother from their earliest infancy in the "recess" is not in fact their mother: Mrs. Marlow tells her own story of being snatched from her mother at birth, amid a political intrigue of her own: "I lost a mother before I was sensible I had one" (1: 28). When she finally falls in love and marries, it is with a West Indian "possessed of considerable fortune, an amiable person, and an untainted heart" (1: 29). When, on their wedding night, it is revealed that they are brother and sister, the couple both collapse in "insensibility," before the result of their nefarious union is spelled out: "we were removed to separate apartments; Mr. Coleville, no longer my husband, had strength of constitution, but not strength of mind, to support this calamity; he fell into a deep melancholy, and shut himself from all the world: as to me, heaven, in mercy, took away my senses by a violent fever" (1: 37). In spite of this extreme repulsion, Mrs. Marlow soon attempts "to satisfy my brother Anthony no levity had erased from my mind the tender ties which once united us, and which time nor reason could ever entirely dissolve, I . . . conjured him to believe, since I could never be his, I never would be another's" (1: 41). Incest, these quotations seem to imply, creates a mood of nostalgic regret rather than self-contempt or horror. From this attitude, the more conventionally "Gothic" elements of the plot almost naturally spring: "I spent many hours in reviewing the ruins with which this place abounded; the gloomy magnificence of those great remains of art, was more suited to my sadness of soul than the softer and more varied scenes of nature" (1:42).[28]

Mrs. Marlow and Anthony, "Father Anthony" to the girls, do manage a cohabitation of sorts in the recess, and when Mrs. Marlow dies, she is conveyed to "a grave [that] was made for her in Father Anthony's cell, whither we conveyed her, wrapt in white, and crowned with the fading produce of this world" (1: 82). Lee evokes a kind of posthumous wedding ceremony to memorialize more than one of the unnatural relations that animate this Gothic place.

Other incestuous and otherwise transgressive sexual relations occur throughout the novel, involving characters such as the Earl of Leicester, whose wife becomes illicitly involved with her brother ("Give me time to breathe, Le Val! . . . for this horrible intelligence unmans me" [1: 140]), and James I, whose unconventional sexual interests are at least hinted at ("Governed by a predilection of the most absurd and singular nature, to a beautiful favourite he always delivered up the reins of empire; readily submitting to a shameful subjection in all important points, provided he might enjoy a ridiculous supremacy in his hours of indulgence and retirement" [3: 247–48]). Lee uses these violations of cultural taboos to create the atmosphere of erotic urgency throughout the work. If Lévi-Strauss can say that "even if the incest prohibition has its roots in nature it is only in the way it affects us as a social rule that it can be fully grasped," then it seems to me that it is as a social rule, as a cultural code, that Lee means to defy it. The world she describes is Gothic because such rules have ceased to apply.[29]

When Matilda and Ellinor first leave the recess, nature seems to them a discordant ruin:

> For a vast space beyond the tomb, the prospect was wild and awful to excess; sometimes vast heaps of stones were fallen from the building, among which trees and bushes had sprung up, and half involved the dropping pillars. Tall fragments of it sometimes remained, which seemed to sway about with every blast, and from whose mouldering top hung clusters and spires of ivy. (1: 85–86)

The "picturesque" effect of this ruined landscape, when given the context of sexual transgression and extreme states of emotional discomfort, becomes more rather than less expressive. The scene bespeaks the forlorn and threatened quality of these motherless girls and the danger which surrounds them and even slips between them as they proceed into the harrowing world.

What gives this novel its special quality, however, is the possibility of female relations it dramatizes. Not just the girls' attraction to the always tantalizingly close mother, Mary Stuart, but also their relations with their foster mother, Mrs. Marlow, with the antagonist, Queen Elizabeth, with friends, with servants, but most especially with each other, render this work female in ways that no other Gothic novel can claim. In many ways like *Millenium Hall, The Recess* celebrates women-centered affection and eroticizes maternal relations with unswerving flair. If this is not a feminotopia, such as those that Felicity Nussbaum describes in *Torrid Zones,* it does at least create the fantasy of a lost world of female-female desire.[30]

I suggested above that Lee was determined to defy culture by her attention to sexual relations that were unacceptable to late-eighteenth-century society. It seems to me that she also defies the position and importance of women in that society. Mary Poovey argues, for instance, that female sexuality was itself a taboo topic.[31] Yet Lee manages to create a historical precedent for the eroticization of female relations: sisterly as well as mother-daughter relations are reexamined in this way.

Together, the sisters experience early happiness, and later the truth of their birth: "She gave birth to two girls—for you, my dear children, are the fruit of this fatal marriage, who scarce had been held to the bosom of a mother, before you were divided from it, I fear, for ever" (1: 65). This "division" becomes the central obsession of their lives. They see her once from a distance "through a grated window" (1: 190), and they work tirelessly on her behalf, even though it places them at times at odds with their friends. Leicester, Matilda's eventual husband, has to resist her pleas on Mary's behalf—"What seems a duty in you, would be the worst of crimes in me" (1: 175); and Ellinor comes into repeated and dire conflict with the Queen of England herself. Each sister returns to the recess as a prisoner. Matilda notes, for instance: "I saw I had been conveyed into the great room of our Recess; sacred once to piety and innocence, but now, alas! the shelter and rapine perhaps murder" (2: 1). And later Ellinor finds herself in the familiar haunts (as it were) of her childhood. She writes to her sister: "[Lord Burleigh] ordered his servants to bear me into the grated room at the end of the eastern cloister. You cannot but remember the dismal place. Half sunk in ruin, and overhung with ivy, and trees of growth almost immemorial, it appeared the very cell of melancholy" (2: 214).

The recess itself becomes the focus of female fears and female desires in this novel. Both Ellinor and Matilda recognize in the recess, however, a kind of solace, a refuge as it were, from political intrigue, from flight, and even from madness and hysteria. The recess is that place that Clare Kahane describes, the secret center, the maternal. It is important here because it becomes the only source of consolation for these brutalized and victimized women. History, as it were, finds its source in a secret female space that retains its magic power throughout the novel. This subterranean world, associated as it is with the sisters and their dreams, becomes equivalent in the novel to female desire itself. Lee dramatizes that desire and feminizes it: real female desire, she seems to say, finds its object in the female. In their love for one another, in their desire for their absent mother, these women become hauntingly powerful in a world that is structured to exclude them. If the conflict between Elizabeth and Mary is suggestive historically, Lee fantasizes what it would be to multiply the maternal implications of this historical situation. In doing so, she gives the Female Gothic its uncanny power.

Part Two

LOVE AND
FRIENDSHIP

FOUR

Sisterly Love in
Sense and Sensibility

Even before Terry Castle's now infamous "outing" of Austen in the pages of the *London Review of Books,* to which I will soon return, academic rumor has run into high gear concerning Jane Austen and her sister Cassandra. Eve Kosofsky Sedgwick had implied as much in her equally controversial MLA talk in 1989. I was in the standing-room-only crowd that came together to hear papers on the "Muse of Masturbation" in Washington that year, and although each of the papers in this panel was stunning, no one in this avant-garde audience was more titillated than by the promise of "Jane Austen and the Masturbating Girl"; nor, it seems, did any paper at the convention receive more attention: Sedgwick herself chronicles public response—what she calls "phobic narratives about the degeneracy of academic discourse in the humanities"—in the version of the essay she published in *Tendencies*.[1] Sedgwick sees not only a peculiar form of academic self-righteousness in the shock of the copulative that her essay addresses, but also a refusal to understand sexuality in historical terms. Sedgwick reminds her readers that "different varieties of sexual experience and identity are being discovered both to possess a diachronic history—a history of significant change—and to be entangled in particularly indicative ways with aspects of epistemology and of literary creation and reception."[2]

For my purposes here, however, it remains interesting that Sedgwick chooses as her first "example" a "particularly devastating bedroom scene" from *Sense and Sensibility* (1811). Before I discuss the passage itself, I want to recall what Sedgwick says about it:

> We know well enough who is in this *bedroom:* two women. They are Elinor and Marianne Dashwood, they are sisters, and the passion and perturbation of their love for each other is, at the very least, the backbone of this powerful novel. But who is in this *bedroom scene*? And, to put it vulgarly, what's their scene? It is the naming of a man, the absent Willoughby, that both marks this as an unmistakably sexual scene, and by the same gesture seems to displace its "sexuality" from the depicted bedroom space of same-sex tenderness, secrecy, longing, and frustration. Is this, then, a hetero- or a homoerotic novel (or moment in a novel)? No doubt it must be said to be both, if love is vectored toward an object and Elinor's here flies toward Marianne, Marianne's in turn toward Willoughby.[3]

Sedgwick here tantalizes her readers with the possibilities of female homosocial relations, a possibility that readers of Sedgwick's earlier work might not have anticipated. Female homosociability is the very social configuration that Sedgwick's *Between Men* seemed to suggest was culturally impossible. In that book, Sedgwick argued, by looking at various eighteenth- and nineteenth-century literary texts, that male-male relations were basic to Western culture. As I mentioned above, she sees "a special relationship between male homosocial (*including* homosexual) desire and the structures for maintaining and transmitting patriarchal power: a relationship founded on an inherent and potentially active structural congruence."[4] This argument leaves little room for female-female relations, and if we take Sedgwick's "homosocial" seriously, it would be meaningless to apply the term to two women in a culture in which they have no access to the exchange economy that gives men both the reason for same-sex desire and an excuse for its intensity. Homosocial relations between women, that is, cannot have the sanction of a culture determined on keeping women at bay.

How then are female-female social bonds to be described? Unlike male homosocial relations, which are public, visible, and "structurally congruent" with the dynamics of patriarchal power itself, female-female bonds will be private, invisible, and structurally opposed, as it were, to the sex-gender system itself. This is why, as I will argue here and in other chapters of this study, the most profoundly emotional and physical relations between women emerge from the family itself. Not only are sisters intimate in ways that Austen's novel dramatizes (and her letters have infamously suggested), other family relations can be read as erotic in any number of contexts. I am speaking of course of mother-daughter relations, which are eroticized not only in the Gothic work of Lee and Radcliffe but also in socially challenging works such as *Millenium Hall*.

What happens when female affection is confined to the family, of course, is that it literally disappears in the structure and ethos of family life. Sisterly affection and mother-daughter love are so central to the ideology of the family in the later eighteenth century that it can seem almost perverse to probe these relations for more than appropriate levels of erotic desire. But who is to set the measure of "love" in these situations? Where love is fully appropriate, that is, as it is in the bonds I am describing, when does it become transgressive? The family is where female-female desire is first articulated precisely because from outside the relationship itself, it is impossible to distinguish love from *love*. In the very invisibility of the family structure, that is, female-female desire can flourish unchallenged, and it can work from the inside, in some circumstances, if not to resist then at least to undermine the successful exchange of women that the sex-gender system demands.

The invisibility of the lesbian in English cultural history has been variously explained. Most recently, Terry Castle has written eloquently about the "apparitional lesbian":

> Why is it so difficult to see the lesbian—even when she is there, quite plainly, in front of us? In part because she has been "ghosted"—or made to seem invisible—by culture itself. It would be putting it mildly to say that the lesbian represents a threat to patriarchal protocol: Western civilization has for centuries been haunted by a fear of "women without men"—of women indifferent or resistant to male desire.[5]

I would argue that the family is the best place to hide lesbian desire, and that although it is "ghosted" because it represents a threat to patriarchal protocol, it has also, it must be admitted, ghosted itself, as a way of answering the demands of culture without expressing outright resistance. Even *Millenium Hall,* which could be seen as resistant in many ways, manages to conceal female-female desire within the family repeatedly throughout the narrative, and the female utopia that it depicts is structured like a family so as to make its challenge to the sex-gender system less rather than more visible. I would claim, moreover, that arguments about what can and cannot be called "lesbian" desire are impossible to resolve, precisely because of the ghostliness that Castle describes and the family structure ensures.

One thing that the recent controversy over Castle's review of the Jane Austen letters reveals is how thoroughly this subterfuge worked. Critics were falling over one another to claim that the sisterly affection between Jane and Cassandra precluded erotic desire because it was a familial bond. Of course, if we are discussing Henry and Sarah Fielding, incest is a possibility because we are dealing with siblings of different genders. But in the case of sisters reared together, and, as even writers such as Marilyn Butler must admit, forced to share the same bed, erotic attachments are never allowed. It would seem to me that erotic attachment between sisters may have been the rule rather than the exception. As Castle argues in that review, "reading Austen's letters to Cassandra, one cannot help but sense the primitive adhesiveness—and underlying eros—of the sister-sister bond."[6]

I am not going to argue the larger cultural case in this chapter. Already writers like Emma Donoghue have begun to explain the vast complexities of female-female eroticism in the eighteenth century.[7] Even her superb book, however, underplays the possibility of the family as the source of female-female desire. In this chapter I hope to show how female-female desire can be articulated within the family at the same time that it resists the kind of narrative closure that the novel demands. The domestication of female desire that results from its placement within the family does not play as naturally into scenarios of cultural closure as heteronormative narratives do. In fact, in these relations, members of the family can be rendered "unnatural" as obviously and dramatically as the beleaguered brother and sister in *David Simple* are. In *Sense and Sensibility*, this difference is articulated through the exigencies of bodily distress as well as emotional indifference, as we shall see.[8] In any case, sisterly love is, as Sedgwick suggests, the "backbone of this powerful novel." In the following pages I want to explore what the novel attaches to this backbone of sisterly affection. For me, Austen seems willing to challenge cultural assumptions, if not to defy them.

This is the passage that Sedgwick discusses:

> Before the house-maid had lit their fire the next day, or the sun gained any power over a cold, gloomy morning in January, Marianne, only half dressed, was kneeling against one of the window-seats for the sake of all the little light she could command from it, and writing as fast as a continual

Sisterly Love in *Sense and Sensibility*

flow of tears would permit her. In this situation, Elinor, roused from sleep by her agitation and sobs, first perceived her: and after observing her for a few moments with silent anxiety, said, in a tone of the most considerate gentleness,

"Marianne, may I ask?"—

"No, Elinor," she replied, "ask nothing; you will soon know all."

The sort of desperate calmness with which this was said, lasted no longer than while she spoke, and was immediately followed by a return of the same excessive affliction. It was some minutes before she could go on with her letter, and the frequent bursts of grief which still obliged her, at intervals, to withhold her pen, were proofs enough of her feeling how more than probable it was that she was writing for the last time to Willoughby."[9]

As Sedgwick points out in the passage quoted above, the quality of affection that Elinor feels for Marianne is unusually rich. Sedgwick talks about "same-sex tenderness, secrecy, longing, and frustration," but she claims that this desire is displaced by the naming of the absent Willoughby. But if Willoughby is named in this context, his name is used as the symptom of Marianne's sensibility, her mistaken indulgence of an extreme feeling that leads her into dangerous excesses and finally drops her into an abyss of isolation and despair. One central strand of the plot of this novel chronicles Marianne's brush with "illness," "madness," and even "death" as the result of her excess sensibility. Throughout this gradual decline and ever so tentative return to "health," it is Elinor who watches and waits with loving patience, and it is Elinor who comes to represent the sisterly love that alone can carry Marianne back from the abyss.

Sedgwick is surely right to say that Marianne's unsettled behavior in the center of the novel is symptomatic of sexual dysfunction. Anti-masturbation tracts were available enough in the later eighteenth century to make a novelist sensitive to effects of self-abuse. Far more readily available to writers and readers of novels at this time, however, was an equally distressing account of female hysteria that earlier critics, myself included, have outlined in Marianne's not-so-gradual decline.[10] More recently, John Wiltshire has made similar claims in his study of *Jane Austen and the Body*. In his discussion of *Sense and Sensibility*, Wiltshire restates the concern that the novel expresses for Marianne's "nervous irritability," and he examines the "sick-bed of sensibility" in some detail.[11]

Accounts of Marianne's "sensibility" remind us that "sense" and "sensibility" establish poles of signification in the text and invite us to interpret behavior within the novel according to the tenets that these terms suggest, yet how those tenets determine judgment the novel keeps revising.[12] The more closely we watch the two heroines, Elinor and Marianne Dashwood, the more uncertain any evaluative dichotomy becomes. Austen defies the simple hierarchy that the title might suggest:

> "What a sweet woman Lady Middleton is!" said Lucy Steele.
> Marianne was silent; it was impossible for her to say what she did not feel, however trivial the occasion; and upon Elinor therefore the whole task of telling lies when politeness required it, always fell. (105)

Austen seems to offer the basis for easy contrast and evaluation in a passage such as this. Marianne becomes the sullen guardian of her own emotions, while Elinor accepts the implications of "polite" society and soldiers on. But from another perspective, Marianne's silence is attractive, dictated as it is by real feeling; and Elinor's polite "lies" seem a questionable basis for honest social interaction. Which response is more to be prized? Popular opinion has always seen Marianne's authentic emotionalism more heartwarming than Elinor's calculated coolness. To be sure, Elinor assumes responsibility in those areas in which she finds Marianne lacking; but Marianne suggests that her "cold-hearted" sister has herself areas of human response that remain undeveloped (17).[13] There is something heroic about Marianne's refusal to speak in situations such as this; speech itself would be tantamount to self-betrayal.

Yet Marianne's refusal "to say what she did not feel" hints at a more serious danger than social awkwardness. For her silence at this moment is a harbinger of that longer and more threatening silence that accompanies her almost total physical collapse later in the novel. There social form is altogether rejected, and the retreat into private feeling becomes absolute. As such, Marianne's situation is indistinguishable from the kind of "hysteria" that an overly excitable sensibility was assumed by contemporary psychologists to cause. Critics who celebrate Marianne's spontaneity perhaps forget that her subjection of public to private value, her reliance on emotion and imagination, can in the Age of Sensibility only lead in the direction of madness and silence. "From now on," Foucault says, "one fell ill from too much feeling."[14]

What is sometimes overlooked in considerations of this dynamic, however, is the relation between the sisters themselves. The copulative of the title, that is, has a resonance similar to the copulative of Sedgwick's title: sense *and* sensibility are at work in this novel, and in a scene such as this, their complementary function is carefully exposed. Marianne retreats into the silence of private feeling while Elinor offers polite lies to the social world of which she is a part. Deep and hidden desires, that is, are masked and transformed by a polite front. It has been a long time since Tony Tanner noticed that Elinor excelled at making screens.[15] What has not been fully articulated, however, is the degree to which the substance of what she hides can be expressed in terms of sisterly affection.

Marianne becomes the victim of her own delusions in this novel: she is so devoted to her fantasies that she establishes them in her imagination as fact; she gives her feelings such precedence that she goes out of her way to create situations that will elicit them. Moreover, she does nothing to curb the pain they cause. "I must feel—I must be wretched—" she says during her first shock over Willoughby's desertion (164). This is a character who has become trapped in her own self-conscious response.[16]

When Elinor attempts to ascertain the truth of the relation between her sister and Willoughby, the complex nature of the sisters' relation is brought into high relief. Elinor taxes Marianne about a letter she is expecting. When Marianne resists, Elinor becomes pointed:

> After a short pause, "you have no confidence in me, Marianne."
> "Nay, Elinor, this reproach from *you*—you who have confidence in no one!"
> "Me!" returned Elinor in some confusion; "indeed, Marianne, I have nothing to tell."
> "Nor I," answered Marianne with energy, "our situations then are alike. We have neither of us any thing to tell; you, because you communicate, and I, because I conceal nothing." (146–47)

We know that Elinor's response to Marianne is less than honest—Lucy has insisted on secrecy regarding her engagement to Edward Ferrars—and that Marianne's accusations are justified. Paradoxically, then, Elinor is more suited to the public world because she has a more highly developed sense of the private. She uses secrecy as a way of protecting her deepest feelings and shielding those closest to her. She understands the nature of her emotions and therefore hides them even from herself. Elinor uses Marianne as a means to execute this disguise and mask her inner self with a surface of sociability. Marianne attempts to break through this reserve by expressing what she feels.[17] Elinor considers private experience in relation to the public context, while Marianne can understand private experience only in relation to itself. Marianne feels so deeply that the novel cannot approve.

Marianne's emotional and physical collapse at the center of the novel gives the novel its peculiar intensity. Her eloquence is transformed by the pressure of self-contempt into "inarticulate sounds of complaint," "feverish wildness," and "sleepless pain and delirium," almost as if her emotional pyrotechnics have been turned on herself (271–73). We are made to feel that her collapse results from a sensibility heightened by the imagination to the point that feeling has started to self-destruct.

In the eighteenth century, the word *sensibility* connoted the physical as well as emotional susceptibility to pleasure and pain, as this passage from George Cheyne's *The English Malady* (1733) suggests:

> Those who stutter, stammer, have a great Difficulty of Utterance, speak very low, lose their Voice without catching Cold, grow dumb, deaf, or blind, without an Accident or an acute Distemper; are quick, prompt, and passionate; are all of weak Nerves; have a great Degree of Sensibility; are quick Thinkers, feel Pleasure or Pain the most readily, and are of most lively imagination.[18]

Marianne's symptoms may not be as extreme as those described here, but the last half of the passage does call her personality to mind. Notice, too, that Cheyne's analysis relates nervous speechlessness to heightened sensibility and a lively imagination. Imagination, in other words, is a faculty, as Hume's analysis suggests, which could easily undermine the coherent structure of thought and speech, rendering the subject isolated in the silence of a world beyond speech, a world of madness.[19]

Cheyne connects amply documented "hysterical" behavior to physical disorders of a particularly suggestive kind:

> I never saw any Person labour under severe, obstinate, and strong *Nervous* Complaints, but I always found at last, the *Stomach, Guts, Liver, Spleen, Mesentery,* or some of the great and necessary Organs or *Glands* of the lower Belly were obstructed, knotted, schirrous or spoil'd, and perhaps all these together.[20]

Michel Foucault, in *Madness and Civilization,* uses descriptions such as this one by Cheyne to suggest a relation between the female sexual organs and early diagnoses of hysteria.[21] In his own chapter "Hysteria and Hypochondria," Foucault centers his discussion on the notion of "irritability of fibers," thereby suggesting the relation between physiology and psychology in the eighteenth century. Foucault says that "all life was finally judged by this degree of irritation," and he shows that physical irritability easily gives way to mental instability: "once the mind becomes blind *through the very excess of sensibility*—then madness appears" (my italics).[22] It is, further, this configuration of madness with a guilty conscience, or really unconscious, that Foucault sees as the origin of modern psychiatry.

Marianne clearly borders on the kind of sexual hysteria that Foucault describes. Her imagination creates a form of desire which is impossible even

Sisterly Love in *Sense and Sensibility*

for Willoughby to satisfy. She focuses her attention on Willoughby because he alone seems able to participate in her private fantasy. But that is only a momentary delusion. The "violent affliction" (64) she suffers when he is separated from her later becomes "excessive affliction" (155) when he has proven false. Marianne's "irritability," moreover, is emphasized throughout the novel. For instance, Elinor wonders "that Marianne, . . . thoroughly acquainted with Mrs. Jennings' manners, and invariably disgusted by them, . . . should disregard whatever must be most wounding to her irritable feelings, in her pursuit of one object" (133). Soon after, Elinor accepts Marianne's plea for silence, made "with all the eagerness of the most nervous irritability" (156); and later she notes "the irritable refinement of [Marianne's] mind" and "the delicacies of a strong sensibility" (175). Although we are repeatedly treated to displays of Marianne's irritability—those frequent outbursts of frustration or disgust—we are perhaps apt to miss their diagnostic significance. I should like to emphasize the degree to which the play of Marianne's private imagination has made her susceptible to the kind of self-delusions in which her character abounds. "Madness became possible," according to Foucault, "in that milieu where man's relations with his feelings . . . are altered."[23] Marianne sacrifices herself to this love for Willoughby because she cannot see how to break through the reserve that "cold-hearted" sister represents.

Whether we go so far as to read Foucault's sexual interpretation of hysteria in terms of sisterly love depends on the degree to which we find it implicit in the details of the novel. When we listen to Marianne's outburst of guilt following her illness, however, such associations are impossible to ignore:

> Do not, my dearest Elinor, let your kindness defend what I know your judgment must censure. My illness has made me think—It has given me the leisure and calmness for serious recollection. Long before I was enough recovered to talk, I was perfectly able to reflect. . . . I saw that my own feelings had prepared my sufferings, and that my want of fortitude under them had almost led me to the grave. My illness, I well knew, had been entirely brought on by myself, by such negligence of my own health, as I had felt even at the time to be wrong. Had I died,—it would have been self-destruction. . . . I cannot express my own abhorrence of myself. (303)

Marianne seems automatically to blame herself here. Guilt arises not so much from what she has done but from her very nature. In Foucault's terms, her illness could be said to be *"the psychological effect of a moral fault."*[24] That her guilt stems from an unconscious fear of her own sexuality is implicit in the terms of her rejection of her earlier self.[25] Elinor is of course the only person to whom she can confide these self-revelations: she is the only person for whom they have real meaning.

If Marianne seems trapped in a response which at first puts her at odds with her own sexuality, we must consider, as Foucault describes in *The History of Sexuality*, that such a process was one of the "strategic unities which, beginning in the eighteenth century, formed specific mechanisms of knowledge and power centering on sex." The "hysterical woman" is for him the "anchorage point" for the "hysterization of women's bodies: a threefold process whereby the feminine body was analyzed . . . as being thoroughly saturated with sexuality; whereby it was integrated into the sphere of medical practices, by reason of a pathology intrinsic to it; whereby, finally, it was placed in organic communication with the social body (whose regulated fecundity it was supposed to ensure), the family space (of which it had to be a substantial and functional element), and the life of children."[26] He sees this process as a further step in the direction of psychoanalysis, the process which for him emerges inevitably as an institutionalization of the familial deployment of sexuality. Marianne's confession is in this sense like a proto–case history.

Like a case history as well is Marianne's willingness to inscribe the signs of her guilt in language, not in the form of the fantastic dreamscapes of her earlier rhapsodies, but as a careful and deliberate reflection on the social implications of her private desire. In terms of Elinor's rehabilitative program, that is, Marianne has begun the all-important process of self-regulation, which for Elinor is a kind of self-realization. Surely we can notice a basic change in the nature of Marianne's use of language here. This speech is the longest and most coherent which she has uttered up to this point in the novel. If she seems at first tentative, centering as she does on self-accusation, she at last becomes calmly assertive of the terms of self-judgment. "I saw that my own feelings had prepared my sufferings": Marianne's ecstatic impressions have given way to careful self-assessment. Her perceptions in regard to her own behavior are as astute as Elinor's would be. She is able to distinguish between emotion and judgment in Elinor's response here, and she applies those distinctions to herself: "My illness has made me *think*" (my italics). Marianne's physical collapse has forced her from her impressionistic response to the world and caused her to look at herself for once objectively. Elinor draws her out in this way, not in violence to the bright, spontaneous creature that she was, but in hopes of establishing a bond with a sister who can finally understand where emotional safety lies. Central to Marianne's rehabilitation, then, is her reconnection with the sister from whom she is isolated in illness. Elinor has never deserted Marianne, and the moment she sees her sister coming back to her is the real climax of the novel's emotional action.

Marianne's illness becomes for both sisters the test of their feelings for each other and the proof that their love can be a bond rather than a barrier separating them from each other and their innermost desire. Throughout the illness itself, as Marianne's pulse races and she cries out in delirium, Elinor is all watchfulness and apprehension. After her interview with Willoughby, however, Elinor has something to communicate. The moment for such communication comes when Marianne has finally accepted the limitations of sensibility and expressed the self-deprecations quoted above. Now Elinor offers her communication not as a lesson to Marianne, but as a way of reaching out to her sister with the power of her own love. Sense and sensibility are reworked in the union of the sisters, which the following passage commemorates:

> [Elinor] managed the recital, as she hoped, with address; prepared her anxious listener with caution; related simply and honestly the chief points on which Willoughby grounded his apology; did justice to his repentance, and softened only his protestations of present regard. Marianne said not a word.—She trembled, her eyes were fixed on the ground, and her lips became whiter than even sickness had left them. A thousand inquiries sprung up from her heart, but she dared not urge one. She caught every syllable with panting eagerness; her hand, unknowingly to herself, closely pressed her sister's, and tears covered her cheeks. (305)

Notice how much attention Austen pays to the manner of Elinor's presentation. We hear much more about how she addresses Marianne than about what precisely she says. The emphasis is on the act itself. Yet this simple act of communication and response quells much of the sisterly uneasiness that the novel has dramatized. Elinor uses tact and concern to enter Marianne's world, and she is welcomed there with a squeeze of the hand to suggest that she understands the significance of Elinor's concern. Feeling is still paramount for Marianne—she presses Elinor's hand "unknowingly"—but now her feeling seems to embrace her sister as well as herself. She edits the "inquiries sprung up from her heart" and produces instead a thoughtful request: "Tell mama," she urges Elinor (305). Surely this is a Marianne who has begun to understand the value of female relations. Moving beyond the incapacitating limitations of entirely private metaphor into a world in which love means communication as well as private fantasy, Marianne enters a world of sisterly love. Many of the early conflicts of the novel are in this scene resolved. Marianne's recovery seems assured and a new basis of self-affirmation seems guaranteed.

What is implicit in this intimate conversation is that Marianne has been saved from her self-destructive self-involvement. She has been saved, however, not for marriage to Brandon but for the sisterly love that Elinor offers and that the novel articulates as the answer to destructive emotion. Sisterly love, like romantic friendship, that is, functions as an alternative to heteronormative desire. In this novel, as critics like Janet Todd and Claudia Johnson as well as Sedgwick and Castle have suggested, the bond between sisters is the only relationship that is emotionally satisfying in the novel.[27] In an earlier version of this chapter, I explained how Edward Ferrars and Colonel Brandon function in a comic resolution.[28] But their importance pales in relation to a scene such as that I have just quoted. Elinor understands her relation to Edward, in any case, in terms that give precedence to her female relations:

> Had Edward been intentionally deceiving her? Had he feigned a regard for her which he did not feel? Was his engagement to Lucy, an engagement of the heart? No; whatever it might once have been, she could not believe it such at present. His affection was all her own. She could not be deceived in that. Her mother, sisters, Fanny, all had been conscious of his regard for her at Norland; it was not an illusion of her own vanity. He certainly loved her. What a softener of the heart was this persuasion! (119–20)

In this narrative exploration of Elinor's thoughts and feelings, Austen deftly represents this self-examination in a kind of public speech which has been crafted to reflect mental processes. The rush of emotional uneasiness, for instance, is mirrored in the choppiness of the prose here, and the self-assurances, timid and prolix at first, become stronger and more direct as this process of reflection continues. Her love for Edward, however, and his love for her, is processed through the perceptions of "her mother, sisters, Fanny," as a way of emphasizing that Elinor's deepest thoughts have never strayed far from those early formative relations. Once she has thereby assured herself of emotional security, she can state to herself what now has value as objective fact: "He certainly loved her." After that has been articulated, she can return to the "heart" and suggest its malleability. Rational persuasion "softens" the heart, which in its pain may have hardened, and allows human feeling to animate her response without causing her to give way to excessive emotion. Elinor finds a way to think *and* feel, without allowing one mode of response to compromise the other.

Sisterly Love in *Sense and Sensibility*

Occasionally, however, Elinor seems in danger of letting masculine-directed desire corrupt her relation with her sister. Consider, for instance, the passage early in the novel when the sisters meet Edward Ferrars in the lanes near Barton cottage:

> "Have you been lately in Sussex?" said Elinor.
>
> "I was at Norland about a month ago."
>
> "And how does dear, dear Norland look?" cried Marianne.
>
> "Dear, dear Norland," said Elinor, "probably looks much as it always does at this time of year. The woods and walks thickly covered with dead leaves."
>
> "Oh!" cried Marianne, "with what transporting sensations have I formerly seen them fall! How have I delighted, as I walked, to see them driven in showers about me by the wind! What feelings have they, the season, the air altogether inspired! Now there is no one to regard them. They are seen only as a nuisance, swept hastily off, and driven as much as possible from the sight."
>
> "It is not everyone," said Elinor, "who has your passion for dead leaves." (75–76)

What Elinor gently ridicules as "a passion for dead leaves" is of course nothing of the kind. For Marianne, the leaves themselves are only the vehicle for a metaphor whose tenor remains finally unexpressed. Marianne is thinking about the air, to be sure, but she is also thinking about love and freedom and the possibility of defying the very limits of selfhood which her current situation circumscribes. Metaphor for Marianne is a means of escape. But it is also a rejection of the means of effecting that escape.

Elinor seems almost brutal in her literalization of Marianne's metaphor, perhaps because she knows that Marianne's passion is leading her away from her. Her own literal-mindedness is really an attempt to liberate herself from the threat of Marianne's imagination. Her aggressiveness on this occasion suggests at the same time a failure of her own imagination, an inability to see beyond the literal. Elinor's response must also be understood in terms of Edward's presence here. She is attempting to censure Marianne's enthusiasm as publicly unbecoming. She wants to compartmentalize and de-romanticize the past as well. All these activities are in the interest of creating a smooth surface and of controlling feeling so that it does not disrupt the tenets of decorum.[29] She is performing for Edward, that is, and in doing so she feels forced to ridicule the lively sister she loves.

That may explain why for many readers the comic ending seems anything but comic. Earlier Marianne had rejected Brandon as dull and uninspiring: "his understanding has no brilliancy, his feelings no ardour, and his voice no expression" (44). Now she gives him her hand out of "strong esteem and lively friendship" (333). Because this is so pale a reflection of other emotions that the novel has articulated, readers feel that Marianne has had to settle for much less than she deserved. The closing paragraphs of the novel really do seem to put her in her place:

> Instead of falling a sacrifice to an irresistible passion, as once she had fondly flattered herself with expecting,—instead of remaining even for ever with her mother, and finding her only pleasures in retirement and study, as afterwards in her more calm and sober judgment she had determined on,— she found herself at nineteen, submitting to new attachments, entering on new duties, placed in a new home, a wife, the mistress of a family, and the patroness of a village. (333)

Foucault has perhaps offered us the terms whereby such a realignment of public and private reality can be explained. He asserts that the hysterization of women was part of "a new distribution of pleasures, discourses, truths, and powers," on the part of the bourgeoisie: "a defense, a protection, a strengthening, and an exaltation . . . as a means of social control and political subjugation."[30] Marianne is "saved" from her hysteria in order to be swept into just such a social resolution at the expense, of course, of her seemingly aberrant private desire. Once her sexuality has been harnessed, she fits more readily into a position of social influence and public power. We feel the sting of what has been sacrificed to achieve this resolution, for Marianne plays her role in a power structure which excludes her as effectively as it celebrates her reconstituted self. Social relations replace the private aspirations of sensibility and establish an unfamiliar public role for the heroine. What private value is not lost is redirected toward "new attachments."

What the novel offers as personal indulgence, then, concerns a set of bonds that, although they do not expose female-female desire, seem at the same time to take them for granted. For the one person who is excluded from the articulation of the resolution is Elinor: "new attachments, entering on new duties, placed in a new home, a wife, the mistress of a family, and the patroness of a village." The sister is not mentioned here because she is the very heart of it all. Whatever else Austen says at the close of the novel, the relationship between Elinor and Marianne is what she means.

Terry Castle has spoken eloquently about the relation between Jane Austen and her sister Cassandra. Of course one cannot make an unthinking connection between the homoerotics of Austen's personal life and that of her fiction. But as Castle points out, even intimate contemporaries thought they saw the Austen sisters reflected in Elinor and Marianne Dashwood. As James Edward Austen-Leigh said in his memoir, "Their sisterly affection could

hardly be exceeded."[31] Castle makes the further point that "men are ultimately insignificant" in the world of the Austen sisters.[32] In *Sense and
Sensibility*, men are more than insignificant. They are the source of bitterness
and self-disgust. They place one in hideously embarrassing social situations
and they deprive one of the consolations of privacy. Both Colonel Brandon
and Edward Ferrars are seriously compromised heroes, even in the terms of
the Age of Sensibility. Austen tidies them away in her novel, in order to
celebrate sisterly love:

> Between Barton and Delaford, there was that constant communication
> which strong family affection would naturally dictate;—and among the
> merits and the happiness of Elinor and Marianne, let it not be ranked as the
> least considerable, that though sisters, and living almost within sight of
> each other, they could live without disagreement between themselves, or
> producing coolness between their husbands. (335)

The relationship between Elinor and Marianne is coded as "natural" here
because it forms the basis of this female homosociability. This is what Austen
accomplishes in this remarkable novel. Women have found one another to be
an almost subversive alternative to the sex-gender system of which they are
inevitably a part. The novel masks female-female desire in the configuration
of family life because that is the only place that it can flourish unmolested.
Sisterly love shimmers with a devotion that exists nowhere else in this work.
It promises that the family can be source of sustenance after all.

FIVE

"Romantic Friendship" in
Millenium Hall

Sense and Sensibility attests to the enduring popularity of novels that treat female-female affection and hints at the cultural complicity that such a trope implies. It also suggests that female self-control and female hysteria are not as easily determined as the culture pretends. In *Millenium Hall* (1762), Sarah Scott had already addressed the questions of female-female affection, female self-control, and female hysteria as a way of resisting the inscription of the female within patriarchal discourse and establishing an alternative to the desexualized/hypersexualized model that historians of sexuality chronicle. *Millenium Hall* attempts to challenge the "sex-gender system" by working within the structure of exemplary narratives, such as were popular in mid-century, to offer an alternative to male-oriented interpretations of female sexual power. In doing so, Scott challenges as well our conceptions of female sexuality in the eighteenth century and our preconceptions concerning female-female relations within that "utterly confused category" of "romantic friendship."[1] I will argue that Scott offers a narrative form that challenges patriarchy with the tales of a group of women who remain at the end of their romantic adventures "happily unmarried."[2]

Although nominally written as a letter from "a gentleman on his travels," the novel establishes an elaborate strategy to resist the authority of the patriarchal narrative voice. Scott's seemingly crude arrangement of internal narration—the novel consists of a series of tales told by or about the inhabitants of Millenium Hall—represents the most obvious of her techniques: the tales create a female subject position within the text in order to undermine the "romance plot" that was already strong enough to determine popular expectation. By challenging the conventions of romantic narrative, Scott is able to reconceive their ideological range. In her personal life, Sarah Scott found an alternative to the ruthlessly limited possibilities available to women in the eighteenth century. In this novel, she dramatizes this discovery in a way that claims narrative authority for women-loving-women and offers women in general an escape from the prison-house of patriarchal narrative.[3]

ROMANTIC FRIENDSHIP AND THE "GAME AT FLATTS"

Lillian Faderman calls *Millenium Hall* "the most complete fictional blueprint for conducting a romantic friendship."[4] Such "friendships" between women were pervasive in late-eighteenth-century England. "Discouragement of romantic friendship seems to have been rare," Faderman tells us, "not only because society believed that love between women fulfilled positive functions such as providing a release for homosocially segregated girls and unhappily married women, but also because men generally doubted that these relationships would be very enduring in any case." Furthermore, Faderman argues, "Because it was thought unlikely that even their sensuality, which included kissing, caressing and fondling, would become genital, romantic friends were permitted to articulate, even during the most sexually conservative times, their physical appreciation of each other."[5] "Romantic friendship," in other words, is assumed to be platonic—homoplatonic, in George Rousseau's phrase—and socially unthreatening.[6]

Anyone who reads the account, though, of Eleanor Butler and Sarah Ponsonby (the "Ladies of Llangollen") will understand the difficulty in deciding the fine distinction between homoplatonic relations and actual sexual involvement. Eleanor Butler writes, for example, that during an illness, "I kept my bed all day with one of My dreadful Headaches. My Sally, My Tender, My Sweet Love lay beside me holding and supporting My Head till one o'clock when I by Much entreaty prevailed with her to rise and get her breakfast." According to Elizabeth Mavor, their biographer and editor: "Very generally speaking symptoms of romantic friendship were 'retirement,' good works, cottages, gardening, impecuniosity, the intellectual pursuits of reading aloud and the study of languages, enthusiasm for the Gothick, journals, migraines, sensibility and often, but not always, the single state."[7] The condescension implicit in such a description, which medicalizes an entire range of social behavior and attempts to render "symptomatic" the few activities that women were free to pursue without censure, reads into the period—perhaps rightly—a distrust of this cultivated homoplatonism that goes deeper than what Faderman suggests.

More recently, Emma Donoghue has established a range of female-female sexual activity that is both widely represented in eighteenth-century popular literature and fully documented in scientific and pseudo-scientific studies. Donoghue makes it clear that people had little difficulty imagining two women having sexual intercourse, although they at times find the details of "penetration" puzzling. She argues, moreover, that "romantic friendship" was not always assumed to be platonic in nature. Donoghue's important study encourages a more careful look at the friendship in *Millenium Hall,* and it warrants a reconsideration of the outlines of erotic interest that obtain within female homosocial bonds.[8] The models for female-female relations were remarkably well articulated at a time when they have been thought to be almost nonexistent.

The popular and well-distributed text *Satan's Harvest Home, or the Present State of Whorecraft, Adultery, Fornication, Procuring, Pimping, Sodomy, And the Game at Flatts . . . And other* SATANIC WORKS *daily propagated in this good Protestant Kingdom* (1749), for example, offers in its almost pornographic fervor a different picture of eighteenth-century attitudes toward female sexuality. The first passage I would like to quote begins with a description of male effeminacy and the habit of kissing in public and proceeds to a diatribe against sexual transgression:

> This *Fashion* was brought over from *Italy,* (the *Mother* and *Nurse* of *Sodomy*); where the *Master* is oftener *Intriguing* with his *Page,* than a *fair Lady.* And not only in that *Country,* but in *France,* which copies from them, the *Contagion* is diversify'd, and the Ladies (in the *Nunneries*) are criminally *amorous* of each other, in a *Method* too gross for Expression. I must be so partial to my own *Country-Women,* to affirm, or, at least, hope they claim no Share of this *Charge*; but must confess, when I see two Ladies *Kissing* and *Slopping* each other, in a *lascivious Manner,* and *frequently* repeating it, I am shock'd to the last Degree.[9]

What I find intriguing about this passage is the immediate connection between male and female same-sex practice: neither is outside the range of social observation nor hidden from the popular imagination in the eighteenth century. By asserting that public displays of affection signify "gross" private behavior, this author reads "criminal" sexuality into the very relations that Faderman suggests were ignored. Far from innocent, romantic friendship becomes, in this description, a sign of the sexual contagion that threatens the fabric of society. These accusations raise a different question from what the "Female Husband" style of notorious court cases do.[10] Here it is the *relation* rather than the *impersonation* that is at issue. Women are seen as dangerously involved with women *as* women: the implications of such relations are if anything *more* radical because they refuse to mimic patriarchal order. Elsewhere this author is not at such pains to exonerate his countrywomen. After cataloguing a variety of sexually transgressive females, for instance, he turns his attention to Sappho:

> *Sappho,* as she was one of the wittiest Women that ever the World bred, so she thought with Reason, it would be expected she should make some Additions to a *Science* in which Womankind had been so successful: What does she do then? Not content with our Sex, begins *Amours* with her own, and teaches the Female World a new Sort of Sin, call'd the *Flats,* that was follow'd not only in *Lucian's* Time, but is practis'd frequently in *Turkey,* as well as at *Twickenham* at this Day.[11]

It is interesting that Sappho's variation on female sexuality is presented as "Reason"-able and that the "Flats" is taught rather than "caught." (These terms demarcate an entire spectrum of homophobic response, viable even today.) Partridge tells us that *flats* is the slang term for false playing cards or counterfeit money. Also current, slightly later according to Partridge, is the use of the term *flat-cock* to describe a woman, "for one of two possible anatomical reasons," and *flat-fuck* for "simulated copulation by a pair of women: lesbian."[12]

It is interesting that *flats* includes a sense both of cheating and deception as well as female homosexuality. It has long been assumed that female homosexuality was considered a "cheat" in the eighteenth century because it claimed for women the social position reserved for men.[13] Here we see, though, that the cheat is of a physical as well as of a social nature: a "flat-fuck" is no fuck at all, from a male perspective. With no penis between them, the women must "simulate" copulation. Thus left out of phallic objectification, however, they may be free to determine sexual signification for themselves.

Emma Donoghue has shown that observations such as those in *Satan's Harvest Home* were by no means isolated. Her study of *Passions between Women* places these remarks in a rich context of "lesbian" visibility in the eighteenth century, and she explores the ways in which "romantic friendship" has been used to "neutralise and de-sexualise textual evidence." The argument, she says, goes like this: "because so many women were passionate friends, . . . passionate friendship between women must have been nothing more than a fashion and could have no connection with sexual identity."[14] Pamphlets like *Satan's Harvest Home* help to give this claim substance: no bond that can be read as sexual is ignored in this lively volume. Donoghue is right to "re-sexualize" the bonds between women that have for so long been claimed to be perplexingly erotic in a nonsexual way.

Later in *Satan's Harvest Home*, the author complains that "in order to render the Scheme of Iniquity still more extensive amongst us, a new and most abominable Vice has got footing among the W——n of Q——y, by some call'd the Game at Flats." Here, the "Turk"ish tale described again involves both sexuality and deception. The tale opens with a description and condemnation of public bathing in Turkey: "But ordinarily the Women bathe by themselves, bond and free together; so that you shall many Times see young Maids, exceeding beautiful, gathered from all Parts of the World, exposed naked to the View of other Women, who thereupon fall in Love with them, as young Men do with us, at the Sight of Virgins." It then proceeds to tell of an older woman who disguises herself as a Man in order to win the hand of her beloved, only to be exposed on her wedding night and eventually condemned for what the judge in the case calls "so notorious a Bestiality, and so filthy a Fact." This does not silence the offender: "Away, Sir, says she! You do not know the Force of Love, and God grant you never may."[15] After this "absurd" reply, the woman is "pack'd away and drown'd in the Deep." But what is the point of this "game" if not to give voice to a protest that rings with the "Force of Love" and challenges conventional wisdom about female sexuality? By condemning the patriarch as lacking knowledge about love, this woman suggests a private world of female desire that threatens patriarchy because it is capable of operating outside the bounds of its control. In any case, it is helpful to notice that lesbian relations were by no means unimaginable in the eighteenth century and were, moreover, assumed to be practiced, even among "Women of Quality" and "at Twickenham at this Day."[16]

"AN AFFECTION QUITE MATERNAL"

Millenium Hall may not be set in Twickenham, but it concerns a series of women who have found in one another more social and emotional support than anywhere to be found in the society that brands them as freaks and shuns them as outcasts. (Among the inhabitants are a group who are physically deformed.) Scott structures the novel by means of a series of "histories" of the individuals in the community at the hall, giving private experience precedence over any overriding narrative shape. The result, however, is a novel with a powerful narrative shape of its own, with personal histories offering irresistible evidence concerning the marginalization of women in eighteenth-century society.

"The History of Miss Mancel and Mrs. Morgan," reflecting Scott's own experience, is the centerpiece of the volume. Narrated by Mrs. Maynard, one of their companions at the Hall, it tells the story of private female misery that is resolved in a romantic friendship. Louisa Mancel and Miss Melvyn (Mrs. Morgan) meet in Mademoiselle d'Avoux's boarding school and find the sympathy in one another that they have not found at home.[17]

In school, the two girls begin as roommates but gradually establish an intimacy that sustains them throughout their lives. Both girls have suffered the loss of a mother or maternal figure (in Miss Mancel's case, an aunt—her mother appears later), and both have learned the personal implications of such a loss. Miss Melvyn has found that without the mother a family can be an unfriendly and even hostile environment: her father, "an easy-tempered, weak man," who after his wife's death remarried a woman with no patience for his daughter's devotion, has sent his daughter to the school as a way of disposing of her. Miss Mancel has had a seemingly luckier fate, for at her aunt's death a certain Mr. Hintman offered himself as her guardian and placed her in the school as a matter of convenience to them both.

Significantly, maternal affection becomes the basis of their deepening intimacy:

> Miss Mancel's dejected air prejudiced Miss Melvyn much in her favour, the usual consequence of a similitude of mind or manners; and when by a further knowledge of her, she perceived her uncommon share of understanding; her desire to learn; the strength of her application; the quickness of her apprehension; and her great sweetness of temper, she grew extremely fond of her; and as Miss Mancel's melancholy rendered her little inclined to play with those of her own age, she was almost always with Miss Melvyn, who found great pleasure in endeavouring to instruct her; and grew to feel for her the tenderness of a mother, while Miss Mancel began to receive the consolation from experiencing an affection quite maternal.[18]

By insisting on maternal desire, Mrs. Maynard highlights the effacement of women in eighteenth-century culture and challenges the conventional patriarchal structure of family relations.[19] "Quite maternal" affection can quite possibly reorder the erotics of the family. In our (twentieth-century) reading of the family as an Oedipal structure, we are assuming a narrative that places the male in the "natural" position of dominance. As various feminist critics have pointed out, female subjectivity is virtually ignored in the Freudian paradigm. The female subject, moreover, is required to de-eroticize maternal relations in order to fit herself into the heterosexual norm. The mother, who for the boy (supposedly) becomes an object of sexual desire, must for the girl be domesticated as a model of responsibility. The mother must for the girl, in other words, be sacrificed to the needs of a society basically in fear of female sexuality and the potential power of female sexual relations.[20]

Mrs. Maynard's narrative resists the patriarchal implications of the Oedipal configuration and the "sacrifice" that patriarchy demands. Instead, the notion of the maternal is recuperated for the purpose of adult emotional (and erotic) pleasure. Mrs. Maynard's description of knowledge, desire, strength, quickness, and sweetness, all leading to extreme fondness—the "great pleasure" that is narrated here—all this vibrates with a new understanding of the maternal. If not specifically sexualized, this description hints at the incipient sexuality of the female bond.

Scott re-eroticizes maternal relations (and "maternalizes" the erotic) as a way of challenging eighteenth-century assumptions concerning female subjectivity and the place of the mother in domestic relations. She insists on the erotic potential of the maternal (and the maternal quality of the erotic) because that is the precise point at which female relations are usually "naturalized." Various feminist critics have argued for a reexamination of the mother/daughter bond. In the eighteenth century, "maternal" affection was one of the few alternatives to the (male) pornographic model that was abusive and demeaning. What Scott has done by maternalizing the erotic is to suggest how deeply she understands the power implicit in a "mother-daughter" relation and how readily it can function for her as a bond both liberating and subversive. Scott complements the implicit "homosexual facet" of motherhood with the motherly facet of homosexuality, opening the possibility of a new kind of female subjectivity that would reorder the priorities of patriarchal culture.[21]

Miss Melvyn is aware of the social implications of their bond, as her concern over "property" makes clear:

> The boundaries and barriers raised by those two watchful and suspicious enemies, Meum and Tuum, were in her opinion broke down by true friendship; and all property laid in one undistinguished common; but to accept Miss Mancel's money . . . appeared to [Miss Melvyn] like taking advantage of her youth; and as she did not think her old enough to be a

sufficient judge of the value of it, she did not look upon her as capable of being a party in so perfect a friendship, as was requisite to constitute that unity of property. (41)

The intimacy that Miss Melvyn expresses here and the very reservations she articulates create the impression of a perfect female friendship that would be in all respects (except one) tantamount to marriage. That Miss Melvyn is sensitive to Miss Mancel's youth and to the difficulties of her emotional situation is itself laudatory, especially in a world in which female delicacy is largely held in contempt. Even more important, however, is the implicit suggestion that two women *could* form "so perfect a friendship, as was requisite to constitute that unity of property." This is a challenge to every assumption about the position of women in eighteenth-century society, where they themselves become property in a male system of exchange.[22]

MEN AND WOMEN—AND ITALIANS

Against this rich context of female bonding, various men attempt to interpose themselves. After Miss Melvyn's father, the three most significant are Mr. Hintman, Miss Mancel's guardian; Mr. d'Avora, their Italian teacher; and Mr. Morgan, Miss Melvyn's suitor and eventual husband. Each of these characters is familiar from patriarchal narrative, but these men are constructed so as to expose the assumptions behind such traditional roles. Scott reworks the value of these male figures according to an anti-conventional scheme. In other words, she insists on conventional narrative roles—father, guardian, suitor, "friend"—in order to problematize the very terms of narrative relations and to undermine the viability of conventional plot structure.

Mr. Hintman has kindly and generously saved Miss Mancel from the horrors of orphanhood, but his kindness quickly shows signs of a darker purpose:

> It is not strange that Mr. Hintman's fondness should increase with Miss Mancel's excellencies, but the caresses which suited her earlier years were now become improper; and Mr. Hintman, by appearing insensible of the necessary change in behaviour, reduced her to great difficulties; she could not reconcile herself to receiving them; and yet to inform him of the impropriety implied a forward consciousness which she was not able to assume. (46)

Narrative convention is so strong that a reader may at first be tempted to dismiss Miss Mancel's alarms. Surely the kindly guardian will see the heroine through a world of woe until the moment of her ultimate achievement as he hands her over in marriage. But such an assumption only forces one into collusion with this wicked and ruthless old man. When Miss Mancel's fears turn out to be more than justified, we are betrayed by our own collusion with patriarchal narrative assumptions.[23]

Such figures are common in eighteenth-century fiction, but only in later Gothic fiction does the paternal figure turn out to be ruthlessly self-serving.[24] Here Scott is suggesting the "gothic" nature of everyday female experience. Women are physically, emotionally, and spiritually abused throughout the novel. What is remarkable about them, however, is that they do not succumb to madness or give in to the unending attempts to hystericize the female body. These women suffer, but they do not allow their suffering to seal their fates as victims of patriarchal narrative. In defiance of eighteenth-century medical "wisdom," they do not lose control: they simply become angry and defiant and learn to rely more exclusively on one another.

The figure who helps the two girls to find out about Mr. Hintman's plans and who befriends them in their anxiety is the Italian teacher, d'Avora. Of course in a conventional narrative the Italian would be the man of whom to be wary. He would either offer the most palpable physical threat or would represent the effeminacy and guile of the Mediterranean temperament. (In the eighteenth century, "Italy" and "Italian" were synonymous with vice.) Instead, Scott makes d'Avora a learned and trustworthy friend of both young girls:

> He took great pleasure in assisting them in the improvement they so industriously laboured for, and as he was a man of universal knowledge, he was capable of being very useful to them in that respect. For this purpose he often read with them, and by explaining many books on abstruse subjects, rendered several authors intelligible to them, who, without his assistance, would have been too obscure for persons of their age. He had very few scholars, therefore had much leisure, and with great satisfaction dedicated part of it to our young ladies, as he saw he thereby gave them a very sincere pleasure. (44)

There is much of interest in this description. First of all, it is the marginalized figure who possesses "universal knowledge." To the degree that d'Avora is powerless, he seems to command personal authority. This is the result, of course, of the selflessness that leads him to devote his time to the improvement of these two girls, and it suggests that his role is analogous to that of a female guardian in this world. As a man at the margins of society, he is free of the phallocentric aggression that would make his honestly advising these women an impossibility. Moreover, he is in an ideal position to offer them a broader culture than that in which they are trapped. His own "tender disposition" (44) qualifies him as an unbiased mentor and trustworthy guide in the world of male prerogative, and his instruction teaches them something about themselves. For his offering of knowledge, his trouble with difficult texts, and his attempts to overcome obscurity, all suggest that his instruction leads these girls beyond the limits of self-knowledge. A kind of anti-Satan, this male offers secret knowledge as a means to freedom: freedom from the ignorance used to isolate women from themselves, and freedom to realize the power of their own relation in a broader cultural context.

Scott creates a vivid contrast between d'Avora and the other men she has portrayed: here the marginalized, feminized, powerless male becomes a sympathetic friend and unthreatening mentor. Note that he teaches them Italian (among other things), at the very least a questionable, even a "sexualized" discourse, being the language, as *Satan's Harvest Home* suggests, of "unauthorized" sexual behavior. (The constant slurs against Italians are hardly limited to such scandal sheets. Samuel Richardson, after all, lists the characters of *Sir Charles Grandison* under the headings: "Men," "Women," and "Italians.")[25] Whether d'Avora's "universal knowledge" extends to the lyric poetry of Sappho is never clear, but certainly he understands that the relationship between these two women has inherent value outside the usual terms for quantification in this society; and he helps them to achieve their desire of mutual independence. He is not threatened by their love; in fact, he participates in the community that grows around it. I would go so far as to suggest that in d'Avora, Scott portrays a sexual outcast like herself, a man defined by his sexual difference, a "gay" man. This is not to say that the male—even the gay male—is in the privileged position here. Rather, Scott acknowledges the limitations placed even on women's movement through the world, to say nothing of their education. D'Avora helps on both these counts; but in the end, he learns from and is supported by them.[26]

The third man to consider in this context is Mr. Morgan, the suitor and eventual husband of Miss Melvyn. "Towards the end of autumn, Mr. Morgan, a man of fortune who had spent above half a year in a fruitless pursuit after health, made a visit to a gentleman in the neighborhood. Unfortunately Miss Melvyn's charms made a conquest of this gentleman, in whom age had not gained a victory over passion" (55). The careless and peremptory nature of this male claim is an alarming detail here; so is the suggestion that it is Miss Melvyn's physical attractiveness that makes her an automatic victim of this diseased "gentleman."

In spite of her disgust at his person and her despair for her own happiness, Miss Melvyn is tricked and threatened into marriage by her stepmother, who uses her daughter's frequent visits to Miss Mancel, who is lodging with a neighboring farmer, to suggest that she has been having an illicit affair with the farmer's son. This woman's violent (and feigned) hysteria at illicit sexuality, so clearly a function of patriarchal control, suggests more than the usual fear of female self-determination. Lady Melvyn insists on marriage as a way of separating the two women, whose relation could be more threatening to patriarchal order (and her own hopes for a secure financial future) than even a liaison with a farmer would be.[27] Lady Melvyn's violent oppression of her stepdaughter secures the ideological imperatives of patriarchy. Here is the "phallic mother": a mother who claims the prerogatives of the sex-gender system and fits her "daughter" into a rigid social hierarchy that places her (the stepmother) on top.[28] In other words, the phallic mother impales the daughter on the diseased penis of the elderly husband as a way of "fixing" her for life. This is the stuff of fairy tales, of course, but it is also the stuff of (family) romance. Scott seems to be distinguishing between the "motherhood" of mutual relations—emphasized in the relations between Miss Mancel and Miss Melvyn and elsewhere in the novel—and the ever-present threat of motherhood as a position in patriarchy, from which the self-hystericizing woman can wield her irresistible and debilitating power.

Significantly, Miss Melvyn's visits to Miss Mancel are what give Lady Melvyn the excuse to make the absurd accusation that her stepdaughter is a disgrace to family. She accuses her of "a strange intrigue; and her frequent visits to Miss Mancel were proofs of it" (58). The success of her plan dramatizes the workings of patriarchy: Miss Melvyn's "innocence" matters little against the familial accusation of "depravity," the family's fear of "infamy," and their concern over what would become her "sullied character." Soiled goods do not fetch a high price at the marriage block. Scott emphasizes the uneasiness both young women feel at their powerlessness and the meaninglessness of their own relation in a sex-gender system that excludes them. This violence with which they are oppressed and threatened seems out of proportion to mere daughterly resistance, unless something about *them* causes anger and anxiety beyond the usual terms of parental control. I think we can call this patriarchal panic *homophobia*.[29]

After the inevitable marriage—"two artless, virtuous young women were ill qualified to contend with Lady Melvyn, especially in an affair which could not be rendered public without hazarding Miss Melvyn's character" (74)—the implicit homophobia of the situation is spelled out in more detail: "Madam," Mr. Morgan tells his bride, "my wife must have no other companion or friend but her husband" (80). For the two women, "this was the severest affliction they had ever yet experienced, or indeed were capable of feeling. United from their childhood, the connection of soul and body did not seem more indissoluble, nor were ever divided with greater pain" (81). The implications of this passage are powerful, and the intensity of the emotion is palpable. Scott insists on an analogy of *body* and soul as a way of suggesting what is really at stake here. By placing the *body* in the second position, Scott signals its precedence in the attachment between them. From early on it has been the attempt of a patriarchal society and patriarchal narrative itself to separate these two women, and who best to effect that separation but the emissary of patriarchy within narrative, the husband? By forcing the women to separate, Mr. Morgan expresses the homophobia inherent to patriarchal narrative. *Millenium Hall,* in other words, begins to make clear the ways in which homophobia would begin to affect women as well as men. Lesbian sexuality is feared because it renders the very terms of patriarchal control meaningless: it is subversive. How can women be commodified, that is, if they do not even go to market? Eighteenth-century society institutionalizes a fear of the sexual exclusivity of women-loving-women and attempts to control the terms of female relations as a way of maintaining the prerogatives of the gender system.

TOWARD A LESBIAN NARRATIVE

By not romanticizing the possibility of marriage as escape from loneliness for these girls, and by dramatizing, as she does, the very real horrors of an unhappy marriage ("Those who know Mrs. Morgan best are convinced that she suffered less uneasiness from [her husband's] ill-humour, brutal as it was, than from his nauseous fondness" [85]), Scott suggests ways in which "romantic" friendship can supplant marriage as a more fulfilling conclusion to private hopes and social consolations.[30]

Of course, Miss Mancel's passionate involvement with a suitor of her own would seem in a sense to contradict the claims that I have been making. In her case, however, there is no more suitable resolution than in the case of her friend. Her suitor is killed after several desperate attempts to end his own life in battle (where he has gone because his grandmother refuses to smile on the match). Miss Mancel in the meantime *rediscovers her mother,* the first step toward the reestablishment of her commitment to Mrs. Morgan. There is no need, it seems, to see female relations as a strict alternative to courtship and marriage. Instead, here as so often elsewhere in this novel, female relations become an active substitute for aggressive and foolhardy male behavior.

When Miss Mancel and Mrs. Morgan are finally freed from the manipulations of the men in their lives, they consider what, as two independent women, they can do for themselves:

> The two friends had agreed to retire into the country, and though both of an age and fortune to enjoy all the pleasures which most people so eagerly pursue, they were desirous of fixing in a way of life where all their satisfactions might be rational and as conducive to eternal as to temporal happiness. They had laid the plan of many things, which they have since put into execution, and engaged Mr. d'Avora to live with them, both as a valuable friend and a useful assistant in the management of their affairs. (110)

Not only are they in control of their own destiny here, but they also find "eternal" happiness in the world of private intimacy. They have redefined the concept of family and the position of the male within it, and they reorder the social world on the same basis. The plans they lay are schemes for helping the indigent and poor and primarily for aiding "the daughters of persons in office, or other life-incomes, who, by their parents' deaths, were left destitute of provision" (111). It need hardly be said for how many nineteenth-century heroines such an establishment would have been a welcome relief from the exigencies of patriarchy. Felicity Nussbaum claims that the novel "supplants the scandalized renderings of lesbian relationships in female communities with an obdurate affirmation of nonsexual attachments, though an undercurrent of homoerotic bonding unsettles the narrative."[31] I would rather emphasize the degree to which these narratives seem to open a space for erotic attachment between women. The degree to which the sexual is underplayed should not blind us to the erotics of the narrative choices that Scott makes in this astonishing novel.

In a discussion of lesbian narrative, Marilyn Farwell cites Lee R. Edwards's attack on "the stranglehold that heterosexuality has exercised on heroines" in a novelistic tradition that has "derived female identity from an equation linking limited aspiration and circumscribed activity to institutionalized heterosexuality." Farwell says that "[o]ther critics have extended this logic and defined certain metaphoric and structural transgressions of the narrative as lesbian."[32]

I would argue that in *Millenium Hall,* we see an example of lesbian narrative in action, not just as a subtext, but as the very structuring principle behind a series of narratives that defy convention. In other words, the disruption of patriarchal narrative opens up the possibility of lesbian author-ity and provides the opportunity for a utopian rethinking of the opportunity of self-determination in patriarchal culture. Throughout *Millenium Hall,* Scott continues to challenge narrative expectations as a way of transgressing the boundaries set for women in the eighteenth century and subverting the laws that contain female experience.

The other narratives work in similar ways to the one I have discussed. Lady Mary Jones escapes marriage because her face is disfigured in a coach accident. Miss Selvyn finds herself too intelligent to be deluded into marriage: "It was impossible Lord Robert could fail of pleasing; but [she] added that it could not be advisable for her to marry: for enjoying perfect content, she had no benefit to expect from change" (161). Miss Selvyn finds this "perfect content" in the company of an older woman who reveals herself at her death to be Miss Selvyn's mother. Separated from her mother in infancy, in other words, Miss Selvyn rediscovers her as a companion and a friend who can offer her an alternative to patriarchal convention. Far from the dark and secret mother that is so familiar in Gothic fiction and more like the sentimental exceptions that shimmer with same-sex desire (as in Radcliffe's *The Italian*), Lady Emilia tells her young "friend" the lesson of paternal abuse and male privilege, at the same time that she bathes her in the affection that society has forbidden and leaves her the money necessary for an independent life.[33] This is a further recuperation of the maternal, here offering an escape from the marriage "market" and a chance for independence. Miss Selvyn uses her money to establish a home for the indigent at Millenium Hall.

Miss Trentham has actually established a friendship with a man, which is mutually supportive until they are pushed to consider marriage. Then there is pain and jealousy, but Miss Trentham contracts smallpox and is therefore delivered from the emotional anxiety and sexual vulnerability that her relationship with Alworth had begun to create. Far from lamenting this fate, Miss Trentham looks upon it as an escape: "In a very short time she became perfectly contented with the alteration this cruel distemper had made in her. Her love for reading returned, and she regained the quiet happiness of which flutter and dissipation had deprived her without substituting any thing so valuable in its place" (199). The "thing" she finds of so little value is of course the phallus: it neither gives her a position in relation to a sexual other nor does it place her in a significant relation to her social context. Instead, it objectifies her, trades in the object she is. By spoiling her quality as an object, her physical disfigurement becomes the guarantee of subjecthood and independent value. It is not so much that she is no longer subject to the order of the phallus, but she is now so far from mattering in that order that she has in fact a degree of self-determination. This is not a conventionally "happy" ending, but Scott makes us see the "happiness" in it again as a way of challenging convention with the possibility of authority in female experience.

It is fitting that the last of the women presented escapes the world of sexual victimization by means of disease. For it is dis-ease with the world of male prerogative that the novel is attempting to dramatize.[34]

Each of the women presented finds her way to Millenium Hall as a refuge from social and personal abuse. What Mrs. Maynard calls the "heavenly society" of the Hall is perhaps an impossible ideal, but it is an ideal that for women in the eighteenth century suggested the only possibility for happiness in a world of ruthless patriarchal values. When, finally, the women involve God as their justification of their enterprise, they are not resigning authority but redefining what constitutes (final) authority in patriarchal culture and restructuring the hierarchy of power. The women create the world, that is, in their own image.

I call *Millenium Hall* a lesbian narrative because it insists on intimate relations between women as an alternative to the male-centered experience of marriage. At every point in the narration when a patriarchal resolution would be possible, Scott offers an alternative in female terms that rewrites the narrative from the position of difference. This disruption of narrative is the most powerful means Scott has of overcoming the assumptions behind patriarchy. Because she articulates a female alternative and gives narrative shape to her own sexual preference, Scott liberates women from the phallic interpretation of female desire implicit in traditional narrative. Lesbian narrative form in other words, offers an escape from "happily ever after."

SIX

Wollstonecraft and the Law of Desire

Mary Wollstonecraft's fictional writings, *Mary* (1788) and *The Wrongs of Woman* (1798), entertain almost all the transgressive possibilities that the other novels in this section articulate. If they reject those possibilities as untenable in later-eighteenth-century culture, then they do so with a full awareness of how much hope must be sacrificed in the determination to see things as they are.

Both novels have been criticized on the level of formal sophistication. As various critics have argued, *Mary* seems at times dependent on a series of conventions that both sentimentalize the female and render her a pawn in an essentially male system of exchange, while *The Wrongs of Woman*, which depends to a greater degree on reasoned argument, seems to at least one critic "muddled and schematic."[1] For some, including perhaps William

Godwin, Wollstonecraft's powers as a novelist did not match her brilliance as a political thinker. When she was working on *The Wrongs of Woman* (4 September 1796), she complained to Godwin that she was "labouring . . . in vain to overcome a depression of spirits, which some things you uttered yesterday, produced. . . . I allude to what you remarked, relative to my manner of writing—that there was a radical defect in it—a worm in the bud—&c. What is to be done, I must either disregard your opinion, think it unjust, or throw down my pen in despair. . . . I have scarcely written a line to please myself (and very little with respect to quantity) since you saw my M.S."[2]

I would argue that these works, as sentimental or as muddled as they might seem, address the issue of female writing in a new way. Indeed, the works are to a certain extent about the discovery that narrative itself assumes a male perspective and that not even the most well-intentioned feminist can write a "novel" without succumbing to its implicit cultural agenda. Wollstonecraft is too intelligent to settle for the easy narrative compromises that some of her contemporaries were willing to adopt, and she is too shrewd to pretend to achieve feminist resolutions to stories that challenge the cultural status quo and are therefore unresolvable in realistic narrative. The process of recognizing these limitations, resisting them, and offering provisional solutions is vividly dramatized in Wollstonecraft's two fictional works. Wollstonecraft struggles, that is, not because she cannot write, but because she does not trust what she is writing. The "worm in the bud" is the male presence in novelistic narrative itself.

The political ferment of the 1790s made feminism a publicly recognizable position from which to speak. Mary Wollstonecraft was not alone in making women's rights a political priority, nor was she the only writer to adopt fiction to her political ends. The politics of the novels of the last decade of the century has begun to be discussed by such writers as Armstrong, Butler, Johnson, and Kelly.[3] What I would like to add to this already rich discussion is a consideration of the politics of novel-writing itself: how do the formal concerns of novel-writing reflect this moment of cultural crisis for women?

Žižek says that ideology works most effectively at the level of form. He argues that in the theories of both Freud and Marx, there is an understanding of the significance of form in the basic structures of psychological or political control. For instance, it is necessary to reveal the "secret" value of commodities not behind commodity-form, where classical bourgeois political economy looks for it: "classical political economy is interested only in contents concealed behind the commodity-form, which is why it cannot explain the true secret, not the secret *behind* the form but *the secret of this form itself*." For Žižek, dreams work similarly—"even after we have explained its hidden meaning, its latent thought, the dream remains an enigmatic phenomenon; what is not yet explained is simply its form, the process by means of which the hidden meaning disguised itself in such a form"—and form itself begins to have a power all its own. When the "forms" are followed, even if they are recognized to be hollow, the ideological effect takes its place.[4] What many of the writers I have been discussing achieve in their fiction is a politicization of the novel form itself. In confronting narrative, that is, they challenge the sex-gender system at its ideological roots. For a culture is most secure in the stories it allows to be told.[5]

Importantly, neither *Mary* nor *The Wrongs of Woman* is really a "novel." Wollstonecraft calls the first work "a Fiction," perhaps in an attempt to distance it from the kinds of fictional projects that went by the name of "novel" in the early 1790s. The second, of course, she never completed; and although she does call it a novel in the "Author's Preface," it was *as a novel* that she never completed it. What exists in published form is different from a novel in several ways, not least of all because it is a fragment. I am not arguing a merely semantic point; Wollstonecraft makes form problematic in her works, it seems to me, because she has an understanding of its ideology. Form is not for Wollstonecraft separate from politics or dissociated from the cultural situation in which she was struggling to create. The formal question in these two works highlights their political agenda.

When one looks at Wollstonecraft's fictional works in the context of other novels of the period, it is easy to see why she might hesitate to embrace the form. As I have demonstrated in various ways in preceding chapters, women novelists struggled to resist the formal compulsion of novels to offer only one version of female experience and their oppression, as it were, of the female character in her movement through the marriage plot. Wollstonecraft's works struggle with the novel form as a way of resisting its ideological power.[6] What stands out most starkly in these works is the failure of female friendship to offer anything but an illusory escape from the oppressive social situation in which the female protagonist finds herself. These works use the conventions of sentimental, romantic, even Gothic fiction in order to represent the oppression of the female in later-eighteenth-century culture. Wollstonecraft understands the political implications of fiction, in other words, and uses fiction itself (not just what it says but what it does) to argue her most deeply felt cultural beliefs. If this is not a happy story, at least it demonstrates how difficult it is to put the tenets of transgressive desire into active cultural practice.

Wollstonecraft understands, in other words, what is at stake in novel-writing. In *The Political Unconscious*, Fredric Jameson notes that "ideology is not something which informs or invests symbolic production; rather the aesthetic act is itself ideological, and the production of aesthetic or narrative form is to be seen as an ideological act in its own right, with the function of inventing imaginary or formal 'solutions' to unresolvable social contradictions."[7] Wollstonecraft is aware of the ideological implications of "the aesthetic act," and that may be why novel-writing was for her so vexed and, at times, unfulfilling. As a politically committed woman of the 1790s, Wollstonecraft was severely limited as to what she could say in her fiction or how she could present it. Both *Mary* and *The Wrongs of Woman* show signs of her struggle to gain ideological control of her projects and to say something, anything, that would aid in her struggle for women's "rights." Narrative itself becomes for Wollstonecraft the ground of her political struggle in these works, and it is at the level of narrative that she confronts most directly the insidiousness of cultural control. A feminist writer cannot succeed unless she is willing to challenge her own imaginative engagement with the plots that her culture provides her. Wollstonecraft also understands that narrative cannot simply be reworked for a feminist agenda, that novels cannot easily succeed at subversion, and that fiction itself is already determined by culture.

Perhaps it would be helpful to return here to de Lauretis's discussion of the place of the female in narrative in *Alice Doesn't.* As I noted above, de Lauretis argues, in the chapter "Desire in Narrative," "that many of the current formulations of narrative process fail to see that subjectivity is engaged in the cogs of narrative and indeed constituted in the relation of narrative, meaning, and desire; so that the very work of narrativity is the engagement of the subject in certain positionalities of meaning and desire." As she goes on to demonstrate, however, the "subject" in this process is necessarily male, and the woman is always, at best, the object: "The story of femininity, Freud's question, and the riddle of the Sphinx all have a single answer, one and the same meaning, one term of reference and address: man, Oedipus, the human male person. And so her story, like any other story, is a question of his desire; as is the teleology that Freud imputes to Nature, that primordial 'obstacle' of civilized man."[8]

What, then, is a committed feminist with a story to do? Wollstonecraft very quickly discovers that the conventions of narrative control the story that she wants to tell: *The Wrongs of Woman* "ends" in a court of law, as I shall demonstrate, because that is where narrative originates. De Lauretis quotes Vladimir Propp and Jurij Lotman to establish connections between narrative and law. Propp first suggests that the "patriarchal state" was necessary to the establishment of certain narrative structures, particularly that involving the murder of the father—as in Oedipus—and later that of the

Wollstonecraft and the Law of Desire

romantic quest. Lotman argues that "the origin of plot must be traced to a text-generating mechanism located at the center of a cultural *massif* and thus coextensive with the origins of culture itself."[9] Both these positions suggest a connection between narrative and the regulatory laws by means of which a culture defines itself. Both theorists argue, however, that narrative is a cultural necessity. Wollstonecraft discovers just how thoroughly the laws of culture—the cultural imperatives, as it were—are gender coded. For a woman, she discovers, there is no narrative; there are no stories to call her own.

Recent critics have taken us a long way toward understanding Wollstonecraft's position on female subjectivity, female-female relations, female education, and the general question of female oppression in marriage and the impossibility of respectability in and around adultery and divorce.[10] One of the most helpful of these investigations into Wollstonecraft's narrative position is Janet Todd's attempt to understand the implications of Wollstonecraft's relation to "sentimental" context. She suggests that Wollstonecraft "was as much under the influence of the late-eighteenth-century conception of feminine sensibility" and that she was at times "trapped in the ideology of femininity and in the myths of the sentimental novel."[11] She argues that Wollstonecraft "tried to bend the sentimental ideology to [her] own purpose, creating unstable stories that proclaimed and castigated women's peculiar sensibility, the emotional vulnerability of the superior feeling heart that twists and turns to irritate and wound itself."[12] While Todd makes these "unstable stories" sound like an unwelcome narrative side-effect of certain ideological assumptions, I would suggest that the narrative volatility of both these works, their refusal to "conform," as it were, to narrative expectation, distinguishes them as narratives about narrative impossibility: female friendship fails to offer the cohesive force of resistance, however vividly it might promise something other than the status quo. It resides in the realm of fantasy, Wollstonecraft seems to say, and can do nothing substantially to improve the lot of women in this world.

Todd attests to the ideological power of literary form when she says that "it is almost a relief when [in *Mary*] the rather disappointing Ann enters the proper sentimental plot of dying heroine, when language and situation, sentiment and plot, can coalesce."[13] What Todd is implicitly suggesting is the power of narrative expectation: her own desire for the death of a character she finds "rather disappointing." Wollstonecraft anticipates this response by creating Ann and killing her off not simply to conform to the conventions of sensibility; she seems rather to be insisting on their ruthlessness. The question to ask at this point in the novel—those of us who do not feel relief at

Ann's death may be the ones to ask it—is what function her death serves in Wollstonecraft's own narrative politics.

Todd's comments make it clear that the early death of a woman of sensibility was by no means unusual in the fiction of the later eighteenth century. But Ann's death is strange in several ways. In the first place, Mary, the central character, has taken up Ann as an attempt to answer for the loneliness she experiences at home: her mother dotes on her brother and hardly tolerates her presence. With Ann, "she hoped now to experience the pleasure of being beloved; but this hope led her into new sorrows, and, as usual, paved the way for disappointment. Ann only felt gratitude."[14] Mary's relation with Ann continues to be more fully realized in her imagination than it ever is in "life":

> She loved Ann better than any one in the world—to snatch her from the very jaws of destruction—she would have encountered a lion. To have this friend constantly with her; to make her mind easy with respect to her family, would it not be superlative bliss? (15)

The answer to this rhetorical question is, of course, yes, but. . . . Mary finds repeatedly that Ann is not the "romantic friend" she seeks. Far from typically sentimental, this friendship is found wanting in various ways throughout its brief tenure—"Before she enjoyed Ann's society, she imagined it would have made her completely happy: she was disappointed, and yet we knew not what to complain of" (16)—and Ann's death, after a period of intense intimacy, is portrayed as more devastating than any dramatized friendship has warranted. Mary goes so far as to question her ability to feel. It is not so much that the misery is false; rather it resonates most profoundly in self-referential fictional terms:

> Ann!—this dear friend was soon torn from her—she died suddenly as Mary was assisting her to walk across the room.—The first string was severed from her heart—and this 'slow, sudden-death' disturbed her reasoning faculties; she seemed stunned by it; unable to reflect, or even to feel her misery. (32)[15]

In mourning for Ann, the potentially romantic friend who never fulfilled her need, Mary laments the fictional construct that should in literary terms have been able to sustain her. Mary is forced to recognize, however, not so much that the fiction is untrue to female experience, but that female friendship, a response supposedly so automatic, is not to be relied upon in a world shaped by (primarily male) desire. Todd says, about Mary herself, that "her sensibility has nothing to do in the world, nothing to create or achieve, and it simply consumes itself."[16] These remarks suggest that because she is a victim of sensibility, Mary's attempt to create herself as a subject is doomed to fictional disappointment, narrative failure, and even critical bemusement.

Mary's love for Ann has rarely been recognized for the deeply coded form of female-female desire that it represents. As Claudia Johnson says in *Equivocal Beings*, "[d]espite the intensity of Mary's love, and the amount of space devoted to its skittish representation, it has received little attention, and is generally passed over quickly to make way for the heterosexual plot later depicted, or discussed as a pathological evasion of such relations."[17] I certainly agree that this relation is of crucial importance to an understanding of the novel, but I would argue that Wollstonecraft's heartfelt sacrifice of Ann to the forces of heteronormativity is deeply embedded in her formal structure. Ann must die and female affection must be overcome, Wollstonecraft seems to say, because heteronormative narrative, like heteronormative culture, simply cannot tolerate such bonds. The fact, as Johnson describes, that she must marry a boy and overcome her "romantic friendship" is a measure of the failure of female utopian ideals to offer a woman like Mary any actual resort from the dominant culture. Johnson says further that "the very gaps in Wollstonecraft's prose afford space to the unspeakable, and as such have an uncanny brilliance all their own."[18] I think that this "impossibility of articulating" the attachment between Mary and Ann is an acknowledgment of the degree to which such an attachment must finally fail to change anything about the culture within which it is constructed. Johnson says that *The Wrongs of Woman* "explodes [the] hope in the emancipatory potential of republican masculinity."[19] I would suggest that *Mary* explodes the hope of the emancipatory potential of female friendship as well. I do not mean to suggest that Wollstonecraft rejected such friendship; on the contrary, it represents the formal center of her work. Rather, it seems to me that she recognizes the inability of such relations to offer any more than a passing solace from the rigors of later-eighteenth-century culture.

"Romantic friendship" is itself the problem here: it leaves Mary as well as Ann dissatisfied because it is itself a euphemism encoded so as to deny female desire and the erotics of female bonds. The odd incoherence between Mary's emotion and the forms of friendship themselves can be explained in this way. Mary's desire for Ann, her need to share a life with her, cannot be contained in the neat invisibility that "romantic friendship" offers. Instead of finding solace in friendship, that is, she finds the torments and dissatisfactions that a more demanding relation might entail. Because this relation must be hidden, must be denied, moreover, the dissatisfactions are all the more likely. Throughout the rest of this novel, Mary may be said to be trying to put her life together again. But the results are never satisfying. Henry can perhaps serve as an alternative "friend" for Mary, but he can never serve as an alternative lover.

The analysis of various critics of sensibility suggests that what had been a literary fashion in the seventeen-sixties and -seventies had become in the eighties and nineties a discourse entirely pervasive in contemporary culture. That is, it not only determined female—and a great deal of male—behavior, but it also offered the only available terms of self-analysis. Wollstonecraft herself, as well as her characters Mary and Maria, confront this "prison-house" of sensibility throughout her life and her fiction.[20] If "politics" (or "the politics of feminism") offers an escape from this prison, or what *The Wrongs of Woman* suggests could only be a madhouse, it does so only by accepting the inevitability of "feeling" and finding a way to politicize that from within.

I have argued elsewhere that "sensibility" is a symptom of the cultural ascendancy of the bourgeois individual in the later eighteenth century. What needs to be articulated more directly in this context is the masculine subjectivity that sensibility presupposes. Feeling as a culturally acceptable indulgence is masculine; feeling as a source of benevolence is masculine; and feeling as the basis of hypochondriacal self-satisfaction is also masculine. For a woman to feel sensibility is hardly an impossibility, as countless female outbursts of feeling in the later eighteenth century attest. But the source of feeling itself is so hierarchized that women learned early on that to survive as an independent individual meant to resist feeling. Sensibility makes the female the victim because it needs to exercise the prerogative of cultural superiority in order to ensure that an outpouring of feeling does not disrupt the hegemony it so ineffectually challenges. Hysteria, after all, an illness associated with an over-abundance of feeling in women, is nowhere celebrated as hypochondria is: Boswell's popular column *The Hypochondriack* could hardly have been written from a female perspective. A journal on *Hysteria* could only be imagined as mocking female sensibility, never celebrating it.[21] For Mary to politicize feeling from a feminist perspective, then, is almost a cultural impossibility.

The most useful emotion in this situation is hatred; for without qualifying one's ability to feel, hatred frees one from the victimization that affection and sympathy automatically entail. In *The Wrongs of Woman*, for instance, Maria has to learn that her feelings toward Venables are political feelings: the hatred and contempt that she feels for this self-important wretch are necessary to resist his power over her. She cannot afford to sympathize with him, even though her instincts, informed as they are by the tenets of sensibility, push her in that direction. By focusing on her negative feelings, she teaches herself how to *imagine* a world beyond him, a world in which she even survives.

When she does allow herself to defy "fiction" in this way, she realizes a kind of power that at other times she lacks. For whenever she feels pity or any of the other forms of fictionalized domestic affection, she is duped and victimized. She *knows* that he is not to be trusted, but her sensibility demands at times that she treat him like a fellow human being. Such moments are her undoing:

> Of Mr. Venables I thought not, even when I thought of the felicity of loving your father, and how a mother's pleasure might be exalted [she tells her daughter], and her care softened by a husband's tenderness. —"Ought to be!" I exclaimed; and I endeavoured to drive away that tenderness that suffocated me; but my spirits were weak, and the unbidden tears would flow. (180)

It is interesting to note that even here, after a series of brutal and contemptible actions, Venables can be treated with that tenderness that Maria seems naturally to feel. Her sensibility, Wollstonecraft seems to argue, always betrays her. A woman may not be able to avoid these feelings, but she must overcome them by reminding herself that the feelings themselves oppress her.

In *Mary* also, the heroine must learn how to keep her sensibility from overwhelming her with misery. She knows that there must be good in an ability to feel sympathy for those suffering around her. But as in other fictions of sensibility, her feelings begin to separate her from the very people she would help. No amount of misery, for instance, can do anything to make up for the loss of Ann. What her emotion does is to create a substitute for the personal relation that might have given her life a center, a meaning. Mary does not understand the political implications of her situation as vividly as Maria does hers, but she knows instinctively that something other than "solitary sadness" must be available to women like herself (68). In the end, she decides that she must look beyond the grave to find it.

Todd suggests that "without the sustaining myth of male desire," Wollstonecraft's heroines find themselves trapped in a world of self-defeating emotion.[22] The mere absence of male desire does not mean that emotion must be self-defeating. Emotion is defeated by the world of male villainy, not by the self. A particular form of male villainy, sometimes in fact coded as sexual power, returns again and again to torment the heroines. Male villainy is complicated in Wollstonecraft's fiction. Writing, as she is, in the eighties and nineties affords her a dazzling array of deceptive and deplorable male figures both in and out of fiction. Her own experiences with Fuseli, Imlay, and Godwin, among others, suggest countless ways of depicting her male characters. Other novelists and other kinds of printed "fiction"—such as the often reprinted *Adultery Trials* and the *Sessions at the Old Bailey*, which I cited earlier—offer her an even more complex vocabulary of male villainy.

Men are villainous not only because they expect women to give up their identity in answer to their own aggressive will, or because they abuse and brutalize the women around them, or because they tease them and torment them in their oppression; men are also villainous because women feel desire in turn, and this desire gives men a power they would otherwise lack. As de Lauretis argues, it is male desire that necessarily structures the female narrative: "women *must either* consent *or* be seduced into consenting to femininity."[23] When a woman refuses, as Maria, especially, tries to, she is driven from narrative itself. Wollstonecraft is not afraid of articulating desire, but as she does so she begins to answer the question of why women have no place in narrative.

In other words, women collude with male villainy on account of the ways in which female desire is constructed in heteronormative culture. A moment that comes rather late in *The Wrongs of Woman* helps to dramatize this point. Maria has finally escaped from Venables, and she has taken a room with a woman who seems sympathetic. When that woman is brutalized by her husband, however, she betrays Maria automatically and thoroughly. Maria flees her abode and searches for another:

> I did not inform my landlady where I was going. I knew that she had a sincere affection for me, and would willingly have run any risk to show her gratitude; yet I was fully convinced, that a few kind words from Johnny would have found the woman in her, and her dear benefactress, as she termed me in an agony of tears, would have been sacrificed, to recompense her tyrant for condescending to treat her like an equal. (173)

The landlady's name is never mentioned, and Maria's "Johnny" gives the expression proverbial force. But what is that force exactly? I have not found a reference to it as such, but Partridge notes that Johnny is a colloquial name for a sweetheart, which suggests a reading of this passage that focuses on *feeling.* "A few kind words from Johnny" fits this nicely, hinting as it does, at a kind of intimate condescension or even contempt, and reminding us with its peremptory flair that the female is abject. Partridge also includes a gloss on "Johnny" as "penis" ("mostly feminine, late c. 19–20.").[24] I think it is worth considering whether such meanings might not have existed earlier

Wollstonecraft and the Law of Desire

than Partridge suggests and whether Wollstonecraft might in fact be suggesting that sexual desire between a woman and a man, not unusually figured in the form of the penis itself, constructs her as a subject of desire who can only betray the women around her. This is not unlike arguments that Wollstonecraft has made elsewhere, particularly in *The Vindication of the Rights of Women,* in which she says that "the sexual attention of man particularly acts on female sensibility, and this sympathy has been exercised from their youth up." The "overstrained sensibility" that Wollstonecraft described is victim to the vagaries of male social and sexual attention, just as this scene dramatizes. And of course *The Vindication* is concerned throughout with the ways in which women betray one another. What the "few kind words" suggest in either case, however, is how condescending "Johnny" can be and how abusive. By giving her comment proverbial force, in other words, Maria demonstrates that she understands she is up against the power of the phallus, so often mistaken for the penis itself and by no means an inconsiderable adversary. As Cora Kaplan says, "for Wollstonecraft, female desire was a contagion caught from the projection of male lust, an ensnaring and enslaving infection that made women into dependent and degenerate creatures."[25]

It is not the man who betrays Maria, then; it is the woman who is married to the man and devoted to the particular feature of his anatomy that controls her. Marriage itself is a problematic and largely victimizing state in both works. But female community also fails the heroine. Fictional desire is painted as unpleasant if not destructive for the woman. Wollstonecraft does not present us with something that might be considered a happy marriage. Nor, for that matter, does she have any interest in happy endings—those that promise marriage and happiness. Female friendship too seems an easily disrupted ideal. Wollstonecraft deals with this repeatedly in her works, as other critics have shown. What I find interesting for the purposes of this argument, however, is the degree to which the narrative possibilities for female success are continually undermined, in this case, and in others, by the power of male presence in the world of narrative.[26]

Mary ends, for instance, with a direct attempt to undermine the "marriage-ending" syndrome:

> Her delicate state of health did not promise long life. In moments of solitary sadness, a gleam of joy would dart across her mind —She thought she was hastening to that world *where there is neither marrying,* nor giving in marriage. (68)

This brings me back to my original point about form in *Mary* and *The Wrongs of Woman*: they are conceived and executed so as to minimize the narrative insistence on the romance plot. In *Mary,* the main character emphasizes female and male friendship and doing good work in the community. Her marriage, as unsatisfying and indeed meaningless as it is, becomes a bother only when Henry's attentions break through the platonic wall that these two characters had established between them. It does not function in the plot as a moment of crisis or culmination of any kind. Nor is there a sense that as a married woman Mary is in any way fulfilled. She defies romance conventions, and when Ann dies, she settles in to live unhappily ever after. This is *not* a tragedy, like Clarissa's or Werther's, because tragedy is no more to be trusted by a woman than comedy or romance.

Wollstonecraft writes a fiction with a conventional form in order to defy convention and assert an independence from its dictates. The narrative feels more like one of the interpolated tales of *Millenium Hall* than like a novel. It may not seem that Wollstonecraft is as clearly or directly advocating same-sex relations as Scott—but I would argue that not only does she argue for such relations, she laments that they are not accorded more significance in culture itself. A woman may love another woman, as Mary so clearly loves Ann, but that love hardly need waste its breath speaking its name because it has no political valence and no substantial place in the dominant fiction of the age. Wollstonecraft nevertheless tries to break through the virulence of the marriage plot to something that represents, if nothing else, the failure of female friendship in the later eighteenth century.[27]

If *Mary* is an apology for this failure, *The Wrongs of Woman,* although just a fragment, anatomizes it in greater detail. This novel attempts to explore the cultural implications of female experience in the age of revolution. There is a structure to the work, but it is the structure of confinement. Maria writes her tale to her deceased daughter within the walls of an insane asylum, where her husband has brutally placed her. This is Gothic in its outlines, and Venables is a demon-lover if there ever was one. But Wollstonecraft has managed to use Gothic conventions to transform the day-to-day story of female experience. Critic Gary Kelly suggests that the work is allegorical; in the pile of buildings in which she finds herself confined, for instance, Wollstonecraft "intended" "to symbolize British political history, thereby turning Burke's well-known symbol of the constitution to her own purposes."[28] This is no doubt true, but it is equally likely that in a work written by a woman in the 1790s, the fortresslike structure would suggest those in which countless other suffering heroines are incarcerated in Gothic fiction: marriage and the home grotesquely disfigured as horrid and painful.

Wollstonecraft insists on this connection, perhaps, because of the degree to which women have been incarcerated in fictional convention as well as in cultural constructions of femininity. That is why it is so significant that the one idea that sustains Maria in her confinement is the idea that her child can learn from experience and have a different life. Her "memoir" to her daughter hovers within this Gothic construct as a hidden source of life, defying convention as well as culture with a female-directed pedagogy.

Maria's maternal desires lie, again, outside the conventional terms of fictional motivation. Shawn Maurer has written interestingly about the implications of maternal feelings in *The Wrongs of Woman*, saying that "Maria's desperate wish to 'instruct her daughter, and shield her from the misery, the tyranny, her mother knew not how to avoid' (82) precipitates what is arguably her most important act—composing the memoir that occupies half of the unfinished novel."[29] The value of the memoir as instruction, as illustration, is not to be overestimated. Again, as in *Millenium Hall*, it is the internal narrations that matter. They defy the attempt to shape female experience into any form other than what it seems here: that is, wretched and abused.

Jemima's own narrative provides an interesting corroboration here. Critics have noted that her story takes only a few pages and have suggested that perhaps Wollstonecraft is not really interested in her.[30] But the very fact that her tale of brutalization complements and heightens the details of Maria's own story suggests that together they make a more powerful and complete analysis—an anatomy—of what it is to be female in a patriarchal society. Jemima's story of underclass life begins with her illegitimate conception and the death of her mother shortly after her birth; she is then subjected to the misery of a poor nurse, who abuses her until she is brought "home" as servant, where she is impregnated by her employer's husband and then cast into the streets. Her story is shocking, but it has a certain logic of poverty all its own: "I was, in fact, born a slave, and chained by infamy to slavery during the whole of existence" (106). Jemima eventually resorts to prostitution to support herself, and finally finds a "protector," who at least offers her a safe place to live. After he dies and she is cast out by his family, she takes a job as a washer-woman; when she is injured and can work no longer, she "[becomes] a thief from principle" (118), is tried and imprisoned in a workhouse, and eventually is employed as a jailer in this house of madness.

The simplicity of her tale of degradation and abuse is a part of its power. Styled as it is in the form of an entry in *The Newgate Calendar*, it offers a vivid example of what a "female narrative" can look like in the later eighteenth century.[31] The tale turns, of course, on male villainy, and it fulfills its "progress" in the contemptibility of the law. These are not accidental events or careless evocation. They provide an object lesson in female narrative: the female story is always controlled by the man. Jemima's encounter with a heartless judge, who tells her he "paid enough in conscience to the poor" (118) and then throws her in the workhouse, foreshadows the scene in which Maria sets her case before a magistrate after her escape with Darnford from the asylum. Maria is accused of adultery and determined to plead "guilty," but at the same time her circumstance "roused bitter reflections on the situation of women in society" (194). Gary Kelly suggests that the trial that follows was based upon the *Trials for Adultery*, published in 1779– 1780. Kelly also notes that "a woman could not obtain a divorce except on grounds of bigamy or incest (there were only four divorces granted to women in two hundred years)."[32]

The motivating impulse behind a volume like *Trials for Adultery* seems to be the inevitability of female fault. As I quoted earlier in this study, the "civilian" who collects this material suggests that "it requires little or no apology for the publication of these trials. It may . . . deter the wavering wanton from the completion of her wishes; it may be of service to the practicers in the law; . . . it will shew to the world in general by what gradual steps affection sinks into indifference, indifference into disgust, and disgust into aversion: the consequences of which are but too apparent from the perusal of these volumes."[33] These cases, however, seem but an excuse for the presentation of primarily female transgression, with rhetoric that exacerbates not only female crimes but female identity itself.

In a typical "case," for instance, John Hooke Campbell, Esq., brings an accusation against his wife, Elizabeth Eustatia. In the opening "Libel," their marriage is noted and their five children, "begotten on her body by the said John Hooke Campbell," are recorded. Then we are told that she "went to Bath, for the benefit of the waters, and the education of her children." The libel then goes on to say that "the said Elizabeth Eustatia Campbell was and is a very loose woman, and of a lustful and wicked disposition, and, during the time she resided at Bath and Richmond, she secretly kept company with William Wade, Esq., with whom she committed the foul crime of adultery." The rhetoric of female wickedness, so common in these "trials," is an inevitable part of the narrative of female degradation, even following, as in this case, several years of marriage and the production of five children. The accusation, moreover, opens the defendant to an invasion of privacy that is breathtaking in its extent and embarrassing in its detail. For nearly seventy pages witnesses, including servants, friends, fellow-lodgers, and so on, record bits of information—doors creaking in the night, lewd behavior in public, whispered remarks in private lodgings, and so forth—all to prove that "the said Mrs. Campbell frequently committed adultery with the said

Mr. Wade." What the case actually reveals, however, is a discreet love affair carried on with tact and concern. The "lewdness" is fabricated for the court-room (and the reader) as a means of conforming to the demands of law. It also seems clear in reading this document that Mrs. Campbell had in fact chosen to separate from her husband and live with Mr. Wade. There is of course no legal grounds for such behavior, and therefore the narrative is a narrative of transgression, and the female finds herself once again outside law, and, as in *The Wrongs of Woman,* outside of narrative.[34] Lawrence Stone claims that "until masculine cultural expectations have adapted to the new situation, the ideology of feminism is likely to put many marriages under exceptional strain."[35] It would also be worth considering the degree to which "masculine cultural expectations" have ever adapted to female inde-pendence. Recent statistics on wife battering bring the issue into high relief.[36]

In *The Wrongs of Woman,* of course, Maria attempts to reclaim the terms of legal narrative for herself. For this purpose, the trial is an ideal narrative device. Here Maria can make her arguments and bring charges "the truth of which is an insult upon humanity" (196). The trial technique had been used by Godwin as well, in *Caleb Williams,* to point up the inequities of the legal system and the inability of judges or juries to determine truth. Wollstone-craft, however, has structured her account from Maria's point of view exclusively: the reader is sympathetic to her complaint and alive to the inhuman treatment she has received. Therefore her claims about marriage—Wollstonecraft's claims, really—have special force. Their logic and reason, however, violate the narrative silences not only of most marriage-plot fictions, but also (and obviously) of the law itself.

After she has made her case, made *the* case, that is, that the book has made, her relation to the law is clearly established. She is an outlaw: "If I am unfortunately united to an unprincipled man, am I for ever to be shut out from fulfilling the duties of a wife and mother? —I wish my country to approve of my conduct; but, if laws exist, made by the strong to oppress the weak, I appeal to my own sense of justice, and declare that I will not live with the individual, who has violated every moral obligation which binds man to man" (197). Wollstonecraft is attempting, in other words, through the arguments of Maria, to defy the law. In a ceremony that is by its nature the very reverse of marriage, Wollstonecraft brings the second volume of her work to a climax. It is logical according to the rule of law that the judge reject her claim:

> The judge, in summing up the evidence, alluded to "the fallacy of letting women plead their feelings, as an excuse for the violation of the marriage-vow. For his part, he had always determined to oppose all innovation and the new-fangled notions which incroached on the good old rules of con-

duct. We did not want French principles in public or private life—and, if women were allowed to plead their feelings, as an excuse or palliation of infidelity, it was opening a flood-gate for immorality." (198–99)

Wollstonecraft ends her work with this final articulation of patriarchal law. Maria has argued reasonably about her situation and she is accused of "plead[ing] her feelings": this is nothing new. But it is new to see the charge leveled against as clearly articulated a case as that of Maria. Law of course cannot listen to reason in this way because law itself is gendered. I said earlier that this is the literal reverse of the marriage with which most romance fictions end. It is the reverse in form and effect, but superficially the result is the same: the woman remains married to "the man [in the judge's words] chosen by her parents and relations, who were qualified by their experience to judge better for her, than she could for herself" (199). Volume 2, in other words, ends with the outrage of the brutal subjection of women to their husbands. In a patriarchy, this is called marriage, and the men control it.

The various attempts to move beyond this recognition that are recorded in the published version of the work suggest, as clearly as any completed narrative would, not only the impossibility of moving beyond the control of, outside of, or even within the law as she has already articulated it, but also the unsatisfactory nature of any narrative device to which she might turn after documenting the end of narrative, as she has.

Among the list of editorial notes of the "few hints . . . respecting the plan of the remainder of the work" (201), we find the following:

> Once more pregnant—He returns . . . Discovery—Interview—Consequence. . . .

> Finds herself again with child—Delighted—A discovery—A visit—A miscarriage—Conclusion. . . .

> Divorced by her husband—Her lover unfaithful—Pregnancy—Miscarriage—Suicide. (202)

All of these "hints" suggest that the woman has no story. History excludes her, and narrative offers her no hope. In *The Sense of an Ending*, Frank Kermode quotes Iris Murdoch: "Since reality is incomplete, art must not be too afraid of incompleteness."[37] Wollstonecraft is not only not afraid of incompleteness, she insists on it as the only form that reflects the impossibility of being a woman in patriarchal society. "Pregnancy—miscarriage—suicide": what more does she need to say?

In the final set of paragraphs entitled "The End," she attempts to write in this area beyond meaning. This conclusion has the quality of fantasy, and that she begins it by taking an overdose of laudanum suggests that it may be just an articulation of the "suicide" noted above. But in the midst of her reverie, Jemima returns with her child—supposedly hidden by her husband—and after "violent vomiting," Maria decides "the conflict is over!—I will live for my child!" (203). It would be tempting to understand this as a final resolution, but in the terms of the work before us, that is not what it is. Whether or not the child is dead, this final outburst has the quality of a hallucination: "I will live for my child"—even this is an impossibility in the world Wollstonecraft has described. As we might realize with bitter irony while reading these lines, Wollstonecraft herself died as the result of the complications of childbirth. Even the hope, the desire, that a child represents cannot sustain a woman in the world: this is the female narrative and here is where it ends. The fragments suggest the force of narrative convention. Any other ending that did not accept the culturally sanctioned terms of closure would be mere fantasy. "Pregnancy—miscarriage—suicide": Wollstonecraft circumscribes the options for her heroine according to the dictates of the social and legal system to which she has been subjected. Even to "live for my child" is more than the law of desire in a masculinist culture allows.

Part Three

EROTIC ISOLATION

SEVEN

Self-Love in *The Female Quixote:*
Romancing the Ego

The Female Quixote (1752) is often read as a romance that defies the tenets of novelistic expression in order to articulate resistance to the cultural situation of women in the later eighteenth century.[1] Romances were considered transgressive because of the sexual expectations they raised and the degree of fantasy they encouraged. Richard Berenger, a classical scholar writing in *The World* in 1754, articulates this cultural expectation with breathtaking accuracy. Berenger first complains about "putting romances into the hands of young ladies." Then he goes on to ask:

> Why do we suffer those hearts, which ought to be appropriated to the various affections of social life, to be alienated by the mere creatures of the imagination? In short, why do we suffer those who were born for the

> purpose of living in society with men endued with passions and frailties like
> their own, to be bred up in daily expectation of living *out of* it with such
> men as have never existed?

The fear of female sexuality is implicit in this diatribe. Berenger feels that
the female imagination needs to be directed, if not absolutely controlled, by
the male. Moreover, the not so subtle suggestion of birth and breeding, upon
which these remarks are based, makes clear how the social function of the
female has been constructed. Whatever else is true about romance, it does
not celebrate childbirth nor does it sentimentalize the family in particular
or domestic values in general. That is partly why it is so threatening to the
cultural imagination. Berenger concludes his argument with a fictional representation. By telling the story of "Clarinda," who is so influenced by her
reading that she falls in love with her suitor's French valet de chambre,
Berenger acknowledges the fictionalization of experience itself. His own
argument depends on fiction in order to make its point. After Clarinda's
father forbids the match and sends the Frenchman packing, she languishes
for decades, and "in the fifty-fifth year of her age prefers the visionary
happiness of reading *Clelia* and thinking on her Antonio, to the real blessings
of those social relations, which in all probability she had enjoyed through
life, if she had never been a reader of romances."[2]

This scenario is reminiscent of the situation in Charlotte Lennox's *The
Female Quixote* (1752), but the moral is spelled out with more brutal
efficiency. In Berenger's account a woman is expected to play a role that is
established for her in society. If she does not play that role, if she is not
"appropriated to the various affections of social life," she is no better than
a failure: the isolation of her own imagination is a measure of her disgrace.[3]

Like her liveliest descendent, Marianne Dashwood, Lennox's heroine
Arabella becomes so enraptured with her own private sexual fantasies that
no worldly relation makes sense to her. Arabella uses these fantasies as a
means of surviving a brutally stifling life. She lives in rural isolation with
her antisocial father and an assortment of adoring domestics. Her reading
has been confined to the voluminous French romances that she has inherited
from her mother, whose own story is one of disappointment and frustration.
From these romances she has learned to give emotional precedence to her
own responses to the world. For Janet Todd, Arabella's "mistake is like
the coquette's, the assumption of too great female significance and social
power."[4] Unlike the coquette, who reassured an earlier generation of the
need for the regulation of female desire, Arabella does not direct her sexual
needs to the gentleman of her common acquaintance. Instead she creates

Self-Love in *The Female Quixote*

sexual excitement in a variety of surprising situations that have as their common denominator only Arabella's imagination itself.

Berenger's remarks suggest that the dangers of reading are the dangers of a kind of sexual introversion that makes a woman unsuitable for the various fulfillments that marriage offers. The transgressive nature of reading for women of the eighteenth century has been widely discussed. Until Sedgwick's discussion of Marianne Dashwood, however, the masturbatory implications of this transgression remained unexplored.[5] Charlotte Lennox takes the threat of sexual introversion seriously; and in her drama of near hysterical involvement in the privacy of the sexual self, Lennox refuses to offer fulfillments that have not first been tested in the heated confines of Arabella's imagination. In the novel, this process does not always undo her heroine; in fact, it quite often preserves her from harm.

In her first "adventure," Arabella's "romantic" notions are brought into high relief. During a visit to church one Sunday, Arabella is *seen* by a stranger, Hervey, who finds her attractive and asks his host about her "obtain"-ability. In the straightforward novelistic mode of their conversation, his friend tells him: "The poor Girl . . . has been kept in Confinement so long, that I believe it would not be difficult to persuade her to free herself by Marriage. She never had a Lover in her Life; and therefore the first Person who addresses her has the fairest Chance for succeeding."[6] However ridiculous Hervey later finds Arabella's high romantic protests of his fantasized attempt to "ravish" her, it would be difficult to imagine a more cynical articulation of the self-satisfactions of male desire than this. Were Hervey to find the vapid and ill-prepared girl that his friend suggests, Arabella's fate would already be sealed. Instead he finds an energetic and self-obsessed young woman, who is too self-involved to become an unwitting victim to the sordid kind of seduction he is planning. Moreover, by resisting his charms, she articulates the specific terms of her fantasy.

After her first response to his advances, he asks, "What do you take me for?" "For a Ravisher, interrupted *Arabella,* an impious Ravisher, who contrary to all Laws both human and divine, endeavour to possess yourself by Force of a Person whom you are not worthy to serve; and whose Charity and Compassion you have returned with the utmost Ingratitude" (20). Arabella may have made a fool of herself, shrieking at his approach and using sublime language to put him off; nevertheless, her nearly hysterical self-involvement not only protects her from his mercenary attentions, but it also ensures her ability to remain the mistress of her own fortune. If she is deluded as to her own importance, at least she has the wherewithal to protect herself from a sordid but novelistically convincing seduction. The rakes expect abject gullibility; instead they find a kind of self-obsession that in its auto-erotic dynamic leaves them powerless. Of course, the narrative seems to mock Arabella's bizarrely inappropriate response. At the same time, however, the private thrills that she takes in protecting herself have an important cultural significance. Her own fantasies prevent her becoming a victim here. If her sexually histrionic response is a "mistake," it is an uncannily appropriate one.

Eighteenth-century antionanistic tracts are vivid in their depiction of female masturbatory practice, and one at least seems to suggest a connection between same-sex desire and the auto-manipulation of sexual organs.[7] Such tracts develop only those notions of female sexuality that are implicit in a range of other concerns as well. In her study of "spectral politics," for instance, Terry Castle suggests that even the solitary practice of reading was seen to harbor "dangers" that included a complex dynamic of self-involvement. She explains that once "reading became dangerous because it prompted obsessional thoughts," it became possible to diagnose the reader as the victim of hallucinatory disease. Moreover, she argues,

> The rationalist attack on the "effeminizing" habit of reverie had powerful buried connections . . . with the medical attack on masturbation waged in the same period: the "criminal reveries" of the vicious and sensual . . . easily modulated into "the pampering of . . . base appetite." "There is certainly no power of the mind that requires more cautious management and stern control," wrote Abercrombie, "and the proper regulation of it cannot be too strongly impressed upon the young." Like masturbation, reverie was a self-indulgent, repetitive activity resulting in a debilitating psychic "discharge": the discharge of hallucination.[8]

In Arabella's case, this analogy seems almost superfluous. As her hallucinatory powers develop, so do the possibilities for sexual transgression of a masturbatory kind. For Lennox, moreover, "the pampering of base appetite" seems at times the only alternative for a woman of Arabella's temperament.

Nevertheless, hallucination and masturbation, however suggestive in this context, cannot explain the details of Arabella's complex self-involvement. If she behaves like someone completely mentally and physically self-obsessed, that does not necessarily mean that she is mad or that her relation to her physical self is abusive. She seems in many contexts quite sane and self-possessed. The combination of hallucination and self-love that Arabella displays might better be termed "auto-affection," as one recent critic has used the term. Auto-affection involves a complex system of self-presence "through alienation and reconfrontation of oneself as an object."[9] The

Self-Love in *The Female Quixote*

implicit fictionalization of her own experiences that Arabella practices involves an implicit "alienation and reconfrontation" as well. The novel repeatedly makes it clear that Arabella loves no one quite so much as she loves
herself. Her willingness to see herself as the heroine of a romantic narrative
is the outward sign of this love. Arabella's auto-affection, in other words, is
the motivating force of most of the narrative. But the brilliance of Lennox's
portrayal resides in her refusal to make a total mockery of this auto-
affection. Lennox could almost be said to celebrate the degree to which
Arabella is able to transform herself into the heroine of her own sexually
transgressive narratives.

The novel abounds in instances in which Arabella's flights of sexual
fantasy help to preserve her personal and political integrity in situations
which, in a novelistic narrative, would undo her. Her situation is not, after
all, as secure as some of her critics have made it sound.[10] Her father has
attempted to subject her to his cynical disaffection with the world and has
left her to fend for herself in what may be a privileged, but is certainly not
an enviable, position. She is as isolated as any tragic heroine of the eighteenth century, yet she educates herself so as to find a way to resist her father.
He assumes that she will follow his will in all things, including the selection
of a husband. His shock at her resistance in this matter is softened only
because he assures himself that she will accede to his wishes in time. But
Arabella determines to resist his choice, and does resist until her own desire
gives her a reason to alter her view.

Her father makes his economically informed choice in terms that display
the sex-gender system at its most virulent. His choice of a mate for his
daughter is her cousin, to whom he will in any case leave a portion of his
estate as a peculiarly ill-chosen threat to force his daughter's hand.[11] The
incestuous potential of this choice has little resonance in this novel, perhaps
because it very quickly becomes clear that Glanville is particularly susceptible to Arabella's maddening charms. Lennox encourages an incestuous
situation, moreover, because Arabella must finally come to recognize the
value of family and the satisfactions of a wealthy estate. Glanville comes
from within the family that Arabella would disown. But he understands that
her eccentricities need the protection of the wealth and power that this
family represents. Arabella's self-involvement needs the protection from the
world that an incestuous union offers. Unlike the incestuous siblings in
David Simple, that is, Glanville represents the safety of keeping it in the
family. It remains for him to naturalize Arabella's idiosyncrasies and to
ground her private flights of emotional fancy in something like heteronormative desire. With this feminized and ineffectual hero, of course, hetero-

normativity is a less rigorous determinant than it might be. His "control," that is, often seems more like indulgence, as we shall see.

When she complains about her cousin's "presumption" in expressing his love for her, her father makes his position clear: "That Presumption, as you call it, tho' I know not for what Reason . . . was authorized by me: Therefore, know, *Bella,* that I not only permit him to love you, but I also expect you should endeavour to return his Affection; and look upon him as the Man whom I design for your Husband" (39). It may at this stage seem quibbling to say that Arabella accepts Glanville as her lover only when he has fulfilled her romantic expectations, but Glanville becomes interesting only to the degree to which *she* educates *him.*[12]

Margaret Doody says that Arabella's "mode of survival in adolescence is to make a fantasy of her own that will not subordinate her to her father's story" and that "[t]hrough reading her romances Arabella frees herself from fearing, or even seeing, the dangers of her position in relation to the paternal inheritance."[13] What Doody calls "her father's story" is the system of male exchange that the "marriage-plot" represents; he wants, that is, to lead her to the ending that he has provided for her: "since you seem to be so little acquainted with what will most conduce to your own Happiness, you must not think it strange, if I insist upon directing your Choice in the most important Business of your Life" (42). Happiness for the Marquis is a "Business," and the degree to which Arabella resists this equivalence is the degree of her romantic delusion. Throughout the novel, Arabella's romantic notions turn out to have the power to preserve her in the various ways that a patriarchal culture might dispossess her, the ways indeed that novelistic realism might find it convenient to sacrifice her to a "happy ending."

In other words, there is a difference between what the novelist *says* and what she *does* in *The Female Quixote.* Arabella is indoctrinated into the values of novelistic realism only after she has been allowed to indulge a different, deviant desire and discover for herself how to render self-love socially acceptable. In spite of a certain amount of narrative disapproval of Arabella's early behavior, there is a great deal of interest in the degree to which she will carry her romance of self-love and how thoroughly she will embarrass, if not subvert, the patriarchal energy that is being expended to contain her. In other words, Arabella defies the cultural imperative to "be," in a limited, "realistic" sense, the kind of female character who is easily contained in the gesture of narrative closure—a woman, that is, who functions well in the marriage-plot.

Catherine Gallagher says that "[t]he difference between Arabella and the . . . reader of *The Female Quixote* is that Arabella does not know she is

Self-Love in *The Female Quixote*

reading fiction and . . . does not value fiction per se, whereas the reader of this book can register that she is reading a satire, can get the jokes, only by understanding that she is reading a fiction."[14] Of course, each reader creates her own Arabella, much as Glanville and her father do. Each reader, that is, decides to what extent Arabella is to be indulged, and indulged she must be if someone is to follow her exploits for several chapters. Since readers of fiction know that she will be married or promised in marriage before the end of the novel, moreover, they might take pleasure in the extent to which Arabella is able to resist the closure that the novel makes inevitable. Gallagher cites Samuel Johnson and Henry Fielding as the normative, judgmental readers that the novel demands.[15] It is surely possible to imagine novel-readers who do not share the fictional values of such august cultural interpreters. There may well have been readers, indeed there must have been readers, who enjoyed Arabella's perversity and celebrated her exotic world of private fantasy. I would go so far as to claim that Lennox had to find a way to bring Arabella through her ordeal of socialization without sacrificing her rich self-appreciation and without rendering her deepest fantasies meaningless. *The Female Quixote,* that is, is finally a novel about self-confrontation and self-respect. Both these encounters with the self can have meaning only to the degree that they emerge from Arabella's self-love.

Her success or failure in the task that the novel sets for her cannot depend on the respect she earns from the men around her. They hover in surprisingly irrelevant attendance on her exercises of auto-affection. They are all—her father, her uncle Sir Charles, her suitors, Sir George, and her cousin Glanville—predisposed to *indulge* her to a certain extent, but none is prepared to take her seriously, least of all the man her father has chosen as her husband. Glanville obviously finds his cousin physically attractive when he first meets her, and he finds he loves her to a certain extent in spite of the woman she is. But her behavior has a decided effect on his sense of his own sanity.

The number of times that Glanville declares that she is driving him mad becomes a measure of his own inability to control his cousin's behavior, to fit her, that is, into the narrative he has prepared for her. In a typical instance, "Mr. *Glanville,* who was at first disposed to laugh at the strange Manner in which she received his Expressions of Esteem for her, found something, so extremely haughty and contemptuous in the Speech she had made, that he was almost mad with Vexation" (33). That this "vexation" occurs shortly after Glanville has aggressively approached Arabella "with a Resolution to acquaint her with the Permission her Father had given him to make his Addresses to her" (31), that it occurs after only "several Days" of their acquaintance, and that he has had to overcome her "pretty Anger" (31) in order to accost her with his "love," all suggest that he is no candidate for the reader's unqualified sympathy. Moreover, whatever the terms of her rejection of her cousin, his presumption on this occasion barely qualifies him for the "vexation" he articulates.

On other occasions, he no less revealingly feels the madness of vexation when Arabella embarrasses him with her romantic flights, typically before her father but also whenever there is anyone in a position to judge him in light of his cousin's odd attitudes. For instance, when Arabella offers to acquaint her "suitor" Sir George with her "whole History," Glanville's reaction is barely civil:

> Mr. *Glanville,* at this Word, not being able to constrain himself, uttered a Groan, of the same Nature with those which are often heard in the Pit at the Representation of a new Play. Sir *George* understood him perfectly well; yet seemed surprised: And *Arabella,* starting up,
> Since, said she, I have given you no new Cause of Complaint, pray, from whence proceeds this Increase of Affliction?
> I assure you, Cousin, answered he, my Affliction, if you please to term it so, increases every Day; and I believe it will make me mad at last: For this unaccountable Humour of yours is not to be borne.
> You do not seem, replied *Arabella,* to be far from Madness already. (120)

This little interchange tells us a great deal about the characters involved. Glanville "groans" at the mention of Arabella's "History." He does so not just (or even?) because he is afraid that it will embarrass him with its depth of self-involvement. He groans at the very idea that Arabella might have a history to tell. Sir George understands the groan, suggesting a conspiracy of male contempt for the young woman, but he masquerades his feeling in order to work his way into her affections. Only Arabella is clear-headed and direct—her ability to transform her cousin's "mad" to "Madness" is a typical example of her wit and self-possession.

Of course, madness is what *she* is accused of throughout the work. Her uncle Sir Charles, Glanville's father, says at one point, not atypically, when she is suffering the loss of her father: "She is in a Delirium. . . . I am persuaded her Head is not quite right" (60). At other times, characters speak in terms of a "cure" for their cousin/niece. Glanville says, for instance, "As he feared it was impossible to help loving her, his Happiness depended upon curing her of her romantic Notions" (117). This idea that her "romantic Notions" are a sickness, at times in remission but often virulent enough to threaten his love as well as her sanity, is equivalent to other attempts to "medicalize" female sexuality that were current in mid-century, as such publications as Cheyne's *The English Malady* (1733) suggest.[16] As John Mullan makes clear, "the writings concerned with hysteria, spleen, nervous disorder—produced in a steady flow between about 1720 and 1770—are remarkable for the conventionality of the versions of cause and effect on which they rely." He says further that "[f]or the eighteenth-century practitioner of 'Physick,' the female body is construed, like the bodies of Richardson's heroines, as an ever-visible corpus of signs given over to their practice of interpretation."[17] Arabella continually undergoes "the practice of interpretation," and her simple acts of auto-affection are coded as a kind of delirium throughout the text. Her fantastic discourse is understood as an unsettling irregularity that heteronormative regulation may cure. As Castle argues, "the same metaphors and the same superstitious fear of haunting thoughts carried over, with little modification, into modern psychoanalysis."[18]

Arabella is not technically hysterical, but her cousin and her uncle at times seem to attempt to interpret her odd behavior as a form of hysteria. This diagnosis of her "problem" is something that Arabella must not only resist but also subvert if she is to remain free from the attempts at curtailing her liberty. Sir Charles makes the danger explicit when he tells his son: "tho' my Niece has some odd ways, yet, upon the Whole, she is a very accomplished Woman; and when you are her Husband, you may probably find the Means of curing her of those little Follies, which at present are conspicuous enough" (179–80). Her diminutive faults are a reflection of her diminutive value: a husband can always cure his wife of being the person she is.

The person who best understands how to make Arabella the victim of her own delusions is Sir George. Unlike Glanville, Miss Glanville, and Miss Groves, Sir George, the neighboring baronet, spends his time "meditating on the Means he should use to acquire the Esteem of Lady *Bella,* of whose Person he was a little enamoured, but of her Fortune a great deal more" (129). He understands the fictional status of "reality." Sir George's romantic account of his own "history," which not so surprisingly offends Arabella exactly where it is meant to charm her, represents an elaborate attempt at emasculation, as the conventions of female-inspired romance seem to require.[19] Sir George, that is, in the character of Bellmour, finds himself in situation after situation in which he assumes a "fantastic" posture such as that in which he quotes a woman describing him as follows: "You was not . . . yet recovered from your Swoon, so that they carried you like one that was dead: They had taken off your Helmet to give you Air; by which means your Face being quite uncovered, pale, languishing, and your Eyes closed, as if in Death, presented the most moving, and, at the same time, most pleasing

Object in the World" (224). Sir George knows enough to try to eroticize himself as a figure in a female erotic fantasy, because he understands how the features of romance participate in the female imaginary. The languishing form of the hero, wounded and pathetic, becomes a conventional figure in Gothic fiction, where the elements of romance are resurrected for popular late-eighteenth-century consumption, as I demonstrate in my discussion of "Female Gothic."[20] This powerlessness could be seen to offer the self-affectionate woman a sense of power that she in other contexts lacks. Indeed, Sir George becomes a "pleasing Object" precisely to the degree that he is pale and languishing; that is, he pleases to the degree that he is unconscious, as he seems so clearly to know.

The elaborate romance that he relates throughout several chapters in the middle of the novel is based on a variety of French romances, particularly *Cassandra,* La Calprenéde's vast seventeenth-century romance, which was fully translated into English in 1661 (second edition 1676).[21] It tells in delightful detail the complications of Sir George's past adventures in love, and in doing so it barely exaggerates the details of its French original. Sir George's tale of his own irresistibility and the story of the extent to which his lovers are willing to go to save him from the vindictiveness of heroic antagonists makes the narcissism of the romance form almost obtrusive. Sir George is put in the position, that is, of making himself the center of an elaborate sexual fantasy that places him as the "languishing" object of desire in a number of different situations. The swoons, the fevers, the wounds, and the bitterness that Sir George suffers in the character of the romantic hero Bellmour all constitute a form of self-aggrandizement that only he and Arabella understand. For only they share the degree of romantic self-possession that gives such expressions meaning in this context. Sir George's preposterous posturing could be read, then, as a parody of Arabella's own self-importance, and his exaggeration of his own worth could be seen as a reflection of her own deep auto-affection.

Where Sir George gets it wrong, however, is in his typically male refusal to suffer in any but his own terms. That he has powerful feelings he convinces Arabella, and that he has been involved in high romantic attachments is clear. But when he cannot remain true even to the fictions he is creating, Arabella loses interest in him. His story, that is, finally becomes the story of his own desire, his own desire for Arabella, and not the story that Arabella would tell, a story of fidelity and trust that would both gratify her and fulfill her own desires. In other words, Sir George becomes the victim of his own fiction. For whatever story he attempts to tell, his "romance" reveals the self-obsession and sexual aggression with which he attempts to violate Arabella's independent position. He can only tell himself in the end. His languishing form becomes a mockery of Arabella's deep self-involvement, and she refuses to countenance his "infidelities" with anything but contempt. When Sir George attempts to defend as a "powerful Impulse" his failure to remain faithful to his fictional lovers, Arabella shows little patience: "Call not, interrupted *Arabella*, that an irresistible Impulse, which was only the Effect of thy own changing Humour: The same Excuse might be pleaded for all the Faults we see committed in the World; and Men would no longer be answerable for their own Crimes" (251). Again Arabella has been able to defend herself by her adherence to a romantic code, and although her condemnation of Sir George's "Humour" might with equal validity be turned on herself, she is at least consistent in her refusal to countenance Sir George's "prostituted Vows," and she emerges from this fictional encounter even more securely the mistress of herself.

Later, when he secretly makes the attempt to "supplant [Glanville] in Arabella's Affection" by "brib[ing] a young Actress to personate a Princess forsaken by [Glanville]" (367–68), he puts his fictionalizing ability to its greatest test. Arabella is fully duped by the suffering Cynecia, "Princess of Gaul," who tells her tale of woe at great length and at last exposes Glanville as her seducer. What better way to expose the failings of her romantic imagination than in such blatant manipulations of her affections? It is difficult to imagine that Lennox is doing anything but poking fun at her heroine here. "Like Cervantes," Ross says, "Lennox enjoys piling up layers of fiction; at one point she has an actress disguised as a princess recite the romance of her life, in which she meets a prince who recites the romance of his life."[22] But there is more than simple enjoyment in this complication of narrative; Lennox reveals the deep complexity of narrative control and the ease with which one can become the victim of stories, either one's own or others'. The fictionality of experience and the impossibility of determining the "truth" of any social experience are emphasized here. Shortly later, when Arabella is nearly drowned and Glanville and Sir George have engaged in a near fatal duel, the implications of unrestrained indulgence of private fantasy become all too clear. At such moments, fact and fiction assume an uncanny identity.[23]

The divine who finally reforms Arabella curbs her desire at the same time that he undermines her sense of self and sense of possibility in the world. After agreeing to the terms of their discussion, Arabella makes the stakes clear when she asks him to "Prove, therefore, that the Books which I have hitherto read as Copies of Life, and Models of Conduct, are empty Fictions, and from this Hour I deliver them to Moths and Mould" (377). Notice that the subject is "fiction": if her books can be construed as fiction, she will have nothing to do with them. Of course, the divine has won his battle before he even begins. For anyone who accepts the false dichotomy of history and fiction as a way of determining "truth" is an appropriately trained "subject" of the patriarchy.[24]

Instead of recognizing, therefore, that what she has learned in the romantic fictions has been a valuable education, if not in the ways of the world, at least in the ways of desire, Arabella succumbs to the "realism" that would limit her options and preserve her for marriage and breeding. The divine condemns what he calls "wild imaginations" and the conduct of the heroes in the romances. Arabella's lively and energetic self-involvement becomes morally questionable, and as she throws aside the fiction that has formed her, she throws aside her sense of herself as well. It is a self, as the divine would explain, infected with romance.[25]

The terms of this infection have everything to do with the power of female sexuality, as the divine's Johnsonian expostulation makes clear:

> Books ought to supply an Antidote to Example, and if we retire to a contemplation of Crimes, and continue in our Closets to inflame our Passions, at what time must we rectify our Words, or purify our Hearts? The immediate Tendency of these Books which your Ladyship must allow me to mention with some Severity, is to give new Fire to the Passions of Revenge and Love; two Passions which, even without such powerful Auxiliaries, it is one of the severest Labours of Reason and Piety to suppress. (380)

Arabella's adventures have in a sense corroborated this estimate of the power of fiction. That is, because of her reading she has filled with incident a life which would appear outwardly uneventful if not appallingly dull. What the "Fire" of fiction has accomplished for Arabella, on the other hand, is to protect her from some of the meaner assaults that her culture automatically provides; it has given her a sympathetic ear to victimized females who are otherwise ostracized from civilized society; it has caused her to see her own experience as valuable, and worthy of report; and it has caused her to see through the most flagrant, and even some of the more subtle, duplicities and meaningless functions of her culture.

It has also enabled her to fictionalize her subjectivity: to create an erotic "I" who can be the subject as well as the object of pleasure. Her exotic fictionalizing of her own experience has been an attempt to find a "self" that represents her private fantasy in the world. According to Benveniste, "*I* can only be identified by the instance of discourse that contains it and by that alone": it is the attempt to create inner experience in the only reality there is, the reality of language.[26] Marie-Paul Laden develops this notion of enunciation to its logical implications for first-person narrative: "two subjects are logically intertwined, with the speaking or writing 'I' a product of the experience it relates, and the situation of enunciation an outgrowth, culmination, or plausible extension of the life the 'I' recounts."[27]

Arabella's "I"—the "I" of ecstatic self-involvement—has been a provisional self in a world that is exercising its power to disinherit her, as it were, from selfhood. Her self-enunciation in narrative is her attempt to take control of narrative and give her self a central place in it. Todd says that "Arabella has to learn that she cannot have the absurd centrality depicted in French romance. She must understand that she will not make the rhetoric that contains her but live instead in the rhetoric of others, the creators of her social reputation."[28] Arabella's ability to accept the dictum of the divine, and her ability at the end of the novel to turn to Glanville with "a Look of mingled Tenderness and Modesty" and to tell him of her "remaining Imperfections" and how grateful she feels "to be desired for a Partner for Life by a Man of your Sense and Honour" (383), all set a fictional pattern that becomes familiar by the end of the century. The heroine undergoes a transformation that renders her so alien from her earlier self, that one is forced to question who it is who participates in this all-too-pat conclusion—in this case, the breathtakingly brief conclusion is in part thanks to the advisory control of the anything-but-abrupt Samuel Richardson.[29] The resolution sits so uncomfortably on the action that has preceded it that the novel seems to challenge the very notion of a resolution.[30] The narrative has a logic of its own that frees Arabella from the dwindling position in which she finds herself at the novel's close. Wendy Motooka argues that "Arabella's sudden reformation in the penultimate chapter may be read as an attempt to salvage social coherence in the face of radical and disturbing, albeit stylized, moral and political diversity."[31] If Arabella is to settle for "every Virtue and laudable Affection of the Mind" (383), the salvage operation would seem half-hearted at best.

Charlotte Lennox explores the position of women in the later eighteenth century by creating a heroine who, for several hundred pages, survives in an antagonistic world on her own terms and in her own way. She offers us moreover a heroine who reads and remembers what she reads, whose intelligence puts the men around her to shame, and who is ready to argue with even the most distinguished intellectual of her day. This heroine functions in spite of a father who is trying to force her hand in marriage; an uncle whom she suspects of harboring incestuous desires; a suitor, also a close relative and implicated in the plot for her property, who spends a great part of the novel in a state bordering on madness, who flies off the handle at anyone who criticizes the heroine and who actually becomes involved in fisticuffs and a duel on her behalf; and a handful of other suitors, who fall at her feet throughout the novel, one especially going to the lengths of creating a fiction that will match her romantic fantasy. By presenting her romance of self-love in a realistic guise, Lennox is able to articulate a fantasy of female power that is rarely matched in the eighteenth century. Critics have suggested that Lennox has remained attached to the romantic conventions she seems to be criticizing. I would go even further to suggest that Lennox has given voice to female desire while paying lip service—plot service, as it were—to the marriage plot that was already determining the fictional options open to women. "Surrounded by such incestuous and greedy demands," Doody says, "Arabella retains the presence of mind that her reading inculcates. Strong in her conviction that she herself is supremely of importance, she resists the hectoring and the bribery."[32] Arabella remains "supremely of importance" throughout this so-called "parody" of romance. She never sacrifices her sense of the value of her own experience; even at the close, when she is arguing with the Johnsonian divine, she remains self-possessed enough to resist his condescending tutelage and even to retain a degree of self-respect after he has clipped her wings and assured her of the tawdriness of her "female" experience.

EIGHT

"Defects and Deformity"
in *Camilla*

A PICTURE OF YOUTH

Camilla: or, A Picture of Youth (1796) is in some ways Frances Burney's most revealing novel.[1] While the youth that is pictured is harrowing in its vicissitudes and terrifying in its psychological torment, the details of private life are richly drawn and refreshingly complex in their ambiguities. As frightening, in its way, as any Gothic novel (Burney herself called it *"Udolphish"*), *Camilla* tells of the changes of fortune of a small group of young people who are comfortably installed in the English midlands, with nothing really to menace them but changes in the weather and the irritability of personality.[2] As in Burney's other novels, there is a female heroine at the center of the action, and in *Camilla,* the title character is surrounded by a range of other young and not-so-young females, who offer interesting comparisons and contrasts to her and her own behavior. In spite of the wealth of friends and family, however, she remains peculiarly, even torment- ingly, isolated throughout the novel and is barely reclaimed for social reha- bilitation at its close.

Camilla is blessed with affectionate parents. She respects her mother and idolizes her father. Paternal affection and sympathetic concern are nowhere exhibited more touchingly than in this novel. Mr. Tyrold, the rector of Etherington, is a generous and gracious father, and his love for his Camilla is never questioned. At the same time, and pointedly, his paternal concern is repeatedly not only wrongheaded, but also cruel and even thoughtless. That this is possible, even inevitable, is central to the novel's feminist thrust. Even the perfect father, Burney seems to say, cannot even begin to understand, much less to feel, the torments of youth, particularly female youth. Burney is at pains to point out the acute embarrassment, the self-ridicule, and the emotional abjection that Camilla's kindly father causes her. When he is angry with her, he curbs his emotion. But when he is trying to help or protect her, he gives her advice that works against her self-interest time and time again. Burney seems to rewrite the meaning of benevolence, which for many eighteenth-century readers was a talisman of goodness and probity, in the character of Mr. Tyrold and to show that all the goodwill in the world, when placed in a figure with paternal authority, is never less than harrowing to those around him.

Mr. Tyrold's benevolent and protective quality is articulated most effec- tively, as various critics have noted, in the sermon he sends to Camilla on the occasion of her supposedly fruitless love for Edgar Mandlebert.[3] As Epstein says, "Augustus Tyrold's letter . . . encodes in the father's discourse the ethos of a society that entraps Burney's women (and some of her men) with its rules not so much about conduct itself, but about the public interpretations of conduct."[4] Interpreting Camilla's conduct becomes Edgar's peculiar obses- sion throughout the novel, as we shall see, and Burney sees his insistence on secret interpretation as the basis of the misunderstandings between these two characters.

This novel is as much concerned with self-confrontation and self-discov- ery, then, as it is about romantic love. This "sermon" really says more about the self-abnegation required of a female:

> Again, if none of these outward and obvious vicissitudes occur, the proper
> education of a female, either for use or for happiness, is still to seek, still a
> problem beyond human solution; since its refinement, or its neglence, can
> only prove to her a good or an evil, according to the humour of the husband
> into whose hands she may fall. (357)

"Defects and Deformity" in *Camilla*

This is not so much a "moral" center of the work as the "political" center. Here we find a position not far afield from that of contemporary feminists such as Mary Wollstonecraft and Mary Hays. As this sermon builds to a climax, and Mr. Tyrold attempts to convince his daughter to stifle her feeling for Edgar, he puts his plea in terms that suggest the basic tenets of patriarchal control: "Struggle then against yourself as you would struggle against an enemy. Refuse to listen to a wish, to dwell even upon a possibility, that opens to your present idea of happiness" (358). He proceeds to counsel her as to how she should appear in public ("Discriminate . . . between hypocrisy and discretion" [361]; "To delicacy, in fine, your present exertions will owe their future recompense" [362]).

That a young woman with feelings should be set against herself in this way would seem surprising, until we consider the assumptions that were current about female sexual voracity. As Mary Poovey makes clear, "The paradox of modesty—and the paradox of female sexuality it simultaneously concealed and revealed—necessarily established the terms in which real women both consciously conceptualized and evaluated their own behavior and even unconsciously experienced their own gender."[5] Poovey's remark is couched in terms so similar to those of Tyrold's sermon that neither the virulence of his remarks, nor their implicit feminism, can go unnoticed. This kindly and encouraging father makes it clear, in other words, that women are neither to be trusted to act independently nor to be encouraged to make decisions for themselves. They live in a kind of self-alienation and self-distrust that causes them to falter in public and to silence their feelings at all costs. "Happiness," that desideratum of later-eighteenth-century culture, is no more than a chimera. For women, at least, it is never really articulated as a possibility. Burney uses Camilla's younger sister, Eugenia, to make this point most dramatically, as I shall discuss. For Camilla herself, the specter of unrealized happiness plays an even more powerful role in determining the erotics of isolation and self-contempt.

"THE LITTLE HUMP-BACK GENTLEWOMAN!"

Female happiness is the obsession of Sir Hugh Tyrold, Augustus's older and titled brother, and his assiduous concern for the welfare of the group of young female characters in his care makes the possibility of their happiness simply grotesque. The darling of the young girls in the work, he devotes himself to their happiness. And in case after case, situation after situation, his attempts to please are ruthlessly destructive and hideously inappropriate. He stages his own version of a beauty pageant among the girls around him.

Indiana, "his first idol," begins to seem dull to him, and she loses her place to Camilla, his "little jewel" (15)—"The tide of youthful glee flowed jocund from her heart, and the transparency of her fine blue veins almost shewed the velocity of its current" (14). Camilla is lively in a way that pleases him greatly. We are never encouraged to read his interest in little girls as particularly pernicious, but passages like this one suggest that his prurience is not far, as it were, from the surface.

To give a little charge to the beauty pageant he holds in his imagination, he offers as the prize nothing less than his entire fortune: "in less than a month after the residence of Camilla at Cleves, Sir Hugh took the resolution of making her his heiress" (15). The immediate result of this choice is the bitter and long-lasting jealousy of the otherwise unprovided-for Indiana, whose name calls to mind spotless sentimental heroines of a generation earlier, but who herself is a vain, covetous, and virtually idiotic female. In this instance, however, she seems to have a legitimate complaint. In his attempt to bestow complete happiness on one of his nieces, he destroys the happiness of another absolutely. However, Camilla herself is in no position to enjoy these favors. She feels the pain of her cousin's jealously more acutely than she experiences the pleasure of her own future prospects. And when her fortune has changed, not only when her uncle has revised his will but when her own chances for happiness seem attenuated, it is these early enmities that return again and again to make her miserable. Sir Hugh, that is, in his attempt to make her happy only ensures her unhappiness.

Indiana, of course, fares no better for the well-wishing of her uncle. In his hope for her happiness, he pairs her, in both his and her imagination, with Edgar and Edgar's estate—"nothing can be a greater pleasure to me than having two such good girls [Camilla and Indiana], live so near that they may overlook one another from park to park, all day long, by the mode of a telescope" (20). What seems here so jocular—and fatuous—returns to haunt these characters later, as do all his schemes for happiness. The tragic isolation of women from one another, the almost lurid relation that the telescope suggests, becomes one of the central concerns of the novel. One thing about this quotation may by now be obvious, however: everything that Sir Hugh does for the happiness of others he is really doing for himself.

When, therefore, he does something that seems really generous, like taking the children to the Northwick fair, it seems a blessed relief from his manipulations. When a fear of smallpox is articulated, and when it becomes clear that Eugenia, Camilla's younger sister, has not been inoculated against the disease, his motives for persisting again seem questionable. In this case, it should be noted that Camilla's brother, Lionel, is the immediate cause of their actually proceeding to fair—he gallops on ahead and it becomes incumbent upon them all to follow. As they do so, however, Sir Hugh articulates a homely approach to the disease: "she will be sure to have it when her time comes, whether she is moped or no; and how did people do before these new modes of making themselves sick of their own accord?" (23). When he cannot keep Eugenia back in the chaise with himself—"he could not answer to his conscience the vexing such a young thing" (23)—he sets her in pursuit of her happiness only to find that she immediately encounters a boy who is just recovering from the illness. When, shortly later, Sir Hugh tries to raise her spirits by giving her a ride on a sort of makeshift teeter-totter, she falls to the ground and is maimed for life. As she lies ill from her fall, the evidence of smallpox infection appears, and inevitably, she is disfigured by the disease to the point that Sir Hugh shrinks back in horror at "the dreadful havoc the disease had made on her face" (29). In his despondence, he alters his will, so that the poor Eugenia may become his sole heiress. Again attempting to provide happiness where none is likely, his gesture only makes Eugenia later the victim of a money-hungry impostor who almost succeeds in actually murdering her.[6]

The fate of Eugenia is especially interesting in the novel, as various critics have remarked. Against all odds, she breaks out of the role of invalid and even turns the attempts at her victimization to her own advantage. When, for instance, Sir Hugh decides that since she can never be a beauty she will be a scholar, and when, therefore, he pairs her with his own nephew, Clermont Lynmere (Indiana's brother), she is doomed to social marginalization and personal abuse. She triumphs above both these disadvantages, however, and emerges not only relatively unscathed but also remarkably self-assured. This pathetic character becomes in fact one of Burney's most interesting creations. A harbinger of later sentimentalizations of misery, she succeeds in a ruthlessly unsentimental fashion to make something of her life and to succeed in areas where everyone has assumed she can only fail.

She does this by learning to love her deformed and debilitated self. Like the various maimed and disfigured heroines in *Millenium Hall*, Eugenia must learn to appreciate the freedom that her accidents afford her. In an amazing series of scenes of public embarrassment and paternal tutelage, Eugenia is taught how to see herself in relation to others. This is no easy task in *Camilla*. As Claudia Johnson suggests, "under male sentimentality, the female in distress . . . is an object either of suspicion or derision." "The most severe suffering in the novel," she says, "has no place in the sentimental economy, and it is especially off-limits to the woman whose experience it is."[7] Eugenia's suffering, her abject relation to the community in which she finds herself, creates a space in which she can learn a different, erotic relation to herself and the world around her. There is nothing sentimental about this process of erotic isolation. The economy in which she finds self-realization possible stands in direct opposition to the sentimental ethos that Johnson and others describe.

When Eugenia is trapped with Camilla in a barn (another of Lionel's tricks), a group of women and a young boy mock her appearance: "What were you put up there for, Miss? to frighten the crows?" "Miss may go to market with her beauty; she'll not want for nothing if she'll shew her pretty face!" "Only take care, Miss, you don't catch the small pox!" (286). Eugenia is "astonished and confounded" that she has such an effect on other people, and she withdraws into a depression from which she cannot be coaxed. Camilla begins to bring her out of herself, but when Sir Hugh proposes an outing to the races, "her face was then again overcast with the deepest gloom; and she begged not to hear of the races, not of any other place, public or private, for going abroad, as she meant during the rest of her life, immoveably to remain at home" (297).

Her father attempts to assure her that "[h]appiness is in [her] power, though beauty is not" (304), but his real lessons come in much more effective form. He insists on taking her out into the neighborhood, "passing, wherever it was possible, close to cottages, labourers, and children" (305). He achieves his desired effect soon enough, when "an unlucky boy called out, 'O come! come! look!—here's the little hump-back gentlewoman!'" (305). This is Mr. Tyrold's cue:

> She then, clinging to her father, could not stir another step, and cast upon him a look of appeal and reproach that almost overset him; but, after speaking to her some words of kindness, he urged her to go on, and alone, saying, "Throw only a shilling to the senseless little crew, and let Camilla follow and give nothing, and see which will become the most popular." (306)

This simple lesson has all the marks of cultural conditioning. Although Mr. Tyrold explains that his example shows "how cheaply preference, and even flattery, may be purchased" (306), it also exposes the dark underside of benevolence and underlines the falseness of sympathy that the novel has in other ways been explicitly questioning. Eugenia's self-love can be based only on an understanding of the "bribery" implicit in public relations. And just as her fortunes later make her the victim of the grotesque courtship and abduction of Bellamy, here her father teaches her that her fortune can make her popular and "save" her from disgrace.

"Defects and Deformity" in *Camilla*

I have argued elsewhere that benevolence is a symptom of the ideological inequalities of bourgeois society, and Mr. Tyrold's advice makes the reiteration of this position almost superfluous. Still useful, however, is Slavoj Žižek's observation that hierarchical relations are repressed in bourgeois society and that the persistence of relations of domination and servitude emerges in "a symptom which subverts the ideological appearance of equality, freedom."[8] Social relations—the relations of domination and servitude—are culturally fetishized in the erotics of benevolence and emotional mutuality that sensibility celebrates. As I have already discussed, Žižek's notion of the symptom suggests that any ideology necessarily contains a fissure that exposes its hidden agenda and that at the same time gives the ideology its substance. I would place benevolence among those features of late-eighteenth-century culture that expose its inner workings most tellingly. Augustus Tyrold gives his "deformed" daughter Eugenia the secret of bourgeois ideology because she needs it to survive. As a commodity in her own right, of course, she is doomed to failure. It is only by refiguring commodification that she can even hope to find happiness.

The details of this refiguration become clearer when Mr. Tyrold takes Eugenia to gaze on a beautiful woman who is sitting at a window. At first his lesson seems to be obvious, as Eugenia describes it: "You would have me, Sir, . . . learn to see beauty with unconcern, by deprecating its value?" Eugenia resists this lesson and all that Mr. Tyrold can say about "faded beauty" (308). When this woman saunters into the garden and displays signs of madness, however, Eugenia is shocked: "Did you lead me thither purposely to display to me her shocking imbecility?" (308). When Mr. Tyrold explains that he thought that this would be "an experiment more powerful . . . than all that reason could urge" (308), Eugenia exclaims, "O my dear Father! your prescription strikes at the root of my disease! —shall I ever again dare murmur! —will any egotism ever again make me believe no lot so hapless as my own! I will think of her whenever I am discontented; I will call to my mind this spectacle of human degradation—and submit, at least with calmness, to my lighter evils and milder fate" (310–11). Eugenia must objectify the mad woman as an abject other who can afford her a sense of her own power and self-possession. This parody of a love scene—the beauty, the gaze, the implicit desire—finally establishes Eugenia herself as the object of her own affection. Her isolation becomes a source of strength.

Eugenia has learned self-love by means of a careful hierarchy of debility that places her above a raving lunatic if implicitly below her lovely and affectionate sister. Eugenia can understand herself, moreover, only by comparing herself to the "other" that her father provides. Her father tells her that "beauty, without mind, is more dreadful than any deformity" (311), but what she has really learned is that even deformities can be measured and assessed in relation to one another and that her position within this cultural construct is doubly assured.

A later chapter in *Camilla* is called "The Computations of Self-Love" (bk. 8, chap. 11). The title might be more appropriate in the context of Eugenia's self-confrontation. She learns how to love herself as a way of surviving in a culture that would mock and marginalize her. Mr. Tyrold offers ways to feel superior—her money, her mind—but these make her no less susceptible to self-delusion, as later events in the novel make clear. When she finds that her love for Melmond is not returned, her self-deprecating remarks are telling: "Believe me, Sir, . . . surprise was the last sensation I experienced upon a late . . . transaction. My extraordinary personal defects and deformity have been some time known to me, though—I cannot tell how—I had the weakness or vanity not to think of them as I ought to have done!" (745). She then frees him to enjoy the love of her cousin Indiana, and as if the earlier paternal indoctrination could finally be realized, she solemnly promises to share her fortune with the happy pair. The effect on Melmond is immediate: "she seemed to him, on the sudden, transformed to a deity, benignly employed to rescue and bless him, but whose transcendent goodness he could only, at a distance, and in all humility, adore" (747). Melmond is different from the cruel boy to whom she threw the shilling only in the sophistication of his response. He is as much a victim of bribery as the boy had been, and Eugenia is no less ready to buy devotion than her father has taught her to be. Of course, a reader might want to create a space for Eugenia's goodness here, but what would that goodness be without the inheritance to back it up? If Melmond will learn to love Eugenia later on, then he could never have done so without this acknowledgment of the power of financial considerations in this most ruthless of cultural transactions. Eugenia's disability is symptomatic of the corrupt and corrupting features of benevolence, and its ideological dimension is clear in the advice that Tyrold articulates. Eugenia embraces the social reality that gives her the power of her purse and towering mental superiority, for it offers her a way to transform her deformity into a force for doing good. She finds in the hideousness that haunts her a key to social relations. By choosing the distance that benevolence affords, she both adheres to the ideology that marks her as different and claims the superiority that such difference allows. It is a cynical, antisentimental reading of private experience, but at the same time a very useful one. For out of isolation, Burney establishes a mutually beneficial relation that is based on esteem rather than love.[9] For Eugenia needs all her love for herself.

"THE VERY THING!"

After exposing, in different ways, mother, father, sister, cousin, uncle, and friend, Burney turns her attention to the members of a fashionable set who use Camilla for their own amusement. Central among these is Mrs. Arlbery, a woman of questionable status. She offers friendship to Camilla and attempts to take her up as the darling of her witty group of bored aristocrats. Mrs. Arlbery's other favorite is the self-confessed fop and would-be libertine, Sir Sedley Clarendel. Sir Sedley hovers around Camilla throughout the novel, particularly when she is in the company of this acerbic lady of fashion. Indeed Mrs. Arlbery and Sir Sedley participate in a verbal repartee that gives the novel much of its life. When Mrs. Arlbery is talking about Sir Sedley to General Kinsdale at the Northwick ball, for instance, he asks her, "Is it then necessary to keep him [Sir Sedley] a fop, in order to retain him in your chains?" "O, he is not in my chains," she answers, "I promise you. A fop, my dear General, wears no chains but his own. However, I like to have him, because he is so hard to be got; and I am fond of conversing with him, because he is so ridiculous. Fetch him, therefore, Colonel, without delay" (75). Both Mrs. Arlbery and Sir Sedley are mocked in such a speech: he, because he seems so emasculated in her description; she, because her basis of community interaction seems so corrupt. Whether or not the "chains" are meant as a reference to Sir Sedley's sexual practices, they function usefully to commemorate the cultural control exerted on a figure as unorthodox as he. What Mrs. Arlbery fails to mention is that this culture takes its gendering so seriously that everyone could be seen to be chained to a community identity that culture cannot afford to make flexible in any way. If I neglect Mrs. Arlbery's own obsessive interest in Camilla's love-life, that is not because it is not a rich source of erotic energy in the novel. Her erotic energy in fact does a great deal to shape the heroine's own experience and to condition Mandlebert's reaction to her. Still, Burney's interest in the fop seems almost out of proportion to his own role in the novel, and I have chosen to focus rather on his queer function here.

Sir Sedley's "chains" become slightly more obtrusive as the novel proceeds, and at one point he seems actually to threaten the heroine with his attentions. By far the most interesting of Burney's fops, Sir Sedley seems, at times, sadly trapped in his posturing. That he cannot admit his attraction to the girl, or even treat her with anything like respect, suggests how conflicted his situation really is. Of course there is ample suggestion that his own sexual make-up may undermine his interest in Camilla—the connection between foppish behavior and sodomitical practices was increasingly available to the public imagination—but nowhere does he see himself as anything but a superior and somewhat detached presence in the world. He cannot succeed in this pose, because the novel seems to know more about him than he knows about himself. In the later eighteenth century, anyway, the "diagnosis" for Sir Sedley's "condition" was already well formulated. In 1749, the author of *Satan's Harvest Home* makes a connection between effeminacy and sodomy that he and Burney both ascribe to the luxury of class as well as the demands of fashion. Randolph Trumbach has made the most complete argument for the association of effeminacy and sodomy in the later eighteenth century, and although his argument is overly schematic for talking about a novelist with the subtlety of Burney, it does help to remember that "[a]fter 1729 the fop's effeminacy, in real life and on the stage, came to be identified with the effeminacy of the then emerging role of the exclusive adult sodomite—known in the ordinary language of his day as a *molly*, and later as a *queen*."[10] Such terminology becomes possible, of course, only when a community has identified its members sufficiently to distinguish them in such a way. Mollies and queens are possible, that is, only when the community agrees to acknowledge them as the symptom, the repressed kernel of desire, that determines their own identities.

At a crucial point in the novel, Mrs. Arlbery invokes her sense of community to set Sir Sedley on "curing" Camilla of her love for Edgar Mandlebert, the tentative hero: "The cure of a romantic first flame," she says, "is a better surety to subsequent discretion, than all the exhortations of all the fathers, and mothers, and guardians, and maiden aunts in the universe. Save her now, and you serve her for life;—besides giving me a prodigious pleasure in robbing that frigid Mandlebert of such a conquest." And later: "You are the thing, Clarendel, the very thing! You are just agreeable enough to annul her puerile fascination, yet not interesting enough to involve her in any new danger" (368). Sir Sedley seems, in other words, an unthreatening sexual presence, a "thing" that will distract Camilla rather than involve her in any "danger." Sir Sedley can play at sexual intrigue; he can even imagine that he has feelings for the young ingenue. The talk of "cure" in this context is suggestive, but it might also seem surprising that Mrs. Arlbery would employ a figure such as Sir Sedley to liberate Camilla from her attachment to Edgar. Trumbach makes the interesting point, however, that the identification of the effeminate fop as a gender outlaw worked to separate the genders rather than blend them: "the molly was a wall that perhaps made possible an unprecedented development of equality between the other two genders, since it was now the case that there would remain a radical separation of male and female experience, no matter how far equality might go in other ways."[11] The community needs Sir Sedley, that is, for the coherence of its own distinctions.

Mrs. Arlbery knows, and Camilla learns that the Sir Sedleys of this world are of no cultural significance except as entertaining distractions from real feeling. There is no place in the late eighteenth century for a man of compromised sexuality, and even Burney suggests that Sir Sedley is wrong to strut before an uninitiated young girl as he does. At other points, however, Burney seems to sympathize with the man who seems most deeply afraid of the implication of who he is.

When Camilla is the victim of a runaway carriage, and Sir Sedley manages to save her from serious calamity, Burney suggests that Sir Sedley experiences a crisis of identity:

> He received, indeed, from this adventure, almost every species of pleasure of which his mind was capable. His natural courage, which he had nearly annihilated, as well as forgotten, by the effeminate part he was systematically playing, seemed to rejoice in being again exercised; his good nature was delighted by the essential service he had performed; his vanity was gratified by the publicity of the praise it brought forth; and his heart itself experienced something like an original feeling, unspoilt by the apathy of satiety, from the sensibility he had awakened in the young and lovely Camilla. (404)

This delightfully condescending description of Sir Sedley's "pleasure" suggests a tension between "natural" courage and an unnatural effeminacy; and it argues further that by shocking him into authentic rather than feigned action, his heroism proved what a real man he could be. As the description continues through "good nature," "vanity," and "original feeling," we can recognize that Burney has pilloried the fop as largely vain, unnatural, and insensitive. Such a complex figure in Burney's narrative as Sir Sedley would seem to deserve more than the "unnatural" label that is usually preserved for insensitive villains of a different order. No, Sir Sedley is unnatural because he does not fit a social code for gendered masculinity, and it seems as if Burney is joining with hegemonic forces to censure and mock him. Community harbors this shocking and unnatural secret that actively threatens the heroine and, in a sense, contaminates her with the illicit desire he comes to represent. It would be possible to suggest that Burney is opposed not to the effeminacy of her fop, but rather to the inauthenticity of his pose. I would argue, however, that the effeminacy itself is what Burney finds offensive. The refusal to enter into a legitimate negotiation with members of the opposite sex renders Sedley ridiculous in Burney's world: at best he is silly; at worst, a dangerous and threatening alternative to gendered clarity.[12]

The nature of this threat becomes apparent when, like other Burney fops before him, he turns from dispassionate onlooker to sexual aggressor in a singularly frightening moment. Sir Sedley and Camilla meet when they are sharing the home of Mrs. Arlbery, who seems always to stay out of the way long enough to allow him to seduce her. On the present occasion, however, seduction gives way to outright sexual aggression. She encounters him in the garden and trembles and looks away as he approaches:

> To the prepossessed notions and vain character of Sir Sedley, these were symptoms by no means discouraging; with a confidence almost amounting to arrogance he advanced, pitying her distress, yet pitying himself still more for the snare in which it was involving him. He permitted his eyes for a moment to fasten upon her, to admire her, and to enjoy triumphantly her confusion in silence: "Ah, beauteous tyrant!" he then cried, "if this instant were less inappreciable, in what language could I upbraid thy unexampled abuse of power? thy lacerating barbarity?"
>
> He then, almost by force, took her hand; she struggled eagerly to recover it, but "No," he cried, "fair torturer! it is now my prisoner, and must be punished for its inhuman sins, in the congealing and unmerciful lines it has portrayed for me."
>
> And then, regardless of her resistance, which he attributed to mere bashfulness, he obstinately and incessantly devoured it with kisses, in defiance of opposition, supplication, or anger, till, suddenly and piercingly, she startled him with a scream, and snatched it away with a force irresistible. (558–59)

Burney clearly suggests that the effeminate man hides in his gender confusion a sexual aggression that is as dangerous as it is disgusting. Sir Sedley tries to "devour" the hand of his darling, it seems, because he cannot explain to himself his attraction to her. Here, the aloof effeminate man is a danger because his sexual urges are uncontrollable and unresponsive to female pathos. What happens is that he loses himself in desire, just as he has lost himself in his desire to be something more than merely masculine. His refusal to subject himself to the codes of masculine behavior, in other words, signals an irresponsibility that is equivalent to a sexual threat. Although Burney could be said to demonize this incomprehensible version of masculinity, her community has made such demonization the only possible response. The community needs this figure, as I have suggested, and they need do nothing to naturalize him. From Burney's perspective, in any case, a libertine of any stripe is by definition a threat to the female. James G. Turner argues that "the social libertine respects the pales and partitions that society has constructed to allow the coexistence of lust and respectability."[13] Burney attempts to deconstruct this uneasy binary by exposing the seamier side of the libertine posture. With Sir Sedley she suggests that masculinity is in crisis and that community makes women such as Camilla only more liable to succumb to the villainy of its darling figures.

Burney must turn this formerly amusing figure of comedy into a villainous threat to her heroine because only a homophobic response, only a rejection of the plaything of the aristocracy, can lead her to the kind of self-determination that this marriageable female would like to claim. Friendship with a fop, that is, has to be defined as sexually threatening even when Sir Sedley seems to threaten only himself. Burney's feminism has to be homophobic, that is, in order to survive. Camilla, it seems, has the power to renaturalize this gender freak and to bring him round by means of his desire for her. Once she accomplishes that, of course, she must reject him. For he is not the proper suitor for the heroine. He comes to represent the dark secret of community itself.

Burney seems to distrust community because of the position that a woman must occupy within it. Sir Sedley helps to make this position clear because he occupies a similarly problematic place in the symbolic structure that the novel poses as community. Burney implicitly understands this no-place that her heroines occupy, just as she sees herself as the no-body of culture.[14] If the woman returns as the symptom of man, as Žižek argues, the "mollie" can only return as the symptom of culture, of the community itself.[15] Homophobia is not gender specific, as Burney's portrayal suggests. Sir Sedley is trapped between the community that makes him its "very thing" and the woman who has the power to naturalize him. An odd exchange, this, but one that makes the victim of the community/individual binarism most explicit. This is not the last time that the effeminate male serves to define cultural distinctions, nor is it the last time that a woman mistakenly labels the "queen" as her most dangerous opponent. Community works its magic in different ways on both the heroine and her effeminate friend, and it ensures that they will be placed at odds. Camilla is right to be afraid of Sir Sedley: he is the "very thing," after all, that the community would use to destroy her.

"REPRESS, REPRESS"

The central hero, Edgar Mandlebert, is to certain critics no more satisfying than the oddly debilitated heroes in Burney's other novels. The other heroes, however, who fail to recognize, or to admit that they recognize, the charm of their heroine, usually have the excuse of carefully articulated practical problems: the obstacles to comic or romantic resolution, in other words, are understandable even if a bit bizarre. Orville, for instance, the hero of *Evelina,* is not aware of the young Evelina's interest because she is so far out of range socially; Mortimer Delvile, in *Cecilia,* falls in love with Cecilia, but he cannot accept the terms of her availability, particularly the "name clause" of her uncle's will; and Harleigh, although sympathetic to the long-unnamed heroine of *The Wanderer,* can never convince her to divulge her inmost secrets and therefore must reject her because she might not be an acceptable wife.[16]

Of all Burney's heroes, only Edgar Mandlebert, seemingly one of the most promising if not the most clear-headed, spends the vast majority of the novel's time in the company of the heroine with a specific interest in her as a possible mate; and he repeatedly and continually decides that she is unworthy of his love. The romantic inevitability of this novel is tormenting, that is, in a particularly frustrating way. As Julia Epstein says, "*Camilla* tells the story of love postponed, thwarted, frustrated, misled, and deliberately unspoken and even disguised."[17] In it, the hero and heroine perform an almost endless ceremony of misapprehension and misconstruction. But they both turn these on Camilla herself: she must continually suffer Edgar's censure as well as her own. This dynamic fills the novel with an odd sort of discomfort: embarrassment and self-contempt are the heroine's constant companions, and she spends a great deal of the novel's vast extent in a puzzled attempt to determine what she might have done to upset her timid friend. This situation results in a personal distress of the most unnerving kind. Erotic isolation becomes more than a trope in this novel: it becomes its very rationale. If Eugenia has taught Camilla that social relations are unde-pendable and even personally dangerous, then the latter heroine moves into deeper gloom and isolation as the novel proceeds. Indeed, the point of the novel seems to be to isolate her so that she can find a self at last outside of the complications of community, family, and friends. At times, for a woman especially, community becomes more a challenge, and a measure of failure, than a source of comfort.

Who is better positioned to answer this doubly disappointing gender-challenge than the other differently gendered male figure in the novel, Edgar Mandlebert? Edgar stands only slightly uncomfortably in the line of Burney's "weak" heroes. Early in the novel the narrator describes him in unexciting, if not outright condescending, terms: "His disposition was serious and meditative; but liberal, open, and candid. He was observant of the errors of others, and watched until he nearly eradicated his own" (57). His brooding watchfulness and tendency toward misapprehension is here presented as a positive quality, but it very quickly becomes the source of much that is distressing in the plot of the nearly doomed courtship between him and Camilla.

Throughout the novel, as well, Edgar appears to be hovering on the edges of scenes, judging those he is watching even while they mock and mimic his seriousness and his self-effacing distance. When he does speak, as he often does, with gravity and authority, he is often (one is tempted to say always) not just wrong but even foolish. Like Harleigh's counselling Juliet against performing in public (in *The Wanderer*), moreover, he gives advice that is unwarranted, unwanted, and clearly in opposition to the best interests of the heroine. Overbearingly arch and self-important at times, he could almost be seen to represent a different kind of supercilious and quasi-sodomitical male from the sexually voracious fop. The homosocially conditioned intellectual is equally dangerous. For in his superiority he threatens the heroine more subtly but more devastatingly than the fop ever could. For example, Edgar heartily disapproves of Mrs. Arlbery as a friend for Camilla. Notwithstanding the fact that Mrs. Arlbery is a powerful woman who could both encourage Camilla's talents and help her position in the world, Edgar feels that she is in some way not respectable. His fear of female homosocial relations is of course symptomatic of the culture as a whole: rather than see Mrs. Arlbery as a sexual predator, though, he vaguely disapproves of her influence. His attempt to control Camilla's female friends because of a standard of which only he is the arbiter is peculiarly male. The scene in which he argues his case to Camilla is pointed:

> "I should be grieved, indeed [he says], to be the messenger of affliction to you; but I hope there may be no occasion; I only beg a day or two's patience; and, in the meanwhile, I can give you this assurance; she is undoubtedly a woman of character. I saw she had charmed you, and I made some immediate inquiries. Her reputation is without taint."
>
> "A thousand, thousand thanks," cried Camilla, gaily, "for taking so much trouble; and ten thousand more for finding it needless!"
>
> Edgar could not forbear laughing, but answered, he was not yet so certain it was needless; since exemption from actual blemish could only be a negative recommendation: he should very soon, he added, see a lady upon whose judgment he could rely, and who would frankly satisfy him with respect to some other particulars, which, he owned, he considered as essential to be known, before any intimacy should be formed.
>
> Wishing to comply with his request, yet impatient to leave the house, Camilla stood suspended till the chaise was announced.
>
> "I think," cried she, with a look and tone of irresolution, "my going this once can draw on no ill consequence."
>
> Edgar only dropt his eyes. (155)

I quote this passage at length because I think it demonstrates the complexity with which Burney handles issues such as Edgar's "knowledge" versus Camilla's "feeling." There is no clear-cut right and wrong at this moment. In context, of course, Edgar is wrong to stop Camilla in her escape from the house where she has been insulted and tormented by her petty enemies Miss Margland and Indiana. He is also wrong to urge action on the basis of half-understood emotional prejudices. He is most wrong, however, to judge as he does both Mrs. Arlbery and Camilla from his position of flawed knowledge. In Burney's fiction, a male rarely has any more secure position from which to judge, and that at least partly explains why their judgments are so often malign.[18] Edgar judges and misjudges throughout the novel, and the effects of this range from mildly unsettling to utterly debilitating.

Edgar may be right that Mrs. Arlbery has the potential to be a bad influence on Camilla, but that matters less in any scheme of assessment than the condescension with which he treats her. I would agree with Claudia Johnson, however, who sees Mrs. Arlbery as threatening precisely because she "makes possible relations to desire to other women that are not mediated by heterosexual gender codes."[19] Edgar is right to feel threatened: Mrs. Arlbery respects Camilla and understands her in ways that he never seems able to. Edgar is not really protecting Camilla by his advice here; he is tormenting her. In fact, he is not usually even nice to her: he has been taught that it would compromise his position. Mortimer Delvile (in *Cecilia*) at least has the excuse for his behavior of Cecilia's insurmountable name clause, and Harleigh (in *The Wanderer*) has Juliet's brooding secrecy. But Edgar Mandlebert has nothing but his own judgment to qualify his handling of Camilla, and as a result his behavior seems more mean-spirited and more contemptible. Edgar, schooled in condescension and trained to think of himself as "naturally" superior to Camilla, can only abuse her in his attempts to instruct. Instruction, itself, here and elsewhere in Burney, is always a process of subjectification, and it never enriches more than it victimizes the (always female) pupil: Burney understands that the novel of education is not a female form.

Throughout the novel Edgar's behavior is no different from what in other contexts we might call voyeurism. When, for instance, the Arlbery group stop at a fairlike exhibit of an "ourang outang" (428), Edgar displays an uncanny genius for being at the wrong place at the right time. Edgar had earlier passed judgment on the animal exhibit as "a species of curiosity not likely to attract the most elegant spectators; and rather, perhaps, adapted to give pleasure to naturalists, than to young ladies" (421). As a result, Camilla had decided not to attend. But on the morning in question, the party make it impossible for her to bow out gracefully. No sooner does the show begin, however, than she and her companion encounter "a general howling . . . not more stunning to the ear than offensive to all humanity" (430). They immediately prepare to leave:

> The audience applauded in loud shouts, but Mrs. Arlbery, disgusted, rose to quit the booth. Camilla eagerly started up to second the motion, but her eyes still more expeditiously turned from the door, upon encountering those of Edgar; who, having met the empty coach of Mr. Dennel, had not been able to refrain from inquiring where its company had been deposited; nor, upon hearing it was at the *accomplished Monkies,* from hastening to the spot, to satisfy himself if or not Camilla had been steady to her declaration. But he witnessed at once the propriety of his advice, and its failure. (430)

What is astonishing here is that Camilla is judged, as it were, for attempting to judge for herself. Edgar takes more pleasure in being right, moreover, than he takes pain at seeing his friend insulted. The structure of the passage, moreover, with Edgar appearing at the moment of greatest embarrassment, suggests a nightmare of surveillance. Doody says that "most of the characters in *Camilla* . . . seem like mad detectives. Their observation and conjecture are driven by anxieties, and their relation to each other is suspicious: Camilla is Edgar's suspect" (249). What we see here is the kind of surveillance that is familiar in Gothic fiction: the heroine is never free from an observer who watches and judges; as Doody says, she is Edgar's "suspect."[20] She is also, in his experiments on the female nature, his subject. In Gothic fiction, however, this figure is rarely the hero.

After Dr. Marchmont tries to cool Edgar's enthusiasm for Camilla by advising "circumspection," this position of distance and distrust reaches a climax: "That her manners are engaging, that her looks are captivating, and even that her heart is yours, admit no doubt: but the solidity or the lightness of that heart are yet to be proved" (594). Marchmont, the voice of patriarchal resistance and unabashed misogyny, pushes Edgar to test and prove Camilla's heart with so little concern for her own feelings that she is forced to conclude that she is "lessened in your esteem"; and in her unflinching way, she acts: "I here, therefore, solemnly release you from all tie, all engagement whatever with Camilla Tyrold! I shall immediately acquaint my friends that henceforth . . . we Both are Free!" (640–41).[21]

Even here, Camilla's motives can be questioned, of course, and Dr. Marchmont does not hesitate to suggest that she may have acted "from a confidence of power that loves to tyrannize over its slaves, by playing with their chains? or a lurking spirit of coquetry, that desires to regain the liberty of trifling with some new Sir Sedley Clarendel? or, perhaps, with Sir Sedley himself?" (642). Marchmont seems as interested as Mrs. Arlbery in the chains with which men bind themselves, and he is blind to any but the homosocial implications of male-female relations. Because he is the most rigorous patriarch in a patriarchal system, it is hardly surprising that he resorts to such a cheap but readily available distortion of Camilla's motives or that he does so in terms that supplant the woman in question with another man.

As a result of this contemptuous misconstruction of Camilla's motives, and perhaps because he has experienced the thrill of jealousy too long for it to hold much fascination for him here, Edgar sees through Marchmont's response and begins to understand the terms of his apprenticeship: "Dr. Marchmont! how wretchedly ill you think of women!" (642). From this moment Edgar attempts to put aside the compulsory misogyny that shapes his culture and begins to look for a way to think for himself. He determines to rely on his own feelings rather than on any abstract notion of "woman" or "the dangers of the female."

Eventually, even as Burney uses Edgar to demonstrate a male contempt for female judgment, she tries to suggest ways in which he is different from the many male villains who populate this work. Often when Camilla and Edgar talk, for instance, he backs down from his aggressively male judgmentality. Burney seems even to suggest that a relationship with Edgar might be preferable to her relationships with the various women who deceive and/or mislead her. The transition of Edgar from a threatening judge to an encouraging lover is accomplished, however, not by eroticizing her hero, but by domesticating him. Camilla and Edgar seem able to communicate only when they have transformed the erotic tension between them into something more like a sibling relation. Of course, that does necessarily diminish the possibility of eroticism, as their later relationship suggests. Within the domestic, Burney finds room for a range of emotion that would in any circumstance be considered extreme.

Before Edgar can be fully domesticated, he causes Camilla a kind of grief which exacerbates her isolation and borders closely on what in the eighteenth century would be called hysteria. Less and less in control of her feelings, Camilla seems in danger of losing her mind or even her life. On one of the few occasions when Camilla's mother gives her advice, she does so in response to Camilla's extreme consternation. The older woman's words are simple and direct: "'Repress, repress,' said Mrs. Tyrold gently, yet firmly, 'these strong feelings, uselessly torturing to us both.'" And again, "'Camilla, . . . it is time to conquer this impetuous sensibility'" (881–82). What better cultural advice could Camilla's mother give her? After all, this clear articulation of a culture's agenda, as described by Foucault and others as the "hysterization of women's bodies," is here accomplished with the doting care of maternal affection.[22] Mrs. Tyrold understands how sensibility functions to undermine female subjectivity itself. I have argued that as sensibility's influence became more pervasive, sensibility itself became a "symptom" of nervous disorders of various kinds. That medicalization of emotional pleasure, however, disguises the ideological symptom with which it is identical. Far from only allowing us to diagnose individual psychological complaints, that is, sensibility offers a means of diagnosing a culture's refusal to acknowledge the repression inherent to its hegemonic realization.[23] For Žižek "it is precisely the symptom which is conceived as . . . a real kernel of enjoyment, which persists as surplus and returns through all attempts to domesticate it."[24] The kernel of enjoyment is memorialized in *Camilla* precisely because the heroine and hero meet after a long absence in the sickroom that best represents the overindulgence in sensibility.

When, for instance, Edgar is actually asked to say prayers at her bedside as she lies apparently dying from the effects of her love, their recognition scene, almost a parody of extreme romantic confrontations, is a bed scene almost Gothic in its implications. Mrs. Marl asks him to pray with the young lady in her care:

> He complied, though not immediately; but no sooner had he begun, no sooner devoutly, yet tremblingly, pronounced, *O Father of Mercies!* than a faint scream issued from the bed.—
>
> He stopt; but she did not speak; and after a short pause, he resumed; but not a second sentence was pronounced when she feebly ejaculated, "Ah heaven!" and the book fell from his hands.
>
> She strove to raise her head; but could not; she opened, however, the side curtain, to look out; he advanced, at the same moment, to the foot of the bed . . . fixed his eyes upon her face; and in a voice that seemed to come from his soul, exclaimed, "Camilla!"
>
> With a mental emotion that, for an instant, restored her strength, she drew again the curtain, covered up her face, and sobbed audibly, while the words, "O Edgar!" vainly sought vent.
>
> He attempted not to unclose the curtain she had drawn, but with a deep groan, dropping upon his knees outside, cried, "Great God!" (877)

This bed scene combines a love scene and a religious ceremony in a way that transforms Camilla's extreme isolation into a mode of seduction. The veiled form of the heroine, the suppliant attitude of the hero, the jerky movements, the ejaculations: this is Burney at her most exotic. This is also the closest Burney comes to articulating desire; as fraught and nearly pathological as it seems, this is what Burney posits as a possibility for male and female relations.[25] It would seem, in the scene just quoted, that Edgar and Camilla have found a way to enjoy their symptom, a way of transforming the threatened debilities of sensibility into the basis of mutual attraction. Their religious scene, moreover, engages the more inescapable exercises of patriarchy in their behalf, transforming a devotion to patriarchal law into a form of devotion to one another.

Later, when the more conventional last phases of the courtship begin, Edgar finds it suitable to court Camilla through her mother. They have all been in the sickroom together, and when Mrs. Tyrold begins to leave, Edgar detains her:

> "Ah yes, stay, dearest Madam!" cried Edgar, again respectfully taking her hand, "and through your unalterable goodness, let me hope to procure pardon for a distrust which I here for ever renounce; but which had its origin in my never daring to hope what, at this moment, I have the felicity to believe. Yet now, even now, without your kind mediation, this dear convalescent may plan some probationary trial at which my whole mind, after this long suffering, revolts." (899–900)

This is an attempt at reconstituting the domestic, the sentimental family that Edgar has long ago violated by his distrust and his own endless testing. If he succeeds, he does so in terms that seem oddly deflating. After the wild erotics of the sickchamber, his approach to Camilla's mother hardly seems promising. Edgar has had to domesticate himself as a son and brother in order to fulfill his heroic role in this novel. This is not particularly exciting, not in keeping with the excitement of sexual possibility that seems always to hover at the edge of this text. But his "dear convalescent" may see things differently.

After the sexual abuse of Sir Sedley; of Bellamy, who threatens the life of Eugenia; and even of Clermont, who shows contempt for women as clearly as Marchmont, this fraternal attraction, underwritten, as it were, by the erotics of the bedchamber, has at least the advantage of not being abusive. One could even argue that with Edgar, Burney has rewritten the male role as unthreatening even as it is sexually promising. But as in other Burney novels, marriage intervenes before the erotic can be realized in any but the most indirect situations.

In *Camilla,* after all the testing and all the distrust, Burney places Edgar and Camilla in a context that is fulfilling in the only terms she has offered her heroine: "Edgar, by generous confidence, became the repository of her every thought; and her friends read her exquisite lot in a gaiety no longer to be feared" (913). No longer is female sexuality to be feared: now that it has been harnessed, as it were, in a fitting patriarchal project—at the center of a marriage, a family, a village, a culture—it can be celebrated and shared.[26] Nor can it integrate the fragmentation and isolation that the novel has so vividly dramatized. This novel posits a more unalloyed "happy ending" than *Cecilia* or *The Wanderer,* but in doing so it gives in to a kind of unabashed wish-fulfillment that the novel belies. The happy families in *Camilla* seem so close to unhappy, schemes for happiness so wrongheaded, and romantic relationships so doomed that when Burney says, "Thus ended the long conflicts, doubts, suspences, and sufferings of Edgar and Camilla" (913), we can perhaps be forgiven a degree of skepticism. But when she says that Dr. Marchmont "saw" his mistaken judgment of Camilla and "acknowledged its injustice, its narrowness, and its arrogance" (913), we know that she is dealing in fantasy. The patriarchy cannot be wished away, even in so impressive a novel as this.[27] Camilla and Edgar may be allowed to be happy, but the world surely does not change. Burney has shown us just too much of it for us to be able to think that it will. We might as well say with Camilla's mother, "Repress, repress."

NINE

The Pleasures of Victimization in
The Romance of the Forest

Ann Radcliffe is an interesting case of a writer who falls between the popular and the canonic: she is never taken as seriously as Jane Austen, but neither is she classed with the bulk of her Gothic-writing contemporaries. If feminist readings of the Gothic have taught us to look deeply into the souls of Radcliffe's characters—more deeply than earlier Gothic critics had asked us to—and if they have taught us new ways of considering the role of the novelist herself, they have not always broken free of the kind critical superiority which sees Radcliffe as an unwitting participant in the drama of her age and which attributes many of the most intriguing features of her novels to authorial lapse.[1] What I would like to do in this discussion of *The Romance of the Forest* is to reconsider the implications of one of Radcliffe's most successful novels as an extreme statement about the limits on female experience and the ruthlessness of paternal concern. In doing so, I hope to continue the process that has already begun of reassessing the contribution of Radcliffe to the early history of the novel and to the woman's novel in particular.[2]

If Coleridge can say about a work such as *The Mysteries of Udolpho* that "the curiosity is raised oftener than it is gratified," for Radcliffe to raise the curiosity is to open the possibility of a response that "realistic" narrative would not encourage.[3] Gothic conventions offer a means of exploring a different world, or rather a world of different desire, than novelists of the "probable" were able to consider. Terry Castle credits Radcliffe with a proto-psychoanalytical account of human subjectivity, and she claims that in her "spectralization" of characters, Radcliffe reconceives internal/external relations.[4] In this chapter I will look a little more closely at the kind of "spectralization" that transpires in *The Romance of the Forest* in an attempt to look at the ways in which Radcliffe transgresses the limits placed on female experience in the later eighteenth century.

Leslie Fiedler has been cited, by Claire Kahane and others, as the originator of the notion of "maternal blackness" at the center of Gothic experience.[5] As I pointed out in chapter 3, Kahane is much more explicit: "What . . . draws me inward," she says, "is the spectral presence of a dead-undead mother, archaic and all-encompassing, a ghost signifying the problematics of femininity which the heroine must confront."[6] Kahane's remarks assert something about the nature of Gothic fiction itself—this feeling of being drawn inward—which is essential to its form, and in a novel like *The Mysteries of Udolpho,* as in *The Recess,* the dead-undead mother is an all-commanding presence. In *The Romance of the Forest,* however, the "problematics of femininity" are at issue in other and quite contradictory ways. This is a novel that works so actively against the notion of a mother, dead or undead, that we are forced to look elsewhere for the real center of Radcliffe's concern. If the novel examines a parental fantasy of any kind, it is a paternal fantasy, and a great deal of the novel's energy goes into the exploration of aggressive as well as benevolent fatherhood. The contours of the paternal, moreover, seem to a certain extent congruent with those of heterosexual eroticism—heteroeroticism—itself. Claudia Johnson makes this point irresistibly: "Fleeing the rage of her father, Adeline finds herself in the households of three different men in each of the three successive volumes of the novel." The implications of this configuration are not difficult to imagine. As Johnson says, "*The Romance of the Forest* effects its social criticism by examining the way society either corrupts or preserves the 'naturally' moralizing properties of male heterosexual feeling."[7] Masculinity is at the center of this novel as it is in perhaps no other Radcliffe novel, and the consequences in terms of female sexuality are never less than surprising.

Adeline, whose seeming lack of a surname dramatizes her isolation, enters the novel in a singularly desperate condition:

> This ejaculation was interrupted by a noise in the passage leading to the room: it approached—the door was unlocked—and the man who had admitted La Motte into the house entered, leading, or rather forcibly dragging along, a beautiful girl, who appeared to be about eighteen. Her features were bathed in tears, and she seemed to suffer the utmost distress.[8]

Adeline's first appearance in *The Romance of the Forest* suggests almost total helplessness. She is dragged into the room, and as it turns out, she is handed over to La Motte, about whom we know little more than that he is fleeing Paris for undisclosed reasons, a man whose "conduct was suggested by feeling, rather than principle" (2), and she becomes in a sense his property from this moment forward. In Gothic terms it is not surprising that Adeline is suffering, that she is brutalized, or that she is alone. But Radcliffe offers us these qualities as Adeline's primary condition. In this case, the female starts from a position of utter abjection, and only gradually does she even come to learn that there might be an alternative to her present torment. It is telling that Adeline does have a "history," which is later unfolded; but her own version of the past turns out to be so far from the truth that its articulation is just a further sign of her helpless condition. Moreover, by presenting it later and in rather vague retrospective terms, Radcliffe ensures that Adeline seems the destitute orphan that she in fact is. Soon after this we are treated to the following reverie: "Adeline felt the forlornness of her condition with energy; she reflected upon the past with astonishment, and anticipated the future with fear. She found herself wholly dependent upon strangers, with no other claim than what distress demands from the common sympathy of kindred beings" (21). It is by now fairly uncontroversial to describe this utter abjection as "masochism" and to see female involvement in Gothic plots as masochistic in specific ways. Michelle Massé, for instance, speaks about "the central truth of women's Gothic trauma and the masochism that so often accompanies it." Massé depends on Ann Grief's description of masochism as a "reification of early trauma in which pain becomes associated with pleasure in all its forms, from sexual pleasure to romantic love." Massé is careful not to insist that masochism represents "simply a capitulation to or resistance against the cultural trauma that denies a woman's identity," but I must question whether the Freudian model of masochism, a model based on nineteenth-century male sexual obsessions after all, can answer all the questions surrounding sexual subjectivity in Radcliffe's fiction, or other examples of "female Gothic."[9]

Still, the "forlornness" of Adeline's "condition" is familiar to readers of Gothic fiction;[10] and it would not be too much to claim that this "condition" is a description of the most salient feature of female Gothic subjectivity. Simple abjection is surely more to the point.[11] Adeline begins this novel in a state of abjection, and only gradually does she find a way to make the violent, dark revolt of being a source of a kind of perverse pleasure. In any case, Adeline's entrance suggests powerlessness, and the novel is animated with Adeline's attempts to create for herself a context in which she might survive the abrupt abandonment into which she is thrown at the novel's opening. This "forlornness," this abjection, is a symptom of sensibility, after all, and it is through the lens of sensibility that Adeline's fears and her desires need most carefully to be articulated.

The tenets of sensibility serve only to heighten our growing sense of the "problematics of femininity," but not in ways that are predictably Radcliffean.[12] For instance, the La Motte group—La Motte and his wife, their son Louis, and servants—offer the possibility of a familial grouping. But this family hides the guilty secret of La Motte's nefarious history and grows in dissension and distrust. Adeline is the key to this dissension, because she is young and attractive, but also because she is typically a cipher, waiting to be filled out, to be written on, with the intentions and desires, as well as the misinterpretations, of others.[13] Family is therefore problematized: it feels corrupt and corrupting, and whatever relations are formed seem doomed to misprision and misconstruction. Inevitably, the young girl is sacrificed to the good of the whole, which in this case is literally equivalent to the survival of the father.[14] Claudia Johnson says that "[m]ale sentimentality erodes the distinction between the sociable and the erotic, and Radcliffe's novels are canniest when showing conventional characters struggling with this anti-conventional phenomenon." Male sentimentality, that is, complicates any notion of female masochism in this text, and it makes masculinity and male victimization as important to think about as the inevitable victimization of the female. Johnson's analysis of the novel makes the case that "[c]ivility and heteroerotic interest *look* the same because they *are* the same."[15] But the novel argues more than one kind of heteroeroticism, and I hope in the pages that follow to make the case that Adeline and Theodore are not the hetero-erotic poster couple that most critics would like to make them. If I call them queer, it is not merely to be provocative. It seems to me that Adeline and Theodore find a space outside, or an isolated space within, heterosexuality that defines them as "different" in ways that I will outline below. The superfluity of fathers in the text, the intensity of paternal concern, both good and bad, creates the backdrop against which Radcliffe's version of queer desire can be vividly displayed.

Adeline, in her friendless misery, often seems in danger of losing her wits or her virginity, or both. Although she is not, as her guardian Madame La Motte suspects, conspiring to have illicit relations with La Motte, she is as destitute of female protection as if she were. Her own sensibility is no less finely honed than that of Madame La Motte, but she must learn to support herself in a world of male aggression. This indirect victimization is but a signal of what is in store for her. Her sensibility does not embitter her, however; it makes her more sensitive to the possibilities of a resolution on her own terms.

The values that will sustain Adeline in the world are nevertheless not to be found in any abstract construct such as duty, family, or home. In this novel, such ideals are always problematic. For no sooner does the La Motte group begin to feel familial than the ruthlessness of family structure becomes apparent. When, therefore, La Motte decides to sacrifice Adeline in order to save himself, it is a confirmation of the sense of family that Radcliffe has been establishing. There is no space in the family for a young and unprotected girl. She automatically becomes the victim of a system that is meant to protect her. In this Radcliffe is surely as radical as any of her contemporaries. For whatever platitudes she articulates in the conclusion to her work, what she makes us feel at its climactic moments is that the family is as dangerous and destructive as any of the Gothic configurations Adeline is forced to enter. In one sense, in fact, the family is the most dangerous configuration of all, because here, at first anyway, Adeline felt safe.

Claudia Johnson has complicated our sense of the security of this sentimental home. In discussing the failure of female relations in this novel, she suggests that "[p]rofessions of female friendship . . . function ideologically as clichés, concealing contradictions in the heteroerotic monopoly on sociable affections."[16] What this collapse of romantic friendship means for Adeline, however, is that she has to turn her beloved Theodore into a friend before she can love him. Before she can do that, however, she has to undermine the paternal threat that haunts her throughout the novel.

Adeline's past is riddled with falsehood and treachery. The man she assumes is her father turns out to have been a hired ruffian; but that does not make any less poignant her feelings of despair when she finds this sham parent insensitive to her needs and desires: "My father came sometimes to Paris; he then visited me, and I well remember the grief I used to feel when he bade me farewell. On these occasions, which rung my heart with grief, he appeared unmoved; so that I often thought he had little tenderness for me. But he was my father, and the only person to whom I could look up for protection and love" (36). This same "father" later imprisons her and leaves her to the ruffians from whom she is "rescued" by La Motte. For the majority of the novel, Adeline remains in fear of this "father," from whom she is in flight and for whom she feels increasing contempt. Whether or not this is her real father, this is the family experience she knows, and it is one that torments her. At one point, for instance, La Motte can press his threats to offer her to the Marquis de Montalt because of her fear of her father. "'As *your* friend, Sir,'" she says to La Motte in response to his suggestions concerning the Marquis, "'I will endeavour to'—treat him as mine, she would have said, but she found it impossible to finish the sentence. She entreated his protection from the power of her father" (125). In *The Romance of the Forest,* familial relations are only to be feared.

La Motte quickly abandons Adeline to the shadowy Marquis de Montalt, and the scene in which Adeline overhears a nighttime conversation in which her fate is discussed between the two men signals her marginal position in a world of male power and prerogative. She hears of the Marquis's desire ("'I adore her,' pursued he, 'and by heaven'—") and a hint of the paternal threat ("'Her father, say you?' said the Marquis. 'Yes, my Lord, her father. I am well informed of what I say.' Adeline shuddered at the mention of her father, a new terror seized her, and with increasing eagerness she endeavoured to distinguish their words, but for some time found this to be impossible" [117]). The Marquis's relation to Adeline's father is more complicated than anything she imagines at this moment—at one point later on it seems that *he* is her father—but the conflation of sexual anxiety and fear of the father expresses the classic situation for the Gothic heroine, a familiar configuration in the Gothic world in general and in Radcliffean Gothic in particular.

The so-called "demon-lover" has frequently been cited as the locus of erotic energy in Radcliffean Gothic. Cynthia Griffin Wolff has put the case more succinctly, noting

> the remarkably violent taboo that enshrouds the entire relationship between . . . eighteenth-century heroines and their demon lovers. Despite the fact that the man is darkly attractive, the woman generally shuns him, shrinking as from some invisible contamination. Too often to be insignificant, this aversion is justified when he eventually proves to be a long-lost relation: an uncle, a step-father, sometimes the biological father himself—lusting after the innocent daughter's chastity. This spectre of

incest (an unself-conscious reminder of the origins of the fantasy that is being rehearsed) hangs over the entire tale and is occasionally reinforced by the presence, not fully developed as a character, of an antagonistic older woman with whose competitive malevolence the heroine must contend.[17]

Wolff's description fits *The Romance of the Forest* perfectly. Not only is the Marquis physically attractive, and unaccountably repulsive to Adeline, he is urbane; and his chateau, unlike the usual Gothic setting, is beautifully, if oppressively, decorated and showy in its luxuriance—"fitted up in the most airy and elegant taste" (156). In Wolff's analysis, this "demon-lover" is set against a less erotically interesting "priest-lover" but continues to "dominat[e] the fiction as its undeniable emotional focus."[18]

Without quibbling over authorial intention, I think it would be worth pausing here to reconsider the terms of Wolff's analysis. The Freudian configuration she describes surely is at work in Radcliffe's fiction, but its implications for the heroine are by no means so patriarchally predetermined. In *The Romance of the Forest,* Radcliffe articulates a relation to the Oedipal myth that is more complex than the simple "repressed-desire" model that Wolff and others propose.[19] If Foucault has taught us to reject the "repression hypothesis" as a means of understanding earlier subjective relation to sexual desire, how can we discuss Adeline's desire in ways that are more in keeping with the actual details of the text?

In the first place, the Marquis is not the only threatening father figure in the novel, he is one of a series of paternal nemeses that haunt Adeline's experience. More than suggesting a simple deep attraction to this figure, Radcliffe insists that these seemingly helpful and potentially threatening figures are everywhere in a world shaped by male desire. Any man, every man, who meets Adeline subjects her to the abuse of his desire. The world, in other words, is a sexual wilderness for Adeline, and masculine ascendancy assures that she is almost always a potential rape victim, that every potential rapist is also potentially a father—Adeline has four different father figures throughout the course of the narrative—and that "paternal" affection offers her nothing but alienation and despair. The "demon" in this case, however, the Marquis de Montalt, is hardly a conventional Gothic villain. As Johnson says, "[t]he marquis's villainy is marked by the elegance, not by the outlandishness, of his conduct."[20] But Radcliffe makes it seem as if his good taste is a sign of unnatural desire: incest after all begins at home, and what surroundings could be in better taste? Anyone familiar with the "Dora" controversy knows that Freudian analysis is in certain ways insensitive to the kinds of threatening situations in which Adeline finds herself.[21] The real danger

The Pleasures of Victimization in *The Romance of the Forest*

here is not the desire that Adeline might be repressing, but rather the male desire that both objectifies and victimizes her in its simplest fantasies.

It would be tempting to say that this world of negative possibility is in some ways deeply attractive to the novelist and her heroine and that Radcliffe gives voice to secret desires in this array of powerful paternal figures. But from another perspective, the world of male prerogative gives rise to Gothic experience throughout the text. The terror invoked is not a thrilling and titillating frisson of emotion, but dark and uncompromising fear. In this reading, Radcliffe portrays female experience as fraught with actual rather than imagined danger.

Mary Poovey argues that "Radcliffe can imagine no force apart from sensibility's feminine principles to control this masculine force."[22] Poovey suggests that the "feminine" principle which Radcliffe proposes as a counter to male domination is unimaginative and unpersuasive. It seems to me on the contrary that what Radcliffe achieves in this novel, and in her later ones, is an articulation of an ideal of female sexuality which rejects the abuses of power that she dramatizes in favor of a possibly "liberating" alternative. The feminine principle that the novel offers is shared between Adeline and her erstwhile lover, Theodore. In order to understand the terms of her protest, it is essential to consider the role of Theodore Peyrou more carefully.

Adeline's attraction to Theodore is immediate and compelling. The structure of the novel, however, requires that they be separated for most of the novel. This is convenient in two ways: first, it allows Adeline to undergo the ordeal of her repeated flight and incarcerations on her own and to discover the kind of power that even her attachment to Theodore would deprive her of; second, it allows her to imagine him, as she does at regular intervals throughout the bulk of the novel, in terms similar to these:

> Adeline . . . would have been happy as she was thankful, had not unceasing anxiety for the fate of Theodore, of whom in this solitude she was less likely than ever to hear, corroded her heart, and embittered every moment of reflection. Even when sleep obliterated for a while the memory of the past, his image frequently arose to her fancy, accompanied by all the exaggerations of terror. She saw him in chains, and struggling in the grasp of ruffians, or saw him led, amidst the dreadful preparations for execution, into the field: she saw the agony of his look and heard him repeat her name in frantic accents, till the horrors of the scene overcame her, and she awoke. (259)

Such moments of fearful imagination abound in *The Romance of the Forest*, and their function is clear. Adeline heightens suspense and her own dread by imagining Theodore in chains, Theodore bleeding, Theodore suffering un-told torments. But she also challenges the assumptions of patriarchy by finding this ineffectual and indeed emasculated hero a desirable alternative to the stern and powerful Marquis de Montalt. Terry Castle argues persua-sively that Radcliffe heroines "spectralize" their absent male lovers and in doing so established "a new phenomenology of self and other." For Radcliffe, Castle claims, "[t]he corporeality of the other—his or her actual life in the world—became strangely insubstantial and indistinct: what mat-tered was the mental picture, the ghost, the haunting image."[23] At the same time, what Radcliffe calls "the exaggerations of terror" offer a means of imagining an alternative to the ideology that places women under the power of men.[24] Spectralization, that is, eroticizes the fantasy of the other as a victim. In this signal case, Radcliffe goes to great lengths to describe these mental pictures, and in doing so she embraces the symptom that would otherwise marginalize Adeline as at least slightly deranged.

Castle says that "[n]ot coincidentally, the most influential of modern theories of the mind—psychoanalysis—has internalized the ghost-seeing metaphor: the Freudian account of psychic events . . . is as suffused with crypto-supernaturalism as Radcliffe's."[25] One might go a step further and say that the pathology of perverse pleasure is itself encoded in these imagin-ings and that to the degree that Radcliffe offers a model for psychological description, she does so with the awareness that to render the other a ghost is not to diminish the power of bodily attraction. Theodore's brutalized form gives her fantasy a coherence that gender alone cannot supply. Adeline takes her pleasure in a picture that is everything that phallic masculinity would reject. Her "man" is never depicted as powerful, nor does he seem particu-larly able to extricate himself from the hold that law and society—in the form of the army and the Marquis (at times one and the same)—have over him. Insofar as the Marquis de Montalt comes to represent the source of power in a phallocentric system, Theodore, pathetic as he is (or as Adeline imagines him), represents a conceivable alternative. In his suffering lies his power, both to capture the heart of Adeline and to undermine the unequivo-cal power of the Marquis. But how does he accomplish this?

Early in the novel, just after she has met Theodore in fact, Adeline has a dream which offers a context in which to interpret anxieties such as those just described:

> While she stood musing and surveying the apartment, she heard a low voice call her, and, looking towards the place whence it came, she perceived by the dim light of a lamp a figure stretched on a bed that lay on the floor.

The Pleasures of Victimization in *The Romance of the Forest*

> The voice called again, and, approaching the bed, she distinctly saw the features of a man who appeared to be dying. A ghastly paleness overspread his countenance, yet there was an expression of mildness and dignity in it, which strongly interested her.
>
> While she looked on him, his features changed and seemed convulsed in the agonies of death. The spectacle shocked her, and she started back, but he suddenly stretched forth his hand, and seizing her's, grasped it with violence: she struggled in terror to disengage herself, and again looking on his face, saw a man, who appeared to be about thirty, with the same features, but in full health, and of a most benign countenance. He smiled tenderly upon her and moved his lips, as if to speak, when the floor of the chamber suddenly opened and he sunk from her view. The effort she made to save herself from following awoke her. (108)

This unnamed figure who seems in retrospect to represent her murdered father (who else?) is in a sense a composite of all the men she has met—kind and attractive, but corrupt and threatening at the same time. Perhaps what she most fears about the paternal ghoul is that he represents her own abjection and that he threatens to burden her independent existence with his irresistible corpse.[26] This is the "demon-lover" with a vengeance. The terrors of patriarchy are vivid enough: the young girl is threatened physically and terrified emotionally, and if she gives her hand to the kindly Chevalier, boyfriend, husband, father, friend, she is doomed. "The effort she made to save herself from following" is what motivates her throughout the entire novel.

As the dream continues, however, something happens. Adeline follows the same man into a "suite of very ancient apartments, hung with black, and lighted as if for a funeral":

> Still he led her on, till she found herself in the same chamber she remembered to have seen in her former dream: a coffin, covered with a pall, stood at the farther end of the room; some lights, and several persons surrounded it, who appeared to be in great distress.
>
> Suddenly, she thought these persons were all gone, and that she was left alone; that she went up to the coffin, and while she gazed upon it, she heard a voice speak, as if from within, but saw nobody. The man she had before seen, soon after stood by the coffin, and, lifting the pall, she saw beneath it a dead person, whom she thought to be the dying Chevalier she had seen in the former dream: his features were sunk in death, but they were yet serene. While she looked at him, a stream of blood gushed from his side, and descending to the floor, the whole chamber was overflowed; at the same time some words were uttered in the voice she heard before; but the horror of the scene so entirely overcame her, that she started and awoke. (109–110)

Adeline gives in to attraction here and, as before, she is confronted with a corpse. This time, however, the corpse engages her not by speaking but by an oceanic gushing of blood from an unspecified "wound" in his side. The coffin itself, this tomb at the center of the forbidden passage, suggests, as Clare Kahane would argue, the female, the maternal body.[27] But this wounded body is male, and the blood flows as the result of a complex emasculation, which suggests that Adeline has at last found a way of eroticizing the father in whose blood she must be swimming. The bloody male completes the fantasy of victimization and emasculation: Adeline's dreams rehearse a fantasy that she has made her own. Blood and desire are promiscuously confounded in this vivid fantasy of origins and disempowerment.

Adeline recuperates the erotics of family life by conflating primal images and castrating her father in her dreams. The demon lover is in other words "domesticated." Kahane discusses the "maternal" quality of "the secret center of the Gothic structure, where boundaries break down, where life and death become confused, where images of birth and sexuality proliferate in complex displacements."[28] Here the boundary between male and female seems also to have collapsed, and the bleeding paternal/maternal figure becomes paradigmatic of Adeline's attractions and her fears. In Theodore, she finds the image of this dead-undead father/mother, and it is the pathetic emasculated hero that sustains her in her moments of most severe distress and buoys her up on the seas of her own imagined bloody end.

When she is with Theodore, the implications of this aggressively pathetic longing are given physical terms. When Adeline and Theodore see each other for one of the few times between the beginning and the end of the novel, they meet briefly in a room at the inn where he is being held for (unmanly) desertion from the army:

> Adeline sat, overcome by the description which Theodore had given of his approaching situation, and by the consideration that she might remain in the most terrible suspense concerning his fate. She saw him in a prison—pale—emaciated, and in chains:—she saw all the vengeance of the Marquis descending upon him; and this for his noble exertions in her cause. Theodore, alarmed by the placid despair expressed in her countenance, threw himself into a chair by her's, and, taking her hand, attempted to speak comfort to her, but the words faltered on his lips, and he could only bathe her hand with tears. (194)

Adeline has been here before. Theodore's suffering, and her imagination of his pain, which here does not even require his absence from her side, places him in the only relation that will allow her to feel attraction. Theodore plays

The Pleasures of Victimization in *The Romance of the Forest*

on Adeline's emotions to the degree that he is restrained, controlled, victimized, and emasculated. To the degree, that is, that Theodore becomes *like a woman,* he is attractive to the heroine of *The Romance of the Forest.*[29] We could understand this in either sexual or political terms, but what seems of paramount importance to this configuration is that Theodore is *different* from the powerful males in the novel and like the one male she has only met in her dreams, her father. This is not then simply a feminine response to the terrors of patriarchy, it is a response that for Adeline at least can embody a male/female alternative to ruthlessness and aggression. That she can replace it only with terror and victimization is a measure of her own powerlessness, but it is also, to a certain extent, an outright rejection of the terms under which power is achieved. These suffering victims will find another way.

In her study of male subjectivity, Kaja Silverman claims that "[o]ur dominant fiction calls upon the male subject to see himself, and the female subject to recognize and desire him, only through the mediation of images of an unimpaired masculinity."[30] What Radcliffe has articulated in *The Romance of the Forest* is an alternative fiction, a fiction of male vulnerability and emasculation, a fiction that rewrites masculinity in a female mold and attempts to eroticize the very fact of victimization. Can the debilitated male function as an object of desire here? In a recent essay on Victorian male "masochism," Carol Siegel turns the masochism question around by articulating the possible attraction of the victimized male:

> Because male sexual display necessarily reveals the lack of an empirical basis for the privilege that accompanies biological difference, the male masochist strips off the (symbolic) phallus as he publicly bares himself for the blow. When he compounds this crime against the Fathers by delightedly embracing the victim's role, he would seem to place himself outside the pale, happily free to undermine society's standards.[31]

Siegel goes on to argue against any such "free"-floating role for the male masochist and convincingly argues that sadomasochistic texts such as *Wuthering Heights* "naturalize male cruelty and female submissiveness as the background against which male masochistic displays are staged and into which the flaunting men ultimately recede."[32] The attractive victimization of *The Romance of the Forest,* however, creates a space of mutuality that mimics "sister"-hood as the ideal for male-female relations. Adeline's vividly sadistic abuse of Theodore in her imagination projects lack onto the male body and eroticizes the possibility of nonphallic sexuality. "Male cruelty and female submissiveness" are challenged by the sentimental resolution, even if they are, to a certain extent, reinscribed. Radcliffe, is not, finally, a radical, but her version of female desire is not simply passive acceptance of the terms of family and domestic role. Adeline has had to resexualize the family and re-create a position of power for herself.[33]

Leo Bersani argues that one reading of Freud's *Three Essays* would suggest that "sexuality would not be originally an exchange of intensities between individuals, but rather a condition of broken negotiations with the world, a condition in which others merely set off the self-shattering mechanisms of masochistic *jouissance*."[34] Adeline and Theodore share the *jouissance* of abjection, and in doing so they suggest where the erotics of a "domestic" resolution might really be found. In cutting themselves off from the phallus, they find pleasure in the lack that they have been so tearfully delighted to create for themselves. This is not a capitulation to the dominant fiction of male power; rather it creates a space for pleasures beyond gender, beyond heterosexuality, and beyond family itself. This plea-sure is queer in its focus on the bloody and the tearful. Abjection, that is, becomes the symptom for a desire that would defy the dictates of the hyperpaternalistic world that this novel represents. Heteronormative rela-tions are not enough. Radcliffe has other objects in mind.

AFTERWORD

Female Gothic (2): Demonic Love

The previous chapters offer a rich context from which to enter the nineteenth century, and in this brief afterword I would like to look at two women's novels from early in that century. These works were written in the spirit of Gothicism, and they share many of the issues and concerns with the writers I have discussed above. At the same time, they articulate the terms of female desire with a greater abandon than any of the works I have considered. Because they are more extreme than other female Gothic writing, they can serve to crystallize some of the recurring nightmares that I have considered. At the same time, they introduce new concerns and different perspectives.

The other Radcliffe, Mary-Ann, whose publications traded on the popularity of her predecessor, can serve to suggest some of the more lurid contours of the Radcliffean "sublime." In *Manfroné, or, the One-Handed Monk* (1809), the demon-lover, who loses his hand in a duel with the heroine's father at the moment of attempting to rape her, then returns as the mysterious monk who mumbles from behind his obfuscating cowl to "haunt" the heroine, Rosalina: first in the candlelit aisles of the abbey adjoining her father's castle, then in the subterranean passages that elaborately connect the abbey and the castle and contain in assorted dungeons pathetic prisoners variously thought to be murdered or otherwise victimized by Rosalina's hot-headed father, and finally as her father's guest in the castle itself. Rosalina laments the loss of her mother and learns the details of her history, only as she comes to recognize her father as a murderous tyrant who stops short of killing *her* in a crucial, central scene solely because he is distracted by the shouts of his soldiers.

The novel is rich in midnight trysts, in threatened sexual violence, in mere physical brutality, and in a Gothic atmosphere rendered almost oppressive by its unrelieved gloom. Nowhere are there the shimmering vistas of Ann Radcliffe or Charlotte Smith, or the picturesque moments that dispel the darkness with rays of hope. Here the misery and the victimization are total. The details of the plot read like a catalogue of the abuses in the most violent Gothic novels. When the uproar of the opening rape attempt and duel has subsided, Rosalina discovers in her bedroom "a human hand, blood-stained, and apparently but lately severed from its limb."[1] This simple dismemberment, issuing as it does from a violent sexual encounter, is more than a little suggestive of castration; and when the one-handed monk glowers from within the inner recesses of the castle, few readers would question the source of his bitter resentment:

> [H]is colossal form standing erect and motionless in the dark shadow of a large column, his features still concealed, his arms folded, and the solemn silence he still preserved, was more than the spirits of Rosalina, weakened by the mournful reflections she had been so long indulging, could support. (1/1: 211)

The sexual aggression here is palpable, and Rosalina, although falling victim to weak spirits more than once in the novel, knows well enough how both to resist the sexual advances of Manfroné and to render him more or less innocuous.

The hero, Montalto, a strong if ineffectual rival of both the father and Manfroné, manages to fight to save Rosalina from the villain who has finally decided to stop at nothing to "possess" her. But like his Gothic predecessors as well as his villainous rival, he too must suffer symbolic castration before earning the right to rescue the heroine: "Twice was the murderous dagger upraised, and twice did it drink the blood of Rosalina's fond lover!—Groaning, he sunk on the pavement, and the shades of death encompassed him" (2/2: 32). Later, surprisingly, he rises from this symbolic death of his masculinity into union with the heroine, but not before she has been abducted from her own castle and dragged bodily to another where Manfroné awaits her and her fate seems sealed. In the end, she is thrown into a dark dungeon as Manfroné once again tries to rape her; but he is stopped by the resurrected Montalto, who floats into the underground cave on a rising sea to deal him his death blow—as if to make final the emasculation with which the novel began. The conclusion is a bracing, if muted, union of Rosalina and Montalto, certainly a less compelling narrative effect than the violence and sexual energy that has animated the tale throughout.

What Mary-Ann Radcliffe accomplishes here is twofold. In the first place, she breaks the sentimental cast of the female Gothic and demonstrates that a woman could write descriptions as ghastly as those of her male contemporaries. Second, in contrast with male authors such as Matthew G. Lewis, who specialize in the victimization of women in scenes of sexual violence, she manages to portray a kind of female survival that earlier Gothic heroines barely approximate. Mary-Ann Radcliffe's heroine has learned the lesson of masochism and has decided to defy it. Rosalina weeps like her predecessors, but she has the grim determination that could earn her a place in novels of the latter part of the century. She redefines what it means for a Gothic heroine to survive. Adversity is the occasion for her triumph.

Of course, survival might not be enough for some readers. A marriage can after all be deflating as a conclusion to a list of hideous crimes. But the conventional alternative to such a conservative ending is hardly more satisfying. The damnation plot device avoids the bathos of an unconvincing marriage, that is, but it offers little more in terms of female self-realization. In novels that involve soul-selling, such as Charlotte Dacre's *Zofloya, or, The Moor* (1806), however, sexual desire is equally central to the damnation of the individual. In this novel, Dacre tells the story of the proud Victoria, who finds herself attracted to her husband's brother's immense servant, Zofloya, who lures her with compliments and flattering asides. In a carefully constructed tale of gradual dissipation, Victoria sacrifices her relations to satisfy her seemingly insatiable desire, slowly realizing that only Zofloya himself can soothe her soul. Even at his first appearance in the novel, she finds herself obsessed with the handsome black servant. "Why *he* should be connected with her dreams, who never entered her mind when waking, she could not divine: but certain it was, that his exact resemblance, though as it were of polished and superior appearance, had figured chiefly in her troubled sight."[2]

Very shortly, in fact, she is not only dreaming about him but gazing upon him, almost compulsively: she "involuntarily stole frequent glances towards him: once or twice she imagined that he looked upon her with a peculiar expression of countenance, and strange, incongruous ideas shot through her brain" (137–38). The sexual implications of this dark attraction are implicit from the first. Indeed, throughout the novel, although a reader might suspect the hero's other-worldly power, what Dacre shows is an increasingly intense act of seduction on Zofloya's part and a reckless display of desire on Victoria's. I would argue that his role as satanic emissary, as useful in the conclusion of the novel as it might be, is less engaging than the transgressive relation that develops between the white aristocratic woman and the black servant:

> The secret of Victoria hovered on her lips; hitherto it had remained un-known to mortal soul; in the gloomy solitude of her own perturbed bosom, had she till now preserved it, where, like a poisonous worm, it had contin-ued to corrode. She was now on the point of betraying her inmost thoughts, her dearest wishes, her dark repinings, and hopeless desires; of betraying them, too, to an inferior and an infidel! The idea was scarcely endurable, and she scorned it; but, in the next instant, she cast her eyes upon the noble presence of the Moor: he appeared not only the superior of his race, but of a superior order of beings. (148–49)

It hardly matters that Victoria's secret is her love for her husband's brother, Henriquez. Indeed, throughout the novel, that attraction itself is rendered less convincingly than Victoria's relation to Zofloya. In the passage just quoted, in fact, the desire could almost be taken for a desire for Zofloya himself. Before the end of the novel, of course, she admits this even to herself.

Be that as it may, what Dacre does so brilliantly here, and what few female Gothicists before her even attempt, is to depict female desire itself as a kind of victimization, suggesting that by giving in to illicit desire, either simply incestuous or, more unusually, miscegenational, she encourages a "worm" that feeds on her very being. These "dark repinings" are as harrowing as any passage in a darkened castle of Smith or Radcliffe, and they are infinitely more dangerous, especially when viewed against the backdrop of a century of colonial expansion and institutionalized miscegenation.

Later, when Zofloya has encouraged her to murder her husband, attempt the seduction of her brother-in-law, Henriquez, and imprison and torture his fiancée, her relations with the Moor become more explicit. As the violence of Victoria's activities increase, so does the intensity of her bond with the Moor. Much later, after she has succeeded in seducing Henriquez and witnessed his hideous self-destruction, and after the body of her husband has been discovered, Victoria flees with Zofloya to the mountains. Here she sees

Afterword

the Moor in "his proper sphere": "dignity, and ineffable grace, were diffused over his whole figure;—for the first time she felt towards him an emotion of tenderness, blended with her admiration, and, strange inconsistency, amidst the gloomy terrors that pressed upon her heart, amidst the sensible misery that oppressed her, she experienced something like pride, in reflecting, that a Being so wonderful, so superior, and so beautiful, should thus appear to be interested in her fate" (233).

The irony of course is that in entrusting herself to the Moor, she has damned herself for eternity. But the damnation itself takes the form of a sexual encounter more explicit than most such scenes in Gothic fiction. When Zofloya takes Victoria into the Alps so that she might avoid the investigation that would bring her to justice, she admits that "I perceive too clearly, how much, how compleatly I am in your power!" (234); and when they encounter a storm, "she drew closer to the proud unshrinking figure of the Moor—he passed his arms around her waist, and gently pressed her to his breast" (234). When this physical barrier is breached, Victoria does not recoil in horror, as many of her Gothic sisters would; instead, she recognizes what has been implicit in her involvement with Zofloya from the first:

> Never, till this moment, had she been so near the person of the Moor—such powerful fascination dwelt around him, that she felt incapable of withdrawing from his arms; yet ashamed, (for Victoria was still proud) and blushing at her feelings, when she remembered that Zofloya, however he appeared, was but a menial slave, and as such alone had originally become known to her—she sought, but sought vainly, to repress them; for no sooner . . . did she behold that beautiful and majestic visage, that towering and graceful form, than all thought of his inferiority vanished, and the ravished sense, spurning at the calumnious idea, confessed him a being of superior order. (234)

Very shortly after this she is mistaken for his wife, and it is hardly surprising that she finds herself completely subject to his desires. Such moments of intense recognition as these are much more powerful than the details of the denouement, in which he "whirl[s] her headlong down the dreadful abyss!" (267). This novel is about selling one's soul, in other words, only to the degree to which the soul is understood as sexual. Victoria wantonly transgresses limits placed on female desire. The novel dramatizes that transgression with astonishing boldness.

The creation of an "imp of the perverse" who is a seductive "moor" has vast cultural and psychological implications. Anyone familiar with eighteenth-century literature knows that miscegenation was as frightening a "perversion" as incest or sodomy to the cultural imagination. In the context of the present discussion, however, it is easy to see how Victoria's "desire" for Zofloya is what leads her to destroy herself as she does. Her desire for the "moor" places her outside what is socially acceptable and therefore subjects her to the Law that marks her as an aberration. In killing her husband and throwing herself at her husband's brother, Victoria is only playing out what desire itself has already rendered inevitable. External evil, in the form of Zofloya, is really only the evil of desire, insofar as it marks Victoria and places her, or rather displaces her, in a social structure. In an effective display of the ways in which private desire can be projected as ruthless Law, Zofloya himself casts Victoria into oblivion with a "loud demoniac laugh" at the novel's close (267). This is the "perverse" laugh of the desiring heroine herself as culture represents her.[3]

What recent critics seem to suggest is that "female Gothic," while not freeing women from the limitations placed on them in contemporary culture, at least suggested ways in which their victimization, inherent to the world outside Gothic fiction as well as within it, can be subverted both to turn patriarchal violence against itself and to claim a space for women. As Michelle Massé explains in her chapter on Gothic masochism, many things can be named as sources of conflict in Gothic fiction, "but all point, in the best Gothic tradition, to something more ominous." In her analysis, that "something" is "the refusal of the heroine's existence as subject."[4] That is why the question of female space is so fraught in these works, both haunted and supported by the spectral mother who challenges patriarchy with the threat of undomesticated female power. Even the more "shocking" of these novels, such as *Manfroné,* insist on a resilient and even at times intrepid heroine. The thrill of survival is matched, what is more, not by a paternal suitor who will protect, but rather a feminized hero who will join the heroine in her experience of the world and its vicissitudes. Admittedly, this seems little better than the patriarchal closure which had become inevitable in novels by the 1790s. But I would argue that this "little" is a "lot" of the reason that "female Gothic" became popular for women in the later eighteenth century and remained so for ensuing generations.

Incest, female abjection, isolation, horror: this is a story of women in pain. It does not, cannot end with the close of the eighteenth century. As these two novels demonstrate, the issues become, if anything, less clear, and the solutions even more elusive. *Manfroné* and *Zofloya* begin to suggest how complicated those questions will become. Between them, they offer a conclusion to this study precisely because they refuse to conclude. Wollstonecraft may have brought an abrupt end to female expectation, but Radcliffe and

Afterword

Dacre remind us that what dies can always be reawakened, especially in the complex world of the Gothic novel. Even at the end of the eighteenth century, women were only just beginning to find their place in fiction. The novelists I discuss have a clear hope of finding a different world for themselves somewhere, but it is not quite clear where that might be. If Radcliffe and Dacre carry their fictional encounters into another world, they do so in the hope, however misdirected, that it might offer a more profound realization of female desire than worldly resolutions have offered. In the nineteenth century women may find a way to put worldly hopes into successful fictional form. In the eighteenth, transgressive desire must be placed in the margins of narrative in order to avoid the implicit dictates of narrative form; the "dominant fiction" replicates a cultural determination of personal meaning after all.[5] If, later on, women learn to speak more directly for themselves, they can do so only to the degree that these intrepid writers opened a space for them.

I have attempted to discuss a range of novels that come very close to defying convention in a number of ways. If I have not been sanguine about their subversive potential, and if I have shown them to end in desultory frustration, I hope that I have not suggested that their efforts were literary or social failures. For what the fiction of the latter half of the eighteenth century shows is the remarkable inventiveness of these novelists, their indefatigable willingness to explore transgressive possibilities, and their insurmountable sense of the obstacles facing women's happiness. If I have been at all successful in teasing out the "queer" possibilities of these texts, if I have helped to make them more accessible to studies of the history of sexuality and gender, I hope that I have done so in the remarkable context that these works suggest and not without an awareness of their particular historical significance.

I have chosen to write about a series of novels that have a certain spirit in common. I would like to call that a spirit of resistance, and I would like to locate it in the affectional relationships that these writers describe. On one hand defying the cultural dictates of domestic ideology and the practical effects of parental control, and on the other eroticizing relations that the family would naturalize—relations, that is, such as sister, brother, father, and mother—these novelists have accomplished more than literary history has ever allowed them. In violating the dictates of conservative culture, these women have opened vistas that our own culture has hardly begun to contemplate. What is queer about these works is their refusal to conform to heteronormative expectation as well as their sheer inventiveness of imagined alternatives. The novelists I have discussed offer romantic friends, effeminized male partners, devoted sisterly affection, mother-daughter bonds, maimed and disfigured heroines, bleeding heroes, abject paternal obsession, and last, but by no means least, lesbian couples. No wonder the novel became the most popular literary form. For the first time, women were able to take a literary form and invest it with some of their own most deeply felt concerns. If the result in these few novels is as complex as I hope my analyses suggest, then the implications for the history of literature as well as culture are nothing less than profound.

NOTES

Introduction

1. Cheryl Turner, *Living by the Pen: Women Writers in the Eighteenth Century* (New York: Routledge, 1992), 39.

2. See Emma Donoghue, *Passions between Women: British Lesbian Culture 1668–1801* (London: Routledge, 1993), 2–3, 7.

3. Slavoj Žižek, *The Sublime Object of Ideology* (London: Verso, 1989), 26.

4. For a further articulation of this argument, see my essay "Amelia's Nose; or, Sensibility and Its Symptoms," *The Eighteenth Century: Theory and Interpretation* 36 (1995): 139–56.

5. See, for instance, Janet Todd, *Sensibility, an Introduction* (New York: Methuen, 1986), 61–62: "By the last decades of the [eighteenth] century, as the tide began to turn against a sensibility which was judged effeminate, destabilizing, marginally provincial and detrimental to Christian precepts, feminine sensibility, when embraced, often had a decadent quality about it, a self-indulgent physicality and a self-contemplating vanity. The aesthetic experience obscured the ethical, and emotion, severed from any kind of rationality or action, degenerated into impulse and sensation."

6. See, for instance, G. J. Barker-Benfield, *The Culture of Sensibility: Sex and Society in Eighteenth-Century Britain* (Chicago: University of Chicago Press, 1992), 37–103; Judith Frank, "'A Man Who Laughs Is Never Dangerous': Character and Class in Sterne's *A Sentimental Journey*," *ELH* 56 (1989): 97–124; Robert Markley, "Sentimentality as Performance: Shaftesbury, Sterne, and the Theatrics of Virtue," in *The New Eighteenth Century*, ed. Felicity Nussbaum and Laura Brown (New York: Methuen, 1987), 210–30; John Mullan, *Sentiment and Sociability: Language and Feeling in the Eighteenth Century* (Oxford: Clarendon, 1988), 114–46.

7. Žižek, *The Sublime Object of Ideology*, 69; see further, "The Dialectics of Symptom," 55–84.

8. Any antisodomitical volume might suggest the form that "worse" might take. In one, for instance, any sign of effeminacy, such as male kissing in public, is conidered the sign of sodomy; see *Satan's Harvest Home* (1749; rpt. New York: Garland, 1985), 50–55. For a discussion of the female implications of sensibility, see Todd, *Sensibility*, 110–28, and Barker-Benfield, *The Culture of Sensibility*, 104–53.

9. Michel Foucault, *The History of Sexuality*, vol. 1: *An Introduction* (1976), trans. Robert Hurley (New York: Vintage–Random House, 1980), 116.

10. As Foucault says in *The Birth of the Clinic,* "Western man could constitute himself in his own eyes as an object of science, he grasped himself within his language, and gave himself, in himself and by himself, a discursive existence, only in the opening created by his own elimination: . . . from the integration of death into medical thought is born a medicine that is given as a science of the individual." Michel Foucault, *The Birth of the Clinic: An Archaeology of Medical Perception* (1963), trans. A. M. Sheridan Smith (London: Tavistock, 1973), 197; for an extended discussion of the gendering of scientific language, see also Londa Schiebinger, *The Mind Has No Sex? Women in the Origin of Modern Science* (Cambridge: Harvard University Press, 1989).

11. Nancy Armstrong, *Desire and Domestic Fiction: A Political History of the Novel* (Oxford: Oxford University Press, 1987), 49.

12. The works to which I refer include Ros Ballaster, *Seductive Forms: Women's Amatory Fiction from 1684 to 1740* (Oxford: Oxford University Press, 1992); Mary Ann Schofield, *Masking and Unmasking the Female Mind: Disguising Romances in Feminine Fiction, 1713–1799* (Newark: University of Delaware Press, 1990); Janet Spencer, *The Rise of the Woman Novelist, from Aphra Behn to Jane Austen* (Oxford: Blackwell, 1986); Janet Todd, *The Sign of Angellica: Women, Writing and Fiction, 1660–1800* (London: Virago, 1989); and Turner, *Living by the Pen.*

13. Nancy Armstrong, *Desire and Domestic Fiction: A Political History of the Novel*; Terry Castle, *Masquerade and Civilization: The Carnivalesque in Eighteenth-Century English Culture and Fiction* (Stanford: Stanford University Press, 1986) and *The Female Thermometer: 18th-Century Culture and the Invention of the Uncanny* (New York: Oxford University Press, 1995); Margaret Ann Doody, *Frances Burney: The Life in the Works* (New Brunswick, N.J.: Rutgers University Press, 1988); Julia Epstein, *The Iron Pen: Frances Burney and the Politics of Women's Writing* (Madison: University of Wisconsin Press, 1989); Catherine Gallagher, *Nobody's Story: The Vanishing Act of Women Writers in the Marketplace, 1670–1820* (Berkeley: University of California Press, 1994); Claudia L. Johnson, *Equivocal Beings: Politics, Gender, and Sentimentality in the 1790s* (Chicago: University of Chicago Press, 1995); Felicity A. Nussbaum, *Torrid Zones: Maternity, Sexuality, and Empire in Eighteenth-Century English Narratives* (Baltimore: Johns Hopkins University Press, 1995); Mary Poovey, *The Proper Lady and the Woman Writer: Ideology as Style in the Works of Mary Wollstonecraft, Mary Shelley, and Jane Austen* (Chicago: University of Chicago Press, 1984); Patricia Meyer Spacks, *Desire and Truth: Functions of Plot in Eighteenth-Century English Novels* (Chicago: University of Chicago Press, 1990); and Kristina Straub, *Divided Fictions: Frances Burney and Feminist Strategy* (Lexington: University of Kentucky Press, 1987).

14. See, for instance, Armstrong, *Desire and Domestic Fiction,* 14–27; Todd, *The Sign of Angellica,* 5; Gallagher, *Nobody's Story,* 145; Poovey, *The Proper Lady,* 38–43; and Johnson, *Equivocal Beings,* 14–19.

15. Gallagher, *Nobody's Story,* xi–xiii.

16. Ibid., 165. Gallagher qualifies the last remark by saying that "a few seventeenth- and early eighteenth-century narratives were forthrightly fictional, just as some late eighteenth-century stories insisted on their referentiality, and still others asked the readers to switch back and forth between referential and nonreferential assumptions. There was no sudden novelistic revolution that purged English narra-

tive of somebody and replaced him or her with nobody. Nevertheless, in the middle decades of the century, fictional nobodies became the more popular and respectable protagonists" (165).

17. Todd, *The Sign of Angellica,* 9.

18. This claim is repeated throughout *Desire and Domestic Fiction*; see, for instance, 14–27.

19. Johnson, *Equivocal Beings,* 14.

20. Johnson makes quite a different point about "maternal" fathers. In discussing Burney's *Camilla,* for instance, she argues that "Mr. Tyrold practices . . . 'melting humanity.' But in a world which privileges the sensitivity of men, anything bordering on stoic self-possession and indifference in a woman . . . is held in much suspicion" (*Equivocal Beings,* 147).

21. See, for instance, Susan C. Greenfield, "Veiled Desire: Mother-Daughter Love and Sexual Imagery in Ann Radcliffe's *The Italian," The Eighteenth Century: Theory and Interpretation* 33 (1992): 73–89; and Johnson, *Equivocal Beings,* 162–63 and 134–35.

22. Foucault, *Introduction,* 103–14.

23. The expression is taken from the opening of Mary Wollstonecraft's *The Wrongs of Woman* (1798), Gary Kelly, ed. (Oxford: Oxford University Press, 1991), 75.

24. Teresa de Lauretis, *Alice Doesn't: Feminism, Semiotics, Cinema* (Blooming-ton: Indiana University Press, 1984), 106.

25. Ibid., 123.

26. Ibid., 106, 133.

27. Ibid., 133.

28. For a discussion of *Dracula* along these lines, see Christopher Craft, *Another Kind of Love, Male Homosexual Desire in English Discourse, 1850–1920* (Berke-ley: University of California Press, 1994), 85–90.

29. De Lauretis, *Alice Doesn't,* 139.

30. Leopold Damrosch, *God's Plot and Man's Stories: Studies in the Fictional Imagination from Milton to Fielding* (Chicago: University of Chicago Press, 1985), 10.

31. My use of the term *patriarchal* from *patriarchy* —"government by the father or eldest male of the family" (*OED*)—is not anachronistic. I am using the term to describe a particular set of historical circumstances as well as the general feeling of male control that many women of the later eighteenth century shared. For a fuller discussion of the implications of "patriarchy," see Michael McKeon, "Historicizing Patriarchy: The Emergence of Gender Difference in England, 1660–1760," *Eight-eenth-Century Studies* 28 (1995): 295–322.

32. Spacks, *Desire and Truth,* 6. This book offers the most useful discussion of plot in eighteenth-century novels that is available to scholars of the period, and it has been of use throughout this study.

33. See Tania Modleski, *Loving with a Vengeance* (New York: Routledge, 1982), 59–84; and Kate Ferguson Ellis, *The Contested Castle: Gothic Novels and the Subversion of Domestic Ideology* (Urbana: University of Illinois Press, 1989), 3–19. See also Anne Williams, *Art of Darkness: A Poetics of the Gothic* (Chicago: Univer-sity of Chicago Press, 1995), 1–24; and Susan Wolstenholme, *Gothic (Re)Visions:*

Writing Women as Readers (Albany: State University of New York Press, 1993), 3–36.

34. Charlotte Lennox, *The Female Quixote, Or, The Adventures of Arabella* (1752), ed. Margaret Dalziel, with an introduction by Margaret Doody and chronology and appendix by Duncan Isles (Oxford: Oxford University Press, 1989), 327.

35. De Lauretis, *Alice Doesn't*, 132–33; see also Laura Mulvey, "Visual Pleasure and Narrative Cinema," *Screen* 16, no. 3 (Autumn 1975): 6–18.

36. Turner, *Living by the Pen*, 130.

37. Johnson, *Equivocal Beings*, 11.

38. See, for instance, Armstrong, *Desire and Domestic Fiction*, 61–69.

39. See Randolph Trumbach, *Marriage, Sex, and the Family in England, 1660–1800*, 44 vols. (New York: Garland, 1985); vols. 9a–g are *Trials for Adultery*, and vols. 21a and b, *Select Trials at the Sessions House in the Old Bailey*.

40. *Trials for Adultery* 1 [9a]: iv.

41. The structures of these "trials" almost all take the shape of a husband's divorcing his wife. They begin with a "Libel" denouncing the woman, followed by an assortment of witness's depositions—the most lurid element in the "case"—and ending in a "sentence." To be fair, there are cases in which a woman divorces her husband (often when she has contracted a life-threatening venereal disease), but these cases are vastly in the minority. For a more complete study of eighteenth-century divorce, see Lawrence Stone, *Broken Lives: Separation and Divorce in England 1660–1857* (Oxford: Oxford University Press, 1993) and *Road to Divorce: England 1530–1987* (Oxford: Oxford University Press, 1990).

42. Rachel Blau DuPlessis, *Writing beyond the Ending: Narrative Strategies of Twentieth-Century Women Writers* (Bloomington: Indiana University Press, 1985), 1–2.

43. See Poovey, *The Proper Lady and the Woman Writer*, 38–43; Armstrong, *Desire and Domestic Fiction*, 42–58.

44. See Armstrong, *Desire and Domestic Fiction*, 28–58.

45. DuPlessis, *Writing beyond the Ending*, 3.

46. For Teresa de Lauretis, "However varied conditions of presence of the narrative form in fictional genres, rituals or social discourses, its movement seems to be that of a passage, a transformation predicted on the figure of a hero, a mythical subject. While this is already common knowledge, what has remained largely unanalyzed is how this view of myth and narrative rests on a specific assumption about sexual difference" (*Alice Doesn't*, 113; see also 111–24). See also Marilyn Farwell, "Heterosexual Plots and Lesbian Subtexts: Toward a Theory of Lesbian Narrative Space," in *Lesbian Texts and Contexts*, ed. Karla Jay and Joanne Glasgow (New York: New York University Press, 1990), 91–103.

47. "Crowded with outrageous and rigidly gendered contests over the dignity of meaningful suffering, the works of Wollstonecraft, Radcliffe, and Burney culminate as well as assail the sentimental tradition at precisely that moment when it was being reasserted in extreme forms as a political imperative" (Johnson, *Equivocal Beings*, 14).

48. See, for instance, Gary Kelly, *The English Jacobin Novel, 1780–1805* (Oxford: Clarendon, 1976).

49. Donoghue, *Passions between Women*, 22.

ONE / Brotherly Love in *David Simple*

1. *The Adventures of David Simple* was published in two volumes in 1744, and reprinted in a revised form with Henry Fielding's preface and changes in the same year. Nine years later, after three sisters had died and just before Henry himself died, Sarah Fielding published *Volume the Last,* a sequel to and in an important sense a revision of the earlier tale. What Fielding does in *Volume the Last,* as I shall show, is to intensify the issues that are struggling beneath the surface of *David Simple* in compelling and perhaps subversive ways. Deborah Downs-Miers suggests some of the ways in which Sarah Fielding works against convention; see "Springing the Trap: Subtexts and Subversions," in *Fetter'd or Free? British Women Novelists, 1670–1815,* ed. Mary Anne Schofield and Cecilia Macheski (Athens, Ohio: Ohio University Press, 1986), 311–13; see also Gerard A. Barker, "*David Simple*: The Novel of Sensibility in Embryo," *Modern Language Studies* 2 (1982): 69–80; and Jane Spencer, *The Rise of the Woman Novelist, from Aphra Behn to Jane Austen* (Oxford: Blackwell, 1986), 92–95.

2. Sarah Fielding, *The Adventures of David Simple,* ed. Malcolm Kelsall (Oxford: Oxford University Press, 1987), 106; further references are included in the text.

3. Robert Markley, "Sentimentality as Performance: Shaftesbury, Sterne, and the Theatrics of Virtue," in *The New Eighteenth Century: Theory, Politics, English Literature,* ed. Felicity Nussbaum and Laura Brown (New York: Methuen, 1987), 211.

4. See Kate Ferguson Ellis, *The Contested Castle: Gothic Novels and the Subversion of Domestic Ideology* (Urbana: University of Illinois Press, 1989), 3–19.

5. For a discussion of the feminist implications of Cynthia's early career, see Downs-Miers, "Springing the Trap," 311–12; see also Spencer, *The Rise of the Woman Novelist,* 93–95. For a discussion of the woman as "goods" to be disposed of, see Gayle Rubin, "The Traffic in Women: Notes toward a Political Economy of Sex," in *Toward an Anthropology of Women,* ed. Rayna Reiter (New York: Monthly Review Press, 1975), 157–210.

6. Slavoj Žižek, *Sublime Object of Ideology* (London: Verso, 1989), 78.

7. See Ellen Pollak, "*Moll Flanders,* Incest, and the Structure of Exchange," *The Eighteenth Century: Theory and Interpretation* 30 (1989): 3–21.

8. Terri Nickel, "'Ingenious Torment': Incest, Family, and the Structure of Community in the Work of Sarah Fielding," *The Eighteenth Century: Theory and Interpretation* 36 (1995): 235.

9. Dr. Susan Forward and Craig Buck, *Betrayal of Innocence: Incest and Its Devastation* (New York: Viking-Penguin, 1979), 83; see also Jean Renvoize, *Incest: A Family Pattern* (London: Routledge and Kegan Paul, 1982).

10. Claude Lévi-Strauss, *The Elementary Structures of Kinship* (1949), trans. James Harle Bell and Richard von Sturmer, ed. Rodney Needham (Boston: Beacon, 1969), 44–45; see also Rubin, "The Traffic in Women."

11. Emile Durkheim, *Incest: The Nature and Origin of the Taboo,* together with "The Origins and the Development of the Incest Taboo," by Albert Ellis, Ph.D. (1898), trans. Edward Sagarin (New York: Lyle Stuart, 1963), 84–86.

12. Julia Kristeva, *Powers of Horror: An Essay on Abjection* (1980), trans. Leon S. Roudiez (New York: Columbia University Press, 1982), 71.

13. Martin C. Battestin has talked at length about the figure of incest in the work of Henry and Sarah Fielding; see "Henry Fielding, Sarah Fielding, and 'the dreadful sin of incest,'" *Novel* 13 (1979): 6–18; see also Martin C. Battestin, with Ruthe R. Battestin, *Henry Fielding: A Life* (London: Routledge, 1989), 27–30.

14. Nickel, "'Ingenious Torment'," 239.

15. Michel Foucault, *The History of Sexuality*, vol. 1: *An Introduction* (1976), trans. Robert Hurley (New York: Vintage–Random House, 1980), 69.

16. John Fry, *The Case of Marriages Between Near Kindred Particularly Considered, With Respect to The Doctrine of Scripture, The Law of Nature, and The Laws of England* (1756), in *The Marriage Prohibitions Controversy: Five Tracts,* ed. Randolph Trumbach (New York: Garland, 1985), 3–4. Further references are included in the text. For further incest tracts, see Nickel, "'Ingenious Torment'," 241–42.

17. Among other interesting tracts in Trumbach's collection, John Alleyn's *"The Legal Decrees of Marriage Stated and Considered in a Series of Letters to a Friend"* (1775) argues with Fry, claiming that "should the attempt to reduce matrimonial prohibitions to the standard of rational law and sound policy, be attended with success, what a vast accumulation of happiness would ensue!" (4).

18. On Collier as the author of the preface, see Malcolm Kelsall, "Notes," in *The Adventures of David Simple,* by Sarah Fielding (Oxford: Oxford University Press, 1987), 435; see Spencer, *The Rise of the Woman Novelist,* 207–208, for a discussion of the feminist implications of *The Cry.*

19. Spencer, *The Rise of the Woman Novelist,* 208.

20. Rachel Blau DuPlessis, *Writing beyond the Ending: Narrative Strategies of Twentieth-Century Women Writers* (Bloomington: Indiana University Press, 1985), 5; see also Teresa de Lauretis, *Alice Doesn't: Feminism, Semiotics, Cinema* (Bloomington: Indiana University Press, 1984), 121: "The work of narrative . . . is a mapping of differences, and specifically, first and foremost, of sexual difference into each text."

21. Spencer, *The Rise of the Woman Novelist,* 119.

22. See R. F. Brissenden, *Virtue in Distress: Studies in the Novel of Sentiment from Richardson to Sade* (London: Macmillan, 1974), 40–49.

23. Leo Braudy, "The Form of the Sentimental Novel," *Novel* 7 (1973): 6–7.

24. Žižek says, quoting Hegel, that "Man is . . . 'an animal sick unto death,' an animal extorted by an insatiable parasite (reason, *logos,* language)"; see *The Sublime Object of Ideology,* 4–5.

25. See Spencer, *The Rise of the Woman Novelist,* 118–22, for a discussion of Fielding's feminism.

26. For a discussion of the difficulties of childbirth for eighteenth-century women, see Deborah D. Rogers, "Eighteenth-Century Literary Depictions of Childbirth in the Historical Context of Mutilation and Mortality: The Case of *Pamela," The Centennial Review* 37 (1993): 305–24.

TWO / Female Abjection in *A Simple Story*

1. Julia Kristeva, *Powers of Horror: An Essay on Abjection,* trans. Leon S. Roudiez (New York: Columbia University Press, 1982), 18; see also Judith Butler, *Bodies That Matter: On the Discursive Limits of Sex* (New York: Routledge, 1993),

1–12, 243 n. 2. For an extended discussion of abjection, see my essay "'The Voice of Nature' in Gray's *Elegy*," in *Homosexuality in Renaissance and Enlightenment England: Literary Representations in Historical Context,* ed. Claude J. Summers (New York: Haworth Press, 1992), 208–209.

2. In addition to these three characters, there are only three others of importance: Mr. Sandford, a stern mentor and spiritual guide to Dorriforth; Miss Woodley, a devoted friend, first to Miss Milner and then to her daughter; and Mr. Rushbrook, nephew of Dorriforth, son of a sister he has disowned, whom Miss Milner has befriended and brought into the family and whom Dorriforth adopts as his heir.

3. See Terry Castle, *Masquerade and Civilization: The Carnivalesque in Eighteenth-Century English Culture and Fiction* (Stanford: Stanford University Press, 1986), 323; Castle also notes a similarity between *A Simple Story* and *Wuthering Heights*. For her it is "because of the way Inchbald succeeds in communicating, with startling economy, reserves of the most intense feeling" (*Masquerade and Civilization,* 291).

4. Castle calls *A Simple Story* "a restlessly anti-authoritarian" work, *Masquerade and Civilization,* 292; Jane Spencer has a similar response, but a different emphasis: "Inchbald links her heroine's shocking desire for Dorriforth to her struggle against his control over her, and thus reveals, what the early feminist position could not acknowledge, the disruptive potential of female desire"; Jane Spencer, Introduction, *A Simple Story* (Oxford: Oxford University Press, 1991), xv. See also Gary Kelly, *The English Jacobin Novel* (Oxford: Oxford University Press, 1976), 7. Kelly argues persuasively that Elizabeth Inchbald was among a group of novelists who "opposed tyranny and oppression, be it domestic, national, or international, spiritual or temporal" in the spirit of English Jacobinism (7). On the problems of using *patriarchal* to describe eighteenth-century culture, see Michael McKeon, "Historicizing Patriarchy: The Emergence of Gender Difference in England, 1660–1760," *Eighteenth-Century Studies* 28 (1995): 295–322.

5. I can only speak for one reader, myself. There is every reason to think that other readers would sense Miss Milner's crisis sooner than I did or indeed be aware of it from the first. I do think, though, that part of the effect of the novel is the brilliant way in which it uncovers emotional distress by little signs and partially hidden expressions.

6. See Cynthia Griffin Wolff, "The Radcliffean Gothic Model: A Form for Feminine Sexuality," *Modern Language Studies* 9 (1979): 98–113.

7. Castle discusses precedents in French fiction; see *Masquerade and Civilization,* 300–301.

8. Ibid., 293.

9. Of course, not all fathers of sensibility are kindly, as novels such as *David Simple* and *Millenium Hall* imply; but nevertheless the ideal of paternal kindness is articulated in a variety of places in eighteenth-century novels by both women and men.

10. Michelle A. Massé, *In the Name of Love: Women, Masochism, and the Gothic* (Ithaca: Cornell University Press, 1992), 18.

11. Kristeva, *Power of Horror,* 85.

12. Elizabeth Inchbald, *A Simple Story,* ed. J. M. S. Tompkins, with an introduction by Jane Spencer (Oxford: Oxford University Press, 1991), 154; further references are included in the text.

13. Spencer, "Introduction," *A Simple Story*, xix.

14. Mary Wollstonecraft, *Analytical Review* 10 (1791): 101–102; see Spencer, "Introduction," *A Simple Story*, xiv.

15. For a discussion of the uses of adultery in fiction, see Tony Tanner, *Adultery in the Novel: Contract and Transgression* (Baltimore: Johns Hopkins University Press, 1979), 3–112.

16. *Trials for Adultery: Or, the History of Divorces* (1779), ed. Randolph Trumbach, in *Marriage, Sex, and the Family in England, 1660–1800*, vols. 9a–g; on the question of the "adultery trials" and "female divorce," see, for instance, Gary Kelly, "Explanatory Notes," *Mary and The Wrongs of Woman*, by Mary Wollstonecraft (Oxford: Oxford University Press, 1991), 230.

17. Massé, *In the Name of Love*, 15.

18. Tompkins notes the "Gothic" atmosphere at the beginning of volume 3; see notes to *A Simple Story*, 344.

19. Castle, *Masquerade and Civilization*, 321.

20. Massé, *In the Name of Love*, 45–46.

21. Ibid., 48; see also Jessica Benjamin, *The Bonds of Love: Psychoanalysis, Feminism, and the Problem of Domination* (New York: Pantheon, 1988), 31.

22. Kristeva, *Powers of Horror*, 15; see also Massé, *In the Name of Love*, n. 45.

23. Massé, *In the Name of Love*, 51.

24. Kristeva, *Powers of Horror*, 2.

25. Castle, *Masquerade and Civilization*, 325.

26. The most useful theorization of such triangulation is that found in Eve Kosofsky Sedgwick, *Between Men: English Literature and Male Homosocial Desire* (New York: Columbia University Press, 1985), 1–27.

27. Castle, *Masquerade and Civilization*, 319.

THREE / Female Gothic (1): Friends and Mothers

1. Horace Walpole, *The Castle of Otranto, A Gothic Story*, 1764, ed. W. S. Lewis and Joseph N. Reed, Jr. (Oxford: Oxford University Press, 1982), 25.

2. Tania Modleski, *Loving with a Vengeance: Mass-Produced Fantasies for Women* (1982; rpt. New York: Routledge, 1988), 20. More recent discussions of "female Gothic" include Claudia Johnson, *Equivocal Beings: Politics, Gender, and Sentimentality in the 1790s* (Chicago: University of Chicago Press, 1995); Anne Williams, *Art of Darkness: A Poetics of Gothic* (Chicago: University of Chicago Press, 1995); and Susan Wolstenholme, *Gothic (Re)Visions: Writing Women as Readers* (Albany: State University of New York Press, 1993).

3. Fredric Jameson, "Reification and Utopia in Mass Culture," *Social Text* 1 (1979): 141; quoted in Modleski, *Loving with a Vengeance*, 27.

4. Williams, *Art of Darkness*, 141.

5. Susan Wolstenholme puts the matter succinctly: "All Gothic fiction might be said to employ a kind of sadomasochism" (*Gothic (Re)Visions*, 11); for the most extensive discussion of female Gothic masochism, see Michelle A. Massé, *In the Name of Love: Women, Masochism, and the Gothic* (Ithaca: Cornell University Press, 1992).

6. Michel Foucault, *The History of Sexuality,* vol. 1: *An Introduction* (1976), trans. Robert Hurley (New York: Vintage–Random House, 1980), 32–35.

7. See "Amelia's Nose; or, Sensibility and Its Symptoms," *The Eighteenth Century: Theory and Interpretation* 36 (1995): 139–41.

8. Slavoj Žižek, *The Sublime Object of Ideology* (London: Verso, 1989), 75.

9. Walpole, *The Castle of Otranto,* 7. I will argue that something different is going on in works by women, and that later heroines, despite outward similarities, are quite different from Walpole's persecuted beauty.

10. See Kenneth W. Graham, ed., *Gothic Fictions: Prohibitions/Transgressions* (New York: AMS Press, 1989), for a variety of essays that address the question of transgression in Gothic fiction; also see Peter Stallybrass and Allon White, *The Politics and Poetics of Transgression* (Ithaca: Cornell University Press, 1986).

11. James Trainer, Introduction, *The Old English Baron* (Oxford: Oxford University Press, 1967), xiv.

12. Ibid.

13. Clara Reeve, *The Old English Baron* (1777), ed. James Trainer (Oxford: Oxford University Press, 1967), 14; further references are included in the text.

14. Terry Castle, *The Female Thermometer: 18th-Century Culture and the Invention of the Uncanny* (Oxford: Oxford University Press, 1995), 10.

15. Eve Kosofsky Sedgwick, *Between Men: English Literature and Male Homosocial Desire* (New York: Columbia University Press, 1985), 25.

16. Maurice Lévy, *Le Roman "Gothique" Anglais, 1764–1824,* Publications de la Faculté des Letters et Sciences Humaines de Toulouse, Serie A, Tome 9 (Paris: Gallimard, 1968), 203 [my translation].

17. See, for instance, Edmund Burke, *Philosophical Enquiry into the Origin of Our Ideas of the Sublime and the Beautiful* (1757), 2nd ed. (Menston: Scolar, 1970).

18. Like the sublime, the picturesque was a fully theorized aesthetic response. See, for instance, William Gilpin, *Three Essays on Picturesque Beauty* (London: 1792).

19. Charlotte Smith, *Emmeline, The Orphan of the Castle* (1788), ed. Anne Henry Ehrenpreis (Oxford: Oxford University Press, 1971), 10–11; further references are included in the text.

20. J. M. S. Tompkins cites Emmeline as the first heroine to be set against the grim backdrop of a Gothic castle; see *The Popular Novel in England, 1770–1800* (London: Constable, 1932), 266. Anne Henry Ehrenpreis argues that Walpole's Isabella was really the first; see Ehrenpreis, Introduction, *Emmeline,* xi. Ehrenpreis says, further, that "for all its structural laxity—which, by contemporary standards, was no vice—*Emmeline* did break new ground. If, to the innovations already mentioned, are added Mrs. Smith's use of her own poetry within a prose narrative, and her sensitive descriptions of landscape, it is possible to see why the public of 1788 felt excited, and why *Emmeline* secured 'a hold upon all readers of true taste, of a new and most captivating kind'" (xv). The quotation is from Sir Egerton Bridges, *Censuria Literaria,* 2nd ed. (London: 1815) vii: 248.

21. Castle, *The Female Thermometer,* 15.

22. See Castle, *The Female Thermometer,* 120–39.

23. See, for instance, Cynthia Griffin Wolff, "The Radcliffean Gothic Model: A Form for Feminine Sexuality," *Modern Language Studies* 9 (1979): 98–113; and

Jane Spencer, *The Rise of the Woman Novelist, from Aphra Behn to Jane Austen* (Oxford: Blackwell, 1986), 201.

24. Ehrenpreis suggests that the character Mr. Stafford is a likeness of her husband: see her introduction, viii–ix.

25. Massé, *In the Name of Love,* 18; see also Nancy Chodorow, *The Reproduction of Mothering: Psychoanalysis and the Sociology of Gender* (Berkeley: University of California Press, 1978), 35; and Freud, "The Uncanny," in *The Standard Edition of the Complete Psychological Works of Sigmund Freud,* trans. James Strachey et al. (London: Hogarth, 1919) 17: 241, 220.

26. Clare Kahane, "The Gothic Mirror," in *The (M)other Tongue: Essays in Feminist Psychoanalytic Interpretation,* ed. Claire Kahane Shirley Nelson Garner and Madelon Springnether (Ithaca: Cornell University Press, 1985), 336; in a recent book, Felicity Nussbaum confronts "maternity as the central metaphor for female difference," *Torrid Zones: Maternity, Sexuality, and Empire in Eighteenth-Century English Narratives* (Baltimore: Johns Hopkins University Press, 1995), 24; see further 21–46.

27. Sophia Lee, *The Recess, Or, A Tale of Other Times,* 3 vols., 1783–1785 (New York: Arno, 1972) 1: 2–3. For an intriguing reading of *The Recess,* see Jayne Elizabeth Lewis, "'Ev'ry Lost Relation': Historical Fictions and Sentimental Incidents in Sophia Lee's *The Recess,*" *Eighteenth-Century Fiction* 7 (1995): 165–84. Lewis points out that "Mary's transformation into a domestic and sentimental icon accompanied and ultimately sped the feminization and domestication of British culture" (181). I hope that this chapter has helped to explain what was at stake in that transformation and what kinds of same-sex erotic energy the term "feminization" continues to mask in eighteenth-century studies.

28. For a more thorough discussion of sister-brother incest, see pp. 26–32, above.

29. Lévi-Strauss, *The Elementary Structures of Kinship* (1949), trans. James Harle Bell and Richard von Sturmer; ed. and trans. Rodney Needham (Boston: Beacon, 1969), 29.

30. See Nussbaum, *Torrid Zones,* 135–62.

31. Mary Poovey, *The Proper Lady and the Woman Writer: Ideology as Style in the Works of Mary Wollstonecraft, Mary Shelley, and Jane Austen* (Chicago: University of Chicago Press, 1984), 21: "Given the voraciousness that female desire was supposed to have, the surest safeguard against overindulgence was not to allow or admit to appetites of any kind."

FOUR / Sisterly Love in *Sense and Sensibility*

1. Eve Kosofsky Sedgwick, "Jane Austen and the Masturbating Girl," in *Tendencies* (Durham: Duke University Press, 1993), 109.

2. Ibid., 110.

3. Ibid., 114.

4. Eve Kosofsky Sedgwick, *Between Men: English Literature and Male Homosocial Desire* (New York: Columbia University Press, 1985), 25.

5. Terry Castle, *The Apparitional Lesbian: Female Homosexuality and Modern Culture* (New York: Columbia University Press, 1993), 4–5.

6. Terry Castle, "Sister-Sister," *London Review of Books* (August 3, 1995): 3.

7. Emma Donoghue, *Passions between Women: British Lesbian Culture, 1688–1801* (London: Scarlett, 1993); see chapter 4, "A Sincere and Tender Passion," 109–50.

8. Although published in 1811, *Sense and Sensibility* displays an interest in the concerns that beset other novels in this study. Early versions of this novel appeared in the 1790s. Recent discussions of this novel which address this issue include the chapter on *Sense and Sensibility* in Tony Tanner, *Jane Austen* (Cambridge: Harvard University Press, 1986), 75–102; Nina Auerbach, *Romantic Imprisonment: Women and Other Glorified Outcasts* (New York: Columbia University Press, 1985), 11–15; and John Wiltshire, *Jane Austen and the Body* (Cambridge: Cambridge University Press, 1992), 24–61; see also Claudia L. Johnson, *Equivocal Beings: Politics, Gender, and Sentimentality in the 1790s* (Chicago: University of Chicago Press, 1995).

9. Jane Austen, *Sense and Sensibility* (1811), ed. James Kinsley and Claire Lamont (Oxford: Oxford University Press, 1970), 155–56; further references to this edition are included parenthetically in the text.

10. See, for instance, Tony Tanner, *Jane Austen*, 75–102.

11. Wiltshire, *Jane Austen and the Body*, 41, 47; see further 41–61.

12. Mary Poovey suggests that "between these antinomies [of sense and sensibility] there is no easy choice but rather myriads of possible combinations, each understood in terms of costs and benefits, sacrifices and opportunities" (*The Proper Lady and the Woman Writer: Ideology as Style in the Works of Mary Wollstonecraft, Mary Shelley, and Jane Austen* [Chicago: University of Chicago Press, 1984], 44).

13. Critics have argued that Elinor is not without feeling early in the novel. See, for instance, Jean Hagstrum, *Sex and Sensibility: Ideal and Erotic Love from Milton to Mozart* (Chicago: University of Chicago Press, 1980), 271–72.

14. Michel Foucault, *Madness and Civilization: A History of Insanity in the Age of Reason* (1961), trans. Richard Howard (New York: Random House, 1965), 157.

15. Tanner, *Jane Austen*, 85–88; this essay appeared earlier as an introduction to *Sense and Sensibility* (Harmondsworth: Penguin, 1969).

16. See John A. Dussinger, *The Discourse of the Mind in Eighteenth-Century Fiction* (The Hague: Mouton, 1974), 37–39; Dussinger uses Hume's version of the "self" as an imaginary construct of continuous perceptions—"merely a habit of thinking, and the fiction of the perceiving ego"—to suggest that much of the literature of sensibility addresses the resulting uneasiness about permanence of selfhood by means of the kind of moment-to-moment expression that Northrop Frye implies by his term "literature of process" (see Frye, "Towards Defining an Age of Sensibility," in *Fables of Identity: Studies in Poetic Mythology* [New York: Harcourt, 1963], 130–31). Dussinger says further that "some of the most 'characteristic' works of fiction in this period portray the mind restless to the end and ever in doubt about the self" (39).

17. See Tanner, *Jane Austen*, 90–93. Edward Joseph Shoben, Jr. talks about the "unbridled expression of emotion" as a danger for Austen; see "Impulse and Virtue in Jane Austen: *Sense and Sensibility* in Two Centuries" *Hudson Review* 25 (1982–83): 338. Susan Morgan suggests that Marianne "collaps[es] the distinction between feeling and expression, thus making expression spontaneous and inevitable" (*In the*

Meantime: Character and Perception in Jane Austen [Chicago: University of Chicago Press, 1980], 121). Later, she calls this Marianne's "personal integrity in language" (123).

18. Cheyne, *The English Malady*, ed. Eric T. Carlson, M.D. (Delmar, N.Y.: Scholar's Facsimiles and Reprints, 1976), 71–72.

19. See Tanner, *Jane Austen*, 109–11; see also Poovey, who demonstrates as a paradox of propriety the fear of sexuality implicit in the praise of a woman's "sensibility of heart" in the eighteenth century (*The Proper Lady*, 18–19).

20. Cheyne, *The English Malady*, 127.

21. Foucault, *Madness and Civilization*, 146–50. I am indebted to Tanner's useful discussion of Foucault's analysis of madness and sensibility (see *Jane Austen*, 82–85); see also Richard Blackmore, *Treatise of the Spleen, Vapours, or Hypochondriachal and Hysterical Affections* (1725); and Robert James, *Medicinal Dictionary* (1743), under "hysteria."

22. Foucault, *Madness and Civilization*, 157–58.

23. Ibid., 220; see Tanner, *Jane Austen*, 83.

24. Foucault, *Madness and Civilization*, 158.

25. Poovey argues that "given the voraciousness that female desire was assumed to have, the surest safeguard against overindulgence was not to allow or admit to appetites of any kind. Thus women were encouraged to display no vanity, no passion, no assertive 'self' at all" (*The Proper Lady*, 21).

26. Michel Foucault, *The History of Sexuality*, vol. 1: *An Introduction* (1976), trans. Robert Hurley (New York: Vintage–Random House, 1980), 103–105.

27. Todd speaks of the love between the Austen sisters in *Women's Friendship in Literature* (New York: Columbia University Press, 1990), 400.

28. See "The Sacrifice of Privacy in *Sense and Sensibility*," *Tulsa Studies in Women's Literature* 7 (1988): 231–34.

29. See Tanner, *Jane Austen*, 86–88; also see Morgan, who says that "decorum . . . is a public avowal of continued feelings and thoughts, a way of behaving which sustains the potential in experience for active and changing relations between others and ourselves" (*In the Meantime*, 129).

30. Foucault, *The History of Sexuality*, 123.

31. James Edward Austen-Leigh, *Memoir of Jane Austen* (1871; rpt. Oxford: Oxford University Press, 1951), 17.

32. Castle, "Sister-Sister," 5.

FIVE / "Romantic Friendship" in *Millenium Hall*

1. "Utterly confused category" echoes Michel Foucault's description of sodomy in the eighteenth century; see Foucault, *The History of Sexuality*, vol. 1: *An Introduction* (1976), trans. Robert Hurley (New York: Vintage–Random House, 1980), 101; also see G. S. Rousseau, "The Pursuit of Homosexuality in the Eighteenth Century: 'Utterly Confused Category' and/or Rich Repository," *Eighteenth-Century Life* 9, n.s. 3 (1985): 132–68.

2. See Jane Spencer, Introduction to *Millenium Hall*, by Sarah Scott (New York: Penguin-Virago, 1986), xii; the most interesting recent discussion of this novel is that

found in Felicity A. Nussbaum, *Torrid Zones: Maternity, Sexuality, and Empire in Eighteenth-Century English Narratives* (Baltimore: Johns Hopkins University Press, 1995), 149–62. Nussbaum calls the world of the novel an "Orientalized feminotopia": "[a]n English counterpart to the seraglio with its mutes, eunuchs, and slaves in a female community, it plays on the connections between domestic femininity and women's structural kinship to the perverse, the monstrous, and the deformed" (151). In this chapter I am interested in the quality of affection between women, particularly those coded as mother and daughter, but the larger claims of Nussbaum's book are surely important to the argument I am making, as I hope this chapter will make clear.

3. The details of Sarah (Robinson) Scott's private life are becoming increasingly familiar. In brief outline: born in 1723 to an established Yorkshire family, Sarah Robinson began writing at an early age; her sister, with whom she was close, was the famous "bluestocking" Elizabeth Montague. In 1748 she met Lady Barbara Montague (no relation to her sister), the daughter of the first earl of Halifax and his wife, Lady Mary Lumley, with whom she maintained an intimate relation until Lady Barbara's death in 1765. In 1751, Sarah Robinson married George Lewis Scott, and she separated from him in 1752. Her first novel, *The History of Cornelia,* appeared in 1750. Between 1750 and her death in 1795, Sarah Scott published four more novels and three histories. *Millenium Hall* (1762) was her most popular work. For further details, see Spencer, Introduction, v–x.

4. Lillian Faderman, *Surpassing the Love of Men: Romantic Friendship and Love between Women from the Renaissance to the Present* (New York: Morrow, 1981), 103.

5. Ibid., 77, 80.

6. See Rousseau, "In Pursuit of Homosexuality," 132–33.

7. Elizabeth Mavor, *The Ladies of Llangollen, A Study in Romantic Friendship* (London: Michael Joseph, 1971), 104–105, 88; also see Mavor, ed., *A Year with the Ladies of Llangollen* (Harmondsworth: Penguin, 1986).

8. See Emma Donoghue, *Passions between Women: British Lesbian Culture 1668–1801* (London: Scarlett, 1993). I use the term *homosocial* advisedly.

9. *Satan's Harvest Home* (1749), in *Hell Upon Earth: Or the Town in an Uproar and Satan's Harvest Home,* ed. Randolph Trumbach (New York: Garland, 1985), 51–52.

10. On Henry Fielding's *The Female Husband,* see Terry Castle, "Matters Not Fit to Be Mentioned: Fielding's *The Female Husband,*" in *The Female Thermometer: 18th-Century Culture and the Invention of the Uncanny* (New York: Oxford University Press, 1995), 67–81. Castle notes that "female transvestism was a far more common phenomenon in the eighteenth and nineteenth centuries than has previously been suspected" (70). Also see Janet Todd, *Female Friendship in Literature* (New York: Columbia University Press, 1980), 324–27.

11. *Satan's Harvest Home,* 18.

12. Eric Partridge, *A Dictionary of Slang and Unconventional English,* 8th ed. (London: Routledge, 1984). Partridge gives these terms nineteenth- and twentieth-century currency.

13. See, for instance, Castle, "Matters Not Fit to Be Mentioned."

14. Donoghue, *Passions between Women,* 109–11.

15. *Satan's Harvest Home*, 60–61.

16. I use the term *lesbian* as a way of directing attention to the erotics implicit in certain female relations. It goes without saying that the term, *as we understand it*, was unavailable to women in the eighteenth century, since the concept of sexual identity was itself only in the process of emerging. But Emma Donoghue makes a reasonable claim both that the term was current in the eighteenth century and that it works as an "umbrella term" for various accounts of female-female desire (*Passions between Women*, 3–9). *Lesbian*, in any case, can help to clarify the euphemism "romantic friendship" as well as to connect eighteenth-century women writers to a tradition that is only beginning to be recognized.

17. D'Avoux and d'Avora, the two most empowering figures in the early lives of these girls, both have names that can be associated with *avowal*—the French directly and the Italian by association. This seems to me suggestive.

18. Sarah Scott, *A Description of Millenium Hall and the Country Adjacent* (1762) (New York: Penguin-Virago, 1986), 35–36; further references are included parenthetically in the text.

19. Nussbaum says that the novel "redefines maternity so that it becomes something that the women generously bestow upon each other" (*Torrid Zones*, 152).

20. For a fuller discussion of mother-daughter relations, see Marianne Hirsch, *The Mother/Daughter Plot: Narrative, Psychoanalysis, Feminism* (Bloomington: Indiana University Press, 1989); see also Kaja Silverman, *The Subject of Semiotics* (Oxford: Oxford University Press, 1983), 141.

21. The quotation is from Julia Kristeva, "Motherhood according to Giovanni Bellini," in *Desire in Language: A Semiotic Approach to Literature and Art*, ed. Leon S. Roudiez, trans. Leon S. Roudiez, Thomas Gora, and Alice Jardine (New York: Columbia University Press, 1980), 239; see also Jane Gallop, *The Daughter's Seduction: Feminism and Psychoanalysis* (Ithaca: Cornell University Press, 1982), 28–30. I mention Silverman, Kristeva, and Gallop, but feminist theorists as wide-ranging as Wittig, Irigaray, and Cixous, on one hand, and Rich, Farwell, and Chodorow, on the other, all stress the potential homoerotics of the mother-daughter bond. Nancy Chodorow says, for instance, that girls *cannot* reject or replace their pre-Oedipal attachment to their mothers and remain instead in a "bisexual triangle" through puberty and beyond. The mother becomes the shadowy third term in female relations (*The Reproduction of Mothering: Psychoanalysis and the Sociology of Gender* [Berkeley: University of California Press, 1978]). Sue-Ellen Case and others have pointed out that there is an implicit homophobia in seeing female relations from a maternal perspective. See "Tracking the Vampire," *Differences* 3, no. 2 (1991): 1–20.

22. See Gayle Rubin, "The Traffic in Women: Notes toward a Political Economy of Sex," in *Toward an Anthropology of Women*, ed. Rayna Reiter (New York: Monthly Review Press, 1975), 180; see also Eve Kosofsky Sedgwick, *Between Men: English Literature and Male Homosexual Desire* (New York: Columbia University Press, 1985), 1–5. For a more detailed discussion of women and property in the eighteenth century, see Susan Staves, *Married Women's Separate Property in England, 1660–1833* (Cambridge: Harvard University Press, 1990); see also Laura Brown, *Ends of Empire: Women and Ideology in Early Eighteenth-Century English Literature* (Ithaca: Cornell University Press, 1993).

23. I am hesitant to use the pronoun *we*. Of course I can only speak about my own response to the novel. But Scott seems to structure the scene so that early approval of Mr. Hintman's behavior makes it impossible to suspect that he has any but honorable intentions. When his pernicious motives are exposed, a reader can be trapped by her or his preconceptions, just as the heroine is trapped and endangered because of her own willingness to trust him.

24. It has been argued that the so-called "demon-lover" is attractive to the heroine in Gothic fiction; see, for instance, Cynthia Griffin Wolff, "The Radcliffean Gothic Model: A Form for Feminine Sexuality," *Modern Language Studies* 9 (1979): 98–113.

25. Samuel Richardson, *The History of Sir Charles Grandison* (1753–54), ed. Jocelyn Harris, 3 vols. (Oxford: Oxford University Press, 1972) 1: 5.

26. See Rousseau, "The Pursuit of Homosexuality," for a discussion of male homosexuality in the eighteenth century; also see my essay "*O lacrymarum fons:* Tears, Poetry, and Desire in Gray," *Eighteenth-Century Studies* 30 (1996): 81–95. I use *gay* here as eighteenth-century writers might have done—Smollett's "gay gentlemen" are distinguished by more than their dress—but I also mean to suggest the continuity between our own understanding of sexual difference and that which was emerging in the eighteenth century. D'Avora, in any case, represents what was coming to be a recognizable "type." Felicity Nussbaum cites this claim in *Torrid Zones* and says, "[d]'Avora seems to me to occupy instead the place of the mediating eunuch" (243, n. 42). My only response would be to point out that the sodomite and the eunuch would by no means represent mutually exclusive categories in the eighteenth century. Think only of representations of the castrato throughout the century. In this regard, see James P. Carson, "Commodification and the Figure of the Castrato in Smollett's *Humphry Clinker,*" *The Eighteenth Century: Theory and Interpretation* 33 (1992): 24–46.

27. Of course in one sense the relations between women were not threatening to patriarchal society *at all;* Mrs. Tighe writes after the attempted elopement of Eleanor Butler and Sarah Ponsonby: "There were no gentlemen concerned, nor does it appear to be anything more than a scheme of Romantic Friendship" (quoted in Mavor, *The Ladies,* 39).

28. I am of course revising Kristeva's concept of the phallic mother here; see "The Novel as Polylogue," in *Desire in Language,* 190–200; see also Gallop, *The Daughter's Seduction,* 117.

29. I am not using *homophobia* in a transhistorical way; as Sedgwick makes clear, following Alan Bray, "once the secularization of terms . . . began to make 'the homosexual' available as a descriptive category of lived experience [in the eighteenth century], what had happened was not only that the terms of a newly effective minority oppression had been set, but that a new and immensely potent tool had become available for the manipulation of every form of power that was refracted through the gender system. . . . " See Sedgwick, *Between Men,* 87; see also Alan Bray, *Homosexuality in Renaissance England* (London: Gay Men's Press, 1982).

30. Luce Irigaray offers a way of talking about the technique of *Millenium Hall* that seems to me very useful: "For what is important is to disconcert the staging of representation according to *exclusively* 'masculine' parameters, that is, according to phallocratic order. It is not a matter of toppling that order so as to replace it—that

amounts to the same thing in the end—but of disrupting and modifying it, starting from an 'outside' that is exempt, in part, from phallocratic law" (*This Sex Which Is Not One,* trans. Catherine Porter and Carolyn Burke [Ithaca: Cornell University Press, 1985], 68).

31. Nussbaum, *Torrid Zones,* 153.

32. Marilyn R. Farwell, "Heterosexual Plots and Lesbian Subtexts: Toward a Theory of Lesbian Narrative Space," in *Lesbian Texts and Contexts,* ed. Karla Jay and Joanne Glasgow (New York: New York University Press, 1990), 93; see also Lee R. Edwards, *Psyche as Hero: Female Heroism and Literary Form* (Middletown, Conn.: Wesleyan University Press, 1984), 237.

33. For a discussion of the specter of the maternal in Gothic fiction, see Claire Kahane, "The Gothic Mirror," in *The (M)other Tongue: Essays in Feminist Psychoanalytic Interpretation,* ed. Claire Kahane, Shirley Nelson Garner, and Madelon Springnether (Ithaca: Cornell University Press, 1985), 334–51.

34. For a discussion of the "dis-ease" infecting the early woman novelist, see Sandra M. Gilbert and Susan Gubar, *The Madwoman in the Attic: The Woman Writer and the Nineteenth-Century Literary Imagination* (New Haven: Yale University Press, 1979), 71. As Jane Spencer points out, however, the women at Millenium Hall "do not break down class barriers." Spencer goes on to note that "there is a big difference between the help they give to peasants' children and that offered to indigent gentlewomen," and she calls their attitudes in certain respects "patronising" (Spencer, Introduction, xiii).

six / Wollstonecraft and the Law of Desire

1. Janet Todd, *The Sign of Angellica: Women, Writing and Fiction, 1660–1800* (London: Virago, 1989), 228, 236–37; for helpful readings of both works, see Janet Todd, *Women's Friendship in Literature* (New York: Columbia University Press, 1980), 191–208, 208–26; on "Self, Social Conflict and Writing," see Gary Kelly, *Revolutionary Feminism: The Mind and Career of Mary Wollstonecraft* (New York: St. Martin's, 1992), 23–54; for a political statement of Wollstonecraft's feminism, see Cora Kaplan, "Subjectivity, Class and Sexuality in Socialist Feminist Criticism," in *Making and Difference: Feminist Literary Criticism,* ed. Gayle Greene and Coppélia Kahn (New York: Methuen, 1985), 150–60.

2. Mary Wollstonecraft, *Collected Letters,* ed. Ralph Wardle (Ithaca: Cornell University Press, 1979), 344–45; see also Susan Lanser, *Fictions of Authority: Women Writers and Narrative Voice* (Ithaca: Cornell University Press, 1992), 235–36. Of course, Wollstonecraft's difficulty with writing was not limited to this one case. She is known to have struggled with political as well as fictional writing. Still, the implications of this remark are pointed and useful in this context.

3. See, for instance, Nancy Armstrong, *Desire and Domestic Fiction: A Political History of the Novel* (Oxford: Oxford University Press, 1987); Marilyn Butler, *Jane Austen and the War of Ideas* (Oxford: Oxford University Press, 1975) and *Romantics, Rebels, and Reactionaries* (Oxford: Oxford University Press, 1981); Claudia Johnson, *Jane Austen: Women Politics, and the Novel* (Chicago: University of Chicago Press, 1988) and *Equivocal Beings: Politics, Gender, and Sentimentality in the 1790s* (Chicago: University of Chicago Press, 1995); and Gary Kelly, *The English*

Jacobin Novel, 1780–1895 (Oxford: Oxford University Press, 1976) and *Revolutionary Feminism.*

4. Slavoj Žižek, *The Sublime Object of Ideology* (London: Verso, 1989), 19, 13–16; see also 28–30.

5. Kaja Silverman calls this story the "dominant fiction" of the age; see *Male Subjectivity at the Margins* (New York: Routledge, 1992), 15–51.

6. See Mary Poovey, *The Proper Lady and the Woman Writer: Ideology as Style in the Works of Mary Wollstonecraft, Mary Shelley, and Jane Austen* (Chicago: University of Chicago Press, 1984), 96–97. In speaking of the structural problems in *The Wrongs of Woman,* Poovey says that "the problem apparently lay . . . in the difficulty she had in reconciling her intended 'purpose' with the genre, which here shapes the 'structure' of the work" (96). See also Mitzi Myers, "Unfinished Business: Wollstonecraft's *Maria,*" *Wordsworth Circle* 11 (1980): 107–14.

7. Fredric Jameson, *The Political Unconscious: Narrative as a Socially Symbolic Act* (Ithaca: Cornell University Press, 1981), 79.

8. Teresa de Lauretis, *Alice Doesn't: Feminism, Semiotics, Cinema* (Bloomington: Indiana University Press, 1984), 106, 133.

9. Ibid., 114–20; see also Vladimir Propp, *Morphology of the Folk Tale,* trans. Laurence Scott, with an introduction by Svatava Pirkova-Jakobson, ed. Louis A. Wagner, new introduction by Alan Dundes, 2nd ed. (Austin: University of Texas Press, 1968), 97; and Jurij M. Lotman, "The Origin of Plot in the Light of Typology," trans. Julian Graffy, *Poetics Today* 1 (Autumn 1979): 161–84.

10. Among the most interesting recent discussions of Wollstonecraft's novels are Johnson, *Equivocal Beings*; Kelly, *Revolutionary Feminism*; Lanser, *Fictions of Authority,* 230–38; Shawn Maurer, "The Female (as) Reader: Sex, Sensibility, and the Maternal in Wollstonecraft's Fictions," *Essays in Literature* 19 (1992): 36–54; Poovey, *The Proper Lady,* 48–113; and Todd, *The Sign of Angellica,* 236–52.

11. Todd, *The Sign of Angellica,* 236–37.

12. Ibid., 238; for another view of sensibility, see John Mullan, *Sentiment and Sociability: The Language of Feeling in the Eighteenth Century* (Oxford: Oxford University Press, 1988).

13. Todd, *The Sign of Angellica,* 239.

14. Mary Wollstonecraft, *Mary,* in *Mary and The Wrongs of Woman,* ed. Gary Kelly (Oxford: Oxford University Press, 1991), 8; further references to both novels are included in the text.

15. The quotation is from Edward Young, *Night-Thoughts,* Night the First, l. 388.

16. Todd, *The Sign of Angellica,* 239.

17. Johnson, *Equivocal Beings,* 53.

18. Ibid., 55.

19. Ibid., 59.

20. See Todd, *Sign of Angellica,* 243; by referring to Jameson's *The Prison-House of Language,* I mean to point up the cultural inevitability of a concept such as sensibility.

21. See my "Boswell's Symptoms: *The Hypochondriack* In and Out of Context," in *James Boswell: Psychological Interpretations,* ed. Donald J. Newman (New York: St. Martin's, 1995), 111–26.

22. Todd, *The Sign of Angellica,* 239.

23. De Lauretis, *Alice Doesn't,* 134.

24. Partridge, *A Dictionary of Slang,* s.v. "johnny." I would argue that Partridge has (not unusually) postdated such meanings. Partridge's historical accuracy is clearly questionable when dealing with women's slang. In chapter five I argue that slang terminology for female-female sexual activity, apparent in a number of eighteenth-century texts, is misdated by a century in Partridge.

25. Mary Wollstonecraft, *A Vindication of the Rights of Woman* (1792; New York: Norton, 1975), 65; Kaplan, "Subjectivity, Class and Sexuality," 157; see also Poovey, *The Proper Lady and the Woman Writer,* 74.

26. See Todd, *Women's Friendship in Literature,* 191–226.

27. Both of the characters Mary and Maria *write,* but it is significant that Mary's vatic prose and Maria's memoirs resist the pitfalls of novelistic narrative by insisting on an internalized female voice and resisting the exigencies of narrative closure.

28. Kelly, "Notes," *Mary and The Wrongs of Woman,* 215.

29. Shawn Lisa Maurer, "The Female (as) Reader," 49.

30. See, for instance, Todd, *The Sign of Angellica,* 250–51.

31. See Kelly, "Notes," 221.

32. Kelly, *The English Jacobin Novel,* 230; see also Lawrence Stone, *Broken Lives: Separation and Divorce in England 1660–1857* (Oxford: Oxford University Press, 1993), 3–29; and *Road to Divorce: England 1530–1987* (Oxford: Oxford University Press, 1990), 1–47.

33. *Trials for Adultery: Or, the History of Divorces,* 1779, ed. Randolph Trumbach, 7 vols. (New York: Garland, 1985) 1: iv.

34. *Trials for Adultery* 4: 3–6. By far the majority of trials in these seven volumes are those in which a man divorces his wife; many involve much more salacious detail than that I have recorded here, but none involves a response of any kind by the woman accused. There are a few cases, often involving venereal disease, in which a woman divorces her husband.

35. Stone, *Broken Lives,* 15.

36. I am writing at a time when marital abuse has been a news item as a result of a celebrity murder case. I hope that the issue will not be forgotten soon.

37. Frank Kermode, *The Sense of an Ending: Studies in the Theory of Fiction* (Oxford: Oxford University Press, 1968), 130; Iris Murdoch, "Against Dryness."

SEVEN / Self-Love in *The Female Quixote*

1. See Deborah Ross, *The Excellence of Falsehood: Romance, Realism, and Women's Contribution to the Novel* (Lexington: University of Kentucky Press, 1991), 95: "Lennox was both a moralist and a realist; and therefore, despite its antiromantic premise, *The Female Quixote* is a romance, and Arabella, the quixote, is a romance heroine. . . . Although Lennox does not resolve the issues she raises here, her formal approach does help to crystallize them, and to point to the real sources of women's frustration and conflict."

2. Ioan Williams, ed., *Novel and Romance, 1700–1800, A Documentary Record* (London: Routledge, 1970), 214, 217.

3. Not all men saw romances in this light. William Whitehead, writing in 1753, argues that "[r]omances, judiciously conducted, are a very pleasing way of conveying instruction to all parts of life" (Williams, *Novel and Romance,* 207); and Hugh

Blair, in 1762, sees in French romance "the heroism and the gallantry, the moral and virtuous turn of the chivalry romance . . . and some small resemblance to human nature." Later, he says, "magnificent heroic romance . . . dwindled down into the familiar novel" (Williams, *Novel and Romance,* 250).

4. Janet Todd, *The Sign of Angellica: Women, Writing and Fiction, 1660–1800* (London: Virago, 1989), 152.

5. Eve Kosofsky Sedgwick, "Jane Austen and the Masturbatory Girl," in *Tendencies* (Durham, N.C.: Duke University Press, 1993), 109–29.

6. Charlotte Lennox, *The Female Quixote, Or, The Adventures of Arabella* (1752), ed. Margaret Dalziel (Oxford: Oxford University Press, 1989), 9; further references are included in the text.

7. See, for instance, *Onania* (1708), 8th ed. 1723 (New York: Garland, 1986), in which women who practice "excessive Lust and the abuse of Parts" (155) become physically as well as sexually hermaphroditic. See Emma Donoghue, *Passions between Women: British Lesbian Culture 1688–1801* (London: Scarlett, 1993), 42. The passage quoted comes from *The Supplement to Onania* (after 1725), which is included in the Garland publication.

8. Terry Castle, *The Female Thermometer: 18th-Century Culture and the Invention of the Uncanny* (New York: Oxford University Press, 1995), 183–84; references include Johnson Grant, "Reverie; considered as connected with Literature," *Nicholson's Journal of Natural Philosophy, Chemistry, and the Arts* 15 (October 1806): 124; John Abercrombie, *Inquiries Concerning the Intellectual Powers and the Investigation of Truth* (Boston, 1844), 131.

9. Eric Rothstein, "Foucault, Discursive History, and the Auto-Affection of God," *Modern Language Quarterly* 35 (1994): 395.

10. Deborah Ross, for instance, says that Arabella "does not know how to value the safety of the real world" ("Mirror, Mirror: The Didactic Dilemma of *The Female Quixote,*" *Studies in English Literature* 27 [1987]: 460); on the other hand, Patricia Meyer Spacks notes that "Arabella's consistent commitment to principle and her contempt for meretricious social enticements make her potentially more threatening to a male-dominated order of things than seventeen-year-old fictional heroines customarily appear" (*Desire and Truth: Functions of Plot in Eighteenth-Century Novels* [Chicago: University of Chicago Press, 1990], 28).

11. A cousin is not automatically acceptable as a marriage partner, even in the eighteenth century. See Randolph Trumbach, *The Rise of the Egalitarian Family: Aristocratic Kinship and Domestic Relations in Eighteenth-Century England* (New York: Harcourt–Academic Press, 1978), 13–18. Doody talks about the "incestuous cosiness of the familial arrangement" here (Margaret Doody, Introduction, *The Female Quixote* [Oxford: Oxford University Press, 1989], xxix).

12. Spencer says that "Glanville's endeavours to guide Arabella towards truth lead him deeper into romantic fiction"; see Janet Spencer, *The Rise of the Woman Novelist, From Aphra Behn to Jane Austen* (Oxford: Blackwell, 1986), 191; that Arabella in her resistance opts for the very man her father has chosen suggests the domestic affirmation of sentimental comedy.

13. Doody, Introduction, *The Female Quixote,* xx–xxi.

14. Catherine Gallagher, *Nobody's Story: The Vanishing Act of Women Writers in the Marketplace, 1670–1820* (Berkeley: University of California Press, 1994), 177.

15. Ibid.

198

16. George Cheyne, "Of the Spleen, Vapours, Lowness of Spirits, Hysterical, or Hypochondriacal Disorders," in *The English Malady; Or, A Treatise of Nervous Diseases of All Kinds* (1733), introd. Eric T. Carlson, M.D. (Delmar, N.Y.: Scholar's Facsimiles & Reprints, 1976), 133–41; see also Michel Foucault, *The History of Sexuality,* vol. 1: *An Introduction* (1976), trans. Robert Hurley (New York: Vintage–Random House, 1980), 103–104.

17. John Mullan, *Sentiment and Sociability: The Language of Feeling in the Eighteenth Century* (Oxford: Oxford University Press, 1988), 202–203, 221.

18. Castle, *The Female Thermometer,* 184.

19. On the valorization of the "feminine" male in French romance, see Ros Ballaster, *Seductive Forms: Women's Amatory Fiction from 1684 to 1740* (Oxford: Oxford University Press, 1992), 42–49.

20. See chapters 3, 9, and 10.

21. See the notes to *The Female Quixote,* 216–39, for a discussion of the various sources of Sir George's romance; see also J. M. Armisted, *Nathaniel Lee* (Boston: G. K. Hall, 1979), 69.

22. Ross, *The Excellence of Falsehood,* 96.

23. See Ballaster, *Seductive Forms,* for a discussion of narrative seduction; also see Ross Chambers, *Story and Situation: Narrative Seduction and the Power of Fiction* (Minneapolis: University of Minnesota Press, 1984), 205–26; Todd calls Arabella's near-drowning "a kind of new baptism" (*The Sign of Angellica,* 159). If so, it is a baptism into the debility of femininity in the later eighteenth century.

24. On such "subjection," see Louis Althusser, "Ideology and Ideological State Apparatuses," in *Lenin and Philosophy and Other Essays,* trans. Ben Brewster (New York: Monthly Review Press, 1971), 127–86; for a Lacanian interpretation of Althusserian interpellation, see Kaja Silverman, *Male Subjectivity at the Margins* (New York: Routledge, 1992), 1–45; also, Slavoj Žižek, *The Sublime Object of Ideology* (London: Verso, 1989), 43–44. Spacks says that "Arabella's interpretation of 'history' in the large sense—the records of the affairs of nations—as well as her readings of individual lives, place women in a new position"; see *Desire and Truth,* 23.

25. Laurie Langbauer talks interestingly about Arabella's "cure": see *Women and Romance: The Consolations of Gender in the English Novel* (Ithaca: Cornell University Press, 1990), 77–78.

26. Emil Benveniste, *Problems in General Linguistics* (1966), trans. Mary Elizabeth Meek (Coral Gables, Fla: University of Miami Press, 1971), 218. For Benveniste: "'I' designates the one who speaks and at the same time an utterance about the 'I'" (*Problems in General Linguistics,* 197); see also Kaja Silverman, *The Subject of Semiotics* (Oxford: Oxford University Press, 1983), 43–53; and Shoshona Felman, *The Literary Speech Act: Don Juan with J. L. Austin, or Seduction in Two Languages,* trans. Catherine Porter (Ithaca: Cornell University Press, 1983), 15–22.

27. See Marie-Paul Laden, *Self-Imitation in the Eighteenth-Century Novel* (Princeton: Princeton University Press, 1987), 4–5, and n. 3.

28. Todd, *The Sign of Angellica,* 156–57; see also Spencer, *The Rise of the Woman Novelist,* 189: "When Arabella does give up her illusions, she gives up her power"; and Langbauer, *Women and Romance,* 81: "The text shows that Arabella's only escape from romance is to stop being a woman."

29. For a record of Richardson's involvement in the completion of the novel, see

Duncan Isles, appendix, *The Female Quixote* (Oxford: Oxford University Press, 1989), 419–28.

30. For the most interesting recent discussion of the ending of the novel, see Wendy Motooka, "Coming to a Bad End: Sentimentalism, Hermeneutics, and *The Female Quixote*," *Eighteenth-Century Fiction* 8 (1996): 251–70.

31. Ibid., 252.

32. Doody, Introduction, *The Female Quixote*, xxi.

EIGHT / "Defects and Deformity" in *Camilla*

1. Frances Burney, *Camilla: or, A Picture of Youth*, ed. Edward A. Bloom and Lillian D. Bloom (Oxford: Oxford University Press, 1991). All references are to this edition. Claudia Johnson calls the novel "arduous," but the chapter in which she discusses *Camilla* suggests that she finds the novel as revealing as I do. See Claudia L. Johnson, *Equivocal Beings: Politics, Gender, and Sentimentality in the 1790s* (Chicago: University of Chicago Press, 1995), 148.

2. For *"Udolphish,"* see Burney, *The Journal and Letters of Fanny Burney (Madame D'Arblay), 1791–1840*, 12 vols., ed. Joyce Hemlow et al. (Oxford: Oxford University Press, 1972–84) 3: 137.

3. See especially Julia L. Epstein, *The Iron Pen: Frances Burney and the Politics of Women's Writing* (Madison: University of Wisconsin Press, 1989), 128–32; and Margaret A. Doody, *Frances Burney: The Life in the Works* (New Brunswick, N.J.: Rutgers University Press, 1988), 246–47; see also Edward A. Bloom and Lillian D. Bloom, "Explanatory Notes," in *Camilla* (by Frances Burney [Oxford: Oxford University Press, 1983], 941), where the sermon is called the "moralistic essence of the novel, setting forth an ideal of ethical conduct."

4. Epstein, *The Iron Pen*, 128.

5. Mary Poovey, *The Proper Lady and the Woman Writer: Ideology as Style in the Works of Mary Wollstonecraft, Mary Shelley, and Jane Austen* (Chicago: University of Chicago Press, 1984), 23.

6. Lionel is again involved: he suggested the seesaw game, and later he introduces Eugenia to the wicked Bellamy. His carelessness of others leads repeatedly to their pain: "A stranger to reflection, and incapable of care, laughter seemed not merely the bent of his humour, but the necessity of his existence: he pursued it at all seasons, he indulged it upon all occasions. With excellent natural parts, he trifled away all improvement; without any ill temper, he spared no one's feelings. Yet, though not radically vicious, nor deliberately malevolent, the egotism which urged him to make his own amusement his first pursuit, sacrificed his best friends and first duties, if they stood in his way" (79).

7. Johnson, *Equivocal Beings*, 152.

8. Slavoj Žižek, *The Sublime Object of Ideology* (London: Verso, 1989), 26; see my essay "Amelia's Nose; or, Sensibility and Its Symptoms," *The Eighteenth Century: Theory and Interpretation* 36 (1995), 140.

9. Žižek says that "[i]deology is not a dreamlike illusion that we build to escape insupportable reality; in its basic dimension it is a fantasy-construction which serves as a support for our 'reality' itself: an 'illusion' which structures our effective, real social relation and thereby masks some insupportable, real, impossible kernel

(. . . a traumatic social division which cannot be symbolized)." And further, "[t]he function of ideology is not to offer us a point of escape from our reality but to offer us the social reality itself as an escape from some traumatic, real kernel" (*The Sublime Object*, 45).

10. *Satan's Harvest Home* (1749) in *Hell Upon Earth: Or the Town in an Uproar and Satan's Harvest Home,* ed. Randolph Trumbach (New York: Garland, 1985), 51–52; Trumbach, "The Birth of the Queen: Sodomy and the Emergence of Gender Equality in Modern Culture, 1660–1750," in *Hidden from History: Reclaiming the Gay and Lesbian Past,* ed. Martin Bauml Duberman, Martha Vicinus, and George Chauncey, Jr. (New York: New American Library, 1989), 134; discussions of the "fop" in the eighteenth century range from Susan Staves, "A Few Kind Words for the Fop," *SEL* 22 (1982): 413–28, to G. S. Rousseau, "The Pursuit of Homosexuality in the Eighteenth Century: 'Utterly Confused Category' and/or Rich Repository," *Eighteenth-Century Life* 9, n.s. 3 (1985): 132–68.

11. Trumbach, "The Birth of the Queen," 140.

12. Johnson argues that "the disruption of gender markers authorized by sentimentality has, in problematizing virtually every mode of femininity, rendered women hard to love." She also notes that at least one passage in the novel "bristles with a homophobic determination to reaffirm the very markers of gender which sentimentality elsewhere blurs." Johnson notes too that "the novel everywhere insists that Indiana's femininity is effeminacy, every bit as put on, caricatured, hyperconventional, theatrical, and undesirable as her brother's"; see *Equivocal Beings,* 160–61. For a discussion of Sir Sedley, see 163–64.

13. James G. Turner, "The Properties of Libertinism," in *'Tis Nature's Fault: Unauthorized Sexuality during the Enlightenment,* ed. Robert Purks Maccubbin (Cambridge: Cambridge University Press, 1987), 84.

14. For discussions of Burney's famous phrase, see Joanne Cutting-Gray, *Woman as "Nobody" and the Novels of Fanny Burney* (Gainesville: University Press of Florida, 1992); see also Catherine Gallagher, *Nobody's Story: The Vanishing Acts of Women Writers in the Marketplace, 1670–1820* (Berkeley: University of California Press, 1994), 203–56.

15. In his discussion of Lacanian lack, Žižek says that "there is a certain foreclosure proper to the order of signifier as such; whenever we have a symbolic structure it is structured around a certain void, it implies the foreclosure of a certain key-signifier. The symbolic structuring of sexuality implies the lack of a signifier of the sexual relationship, it implies that 'there is no sexual relationship', that the sexual relation cannot be symbolized—that it is an impossible, 'antagonistic' relationship. And to seize the interconnection between the two universalizations, we must simply again apply the proposition 'what was foreclosed from the Symbolic returns in the Real of the symptom': woman does not exist, her signifier is originally foreclosed, and that is why she returns as a symptom of man" (*The Sublime Object of Ideology,* 73).

16. For Kristina Straub "Both *Camilla* and *The Wanderer* are premised on the rigidity—and illogic—of a system of economically motivated social customs that subordinate female action to male authority" (*Divided Fictions: Fanny Burney and Feminine Strategy* [Lexington: University of Kentucky Press, 1987], 183–84).

17. Epstein, *The Iron Pen,* 127.

18. Joanne Cutting-Gray says that "Edgar can only validate [Camilla] by forcing

her to conform to his positing of her. The value positing activity, a form of subjectivism, is what Heideggger sees as the heart of the empirical demand for proof: 'What a thing is in its Being is not exhausted by its being an object, particularly when objectivity takes the form of value. Every valuing, even where it values positively, is a subjectivizing. It does not let beings: be. Rather, valuing lets beings: be valid— solely as the objects of its doing.'" See Cutting-Gray, *Woman as "Nobody,"* 76; see Heidegger, "Letter on Humanism," in *Basic Writings,* ed. David Farrell Krell (New York: Harper, 1977), 228.

19. Johnson, *Equivocal Beings,* 162.

20. Doody, *Frances Burney,* 249; see also Straub, *Divided Fictions,* 191–92. As Straub says, "On several occasions throughout the novel, Camilla accepts an invitation to some place of public diversion on Edgar's account: either to see and reattach Edgar or to avoid him in the interests of getting over and concealing her attachment. The twists and turns in Camilla's courtship make her economically vulnerable in a manner that is specific to social expectations linked to her femininity. Although she is by no means extravagant, the decorum of the public feminine role demands expenses beyond her means."

21. For Johnson, "the hideous logic of [the] familiar system whereby . . . a man chooses a woman and a woman retires to be chosen, is disclosed through the exaggerated suspicion authorized by Marchmont" (*Equivocal Beings,* 167).

22. See Michel Foucault, *The History of Sexuality,* vol. 1: *An Introduction* (1976), trans. Robert Hurley (New York: Vintage–Random House, 1980), 103.

23. "Amelia's Nose," 140–41; see also John Mullan, *Sentiment and Sociability: The Language of Feeling in the Eighteenth Century* (Oxford: Clarendon, 1988), 201–40.

24. Žižek, *The Sublime Object of Ideology,* 69; see further "The Dialectics of Symptom," 55–84.

25. Joanne Cutting-Gray says that "[i]f Burney's description of desire as that which is grafted upon what is denied were translated in modern terms, it would come very close to Lacan's description of the process of desire. . . . Only if Edgar and Camilla learn to negotiate with desire as a principle that always, elsewhere grafts onto what it denies can they recognize the Other's desire and accommodate it." See *Woman as "Nobody,"* 65; see also Jane Gallop, *Reading Lacan* (Ithaca: Cornell University Press, 1985), 184. For a different perspective on desire, see "Commerce and Masochistic Desire in the 1790s: Frances Burney's *Camilla,*" *Eighteenth-Century Studies* 31 (1997): 69–86.

26. Cutting-Gray says that "Burney's narrative presents marriage as the only narrative that can tell the *logique du coeur.* . . . Marriage is here a feeble attempt to repair the human, fragmented into gender, dissociated from feeling; but because marriage is also an extrinsically contrived union of duality, it cannot integrate reason and feeling reified as psychological states." See *Woman as "Nobody,"* 80–81.

27. Johnson says that "the plethora of concluding marriages . . . flouts the convention by glutting it incredibly"; see *Equivocal Beings,* 164.

NINE / The Pleasures of Victimization in *The Romance of the Forest*

1. See, for instance, Elizabeth Napier, *The Failure of the Gothic: Problems of a Literary Form* (Oxford: Clarendon, 1987).

2. Recent interesting discussions of Radcliffe are included in Terry Castle, *The Female Thermometer: 18th-Century Culture and the Invention of the Uncanny* (New York: Oxford University Press, 1995), 120–39; Claudia Johnson, *Equivocal Beings: Politics, Gender, and Sentimentality in the 1790s* (Chicago: University of Chicago Press, 1995), 63–140; and Anne Williams, *Art of Darkness: A Poetics of Gothic* (Chicago: University of Chicago Press, 1995), 141–72. Both Michelle Massé's *In the Name of Love: Women Masochism and the Gothic* (Ithaca: Cornell University Press, 1992) and Judith Halberstam's *Skin Shows: Gothic Horror and the Technology of Monsters* (Durham, N.C.: Duke University Press, 1995) discuss Radcliffe only indirectly, but they both make very useful comments about Gothic fiction in general. Also of interest is *The Critical Response to Ann Radcliffe*, ed. Deborah D. Rogers (Westport, Conn.: Greenwood, 1994).

3. Samuel Taylor Coleridge, *Miscellaneous Criticism*, ed. Thomas M. Raysor (Cambridge: Harvard University Press, 1936), 357; see also Castle, *The Female Thermometer*, 120–24, for a discussion of Radcliffe's "explained" supernatural.

4. Castle, *The Female Thermometer*, 120–39.

5. Leslie Fiedler, *Love and Death in the American Novel* (New York: Dell, 1966), 132; see also Kahane, "The Gothic Mirror," in *The (M)other Tongue: Essays in Feminist Psychoanalytic Interpretation*, ed. Shirley Nelson Garner, Claire Kahane, and Madelon Sprengnether (Ithaca: Cornell University Press, 1985), 336.

6. Kahane, "The Gothic Mirror," 336.

7. Johnson, *Equivocal Beings*, 75, 77.

8. Anne Radcliffe, *The Romance of the Forest* (1791), ed. Chloe Chard (Oxford: Oxford University Press, 1986), 5. Further references are included in the text.

9. Massé, *In the Name of Love*, 42–43; Ann C. Greif, "Historical Synthesis," in *Masochism: The Treatment of Self-Inflicted Suffering*, ed. Jill D. Montgomery and Ann C. Greif (Madison, Conn.: International Universities Press, 1989), 3.

10. Jane Spencer, on the other hand, says that "in the comparatively neglected *The Romance of the Forest* (1791), we can see how the Gothic novel presented a fantasy of female power"; see *The Rise of the Woman Novelist, from Aphra Behn to Jane Austen* (Oxford: Blackwell, 1986), 201.

11. In *Powers of Horror*, Julia Kristeva describes this state as abjection, a term that, after all, was familiar to Radcliffe and her contemporaries. For Kristeva, "There looms, within abjection, one of those violent, dark revolts of being, directed against a threat that seems to emanate from an exorbitant outside or inside, ejected beyond the scope of the possible, the tolerable, the thinkable. It lies there, quite close, but it cannot be assimilated. It beseeches, it worries, it fascinates desire" (*Powers of Horror: An Essay on Abjection*, trans. Leon S. Roudiez [New York: Columbia, 1982], 1).

12. The most sustained discussion of sensibility in Radcliffe is that in Johnson, *Equivocal Beings*, 73–140.

13. Castle has described a similar situation in *Clarissa*; see *Clarissa's Ciphers: Meaning and Disruption in Richardson's* Clarissa (Ithaca: Cornell University Press, 1982), 57–80.

14. Mary Poovey, in her study of *The Mysteries of Udolpho*, says that "[i]n a society in which a single woman's value is intimately tied to both sexual purity and endowed property, the consequences of sexual and economic exploitation are effec-

tively identical" ("Ideology and *The Mysteries of Udolpho*," *Criticism* 21 [1979]: 323). Recent critics have explained how the Freudian "family romance" victimizes the female; see, for instance, Kaja Silverman: "the female subject is obliged to renounce her first object choice, to effect a violent break with the source of her earliest pleasures" (*The Subject of Semiotics* [Oxford: Oxford University Press, 1983], 141). Patricia Meyer Spacks argues that "Radcliffe's novels debunk men's phallic but not their social power"; see *Desire and Truth: Functions of Plot in Eighteenth-Century English Novels* (Chicago: University of Chicago Press, 1990), 174. *The Romance of the Forest* makes clear that it is never all that easy to separate the two.

15. Johnson, *Equivocal Beings*, 81.

16. Ibid., 80.

17. Cynthia Griffin Wolff, "The Radcliffean Gothic Model: A Form for Feminine Sexuality," *Modern Language Studies* 9 (1979): 103–104.

18. Ibid., 103.

19. See also Toni Reed, *Demon Lovers and Their Victims in British Fiction* (Lexington: University Press of Kentucky, 1988); and Kenneth W. Graham, "Emily's Demon Lover: The Gothic Revolution and *The Mysteries of Udolpho*," in *Gothic Fictions: Prohibition/Transgression*, ed. Kenneth W. Graham (New York: AMS Press, 1989), 163–72.

20. Johnson, *Equivocal Beings*, 82.

21. See, for instance, Toril Moi, "Representation of Patriarchy: Sexuality and Epistemology in Freud's Dora," in *In Dora's Case*, ed. Charles Bernheimer and Claire Kahane (New York: Columbia University Press, 1985), 181–99.

22. Poovey, "Ideology and *The Mysteries of Udolpho*," 310.

23. Castle, *The Female Thermometer*, 125.

24. Fawcett discusses similar moments in *The Mysteries of Udolpho* in terms of a primal scene: "Each of these bed-manifestations is finally explained in the style of rationalized gothic. But even the explanations add something to the mystery and complexity of the image itself, since in each case the horrible sight has, for Emily, a profound sexual ambiguity. . . . All of Emily's 'mistakes' about the sexual identities of the corpse figures indicate the *real* content of these visions: behind the veil is an image of the generating marriage bed of parents, of the violence and 'death' of the sexual act. The single image is composed of the two sexes, the beast with two backs. The contorted, wounded or gnawed faces are like faces in orgasm" (Mary Laughlin Fawcett, "*Udolpho*'s Primal Mystery," *Studies in English Literature* 23 [1983]: 487).

25. Castle, *The Female Thermometer*, 125.

26. On this aspect of abjection, see Kristeva, *Powers of Horror*, 90–112.

27. See Kahane, "The Gothic Mirror."

28. Kahane, "The Gothic Mirror," 338; see also Fawcett, "*Udolpho*'s Primal Mystery," 485–89; and Wolff, "Radcliffean Gothic Model," 100.

29. Claudia Johnson sees this "feminization" of the male as an attempt to limit the possibilities for female expression; see *Equivocal Beings*, 83–87; for Anne Williams, "[b]y the time Radcliffe began to publish in the 1790s, the 'man of feeling' was a familiar character in popular fiction. Though one might tend to assume that in terms of gender codes he is a 'feminized male,' it is more useful to [see] him as a 'mascu-

linized female': that is, a projection of female definitions of the self into the realm of masculine endeavor" (*Art of Darkness,* 167). Where but in Radcliffe could the distinction between a "feminized male" and a "masculinized female" seem almost insignificant?

30. Kaja Silverman, *Male Subjectivity at the Margins* (New York: Routledge, 1992), 42.

31. Carol Siegel, "Postmodern Women Novelists Review Victorian Male Masochism," *Genders* 11 (1991): 2.

32. Ibid., 8.

33. Johnson reads this situation differently: "The waywardness of women's pleasure must be broken," she says, "and their homoerotic and autoerotic tendencies extirpated in order to fix their desires within a heterosexual matrix whose authoritarian character is concealed" (*Equivocal Beings,* 89). I would place less emphasis on the hetero/homo distinction here and look instead at the vividly "perverse" pleasure that is articulated throughout the text.

34. Leo Bersani, *The Freudian Body: Psychoanalysis and Art* (New York: Columbia University Press, 1986), 41; see also Kaja Silverman, "Masochism and Male Subjectivity," in *Male Subjectivity at the Margins,* 185–213.

Afterword

1. Mary-Ann Radcliffe, *Manfroné; Or, The One-Handed Monk* (1809), 2 vols. (New York: Arno, 1974) 1/1: 10; each of the two volumes of this facsimile of the 1828 edition incorporates two volumes of the original with separate pagination; references therefore cite volume (1 or 2) and part (1 or 2) separated by a slash.

2. Charlotte Dacre, *Zofloya; or The Moor* (1806), ed. Kim Ian Michasiw (Oxford: Oxford University Press, 1997), 137. Further references are included in the text.

3. On the laugh of Medusa, see Hélène Cixous, "The Laugh of the Medusa," in *New French Feminisms,* ed. Elaine Marks and Isabelle di Courtivron (Amherst: University of Massachusetts Press, 1980), 245–64.

4. Michelle A. Massé, *In the Name of Love: Women, Masochism, and the Gothic* (Ithaca: Cornell University Press, 1992), 11.

5. For a discussion of this concept of "dominant fiction," see Kaja Silverman, *Male Subjectivity at the Margins* (New York: Routledge, 1992), 15–51.

INDEX

Abercrombie, James, 197n.8
Abjection: definition of, 37–38, 202n.11; deformity and, 141–42; female desire and, 18–19, 40–43; gender expectations and, 45; of Gothic heroine, 160–61, 176–77; male, 49; as novelistic resolution, 50–51; self-obsession as alternative to, 125–26; as survival attempt, 46–47
Adultery: culture and, 45, 118; the novel and, 186n.15; *Trials for Adultery*, 15–16, 44, 116–17, 186n.16
Alleyn, John, 184n.17
Althusser, Louis, 8, 198n.24
Armisted, J. M., 198n.20
Armstrong, Nancy, 5, 6, 104, 180nn.11,13–14, 181n.18, 182nn.38,43, 194–95n.3
Auerbach, Nina, 189n.8
Austen, Jane, 158; *Sense and Sensibility*, 13, 19, 73–87, 88, 125, 189nn.8–9
Austen-Leigh, James Edward, 86–87, 190n.31
Authority: in the home, 7; in narrative, 89, 101; through novel-writing, 16; paternal, 40–43, 48, 50, 65, 138
Auto-affection, 126–27, 129, 132. *See also* Masturbation; Self-love
Auto-eroticism. *See* Auto-affection; Masturbation

Ballaster, Ros, 5–6, 180n.12, 198nn.19,23
Barker, Gerard A., 183n.1
Barker-Benfield, G. J., 179n.6
Battestin, Martin C., 184n.13
Battestin, Ruthe R., 184n.13
Behn, Aphra, 26
Benevolence: as masculine, 110; paternal authority and, 138; sensibility and, 3–4; as spectacle, 24; as symptom, 142–44
Benjamin, Jessica, 186n.21

Benveniste, Emil, 198n.26
Berenger, Richard, 123–24, 125
Bersani, Leo, 170, 204n.34
Blackmore, Richard, 190n.21
Blair, Hugh, 196–97n.3
Bloom, Edward A., 199n.3
Bloom, Lillian D., 199n.3
Boswell, James, 110
Bourgeois culture: the family and, 40; form and, 104; happiness and, 36; hysteria and, 86, 110, 143; the novel and, 5; sensibility and, 3, 54, 110, 143–44
Braudy, Leo, 35, 184n.23
Bray, Alan, 193n.29
Bridges, Sir Egerton, 187n.20
Brissenden, R. F., 184n.22
Brontë, Emily: *Wuthering Heights*, 38, 46, 169
Brown, Laura, 179n.6, 192n.22
Buck, Craig, 183n.9
Burke, Edmund, 187n.17
Burney, Frances (Fanny), 12, 20, 182n.47, 199n.2; *Camilla*, 20, 26, 137–57, 199n.1; *Cecilia*, 150, 152, 157; *The Wanderer*, 150, 151, 157
Butler, Eleanor, 89–90, 193n.27
Butler, Judith, 37–38, 104, 184–85n.1
Butler, Marilyn, 194–95n.3

Calprenède, Gautier de Costes de la (1610–1663), 132
Carson, James P., 193n.26
Case, Sue-Ellen, 192n.21
Castle, Terry, 6, 38–39, 45–46, 48, 51, 57, 61, 73, 76, 84, 86, 126, 131, 159, 166, 180n.13, 185nn.2–4,6–7, 186nn.19,25,27, 187nn.14,21–22, 188n.5, 189n.6, 190n.32, 191nn.10,13, 197n.8, 198n.18, 202nn.2–4,13, 203nn.21,25

Index

Index

Index

Index

Index

Index

GEORGE E. HAGGERTY, Professor of English at the University of California, Riverside, is the author of *Gothic Fiction/Gothic Form* and co-editor of *Professions of Desire: Lesbian and Gay Studies in Literature*. His other writings include work on masculinity and sexuality in the eighteenth century.